P9-CQD-610

"A gifted writer
with an eye for telling detail."
—*Chicago Tribune*

"When it comes to
pacing, suspense, and control,
Eileen Goudge is a pro."
—*Newsday*

Mary K - 110

"A gifted writer with an eye for telling detail."—*Chicago Tribune*

"When it comes to pacing, suspense, and control, Eileen Goudge is a pro." —*Newsday*

"Bestselling author Eileen Goudge again displays her storytelling skills in this engrossing novel. . . . The carefully paced plot quickens near the end and calls for some rapid page-turning and late nights to reach the satisfying conclusion. This novel with the right touch of intrigue, love, romance and lively dialogue makes an ideal vacation companion." —*Denver Rocky Mountain News*

"Fast-paced and intriguing . . . [a] believable depiction of a family in crisis . . . Goudge has the remarkable ability to describe sentiments that are difficult to put into words. Her novel—both entertaining and encouraging—ably demonstrates that good can arise from even the worst of circumstances." —Associated Press

Continued on next page . . .

Praise for the novels of Eileen Goudge . . .

Trail of Secrets

"A walloping novel . . . satisfying."
—*New York Daily News*

"Goudge keeps you cheering for the book's three women protagonists." —*People*

"Maximum drama . . . will keep all who love a secret riveted." —*Publishers Weekly*

"[A] treat . . . Goudge hits the mark."
—*Kirkus Reviews*

"Excellent . . . for summer beach reading, it doesn't get much better."
—*San Antonio Express-News*

"A romantic novel sure to please." —*Booklist*

Blessing in Disguise

"As rich as a chocolate truffle."—*Buffalo News*

"Powerful, juicy reading."
—*San Jose Mercury News*

"Shocking . . . a bittersweet story of love. . . . Readers of Anne Rivers Siddons and Rosamunde Pilcher will not be able to put it down." —*Library Journal*

"A snappy, entertaining novel."
—*Kirkus Reviews*

Garden of Lies

"A successful entertainment."
—*New York Times Book Review*

"Pretty terrific . . . satisfying . . . heart lifting."
—*Chicago Tribune*

Such Devoted Sisters

"A treat." —*San Jose Mercury News*

"Irresistible." —*San Francisco Chronicle*

"Entertaining . . . Goudge is a gifted writer."
—*Chicago Tribune*

Thorns of Truth

"Eileen Goudge writes like a house on fire."
—*Nora Roberts*

"Fans of [*Garden of Lies*] will not be disappointed." —*Publishers Weekly*

"A likable cast . . . Goudge's adroit handling of sex and love should keep her legion of fans well-sated." —*Kirkus Reviews*

ALSO BY EILEEN GOUDGE

Thorns of Truth

Trail of Secrets

Blessing in Disguise

Such Devoted Sisters

Garden of Lies

One
Last Dance

Eileen Goudge

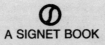

A SIGNET BOOK

SIGNET
Published by New American Library, a division of
Penguin Putnam Inc., 375 Hudson Street,
New York, New York 10014, U.S.A.
Penguin Books Ltd, 27 Wrights Lane,
London W8 5TZ, England
Penguin Books Australia Ltd, Ringwood,
Victoria, Australia
Penguin Books Canada Ltd, 10 Alcorn Avenue,
Toronto, Ontario, Canada M4V 3B2
Penguin Books (N.Z.) Ltd, 182–190 Wairau Road,
Auckland 10, New Zealand

Penguin Books Ltd, Registered Offices:
Harmondsworth, Middlesex, England

Published by Signet, an imprint of New American Library,
a division of Penguin Putnam Inc. Previously published in a Viking
edition.

First Signet Printing, May 2000
10 9 8 7 6 5 4 3 2 1

Copyright © Eileen Goudge, 1999
All rights reserved

Grateful acknowledgment is made for permission to reprint
"The Secret Sits" from *The Poetry of Robert Frost*, edited by
Edward Connery Lathem. Copyright 1942 by Robert Frost.
Copyright © 1970 by Lesley Frost Ballantine.
Copyright © 1969 by Henry Holt and Co. Reprinted by
permission of Henry Holt and Company, Inc.

Ⓟ REGISTERED TRADEMARK—MARCA REGISTRADA

Printed in the United States of America

Without limiting the rights under copyright reserved above, no part of this
publication may be reproduced, stored in or introduced into a retrieval
system, or transmitted, in any form, or by any means (electronic, mechanical,
photocopying, recording, or otherwise), without the prior written
permission of both the copyright owner and the above publisher of this book.

PUBLISHER'S NOTE
This is a work of fiction. Names, characters, places, and incidents either
are the product of the author's imagination or are used fictitiously,
and any resemblance to actual persons, living or dead, business
establishments, events or locales is entirely coincidental.

BOOKS ARE AVAILABLE AT QUANTITY DISCOUNTS WHEN USED TO PROMOTE
PRODUCTS OR SERVICES. FOR INFORMATION PLEASE WRITE TO PREMIUM
MARKETING DIVISION, PENGUIN PUTNAM INC., 375 HUDSON STREET, NEW
YORK, NEW YORK 10014.

If you purchased this book without a cover you should be aware that this
book is stolen property. It was reported as "unsold and destroyed"
to the publisher and neither the author nor the publisher has received
any payment for this "stripped book."

To my children,
Michael and Mary,
and for all those who know that
to seek answers, you must first
know which questions to ask.

We dance round in a ring and suppose,
But the Secret sits in the middle and knows.

—ROBERT FROST

Acknowledgments

This novel was an adventure from start to finish . . . including the handful of manuscript pages that got waterlogged during a rainstorm that sent buckets of water pouring down through my office ceiling. For making it as fun and painless as possible, I would like to thank, first and foremost, my dear and endlessly supportive husband, Sandy, who has been lulled asleep at night on more than one occasion by the furious tapping of my keyboard. He also supplied key editorial commentary and was instrumental in challenging me on scenes that didn't ring 100 percent true emotionally. I hope the story you are about to read will reflect that honesty.

I would also like to thank the women at Viking who helped guide me to safe shores. Susan Petersen, for her grace and firm hand. Barbara Grossman, for her support and encouragement. And my editor, Molly Stern, who often leaves me wondering how I got by for so long without her.

Thanks, too, to Louise Burke at Signet, for her enthusiasm, keen eye, and impressive batting average. I'm privileged to be on her team.

And last, but not least, I'm deeply grateful to my wonderful agent and friend, Susan Ginsburg, who is as dynamic as she is diplomatic. Thank you, Susan, for listening.

One
Last Dance

Chapter 1

The moment she walked in, Daphne knew she was doomed. The store was pretty much deserted . . . even on a rainy Monday night in April with a lackluster basketball season dribbling to a close and most of the hit TV shows in presweeps rerun. She gazed out on row upon row of bookshelves—pale oak that gleamed under fluorescent lighting designed to resemble the kind of opaque hanging fixtures seen in old-fashioned public libraries and apothecaries. There were only a handful of browsers, most of them huddled over steaming mugs in the café section with their faces submerged in books.

Oh Lord, not again. Daphne took a deep breath, holding herself tightly clenched to keep from darting an apologetic glance at her husband. Roger would need no reminding that he'd sacrificed his monthly poker game with the other doctors in his practice to ferry her all the way out here for this.

Stepping away from the puddle that had gathered on the corrugated black rubber mat just inside the door, she felt the mean pinch of a long-forgotten memory: the ancient public library in her hometown of Miramonte, where as a child she'd had to balance on tippy-toes to reach the top shelf, and the loudest noise was the smack of Miss Kabachnik's forcefully applied rubber stamp. Back then, Daphne would sooner have drunk out of the drinking fountain after Skeet Walker had spit into it than dare keep a book past its return date, and thus invoke Herr Kabachnik's wrath . . . and that's just how she felt now, coming in out of the rain, her heart rising in her throat like water nearing its floodmark: as if she were about to be publicly humiliated.

Proof of what lay ahead stood at the far end of the store, in the open carpeted area between the children's and cookbook sections: five rows of gray metal folding chairs, six to a row, each one as empty as a faithless lover's heart.

The assistant manager looked as if he, too, would rather be anywhere but here in Port Chester, Long Island, hosting yet another poorly attended event for yet another obscure author. Clearly, a show of enthusiasm wasn't part of the deal.

Daphne felt a stone of panic lodge in her throat. The young man offered her a handshake as limp and clammy as the coat she was struggling out of. That company-manual smile of his, she thought, might have been coming at her from behind the cash register at a McDonald's. Scarlet clusters of acne stood out on his cheeks, and his glasses, retro Buddy Holly, were smudged at the corners where he was fiddling with them.

But even as he was giving her the lowdown—something about Mrs. Temple, the manager, being home with the flu and sending her apologies for not being able to make it—his eyes kept straying toward Roger, at the moment engaged in thoroughly shaking out their umbrella. He thumped it hard against the doormat, twice, then once more for good measure, before carefully fastening the Velcro tab and dropping it into the bucket by the security gate.

Daphne was used to people deferring to Roger. Her husband's size and authoritative presence commanded attention like a drumroll. She half expected the assistant manager to salute. "Anyway, you're right on time," the boy said, flicking his gaze back to her. "We're all set up for you in back."

"Yes, I can see that. But I'm afraid there's been some sort of misunderstanding." She was careful to strike a friendly, relaxed tone. "My publicist was supposed to have called. I asked that no chairs be set out until we had more of a . . . a feel for the turnout."

The boy absently probed a zit on his chin. "I don't know about that," he said. "All I know is Mrs. Temple told me to put out the chairs. You *are* giving a reading, right? Anyway, that's what it says in the bulletin."

Roger leaned over to give the boy's shoulder a fatherly pat. "Hour and some in the pouring rain on the expressway, I don't imagine a few empty chairs are going to scare us off." He chuckled, a bit too heartily. "You've read it, of course? Her novel?"

He flashed the kid his patented pediatrician's smile. It was the same manner Daphne had once watched her husband use to coax a giggle from a traumatized six-year-old with a broken arm. It worked like a charm on mothers, too. Roger seemed to know instinctively when to listen and soothe . . . and when to firmly seize the upper hand with a hysterical mom who was only making things worse. He even *looked* reassuring: as big and solidly built as a brick church, with thick graying hair that swooped back dramatically from his imposing forehead. Now, leaning forward slightly, he added in a voice low with meaning, "In case you missed it, *Walking After Midnight* got a starred review in *Publishers Weekly*."

In that moment, Daphne nearly turned around and walked back out into the pouring rain. She wasn't sure she could bear it, not tonight, his blustering attempt at leavening what was so clearly a hopeless situation.

"Good heavens, who has time to read all these books?" She smiled too warmly at the clueless assistant manager, glancing at the badge pinned to his lapel. LEONARD. "I'd consider it a personal favor, though, Leonard," she went on in her most reasonable voice, the voice she used when coaxing Jennie into her car seat or convincing Kyle that letting his sister hog the VCR with her beloved *Aristocats* would be a better bet for him in the end than if he bullied her into the *Power Rangers*, ". . . if you'd take down some of those chairs. It's obvious we won't be needing so many."

The reading had been set for eight. It was already five past, and on her way in, slogging across a parking lot that had become a marsh, Daphne hadn't noticed any velvet ropes holding back the fans that any minute would come spilling through the door.

Leonard shrugged, consulting his black Swatch. Some-

thing in the impatient flick of his wrist just then made
her think of her husband. Not just Roger, but every man
who'd ever made her feel this way: as if her every request, however small, had to be served up on a bed of
apologies and feminine wiles. Where had she learned
to behave this way? From Daddy, she supposed. In the
gingerbread house by the sea, where she and her sisters
had kowtowed to their father like the servant girls in
the fairy tales he'd read aloud to them when they were
little. Not the watered-down *Hans Christian Andersen*
versions, but the original tales from an earlier, more
bloodthirsty century, in which the heads of Bluebeard's
wives were revealed in gruesome detail, and Cinderella's
ugly stepsisters hacked off their toes to squeeze into the
glass slipper.

Her mind's eye formed a picture of her father seated
in the brocade wing chair by the fireplace with his head
bent over the heavy leather-bound volume in his lap.
The light from the fringed silk lamp shade played over
his long surgeon's hand as he slid it lengthwise between
the gilt-edged pages with the careful slicing motion he'd
taught them, counseling, *A dog-eared book is the sign of
a lazy, undisciplined person.* His hair, the pale amber of
the single scotch and water he allowed himself each
night before supper, was thinning on top and every so
often he stroked it carefully as if to make sure it hadn't
deserted him altogether. One long gabardine-clad leg
crossed languorously over the other as the words rolled
off his tongue—rich, fulsome, shiver-inducing.

The day after tomorrow she and Roger and the kids
were flying out to California for her parents' fortieth
wedding anniversary. Her sisters would be there, along
with members of their extended family from across the
country. Daphne suddenly couldn't wait. It felt as if everything she treasured most was tied up in the big gabled
house on Agua Fria Point, where little had changed in
the years since she'd left for college. Like the stories
contained in the volumes lining the mahogany bookcase
in her father's study, their yellowing pages rustling like
autumn leaves in the twilight of a seemingly endless
golden summer, a summer of sandy bathing suits slung

over the porch railing and peeling sunburns and homemade lemonade by the gallon.

As if from a distance, she heard the assistant manager
say, "There's usually a few who show up late, though,
like, you know, the regulars . . . the ones you can pretty
much count on."

Daphne nodded. The same loyal handful who showed
up at every one of her readings: pensioners eager to be
entertained as long as it didn't cost a dime, the ponytailed grad student who considered it his moral duty to
support a member of the literary underclass, the would-
be novelists desperate for any thread of hope she might
have to offer, however slender. And like a fleck of gold
amid the silt, the occasional voice piping, "Miss Seagrave, I've read *all* your books. It's such an honor to
meet you."

There were never more than a dozen or so. She simply
wasn't that kind of author. Though generally reviewed
well, her novels had never been on any best-seller list.
Her tales of family unrest, and the quiet desperation that
can lie at the heart of a seemingly fulfilled life, sold only
enough copies to provide her publisher with a legitimate
excuse to offer her a contract for the next book.

At this particular moment, though, Daphne would
have traded half her modest advance for a single warm
body. A lonely widower looking to kill an hour. A
starry-eyed hopeful with a drawerful of rejection slips at
home. A tired shopper stopping to rest his or her feet.
Anyone. Anyone at all.

Her husband even.

But Roger was already wandering off in the direction
of the biography section. She watched his back, the tec-
tonic shift of its broad flat planes under his tweed blazer,
the way he pitched from side to side as big men do—as
if merely assuming that whoever stood in his path must
either step aside or fall in behind him. Don't you dare,
she called to him in silent outrage. *Don't you dare leave
me stranded.*

She caught up with him by a freestanding aisle dis-
playing every kind of computer title imaginable—all of
which appeared to be geared toward a fifth-grade men-

tality. When Roger turned to offer a smile—more pa-
tronizing than encouraging, it seemed to her—Daphne's
cheeks burned.

"Don't worry. You'll do just fine," he reassured her.

"How can you say that?" she hissed under her breath.
"*You're* not the one swinging in the wind here. Roger,
I can't do this alone."

He gently shook his large shaggy head. Daphne distinctly recalled when they'd first met, back in college.
Fittingly enough, Roger had been her TA in Logic I.
Only a few years older, he'd nonetheless struck a profes-
sorial stance even back then. All he'd needed were a
pipe and leather elbow patches to complete the picture.
Once, when she'd asked his help on a take-home exam,
he'd been as exasperated with her inability to grasp
what, to him, was so abundantly clear as *she* had with
the questions themselves. "Don't you see? Without A
and B there *is* no C," he'd cried in frustration at one
point.

What had attracted her to him? Ironically, the very
solid predictability she now found so irritating. After
Johnny, there had been only the pain, each day blending
into the next like waves overlapping one another in a
vast, uncharted sea. Roger had provided an anchor.
Something to hold her in place whenever the sharp tugs
of memory threatened to set her adrift.

Johnny . . .

The clear image she'd carried for so long had faded,
like a wallet photo creased and worn from handling; in
its place was a mosaic of fleeting impressions and sense
memories. The faint acrid scent of the Winstons he
smoked. The self-conscious way he smiled, more like a
sneer, to hide his crooked front teeth. The low cynical
laugh that came from a place inhabited by someone far
older than seventeen, someone who wore his jeans tight
when everyone else at Muir High was into baggy, and
didn't give a rat's ass if he got heat—as if anyone would
dare—about his motorcycle boots and the army jacket
that was more his uniform than that of the older brother
who'd gotten his guts blown out in Nam.

Daphne took a deep breath to ward off the memories,

and turned her attention to Roger. He wasn't unkind, she told herself. He wasn't abandoning her. Hadn't he forgone his poker game to drive her all the way out to Port Chester in the pouring rain?

"Last time, six people showed up, and every one went away satisfied," he recalled, annoyingly accurate as always. "Anyway, I'm not going anywhere. Just give a shout if you need me."

Daphne cast a panicked glance at the empty chairs, which Leonard was in the process of folding and stacking against the wall. He seemed in no particular hurry, and was making more noise than a brass band clanging its way up Fifth Avenue.

She clutched Roger's arm in desperation. "Sit with me," she pleaded under her breath. "Just for a few minutes. Until at least one other person shows up. That's all I ask."

He patted her hand in a gesture of fond indulgence. "I'll stay right where you can see me. I promise. I won't even duck into the men's room."

"It's not *you* I'm worried about," she whispered, squeezing his arm harder than she'd intended, hard enough to make him wince. "*I'm* the one who's going to look like a fool."

"You could never look like a fool."

"Easy for you to say."

A faint look of annoyance creased his broad face. "Really, Daphne," he admonished gently. "You're a serious author, not some fly-by-night pulp sensation. No one whose opinion matters expects you to hold court for a cheering crowd."

"Roger, I am not talking about a *crowd*. Just one friendly face." Daphne hated the way she sounded, as if she were begging, like when three-year-old Jennie pleaded with Daphne to walk her, not just to the door of her nursery school, but all the way inside.

Roger stood with his head bent as if in contemplation, lightly stroking the bridge of his nose between his thumb and forefinger. "It's the principle of the thing," he explained with elaborate patience. "You don't need any-

one to hold your hand. What you *need* is to have more
confidence in yourself."

Suddenly, it was her father's voice she was hearing.
*Stand up straight, shoulders back, you'll never get anyone
to notice you walking all hunched over like that.* She
could see Daddy as if he were standing before her now—
lean, handsome, impatient in the way of someone who
knows there is only one correct way of doing something:
his way. She saw the bony ridge of his nose and the
muscles belting his wiry forearms, his carbon-blue eyes
as sharp as the instruments he used on cadavers no more
equipped to resist his iron will than his family had been.
She supposed her father, like Roger, had had only her
best interests at heart, but at fourteen, painfully conscious of her flat chest and mouthful of metal, the last
thing on earth she'd wanted was to be noticed. Even
now, more than twenty years later, she could feel herself
stiffening in resistance, as if Daddy's thumbs were pressing into her shoulder blades, attempting to pry her
upright.

Roger was right, she told herself. What was there to
be ashamed of? She was an accomplished author as well
as wife and mother. A woman who, at thirty-nine, could
still catch the eye of men half her age. And that, she
thought with a hastily scraped-up measure of pride, was
without dieting or coloring her hair—a naturally wavy
chestnut that tended to frizz with the damp. She reached
up now to rake her fingers through it and could almost
feel the kinks springing up under her touch. But who
would notice? Best to simply grit her teeth and get
through this with as much dignity as she could muster.

Watching her husband stroll off, his large capable
hands stuffed idly in the front pockets of his wide-wale
corduroy trousers, she nevertheless felt a wild urge to
seize the nearest book—*Windows 98 for Dummies*—and
hurl it at him.

The ensuing ordeal turned out to be every bit as ex-
cruciating as she'd imagined—like being skewered on a
spit in one of those glass-front supermarket rotisseries,
endlessly turning. In lieu of the podium she'd declined,
she sat at a small table stacked with copies of *Walking*

After Midnight, on which some thoughtful employee had placed a coffee mug stuffed with half a dozen pens. Just in case, she observed drily, there wasn't enough ink in a single Bic Soft Feel for all the books her legions of hungry fans would be lining up to have her autograph.

A few browsers glanced at her, then just as quickly looked away, as if from a car wreck. It was like the eighth-grade dances she recalled in agonizing detail, the hour upon hour of sitting motionless against the wall, the muscles in her face aching from her monumental effort to keep on smiling as if she were having a good time.

Daphne would have welcomed even the company of the pimply assistant manager, who seemed to think it was enough just to breeze past every ten minutes or so to see if she had everything she needed. She wanted to shriek at him, *What could I possibly need other than a two-by-four to hit you and my husband over the head with?*

Roger, engrossed in a book at the far end of the store, seemed equally oblivious to her torment.

Daddy would never have left Mother stranded this way, she thought. As strict as he'd been with his daughters, he was always tender and solicitous with their mother. Courtly, even. Mother and Daddy had always been the envy of their friends. Well, they must be doing something right. Forty years, she thought. Daphne tried to imagine celebrating her fortieth anniversary with Roger, but in her present state, she wasn't at all certain her marriage would last beyond tonight.

Her gaze strayed once more to Roger, who now was chatting with someone he appeared to know—a woman with short blond hair, not especially pretty, but attractive in the way of suburban wives who jogged five miles before breakfast and drove into Manhattan every other month to have their hair professionally styled. She was smiling at some comment Roger had made, her head slightly cocked, wearing an expression that brought to mind a word Daphne associated with romance novels: coquettish.

Watching them, Daphne felt herself grow even more

tense. Roger seemed in no hurry to get back to the book tucked leisurely under one arm. Nor did he so much as glance Daphne's way. If this woman was such a friend, why didn't he bring her over and introduce her to his wife? Roger didn't have a moment to spare for *her*, but seemed to have all the time in the world for someone he barely knew.

Fuming inside, she watched him lean into the bookcase, draping his arm over the uppermost row of books the way she imagined he might have, at age fifteen, slung it over the back of his date's seat in a movie theater as a preliminary to working his way down to her shoulders.

Five minutes slipped into ten before the woman glanced regretfully at her watch. She said something to Roger and was turning to go when he slipped her his business card. Surreptitiously, it seemed to Daphne. Or was she just imagining the furtiveness with which it flickered between them before being swallowed up by the woman's navy Chanel bag?

Daphne felt as if a car she was riding in had hit a pothole, jarring her so hard she could feel it in her tightly clenched jawbone. Was Roger working up to some sort of—

Her mind refused to form the words, but the wave of panic spreading through her said it all. Even so . . . an affair? Roger? It didn't seem likely.

A fractured memory teased at the edges of her mind— she'd been what? Eight . . . nine?—of a dark room, perfumed fur tickling her cheek. There had been party sounds down the hall, and a couple silhouetted in the doorway . . .

She wanted to cover her eyes now as she had then. *Silly,* she scolded herself. *You're overreacting because you're upset with Roger.*

"Excuse me. Miss Seagrave?"

Daphne looked up at the elderly woman who'd appeared before her, clutching a copy of her book. Small, gray, shopworn, she stood hunched over as if apologizing for taking up space—the kind of person, Daphne suspected, who, when someone cut ahead of her in line, chose to remain silent rather than kick up a fuss. She glanced at the photo on the back, then back at Daphne, and sighed before reluctantly placing the book back on the pile.

"It *is* you," she exclaimed, one hand fluttering to a cheek rosy with unaccustomed excitement. "Oh, heavens, I don't know what to say. I'm so honored to meet you! I've read every single one of your books. In fact," she leaned forward as if about to share some highly confidential piece of information, "I'd have to say you're my favorite author. Next to Iris Murdoch, that is."

"Thank you." Daphne mustered a smile. "That's the nicest compliment I've gotten all evening."

The woman glanced about, and for a stricken moment Daphne wondered if she was going to make mention of the fact that she was the *only* one paying her any compliments, but the enraptured fan only murmured, "I was afraid I'd be too late. That you'd leave as soon as the reading was over. But here you are. I'm Doris, by the way. Doris Wingate."

"Nice to meet you," said Daphne, reaching across the table to shake a soft, shy hand. "Would you like me to autograph a book for you?"

The color in Doris's cheeks deepened to an alarming shade of red. "Oh. Well. I didn't mean . . . but, of course, how stupid of me, you're here to sell books. I wish . . . but, you see, I check everything out of the library."

Anxious to relieve the poor woman's misery, Daphne confided in a low voice, "I know just what you mean. I get away to the library whenever I can. I have two kids, three and seven, and it can get a bit hectic around my house at times." The two women shared a knowing smile, and Daphne saw Doris's hunched shoulders relax ever so slightly. On impulse, she reached into the shoulder bag at her feet. From her wallet, she extracted two bills, a twenty and a five, which she then slipped into the topmost copy of *Walking After Midnight*. Scrawling a few words on the title page, she handed it to Doris. "Here. This one's on me."

The old woman stared in disbelief before slowly extending a trembling hand to accept what might as well have been the holy grail. "Oh. My. I don't know what to say. This . . . this is the nicest thing anyone's ever done for me." She looked as if she was about to cry.

Daphne felt a wave of uneasy sympathy. Would she one day be reduced to this: an old woman grateful for any crumb tossed her way? Any small sign that she was worthy of notice, of time and money spent on her behalf? Someone like . . .

Mother . . .

She quickly brushed away the thought. Her mother wasn't like this woman at all. And neither was she. *I'll talk to Roger. Let him know exactly how I feel.*

As soon as she was able to make her escape, and they were alone in the car, inching along the Long Island Expressway, Daphne confronted her husband.

"Who was that woman I saw you talking to?"

"What woman?" He flipped the turn signal, and eased into the next lane.

"You seemed awfully friendly with one another."

Roger flashed her a grin. "I don't believe it. You're jealous? Of Maryanne Patranka?"

"*Now* we're getting somewhere."

"She's the mother of a former patient. Haven't seen her in years." Roger drummed on the steering wheel, a nervous habit of his. He hadn't mentioned slipping Maryanne his card. If she *was* only a professional acquaintance, it wouldn't make sense, their staying in touch. Unless . . .

"You might have introduced me," she remarked coolly. "It would have been nice just to have the company. It wasn't as if I had anything better to do."

"You sold one book, I noticed," he hedged. "*That's* something."

Daphne didn't tell him the book had been a gift. She suddenly couldn't bear the idea of his knowing. Of appearing foolishly sentimental in his eyes. Even desperate. If she gave up any more ground than she already had, she'd be treading air.

She stared out the window. The rain was still coming down hard. Watching it crawl in dark creeks across the windshield, she found herself thinking, perversely, not of tonight's betrayal, or the affair Roger might or might

not be entering into, but of her satin dress and Roger's
tux at the dry cleaner's waiting to be picked up. Before
packing for their trip to California on Friday, she'd have
Kyle, seven years old and growing like a weed, try on
his trousers to see if they needed to be let down another
inch. Oh yes, and check with her travel agent to make
sure the rental car reserved for them in San Francisco
was the four-door sedan she'd requested. She'd call
Kitty, too, and ask if her sister would baby-sit the kids
the afternoon of their parents' party, so she'd be free to
help with any last-minute arrangements.

This is your life, she thought. All the little routines
and mundane plans piled like bricks, one atop the other,
mortared together with caution to form a house even
the big bad wolf couldn't blow down. A house strong
enough to keep her from thinking about the life she
could have had. With Johnny . . .

Was that the reason she mistrusted Roger? Because
she herself had so often felt guilty of being unfaithful,
in mind if not in body? Did the real reason she was so
angry at him for deserting her tonight boil down to the
simple fact that all those years ago he wasn't the one
she'd chosen? Rather, fate had chosen him for her.

Let it go, Daphne. Her mother's voice, soothing as a
cool hand against a hot forehead. Had Mother ever felt
this way? God knew she'd put up with plenty. Daddy
wasn't the easiest, not by a long shot. But they loved
one another, truly and passionately; she was convinced
of it. *Forty years . . .*

Whatever Daphne might have witnessed that long-ago
night, crouched in the closet of her parents' bedroom,
had to have been her imagination . . . or an innocent
embrace she'd somehow misinterpreted. And if not,
Mother and Daddy had long since resolved any differences they might have had. While visiting last summer,
Daphne had been amused, and yes, a little embarrassed
even, by the way her parents carried on after all these
years. Her mother lighting up like a teenager when
Daddy, who at sixty-seven continued to reign as chief
pathologist of Miramonte General, arrived home at the
end of each day.

"Traffic is really easing up," Roger remarked. "We should be hitting the tunnel in a few minutes. I'll have us home in no time at all."

Home. That was exactly where she wanted to be right now. But not their Park Avenue apartment. She yearned for her room upstairs in the house on Cypress Lane, lying on her bed gazing out the tall, salt-silvered window at the sun setting fire to the high grass along Agua Fria Point.

Daphne saw herself walking up the front path trailed by her husband and children. Mother emerging from the shadows onto the porch steps with one hand cupped over her eyes to shade them from the bright sun, the other pressed to her heart as if half expecting bad news of some kind. And Daddy, accustomed to the kind that usually ended with a body on a stainless-steel table in the hospital morgue, would be there to give her a quick, hard embrace before holding her at arm's length to exclaim gruffly, "You made it. Good."

Tonight, riding up in the elevator alongside Roger to their penthouse on the twenty-fourth floor, Daphne was flooded with relief, an irrational sense of having narrowly averted some unseen disaster. She felt foolish all of a sudden, imagining that a few minutes of embarrassment in a bookstore was the end of the world. That Roger slipping some woman his card spelled an affair. She ought to be grateful, *grateful,* for the life she had. Her husband, and two beautiful children. Her parents, neither of whom showed any sign of succumbing to old age. Her sister, Kitty. And yes, even Alex.

Yet the moment she walked in to find their baby-sitter on the phone wearing a troubled look, some deep instinct told Daphne that she hadn't averted a disaster after all, that whatever it was, she was about to receive some very bad news. She felt it in her gut . . . even before Susie held out the receiver to her as if it were a small, vicious animal that might bite, offering in a queer, hollow voice, "It's your sister. She sounds really upset."

Kitty. And she wasn't merely upset. She was hysterical, gasping for breath between sobs, barely able to speak. And even when Daphne began to grasp what

Kitty was saying, it made no sense. No sense at all. Her sister's words were like the rain dribbling down the darkened window she faced with the receiver pressed hotly to her ear.

"Daddy. It's Daddy," Kitty cried from three thousand miles away. "Mother sh-sh-shot him. The police. Took her away. Come now, Daphne. We *need* you."

Chapter 2

As the sun rose on the Monday that would be remembered in years to come as the watershed that severed her family's history into Before and After, Kitty Seagrave was kneading dough for cinnamon sticky buns.

Her parents' fortieth anniversary was this coming weekend, and she'd volunteered to bake the cake, a triple-layer Lady Baltimore, for the gala Mother and Daddy were throwing at the club. Only now it occurred to her that she'd forgotten to order extra eggs and butter. Like so much else over the past week or so, it had simply slipped her mind. Kitty was ashamed to realize she hadn't given her parents, or the party, more than a passing thought.

And that wasn't like her. Not the Kitty Seagrave who gave out tins of homemade cookies at Christmas, and remembered every family birthday with a card and a gift. The Kitty who doted on her nieces and nephew, and seldom failed to carry out her role as dutiful daughter—a role inscribed in stone that had less to do with the real Kitty than either of her parents might imagine.

But how could she concentrate on anything when, running through her head—endlessly, maddeningly, like those continuous loops on airport TVs—was the introduction scheduled for later today? This afternoon she was to meet the sixteen-year-old girl who held the power either to crush her . . . or offer the gift of a lifetime.

Standing at the flour-dusted butcher block that formed the hub of her roomy old-fashioned kitchen, her heart beating high and fast in her chest, Kitty glanced at the round clock on the wall. *In exactly nine hours and thirty-six minutes, I'll be face-to-face with the mother of my future child,* she thought. If all went well . . .

But what if the girl took one look and ran in the other direction? Kitty was well aware of how she might appear to someone who didn't know her—a single woman living alone with her pets, a Miramonte earth mama with just enough good sense to have turned her homespun talents into something she could make money at: a tea salon supplied by baked goods from her own kitchen. In short, someone you'd be happy to have baby-sit your children . . . but not necessarily to raise them.

Should she have packed up the seashells and bits of worn, pitted glass lining the windowsills of her rooms upstairs? Folded away the fringed silk shawl draped over the bentwood rocker? Taken down the piatas that hung from the gabled ceiling like bright, oversize fruit?

Would it make a difference?

She doubted it. Some things you can change, she thought. Others are as much a part of you as the texture of your skin or the timbre of your laugh. What Kitty saw reflected in the mirror each morning when she rose shortly before dawn was a thirty-six-year-old woman whose appearance had changed remarkably little in the decades since she herself had been a teenager. Other than a certain youthful luster that had begun to fade, like an old satin pillow rubbed to a dull sheen, she was essentially the same Kitty Seagrave who'd harbored a wild crush on her sister Daphne's boyfriend, and once, on a dare, waltzed into a drugstore in her nightgown to buy the June issue of *Mademoiselle*. A creature of habit who wore her waist-length ginger hair exactly as she had in high school: a feathery cascade anchored at each temple with a tortoiseshell comb. And who weighed not an ounce more or less back then—just under a hundred pounds in her stocking feet—a lucky throw of the genetic dice she shared with Daphne, but which drove their younger sister, Alex, who was constantly watching her waistline, nearly insane with jealousy.

Her eyes were the one feature most often remarked on: a blue so deep they were almost purple, the dusky shade of damson plums. A former boyfriend had once said they made him think of swimming at night in the

Old Sashmill Road Reservoir out near Route 32. She supposed it was a compliment.

The fact was Kitty didn't particularly care how she looked. Year after year, the winds of fashion blew past her virtually unnoticed. She wore only what was comfortable—loose cotton tops and drawstring pants, hand-knit sweaters in natural hues, silk kimono tops that fluttered like butterfly wings when she gestured exuberantly, which she was prone to do. And the one pair of shoes she practically lived in served no purpose other than to save her from having to hobble about in agony after endless hours on her feet: Naot sandals that, let's face it, gave her the look of a retro seventies Peace Corps volunteer.

Oh please, let her like me, Kitty prayed, squeezing her eyes shut for just a moment, and bringing her floury hands to rest on the dough mounded in front of her. *Let her see how much I have to give.* Because what was so perfectly clear to Kitty might not be to a perfect stranger: that this baby would be more than a way to fill the cavity in her heart; it would be a bright halo about a life already rich and bountiful.

She drove a fist into the dough, sending a gust of flour spinning up into the pale light that slanted in through the windows. Out back, where Harbor Lane sloped down toward the ocean, the fog clung stubbornly to the houses descending in a crooked staircase to the ghostly thicket of the marina. But higher up where her house sat, it was much thinner, like moisture evaporating from a chilled glass. Under the warm kiss of the rising sun, her garden sparkled as if freshly polished—the tangle of jasmine and honeysuckle and nasturtium along the fence, the thyme and rosemary bordering her small brick patio, the Meyer trees that provided an endless supply of lemons for tarts, cakes, tea breads, and pies, not to mention gallons of lemonade.

This was what she loved best about Miramonte, what she could offer a child: a house by the seashore, where it was seasonable year-round except during the coldest winter months, when the wind sneaked in like a heartless intruder around the loose panes and fog-buckled door frames of the post-Victorian homes originally built for summer use along Oceanside Avenue. Kitty could see her daughter (she was convinced, for reasons that had nothing to do with preference, the baby would be a girl) curled up with her on the old plush sofa in the bay window upstairs, cradling mugs of hot cocoa in which marshmallows bobbed like tiny buoys.

Her gaze fell on the doghouse that stood abandoned beneath an arthritic loquat in need of pruning. Even from here, she could make out the shallow crater worn in the grass by her old chocolate lab's endless doggie circling. When Buster died last year, she hadn't immediately replaced him with a puppy, as her friends had strongly urged. Instead, she'd taken under her wing the pair of stray kittens she found curled up one morning on a scrap of old blanket inside his doghouse. Or maybe it was the other way around: Fred and Ethel had adopted *her*. Traipsing after her as if she were their mother, springing onto her lap whenever she sat down— once when she was on the toilet—even crawling up into her hair and attempting to nurse on her earlobes.

Then six months ago, when Ivan announced out of the blue that he was moving to Santa Fe, she'd received a second consolation prize: a sweet-natured Samoyed-shepherd mix named Romulus. Her boyfriend had given the excuse that his dog's thick fur would be a misery to him in the baking heat of the Southwest. And Kitty, knowing an attack of eleventh-hour guilt when she saw one—even in someone as self-centered as Ivan—had refrained from pointing out that Santa Fe was high desert, where it snowed in winter. What good would it have done for him to know she'd have been far more broken-hearted to let go of Rommie?

Kitty could see her dog out back now, his thick gray Elizabethan ruff bristling as he busily investigated something lurking under the toolshed. One of the cats, no doubt. Rommie was like a truant officer, the way he chased after those two. But with children he was as gentle as a kitten himself. Her baby wouldn't lack for companionship.

Watching his black muzzle surface in triumph with its

prize—an ancient mud-encrusted tennis ball—she felt the corner of her mouth lift in a smile. Then she remembered what lay ahead . . . and her anxiety came rushing back in with a suddenness that left her breathless, as if someone had sneaked up behind and given her apron strings a good hard yank.

With a sigh, Kitty plopped the now thoroughly pummeled dough in a ceramic bowl to rise. She'd long since given up trying to gauge how much to make. No matter how many trays came out of the oven, they were always picked cleaned by midmorning. Her cinnamon sticky buns, it seemed, had developed an almost cultlike following. She'd even heard it rumored that the recipe was a closely guarded secret, passed down through the generations of Seagrave women who'd made their home here, all the way back to the mid-1800s, to Kitty's great-great-grandmother, Agatha Rose.

But there was no secret to Kitty's baking. Had she been pressed to name a magic ingredient, she'd have said simply: *patience.* Taking the time to nurture each batch of dough and letting it rise in a quiet warm place. Knowing it was a form of respect and, yes, affection even, toward those who would savor the end result. Another word for it, she supposed, was love. But that would sound corny.

And maybe even a little foolish.

Kitty covered the bowl with a damp towel, then without pausing to rest, began measuring out flour and sugar for muffins. No time to obsess about things over which she had no control; she had a business to run, hungry customers who would soon be showing up at her door.

Briskly, she stepped around Fred, the largest of the two calicoes, asleep on the braided rug by the stove, to fill her apron with eggs from the basket atop the antique pie safe. The eggs were delivered twice a week, every Saturday and Wednesday, packed in layers of straw by a brussels sprout farmer who tended a few acres up near Pescadero. Every so often, Salvadore, whom she suspected of having a minor crush on her, threw in for free a stewing hen he claimed was too stringy to sell . . . but which always cooked up tender and delicious. She

wondered what the poor man might think if he knew
how often she'd fantasized about his offering instead one
of the fawn-colored children who peeked with shy brown
eyes from the cab of his battered pickup.

When the muffin batter was loosely mixed, she divided
it into three smaller bowls. Into the first she tossed handfuls of chopped apples and walnuts. Into the other two
went frozen blueberries and peaches left over from last
summer's harvest. By now she knew how many of each
kind to bake so that no one went away disappointed.
Only the pumpkin-cranberry muffins she made at
Thanksgiving and Christmas, from sugar pumpkins she
picked and roasted herself, flew out of here faster than
she could keep up with.

Kitty marveled at the popularity of her tea room. Four
years ago, armed with little more than a bright idea and
the need to augment her kindergarten teacher's salary,
she couldn't have foreseen that this place would evolve
into a local institution of sorts. A watering hole where
neighbors met to strategize about a traffic light they
were circulating a petition for . . . and the Ladies' Garden Society gathered to plan their annual begonia festival. Where town councilmen and church deacons and
doctors rubbed elbows with minimum-wage workers
from the tannery, and children trooped in after school
for something to sweeten their walk home.

Here, professors from the university found solace and
civilized company away from pierced tongues and purple
hair. And young lovers traced their initials in steamy
windows. Kitty knew of several marriage proposals that
had been made under this roof. And who could forget
the Ogilvies' tearful breakup last winter after Everett
Ogilvie confessed to his wife of fourteen years that he
was in love with their Finnish au pair?

Yet the concept behind Tea & Sympathy was so simple that when people called it a stroke of genius, Kitty
had to bite her lip to keep from laughing. The idea had
come to her in the most mundane way possible—while
eating lunch in the staff room of Miramonte Elementary.
Nibbling on a stale Fig Newton, she'd idly mused about
how much she missed her grandmother's icebox cookies.

Where had they gone, she'd wondered, all those remembered treats from childhood? Baked goods as heart-
warming as they were toothsome, that you didn't need
a culinary degree and a half a day to prepare. What
insidious plot had succeeded in abolishing them from
cupboards and cookie jars where they'd once reigned
supreme?

That was six years ago. She'd been just shy of her
thirtieth birthday, an age when most people begin to
wonder if it might be worth taking a second look at life's
map to see if they're headed in the right direction. Kitty
was no exception. Fired with inspiration, she set off in
search of Nana's old cookbooks, conveniently packed
away in a box in her parents' attic. Several months and
dozens of trials later, armed with tentative orders from
a handful of restaurants and delis, she had gone about
re-creating a sort of fifties-style kitchen. In the beginning, yes, her more sophisticated friends had laughed.
Pineapple upside-down cake? Apple brown Betty? Rice
Krispies treats? That wasn't what people wanted these
days, they'd said. Black bottom pie had gone out with
Hula Hoops and backyard bomb shelters.

Kitty had merely smiled and gone about filling her
orders, which soon swelled to a flood. In two years' time,
she'd saved enough to open her own business, and had
lucked onto this house, commercially zoned and only
two streets from downtown's main shopping street.

Now there was only one thing missing in her life.

With a mighty effort, Kitty once again pushed
thoughts of today's meeting aside. There was plenty to
do still before Willa arrived to stock the counter out
front—apples to peel, nuts to chop, lemons to squeeze.
And, really, she reasoned with herself, would it be so
terrible if her life went on just as it was?

She loved what she did. She loved just leafing through
the stained, dog-eared pages of her mother's and grandmother's cookbooks, *Fannie Farmer* and *Betty Crocker*,
from a more innocent time, before it became fashionable
to list carbs and fat grams, when all of life had seemed
as simple and straightforward as a blueberry buckle
warm from the oven. She cherished most those recipes

turned to so often they'd come loose from their bind-
ing—banana-nut bread, oatmeal cake with broiled coco-
nut topping, molasses crinkles. Her own specialties were
pies and turnovers filled with whatever fruit was in season locally—strawberries and rhubarb in the spring;
peach, apricot, and plum in summer; raspberries and lo-
ganberries in the fall. During the winter months, when
her mainstays were apples and pears, her mother's
home-canned peaches brought relief from the endless
peeling and slicing.

Mother. *I really ought to give her a call,* Kitty thought
with a twinge of guilt. Lately, though, whenever she
reached for the phone, something always seemed to
come up. Or maybe that was just an excuse. She loved
her mother, honestly she did, but . . .

But. Why did every sentence or thought beginning
with her mother seemed to end with a "but"? Mother
never pushed. She would always cluck in sympathy when
told you were too busy to come . . . but the next minute
she'd be on the phone to Alex or Daphne, declaring
bravely and at great length that Kitty had her own life,
her own plans, *just as it should be.* And, oh Lord, those
Sunday dinners up at the house. However little she ate,
Kitty was constipated for a week. Maybe what she was
full of, up to her eyeballs, was the sticky sweetness of it
all—the image of them all as this picture-perfect family
that Mother served up with such gusto.

Wearied by the mere prospect of what lay ahead—the
party with its endless round of toasts, and her parents
basking in the glow of all that admiration, and yes, envy,
too—she stopped stirring and brought her wooden spoon
to rest against the countertop. An old memory flutter-
kicked to the surface. From out of nowhere, she had a
sudden clear image of Daddy lining them all up for a
camera shot in front of the lodge at Lake Modoc.

They'd been on the road for hours, she recalled, and
it was approaching dark. Their warm jackets still packed
away, they'd stood shivering in the deepening shadows
of the pines as Daddy arranged them according to
height, with Daphne, the tallest at thirteen, wedged between her and Mother, and Alex at the tail end. He'd

insisted on shot after shot, complaining that someone had blinked or wasn't smiling, until they were all freezing and close to tears. Afterward, they'd unpacked, and her father had driven them into town where they'd stuffed their faces at an all-you-can-eat smorgasbord, with Daddy ordering rounds of Shirley Temples and telling funny stories throughout supper. By the end of it, she and Daphne and Alex were scrambling over each other for the privilege of sitting next to him on the drive back.

The pictures, though—the four them huddled together, a frozen quartet of squinched eyes and cheese-eating grins—they hadn't lied. It wasn't the real story, of course, only a facet of it. The real story of their family was made up of dozens of such facets, like those in a diamond that glitters brightly but is hard enough to cut glass.

She'd call home tonight, Kitty decided. She hadn't told her family about Heather. She hadn't wanted to jinx anything. But if today's meeting went well, Mother would know soon enough. She'd wonder, too, why Kitty had waited so long to say something.

And if things didn't turn out as Kitty hoped?

Something in her chest squeezed into a hard fist.

I'll cross that bridge if and when I get to it, she told herself. Either way, she ought to see if Mother needed help with any last-minute details—something, she hoped, she and Daphne could do together.

All at once Kitty couldn't wait to see her older sister. Of course, she could do without Roger, whom she found overbearing, but her sister was the best, and Daphne's children precious beyond belief. When they visited last summer, Kitty had made a batch of cookie dough just for Kyle and Jennie, which they'd decorated with sprinkles and colored stars and bits of candied fruit.

She wished it were as uncomplicated as that with her sister. But even with Daphne—the only person in the world who knew Kitty had slept with her English teacher the night of her high school graduation—she had to tiptoe around certain subjects. Roger, for one. And their parents . . . well, that was the biggest blind spot of all.

There was a reason Daphne lived in New York, Kitty thought darkly. Being three thousand miles away was easier than having to run from hard truths close to home.

"Something sure smells good!"

Kitty turned to find Willa standing outside the open back door, prying a ratty sneaker from one foot while hopping about one-legged on the other. When the shoe was off, she turned it upside down and gave it a good smack, dumping a small river of sand over the porch railing.

Kitty smiled at the same dopey greeting her helper called out *every* morning, and the fact that Willa never arrived without bringing a piece of the outdoors with her—if not sand, then clots of mud, or snips of mown grass. For weeks every spring, the kitchen's rust-colored tiles bore faint golden tracks of pollen from the acacias that lined the narrow dirt roads out where Willa lived, about ten miles north of town in Barranco, a community commonly (and rudely, in Kitty's opinion) referred to as Flipville, due to its large concentration of Filipino farmworkers.

But the girl was so hardworking and good-natured Kitty never complained. She watched as Willa snagged one of the aprons that hung from a row of wooden pegs by the door, then began the morning ritual of winding her waist-length black hair into a knot at the nape of her neck.

"Wan' me do 'ose app-uhs?" she mumbled around a mouthful of bobby pins, jerking her head toward the wooden box of Granny Smiths on the floor outside the walk-in pantry. Kitty nodded, and the girl grinned as if she'd been awarded some sort of prize.

At nineteen, Willamene Aquino tipped the scales at two hundred forty pounds—more than twice Kitty's weight—and had already borne two babies by two different men. Yet life was good as far as Willa was concerned. Her mother, with whom she lived, took care of the children while Willa worked. And Kitty sent her home each day with sacks of fruit, and whatever baked goods were left. She saw no reason not to smile.

It was a cheerful disposition not even the grumpiest customer could shake. Willa was the only person Kitty knew who actually whistled while she worked. She loved to talk, too—nonstop chatter that at times drove Kitty a little crazy. Not so much because she found it distracting . . . but because Willa seemed to have only one interest besides her two little boys, whom she adored: men.

". . . He's got this cute little birthmark, shaped like a heart, right *there*." She paused in the midst of peeling an apple to press a finger into one cheek of her ample behind. "I'm always razing him about it, and man, you should see how red he gets; I'm serious, big tough dude with a tattoo . . . like, what, I'm gonna tell his buddies or something? That's Frankie for you, just a big old teddy bear. Know what he did last night? See if you can guess. Brought me a bunch of flowers he picked himself. Who cares they're from a vacant lot, it's the thought that counts . . . Whew, is it hot in here, or what? Did somebody turn up the heat? It feels like a hundred degrees!"

That was another thing: Willa was always too hot. Usually, Kitty just cracked a window, then threw on a sweater if it got too chilly. Today, she propped open the door that led to the front room, where any minute now her morning regulars were due to arrive.

Josie Hendricks was the first to make her entrance, just as Kitty and Willa were filling the baskets that lined the marble counter out front—a vintage soda fountain, complete with brass spigots, that Kitty had salvaged from the old Newberry on Water Street when it was being torn down.

"Good morning, ladies." The elderly woman, a retired schoolteacher, paused to plant her rubber-tipped cane inside the doorway before hitching herself over the threshold. "Glad to see you fixed that squeak. Did you use WD-40 like I told you?"

Josie, in her mideighties, got around fairly well for someone nearly crippled with arthritis, but lately had become fairly obsessed with all the little repairs she couldn't seem to keep from pointing out—squeaky hinges and wobbly chair legs, the window that stuck, the crack in the ceiling, the porch railing that could use a coat of paint.

"Worked like a charm," Kitty told her. Actually, what she'd used was plain old sewing machine oil, but what was the harm in a little white lie?

She watched Josie ease into a chair at her favorite table by the window, and cast a sharp glance about the room. Jerking a crabbed finger toward a corner of the ceiling where the flowered wallpaper had begun to peel away, she warned, "Let the little things slip, and before long you're looking at big headaches. Trust me, I know."

Kitty merely smiled, and brought Josie the tray that was waiting for her on the counter. The old woman showed up every morning like clockwork at five past seven, and always had the same thing: a peach muffin, and a pot of Darjeeling tea brewed strong enough, in her words, "to slice with a bread knife."

The bell over the front door tinkled again, followed by a gust of cool, damp air. Leanne Chapman, in her nurse's whites, sidled past Bud Jarvis, who'd paused to wipe his muddy boots on the doormat. They both ordered muffins to go. A single blueberry for Leanne, on her way home from the night shift at Miramonte General, and an assorted dozen for Bud, heading off to his job as foreman at the tannery.

"Don't I wish I had it as good as you," Leanne remarked with a dry laugh as Kitty was counting out her change. "Just like home ec all over again, huh?"

She thought she detected a flicker of resentment in Leanne's weary blue eyes. As if what Kitty did wasn't *real* work! Only loyalty to her sister Alex, Leanne's best friend since the first grade, kept her from saying anything.

Besides, she supposed Leanne had reason to be bitter with an ex-husband who'd run out on her when she was pregnant, and a child who was hopelessly brain damaged. Kitty knew from Alex that Leanne was only barely making ends meet. Who *wouldn't* resent someone better off?

It was Kitty's theory that just as there are those who

are born with silver spoons in their mouths, more than
a few could make the opposite claim: that they'd been
short-sheeted at birth. Leanne, she suspected, fell into
the latter category. The kid who'd tagged along on her
family's excursions and spent more time at *their* house
than at her own; who was forced to spend summers in
Iowa with her father rather than at the beach like everyone else her age. In school, no matter how hard she
studied, Leanne had never gotten higher than a B minus.
And the one time she'd let a boy go a little too far,
Stu Harding had spread it all over campus that Leanne
Chapman was "easy."

And that was before her *real* problems had started.

You wouldn't know it to look at her, though. Leanne
was still pretty in a washed-out sort of way, with the
same don't-mess-with-me walk: elbows tucked in against
her sides, with her head cocked slightly to one side as if
to keep an eye out for anything that might trip her up.

It wasn't until she was halfway out the door that Kitty
remembered to ask, "By the way, how's the Ferguson
baby doing?"

Leanne paused to push a wisp of strawberry blond
hair from her forehead. "Poor thing. He's having trouble
breathing on his own," she said. "We've got him on
a respirator, but it doesn't look good." Her expression
softened, and Kitty was reminded of the little girl whose
knees had been perpetually scabbed from falling off her
bike while swerving to avoid every beetle and snake and
land crab crossing the road. It was no accident Leanne
had decided to become a nurse.

"Poor Carole. She must be a basket case." Carole Ferguson had been in Kitty's class at Muir High—one of
the cheerleaders, the kind of girl you wouldn't in a million years imagine something like this happening to.
"Soon as I get a chance, I'll drop by, bring her something for the freezer." Kitty couldn't help thinking of
the baby that might soon be hers and felt a quickening
in her rib cage, just below her heart.

Her mind flew back to the day Cybill Rathwich had
taken her aside, saying she'd heard Kitty was looking to
adopt. Kitty wasn't sure how to respond at first. Her

regular customers were doing their best to be supportive, but so far had only succeeded in making things worse. Professor Ogden claimed to have seen her in a dream, waving to him from a Rose Bowl float with a baby in her arms. Josie Hendricks asked why she didn't just adopt an older child. Father Sebastian gently suggested she try artificial insemination.

What none of them knew, what was too painful for her to talk about, was how long and hard she'd been trying already. For years, all through her late twenties and early thirties, with a succession of lovers, hoping to get pregnant . . . only to have her hopes dashed each month. Then the endless round of tests in doctors' offices, where she'd been told the chances of her conceiving were remote. And more recently, weeding through a series of adoption agencies before finally arriving at two that had no objection to placing a single woman on their waiting list—as long as she understood it might be *years* before her name came up.

And now here was Cybill, with her chapped hands and square, unadorned face, gazing serenely at her like someone offering the world wrapped in a plain brown parcel. Not just another well-meaning soul handing out unwanted advice, but the local midwife. Cybill said she knew someone—an unwed teenager, six months pregnant—who was thinking of giving her baby up for adoption. Was Kitty interested? Standing there, her arms trembling with the weight of a tray holding a wedge of banana bread and a pot of lemon-verbena tea, Kitty had given the only answer possible.

"Yes," she'd breathed. "Oh, yes."

The girl's name was Heather, and she had no intention of marrying the boy who'd knocked her up. There was only one catch: she wouldn't be rushed into making a decision. First, before she would even agree to meet with Kitty, Heather had to know something about her.

At Cybill's suggestion, Kitty put together a scrapbook, complete with photos. She wrote about her house—the tea salon that occupied what had once been the living and dining rooms, and the second floor she used as her living quarters, with its guest room that could be converted into a nursery. She wrote a short, funny description of each of her pets: Byron, her Amazon parrot, who did a pretty fair rendition of "Pop Goes the Weasel" and could chew his way through a lamp cord faster than you could bite off the end of a hot dog; her calico cats that hadn't yet caught on to the fact that they weren't people; and Rommie, the amazing wonder dog, capable of leaping tall fences in a single bound.

What she *didn't* say was how desperately she wanted this baby. What could a sixteen-year-old girl know of this need that was like a slow starvation of the soul? Heather couldn't have experienced the yearning that would overtake Kitty sometimes while in the arms of a lover, causing her to tilt her hips so as to catch his seed, the whole time praying that this time it would take?

She would be thirty-seven in July. The last time she'd lain with a man was six months ago, the day Ivan strapped his drafting table to the roof of his Chevy Suburban, and took off for New Mexico. This might be her only chance.

Kitty thought once again of Leanne's poor little boy . . . and of Carole Ferguson's premature infant fighting for its life. *I'm fighting for a life, too,* she thought. Because wasn't no child at all a kind of death?

Work was the only thing that kept her from going crazy. Staying so busy she barely had time to think of anything except keeping the orders straight, and making enough muffins and cakes and pies to go around.

By nine, every table in the spacious front room was occupied, thirteen in all—a baker's dozen. And like her muffins, no two tables alike. A Victorian oak pedestal nestled beside the delicate draw leaf she'd inherited from Nana. A pine trestle that seated eight stretched alongside a sixties maple dinette. There was even an old Singer sewing cabinet refashioned into a quaint scroll-legged table for two. The overall effect, Kitty decided, was more eccentric than eclectic, but it worked somehow.

Kitty waved hello to Gladys Honeick, proprietress of Glad Tide-ins, the beachwear shop two doors down. Gladys, a shapely henna-haired divorcée who'd seen the better side of fifty, liked to joke that these days any man she could get to sleep with her would need a glass of water by the bed to hold his teeth. She appeared not to have noticed that Mac MacArthur, editor in chief of the *Miramonte Mirror*, always happened to show up around the time she usually did. Along with having all his teeth, Mac had buried two wives rumored to have been worn out trying to keep up with him. Gladys, she suspected, wouldn't have any trouble in that department.

Then there was Father Sebastian, his curly dark head tucked low, a pencil poised over a folded-over section of newspaper containing today's crossword puzzle. In another lifetime, the priest had been a resident of the Bonny Brae Youth Facility—before he decided to clean up his act and enter the local Jesuit seminary. But even in his black shirt and dog collar, he wasn't entirely free of old vices. Father Sebastian once confessed to Kitty with a wink that a world without horse racing and her rum-pecan tarts wouldn't be worth living in.

Kitty usually stopped to chat with the priest, but on this particular morning she found herself gravitating toward Serena Featherstone instead. Serena sat at a table in the far window, studying the tarot cards spread out on the table in front of her. Without looking up, she intoned ominously, "I see great disappointment ahead."

Kitty nearly jumped. Could this woman actually predict the future? Serena, with her long black hair and Indian cheekbones certainly *looked* the part. Then she noticed the smile peeking out from one corner of Serena's wide mouth.

"My sticky bun." Serena lifted her crinkled brown eyes to meet Kitty's startled gaze. "Willa must have forgotten. And if I don't get one before they're all gone, I'll be *very* disappointed."

"Hang on." Kitty hurried off, returning a moment later with a fat walnut-sprinkled bun oozing melted brown-sugar topping.

Serena gave a rueful laugh. "I know," she said. "It doesn't go with my image. My clients like to picture me living off herb tea and rice cakes."

"Speaking of which, you ready for a refill?" Kitty removed the top of Serena's flowered teapot, and peered inside. The perfumed scent of Earl Grey came wafting up at her.

"No, thanks. I have enough here to keep me in tea leaves." Serena indicated the still-full cup at her elbow, adding with a wink, "You could tempt me with another sticky bun, though. I'm only human, after all."

Kitty was turning to go when she suddenly thought to ask, "Do you have many? Clients, that is."

"You'd be surprised, though not many will admit to it." Serena flipped a sheaf of black hair threaded with gray over one shoulder, and regarded Kitty intently. "What about you? Ever been curious about what the future holds?"

Kitty wasn't sure. Until now, she'd never really given it much thought. "I guess that would depend on whether it was good or bad," she ventured.

Abruptly, Serena pushed her plate aside, and reached for Kitty's hand. Peering into her palm, she frowned and said, "One thing's for sure: you're going to fall in love, very soon, and this time for real. Those others . . . they weren't for keeps."

Kitty smiled to herself. Wasn't that what they *all* said?

"What about children?" Despite her natural skepticism, Kitty felt her heart begin to race.

"I see a child. Just one . . . only . . . there's some sort of complication." Serena's frown deepened as she gently rotated Kitty's hand this way and that—as if it were a rudder she was using to guide them to a distant, and possibly unfriendly shore.

"What?" Kitty breathed.

The psychic shook her head, the ends of her long coarse hair tickling the inside of Kitty's forearm. "It's strange . . . I've never seen anything quite like it . . ." When she glanced up, there was a strange, almost guilty look in her tea-colored eyes—like someone who's unwittingly pulled the cork from the genie's bottle, and now wants to jam it back in. "Look, are you sure you want to hear this?"

Kitty thought for a moment, then said, "Yes. I'm sure."

"I see a death in the family. Very imminent." Serena hastened to add, "Someone close to you." She glanced up sharply, slashes of color standing out on her high cheekbones. "I'm sorry, I shouldn't have told you. When it's bad news, I usually keep it to myself."

"Please." Kitty began to shiver, not at all certain what she was pleading for. Mercy? Or more details?

Serena let go of her hand, and sat back. "Nothing is written in stone. I could be wrong. Anyway, that's all I know."

Kitty took a step back, and absently rubbed her palm against her apron—as if wiping away something sticky. "Thanks for the warning. I'll keep an eye out." She struck a light-hearted tone, as if it were all just a silly parlor trick, but the damage was done. Her mind wheeled with questions.

What if the baby was given to her . . . then snatched away?

Serena had predicted a death—but whose? *Not Daphne . . . please don't let it be Daphne.* Kitty was struck with horror when she realized what she was praying for: that it be some other member of her family, someone she didn't love quite so much. Her mother or her father, both of whom were in good health but, let's face it, getting on in years. Or—

"Hey, Sis."

Kitty started, and looked up to find her younger sister poised just inside the door, perfectly turned out in a beige Armani suit and cream silk blouse. Here, where the dress code tended toward batik and tie-dye, where many acted as if cell phones and fax machines had yet to be invented, Alex stood out like a manicured sore thumb.

Her sister, Kitty knew, not only carried a cell phone in her shoulder bag, she'd also had a portable fax machine installed in her car—a late model BMW she leased for a small fortune, claiming it was essential in her line of work. She had a point there. Kitty doubted whether the wealthy Silicone Valley executives to whom Alex showed all those fancy houses would have been as eager to be chauffeured about in her own rust-speckled Honda Civic.

Once a month, too, Alex drove up to San Francisco to have her light brown hair styled, and its natural highlights "restored." On her way home stopping at I. Magnin, where, like a bedouin loading up his camel before heading back out into the Sahara, she stocked up on such essentials as designer pantyhose and Clinique cosmetics. Needless to say, it showed; she was a vision.

"Hey, yourself." Kitty greeted her sister more enthusiastically than she might have otherwise, certain her guilt was written all over her face, that her sister could see how quick Kitty had been to wish for Daphne's safety without giving a thought to Alex's. "What are you doing here this time of day?"

"I was showing a house just down the street." Alex pushed her sunglasses up, parking them above her fashionably wispy bangs. Glancing around the packed tables, she added, "If you're too busy, I can come back later."

"Never mind, you're here now." Kitty seized an empty chair and dragged it over to the counter. "Sit down. I'll bring you something to nibble on.

"Thanks, but I think I'll pass. I'm fat enough as it is." Ignoring the chair, Alex looked over the array of baked goods, her nose wrinkling.

Kitty didn't comment except to say, "Well, you look good."

Alex shrugged. "Good isn't the same as thin. I'm still working on those last five pounds."

In Kitty's opinion, the only thing Alex needed to lose was that tense look holding her in like a too-tight zipper. _If she's so unhappy with the way she looks, what on earth must she think of_ me? Kitty suddenly felt as if she were under a magnifying glass, every tiny line, freckle and untweezed hair blown up ten times its size. Would Heather expect someone more like Alex, who earned six figures and looked like a QVC pitchwoman?

She felt the knot in her stomach tighten.

"I figured since I was in the neighborhood, I'd pick up those cocktail napkins for the party," Alex said, add-

ing with a faint edge of mistrust, "Mother was afraid
you might have forgotten."

A familiar panic descended on Kitty. Napkins? Oh
God, she *had* forgotten. She'd promised to order them
from her wholesale supplier. She could still put in a rush
order, but it was probably too late to have them person-
alized. Damn . . .

She realized Alex was glaring at her, a low shimmer
like the radioactive glow from buried nuclear waste.
"You didn't get them," she said in a flat voice, her hazel
eyes narrowing ever so slightly.

"I didn't forget exactly. I just . . ." *Stop this,* Kitty commanded. *You always cave in, just because she's the one
getting angry, whether she has a right to or not.* ". . . I've
been really busy. I'll take care of it, don't worry."

"Well, if you were too *busy,* you should have said so
in the first place." Alex crossed her arms over her chest.
"As if *I* have one minute of free time. This week alone,
I have three closings, and a deal that won't go through
if I can't convince the seller not to dig up all his rose
bushes when he moves. And who do you think drove
the girls all the way to the airport and back so they
could have five precious minutes with their father before
he took off for Hong Kong?"

"What's Jim doing in Hong Kong?"

Alex frowned. "Changing the subject won't help."
When Kitty didn't respond, she sighed and said, "Something to do with his overseas suppliers. Then he's off to
Hawaii for a couple weeks, where I assume he's meeting
one of his girlfriends."

Looking at her sister, with her glossy lips rolled in
tight against her teeth, Kitty was reminded of the summer Alex had turned sixteen, when their father had
taught her how to drive. Kitty could see Alex in her
mind, hunched grimly over the steering wheel as she
attempted to parallel park between the pair of garbage
cans Daddy had set out in front of the house. So intent
on pleasing him she'd kept at it for more than an hour,
throwing the car into reverse again and again, her face
slick with sweat—each time Kitty looked out the window, she had to turn away, as if from someone stripped

naked—until she'd gotten it just right. Exactly eighteen inches from the curb, by Daddy's measuring tape.

Poor Alex. She's the real casualty of this family, Kitty thought.

Maybe it was the price she paid for being Daddy's favorite. For just as Daphne had always been closest to Mother, there was no doubt who their father doted on. Kitty might have resented it when they were little, but now she saw it in a different light. There was something unnatural in her sister's attachment to their father, in her need for his approval. An attachment that had left room for little else in her life, including Jim.

Kitty wanted to ask: *When you're roasting your ex-husband over the coals, does it ever occur to you that you might have driven him into that woman's arms?*

"Well. It's a good thing you're so busy then," she pointed out cheerfully. "This way you won't have time to sit around wondering what Jim might be up to."

Her sister snorted. "I should hope not. It's been *two* years. Do you think I give a shit what that man does to stroke his ego?" She glanced at her watch—slim, gold, expensive-looking. "Look, I've got to run. Can I count on you to at *least* call Daddy and remind him to pick up his tux at the cleaner's?"

Kitty felt a flash of resentment. "What for? He'd be perfectly capable of looking after himself if you and Mother weren't always running after him like a pair of handmaidens."

Fortunately, Alex was in too much of a hurry to stick around and argue. She merely shot Kitty a disgusted look on her way out, snapping, "Think what you like. I just wouldn't want to be you if Daddy ends up having to wear his next-best suit."

Kitty felt her cheeks grow hot. Why did she let Alex get away with it? This warped version of mother-may-I, with Kitty the one taking two giant steps back? Weren't they too old for all that by now?

She took a deep breath, and rocked back on her heels. *Only a few more hours.* Then she'd know if her dream was going to come true . . . or if she might one day end up like Alex—bitter and disappointed with her smaller, low-cal helping of life.

The rest of the morning passed in a blur. By the time Kitty brought the faces at the tables back into focus, most of them had changed. The after-lunch crowd came and went, and the cakes and pies set out on the counter dwindled to a few slices. Even so, she purposely avoided glancing at the clock. The time would pass more quickly, she told herself, if she concentrated on counting out change instead of minutes.

Shortly after four-thirty, when a pretty dark-haired girl walked in accompanied by a boy around her age, Kitty looked at them in surprise. Could this be Heather? But she was supposed to have come alone. Unless, unless . . . oh God . . . . unless that boy with her was the one responsible for the small, but unmistakable bulge under her baggy sweatshirt.

Kitty, her heart pounding, walked over to greet them. "You must be Heather," she said, smiling warmly.

The girl nodded shyly, and cast a nervous glance at the rather fierce-looking young man standing guard at her elbow. "This is Sean," she introduced. "My older brother."

Yes, come to think of it, there *was* a resemblance. Both had the same dark hair and wide-set brown eyes. But where Heather looked merely nervous, her brother was scowling as if he'd like nothing more than to give Kitty a piece of his mind.

"May I offer you some lemonade?" she asked in what she hoped was a normal voice. "I make it myself from lemons off my own trees." When they didn't respond immediately, Kitty wondered if she was being too pushy. What was she trying to prove? That she was some kind of superwoman who could do it all?

Heather asked shyly, "Do you have any diet Coke?"

She's too young to be pregnant, Kitty thought. Unformed somehow, with her soft mouth and freckled cheeks that hadn't quite lost their baby fat. Not the mature sixteen-year-old Kitty had been expecting; more like a little girl who still slept with a teddy bear, and took chewable vitamins. Heather's fingers were an angry pink where she'd chewed the nails to the quick, and her baggy jeans looked as if they might have belonged to her brother.

Sean, on the other hand, looked to be in his midtwenties. Leaner, more honed, his dark eyes seeming to take everything in while giving nothing back. His open-necked sweater revealed a collarbone badly broken at one time—*not* from some skiing accident, she guessed. Kids from families like his didn't vacation in Vail and Sun Valley. They were lucky if they got a trip to Disneyland.

"We're fine. We don't need anything." His clenched jaw made it clear their visit wasn't exactly social.

Kitty felt herself flush and was suddenly, acutely aware she was on trial here. Still, that was the whole point, wasn't it? She needed to win them over. Not just Heather, but now her brother, too. *Courage,* a voice whispered.

She cleared her throat and suggested, "Why don't we go upstairs where it's more private. We can talk, get to know each other a little bit."

Sean cast a glance about the room that seemed to dismiss the sprigged wallpaper and whitewashed wainscoting, the quaint fixtures and marble soda fountain as so much pretentious bullshit. Then he nodded, as if to say, *Let's get this over with,* and started up the staircase after Kitty, his sister meekly bringing up the rear.

It wasn't until Heather stepped into the large, sunny bedroom that doubled as Kitty's living room that she broke into a smile. "Oh. It's so . . . homey."

Through Heather's eyes, Kitty took in the rag rug by the fireplace. The humpbacked sofa, draped in an old Navajo blanket worn soft as fleece. The pewter pitcher on the square mission table by the window, with its spray of pussy willows. In the late afternoon light, the lozenges of colored glass dotting the sills glittered like ship-wrecked treasure, and even the piñata hanging from the sloping ceiling—a souvenir of a long-ago trip to Mazatlán—seemed more playful than eccentric.

She felt some of the tension go out of her. Maybe, just maybe, this would turn out okay after all. "Do you

like cats?" she asked, beckoning toward the sofa, where
Ethel and Fred crouched at either end like a pair of
sphinxes. "These two are the real landlords here. They
only put up with me because I feed them."

The moment Heather sat down, Fred jumped onto her
lap and began to purr. "Aren't you cute?" she cooed,
stroking his silky calico fur. Smiling up at Kitty, she said,
"We used to have a cat, but it got run over. Sean says
we live too near the freeway to get another one. It
wouldn't be fair." She darted a cautious glance at her
brother, who sat in the easy chair across from her, staring out the window.

Lots of things aren't fair, Kitty wanted to cry. Instead,
she asked, "You're a junior, right? I went to Muir High
myself. It hasn't changed much since then, at least that's
what my nieces tell me. Do you know them? Nina and
Lori Cardoza?"

Heather nodded. "I see them around. They're in ninth
grade, right? It's weird, they don't look anything like
twins." She peered up at Kitty shyly from under floppy
dark bangs. "Have you always lived in Miramonte?"

"Pretty much my whole life, except for college."

Sean turned away from the window. "Why did you
come back?" His voice seemed to carry a note of
reproach.

Kitty suddenly saw Miramonte the way he must: as a
small town rife with snobbery and injustice. For someone
like Sean, were he lucky enough to escape, there would
be no going back. She felt a pang of misgiving. This was
all wrong. She was going about it all wrong, somehow.

Yet how could she think straight with those dark,
faintly accusing eyes boring into her? Sean was no kid,
she realized. Maybe he'd never had a chance to be a
kid. It wasn't just his attitude toward his sister, more
like an overly protective father than an older brother, it
was in the charged air that clung to him like static, and
the clear sense of mission wired into every flexed muscle.
He sat kneading his knees as if to keep from jumping
up, and she noticed the deep scratches, just beginning
to heal over, scoring the backs of his callused hands.

"I don't mean to be rude." Sean's deep voice cut into

her thoughts. "But when Heather told me she was thinking of giving up the baby . . ." He stopped, the muscles in his throat working, as if trying to swallow something that wouldn't go down. "Look, whatever you might think, we take care of our own. Our dad's on disability, but I have a job. My sister won't have to go on welfare."

Kitty looked at Heather, who sat very still, eyes downcast. A wave of hot confusion swept over her. "I thought . . ."

"You thought wrong," he stated flatly.

Sean stared at her with a defiance that made Kitty want to slap him. At the same time, she couldn't help seeing it from his point of view. The years of scraping by on their father's disability, and the pride that had become as hardened with each new assault as the calluses ridging his fingers. Kitty knew the neighborhood where he and Heather lived, out by the mushroom factory—a wasteland of trailer parks and small shabby houses on postage-stamp-size lots.

But before Kitty could reassure him that it wasn't an indictment on his way of life, her wanting to adopt his sister's baby, Heather suddenly jerked upright. "Stop it!" she cried. "Sean, you always think you know what's best. But this time you're not the one who gets to decide!" Her eyes were bright with unshed tears.

"Hey, calm down. It's okay." Sean lurched to his feet and went over to his sister. Sinking down next to her on the sofa, he threw a protective arm over her shoulders. He cast a glance at Kitty that was only marginally contrite, muttering, "Sorry. I just get so damn *fried* whenever I think about it. That jerk dumping her the minute she told him she was pregnant."

"You don't have to apologize," Kitty told him. "I'd be mad, too."

"I know it's Heather's decision," he sighed, his tension easing somewhat, like a foot lifting from some invisible accelerator. "But I wanted to come along anyway. To see if all that stuff you wrote was true."

Kitty waited, hardly daring to breathe. In his cage in the corner, Byron, the parrot, broke into a rusty rendition of "Pop Goes the Weasel," and Ethel slunk in and out between her ankles, mewing with reproach. From downstairs came the faint sound of Willa's tuneless whistling.

At last, she said, "I'm thirty-six. I'm not married, and I don't know that I ever will be." She spoke softly, but with emphasis, forcing herself to look directly at Heather. "I *like* my life . . . though to be honest there are days I wonder how I ended up here, doing what I do. The only thing I've ever been one hundred percent sure of, my entire life, is that I want to be a mother."

Silence. Kitty felt as if she were floating—her heart descending in a lazy spiral, like a coin tossed into a wishing well. Then Sean cleared his throat with a harsh-sounding laugh. "We're not exactly your average TV family either. Our mom walked out on us when Heather was six. We haven't heard from her since."

"It's mostly Sean who takes care of stuff," volunteered Heather, her outburst of a moment ago eclipsed by her obvious worship of her brother. "He's a way better cook than Dad or me."

Now it was Sean's turn to look uncomfortable. "It's not that big a deal." He dropped his gaze, rubbing a hand self-consciously over one knee of his jeans—jeans faded in a way that could only have come with wear. Kitty didn't see him as the type to blow fifty bucks on a brand-new pair stonewashed to look secondhand.

He doesn't need to spend money on jeans to look great in them.

The thought came out of nowhere, and Kitty blushed. What difference did it make that he was good-looking? The only thing that mattered was that Heather had a big brother who loved her dearly . . . and in the end would go along with what was best for her.

Seizing the moment, Kitty blurted, "Would you . . . I mean, do you have plans for tonight? I'd love it if you could stay for dinner." She smiled at Sean. "I'm a pretty fair cook myself."

Heather brightened, and looked eagerly toward Sean, who sat there shaking his head. "I don't know . . ."

"*Please*, Sean." A hand flew up to graze her soft, seeking mouth before she remembered to yank it back into her lap. Kitty couldn't help wondering what other bad habits she might have besides biting her nails.

"I don't like leaving Dad alone," Sean said, frowning. To Kitty, he explained, "It's his back. He hurt it moving those heavy barrels at the tannery. It's not so easy for him to get around."

"He's welcome, too," Kitty offered.

"I guess there's no harm in asking," he relented, his flinty eyes fixing Kitty with a look that said, *Just so long as we all know where we stand, that nothing's been decided.*

She nodded, feeling herself sag with relief. Okay, so the final decision was yet to be made, but . . .

There was still hope.

Hope that one day soon she would wake to the cry of a newborn, instead of the jangling of her alarm clock. That there would be snapshots of her child tucked in among the gallery of framed family photos on the mantel. And an end to the yearning that whistled through her like wind through an empty building.

It wasn't until Sean and Heather had gone home to pick up their father, and Kitty was excitedly clanging about in her kitchen—as if she hadn't spent all day in it—that it occurred to her: she hadn't called Daddy to remind him about picking up his tuxedo. She felt a pang of guilt before her natural stubbornness kicked in.

Just because Mother and Alex chose to cater to his every need, it didn't mean *she* had to follow suit. The funny thing was, she got the feeling Daddy respected her for it. Just the way he looked at her sometimes— like maybe he knew enough to keep his distance. Kitty had never confronted him with what she'd witnessed when she was fifteen, riding her bike home one evening from a football game: Daddy and Mrs. Malcolm in his gray Plymouth sedan, parked behind the Masonic Hall where her father went every Tuesday night. They were kissing. She couldn't see their faces very well, but scorched into her mind were the paintbrushlike streaks in the steamed-over passenger-side window left by Mrs. Malcom's curly blond hair.

The only thing Kitty remembered after that was pedaling home like the Furies, up the hill to Agua Fria Point with her breath coming in dry, hot bursts, and a stitch burning like a needle stuck in her side. Then skidding into the driveway of her house, where she parked her bike and promptly threw up in the bushes.

She hadn't been able to look at her father the same way after that. Had Mother guessed? Probably not. And knowing her, it was probably just as well she remain clueless. A thing like that would just kill her.

Off in the distance, Kitty could hear an ambulance wailing. In that instant, Serena Featherstone's creepy premonition of this morning came rushing back. What if it hadn't been just a silly parlor trick after all? What if the woman turned out to be right?

You're being morbid, Kitty scolded herself. Nonetheless, as she stood in the kitchen with the evening's cool seeping up through the soles of her bare feet, and her head slightly cocked listening to the siren fade to a distant bleating whine, she couldn't help feeling as if a goose had walked over her grave.

Chapter 3

A lex Cardoza, winding her way along Quartz Cliff Drive in her BMW, heard the siren, too. She pulled over as far as she could without smashing through the wooden guardrail and into the ocean below, and caught a flash of red in her rearview mirror as the ambulance rocketed past. Probably headed for Pasoverde Estates, where she'd wasted the better part of the afternoon. Those blue-chip retirees with nothing better to do than dupe a hardworking realtor into showing them houses they had no intention of buying—one of them had probably keeled over on the golf course.

She pictured the Hendersons: Dick, with his gold Rolex and Naugahyde tan, and his cheery wife, Pat, wearing a blue terry headband that matched the trim on her tennis whites. They'd insisted on her showing them every available property in the club, the highlight of the tour, of course, being the Brewster estate. Like all the other thrill-seekers before them, the Hendersons had wanted nothing more than to peek into the palatial home where Brick Brewster—star of the popular seventies TV series, *Jericho Valley*—had put a bullet through his head.

Alex's hands tightened on the leather-laced steering wheel. A headache was burrowing into one temple, a real extrastrength Excedrin special. Squinting hard behind designer sunglasses that were more for show than protection, she didn't spot the bicyclist until it was almost too late. The guy shot out in front of her, and she had to stamp hard on the brakes to keep from plowing into him.

The ponytailed kid flipped her the bird as he whizzed past.

Alex let out a ragged sigh. Damn. That was close. She needed to watch it when she was this burned out. Trouble was, she couldn't recall a single day in months when she *hadn't* been. Mornings, if she wasn't the first to hit the office computer, some young hotdogger was sure to beat her to the most current listings. Which meant having to leave for work before the twins were off to school, then all day long dashing from pillar to post—sellers refusing to come down in price, buyers who couldn't make up their minds, and closings that meant sitting around for hours before she could collect her commission check.

All of which she could have handled . . . if it weren't for the sword dangling overhead. In her mind, she pictured a wickedly gleaming scimitar like in *The Arabian Nights* storybook that had given her nightmares as a child. A sword of Damocles forged by the IRS, and sharpened on the Visa and Mastercard statements that showed up faithfully in the mail each month with their minimum payments that didn't even cover the goddamn *interest*.

In hindsight, which was always twenty-twenty, she could see where she'd gone wrong, see it bearing down like a ten-wheeler she might have been able to dodge had she taken a moment to glance in her rearview mirror. But events are seldom that clear-cut while they're unfolding, she knew. Somehow, with the expenses involved in buying and furnishing a house—not to mention the flurry of moving and unpacking, and, oh, let's not forget that nasty piece of unfinished business called divorce—Alex had managed to spend not only every penny from her share of the Myrtle Street house, but all of her savings as well. She'd planned on making up the difference by tax time . . . but house sales had been down the last couple of years. Her commissions covered her mortgage and credit card payments, with barely enough left over for household expenses. Now, with interest and late charges, her debt to Uncle Sam stood at close to forty thousand.

Every time she thought of it, her stomach buckled as if she'd been kicked. Her accountant had been stalling the agent assigned to her case . . . but if in the next couple of months she didn't come up with what she owed, Brett warned, she could lose everything: house, car, furniture. Even her wages would be attached.

Alex's chest grew tight, and her heart began the rapid-fire hammering that in these past weeks had become almost as familiar as breathing. That was partly why she'd lost her temper at Kitty today. While she'd been run ragged helping to arrange this party—choosing which wedding photos to have enlarged, finding a seamstress to hem the seventeen custom-dyed tablecloths delivered in the wrong size, making motel arrangements for out-of-town relatives—her sister couldn't even remember to order the stupid napkins. And, dammit, Alex *needed* this party to go off without a hitch.

If the evening went well, her father would be in the perfect frame of mind to approach for a loan. Daddy was generous, often to a fault, when it came to small and even medium-size favors, but he could get prickly about loaning large sums, especially when it was to cover a debt incurred by what he deemed the deadliest of sins: profligate spending. And if he refused . . . she might as well kiss off the next ten years of her life.

Which was why, instead of heading straight home from work, she was at this moment driving too fast along Quartz Cliff Drive in the direction of her best friend Leanne's house. There was one more loose end Alex needed to tie up, a loose end that might turn out to be the fuse on a bomb that could blow them all sky-high if she didn't watch out.

Yesterday, while going over the guest list, she'd been surprised to note that Leanne's mother wasn't on it. Beryl Chapman had been her mother's closest friend for nearly forty years, almost as long as Mother and Daddy had been married. *It must be an oversight,* Alex had thought. But when she'd brought it to her attention, Mother had grown suddenly evasive. Leaping up to rearrange the throw pillows on the sofa, she'd replied primly, "The reason Beryl isn't on the list is because I didn't ask her." That was it. Subject closed. When Alex pressured for more details, she had simply clammed up.

Did she find out? About Beryl and Daddy? Alex didn't see how. All that had happened ages ago. If Mother hadn't caught on back then, why would she suddenly put two and two together? It didn't make sense. Probably she and Beryl had had some sort of fight. Yes, that had to be it.

Which was where Leanne came in. Maybe *she* knew something. She and her mother weren't that close, true, but since Tyler's birth four years ago, Beryl had been coming around more often, lending a hand here and there—that is, when she wasn't afraid of breaking a fingernail, or something. If their mothers had had a fight, wouldn't Beryl have at least mentioned it to Leanne?

Maybe Leanne knows more than she's ever let on. Leanne had been just a baby when her parents split up, but suppose at some point her father had told her the *real* reason they'd gotten divorced.

It didn't seem likely. Wouldn't Leanne have at least mentioned it by now? They knew *everything* about each other. Alex was the first person Leanne had told when she started her period, the summer they'd both turned thirteen . . . and in college, when she was raped by a blind date who'd had too much to drink. It wouldn't be like Leanne to hold back on something this huge.

And that raised another, perhaps even thornier issue. If her friend truly *was* clueless, how much did Alex dare dig up? Would it be fair to drag Leanne into this when she already had more than she could handle?

Alex shivered in the damp air slipping through the vents, wishing suddenly that she were as blissfully ignorant as Leanne. As her sisters, too. She'd bet anything *they* didn't wake up in the middle of the night in a cold sweat, with their hearts going a mile a minute, wondering when and where the other shoe was going to drop. *She* hadn't done anything wrong, Alex told herself. So why did she feel so guilty?

She remembered the first time her father had taken her into his confidence. She'd been eleven, going on twelve. It had been their habit to take a stroll on the beach every evening after supper, just the two of them—a habit that developed more out of default that any obvious favoritism. Daphne and Kitty, when asked, always had something more important to do; and Mother . . . well, naturally, she wouldn't have *dreamed* of leaving the dishes to go for a walk.

Alex had another theory as well: it had worked out that way simply *because it was meant to be.* She was her father's favorite, after all. Deep down, she'd always known it. Proof lay in the fact that she could tell him anything, and Daddy never became impatient the way he sometimes did with Daphne and Kitty. He merely advised her as best he could, not talking down to her like her friends' fathers did to them. So it had seemed perfectly natural to her on that long-ago day, as they meandered along the wet tide line in their bare feet, with their pant legs rolled up to their knees, to ask about something that had been troubling her—a remark the school nurse had made earlier that day during a special girls-only class on human reproduction.

Mrs. Leidecker had drawn an outline on the blackboard that resembled the head of a long-horned steer but was supposed to have been the female reproductive system, and was in the midst of explaining about the egg dropping from the Fallopian tube, and becoming fertilized by one of the minnowlike squiggles swimming up to meet it, when Lana Boutsakaris had raised her hand to ask, "But how does the sperm get *up* there in the first place?"

At which point Mrs. Leidecker had turned beet red, and stammered what had to have been the first thing to pop into her head. Had any of them ever seen dogs mate? It was like *that,* she'd said before rushing on to the next topic. But while the other girls snickered and made faces at one another, Alex had merely sat there, too sickened to say a word. She couldn't picture her parents doing anything like that—Daddy mounting Mother from behind the way she'd once seen their Irish setter, Otis, do to a neighbor's dog. If *that* was how babies were made, she was never getting married or having children.

Daddy didn't laugh when asked if it was true. Nor did he blush the way Mother did when the kissing in movies went on a little too long. He'd smiled gently, and said, *Never, ever be ashamed of what's a normal, natural function of the human body, Alex.* He went on to explain that what happened between a married couple when they made a baby was special and wonderful, not something dirty or disgusting.

Except Alex knew it wasn't just married couples who did It. The weekend before, she'd seen an old black and white movie on TV in which a couple, each of whom was married to another, fell in love. It ended up ruining everyone's lives, including their own. She'd asked Daddy about that, too.

For a long time he didn't say anything, just stood there gazing out at the waves tossing in silvery arcs under a sky the color of rainbow sherbet. Their elongated shadows glimmered on the wet sand, and the breeze lifted the hair on top of his head in a little raft—his one vanity, the way he combed and sprayed his thinning hair to make it look fuller. When he finally spoke, his gaze was so distant she wasn't sure if he was addressing her or simply voicing his thoughts out loud.

Sometimes, Alex, even when a husband and wife love each other, it isn't always enough. Certain women, through no fault of their own, find intercourse painful or unpleasant . . . in which case their husbands have no choice but to seek that sort of companionship elsewhere.

Alex didn't know what had prompted her into making the connection, but she found herself asking, *"You've* never had to do that, have you?"

Daddy had turned to look at her then, his eyes black with shadow against the deepening rose-purple sky, and one side of his mouth screwed down in a small pained smile. *I love your mother very much,* he said. *You know that. Whatever I tell you must be held in the strictest of confidence, now and forever. Do you understand?*

She'd nodded, feeling suddenly weightless, her skin tight with goosebumps like when something really, really big was about to happen.

I've been with other women, yes. But I didn't love them

*the way I love your mother. If you ever hear anything . . .
other kids talking at school, like your friend, Leanne, for
instance . . . I want you to keep that in mind.*

And she had.

The rest hadn't come out until much later, of course.
The whole history with Leanne's mother . . . and the
women who'd succeeded Beryl. As Alex matured, her
father's confidence in her had grown. Without being
privy to any of the embarrassing details, she always
knew when he was seeing someone.

The first to make any kind of impression was Anne
Stimson, a pixie-haired intern doing her pathology rota-
tion under him—that had lasted only eight months, until
Anne left for pediatrics. To the best of Alex's knowledge
they'd parted friends. Then there was Leonore Crabbe,
who owned a pottery shop on Locust called Mud,
Sweat & Tears, and read "The Rubáiyát" for fun; Leonore, a true believer in come-what-may, he'd seen off and
on for years, until she took up with a local stained-glass
artisan, with whom she'd since borne two out-of-wed-
lock children.

The early eighties, Alex recalled, were dominated by
Mary Kate Klausen, a pretty, dark-haired nurse with a
history of instability, who'd threatened to kill herself
when he finally broke it off. There had been a long period after Mary Kate when he didn't see anyone. Then
there was a married woman, a pharmaceutical salesper-
son from out of town—the name escaped Alex. Was
he still seeing her? If so, she hadn't heard about it in
some time.

Months, even years, might go by without any mention
of someone new. Yet when Daddy did confide in her, it
seemed perfectly natural to Alex that he do so. After
all, he had to tell *someone.* Who else could he trust?

The only thing she minded was the burden of so many
secrets, like a minefield she had to tiptoe through in
order to remain in one piece. A minefield that on some
days, like today, she felt sure was going to explode in
her face.

Jim had once joked acidly that if she was any more
tightly wound she'd snap in two like a frayed fan belt.

She had to chill out, as the twins would say, or she would blow this.

Alex cursed under her breath as she took a sharp curve and felt the back end of her BMW start to fishtail on the sand-ribboned blacktop. She slowed at once, gripping the steering wheel so tightly her knuckles stood out like bleached sailor's knots against the perforated tan leather.

Jim, she thought. *I wouldn't be in debt up to my eyeballs if he hadn't left me.*

She wouldn't have had to sell their mostly paid-off house and take on a mortgage at a much higher interest rate. Or struggle to provide Nina and Lori with everything they were used to—nice clothes, decent allowance, tennis and horseback-riding lessons, membership at the club.

Worse, she was without the one person with whom she could share her worries. For when Jim walked out, she'd lost the only man she'd ever loved, since she'd first laid eyes on him at the age of seventeen.

Her eyes filled with hot, angry tears. In June, they would have been married sixteen years—the date ought to have been circled on her calendar. Instead, here she was getting all worked up over a party to celebrate her parents' anniversary, not hers.

Maybe they'd had the right idea after all, she thought. Maybe the secret to a long-lasting marriage was to focus on just what was on the surface and turn a blind eye to the rest. Illusions, it seemed, were more sustaining than whatever dark truths pulsed underneath.

Alex took a deep breath, forcing her mind off those thoughts . . . and after several minutes felt her tension begin to ebb. This particular stretch of coastline—where sandstone cliffs plunged in a sheer drop to the bay that lay nestled in the arms of two promontories like a vast silver bowl—always had that effect on her. Like tuning into a favorite golden oldie on the radio, or remembering something nice waiting for her at home.

To her left, facing the road, stretched a row of houses on postage-stamp lots that enjoyed some of Miramonte's best ocean views. Houses that might at one time have been on the dowdy side, but that over the years had been added onto or replaced by a succession of owners. What remained was a hodgepodge of styles and price range. Like the soaring A-frame she was coming up on now, beside which a small cottage with peeling gray shingles appeared to flounder like a skiff beneath the prow of a mighty ship. And that cedar-shake rustic she'd always admired, with its banks of sliding glass doors and wraparound deck; minus the dump next door she could have gotten three quarters of a million for it, no sweat.

Snug Harbor Lane, on the other hand—two miles north, and a quarter of a mile inland—was another story. Bumping along the weather-buckled strip of asphalt lined with modest frame houses, most of which had seen better days, she suppressed a shudder at the thought, *There but for the grace of God go I.* And if soon she didn't see her way clear of the avalanche of debt that had her snowed under, she might very well be reduced to this: twelve hundred square feet of peeling clapboard, with a dandy view, not of the ocean, but the salt marsh with its faint but persistent odor of rotting vegetation.

The houses in this subdivision—a relic of the sixties, when beachfront property was still reasonably affordable, and Miramonte was just starting to come into its own as a summer resort—had been built to withstand nothing more taxing than a summer squall, or the occasional weekend of too many people squeezed in under one roof. As well as being ridiculously expensive to heat in winter, they were damp year-round. But unlike the lion's share of older summer housing, Snug Harbor Lane had failed to attract developers eager to tear down and rebuild. The fly in the ointment—Alex had been through it with prospective buyers so many times she could recite it in her sleep—was that the marsh that picked up where the road ended, stretching as far as you could see, fell under the long arm of the Coastal Commission. Larger homes would mean putting in more sewer lines, which in turn would endanger the marsh's delicate ecosystem. In short, while the population of mud hens stood at an all-time high, homeowners like Leanne, who might have been able to sell at a hefty profit, could go fly a kite.

Her friend's house was the last one on the left, where the road dead-ended in an abbreviated turnabout—a dinky two-bedroom, once yellow but since faded to the anemic hue of dried egg yolk. Pulling up at the curb, Alex waved to her friend, standing out front with a muddy hose looped like a lasso over one arm, watering the scrap of parched grass that passed for a lawn. Leanne waved back before sauntering over to crank off the hose.

The afternoon had turned unseasonably warm, and she was dressed in cutoffs and a stretchy blue halter top, her pale gold hair caught up in a ponytail from which stray wisps escaped to trail down her neck. *She's lost weight,* Alex observed as she bent over the faucet half hidden behind a clump of overgrown hydrangeas. Leanne had always been slim, but now she looked merely worn down, tendons forming grooves on the backs of her pale legs, and a butt that barely pulled at the back pockets of her cutoffs. The night shift was clearly taking its toll, not to mention the malpractice suit that had been pending since Tyler's birth. And that was another thing—a little boy who, at four, was unable to sit up, eat with a spoon, or even recognize his own mother.

Leanne straightened, squinting at her with one hand cupped over her eyes. "Well, look who's here. It's the Avon lady dropping by with the latest breakthrough in pore cleansers." She grinned.

Alex grinned back. "Why, do your pores need cleansing?"

"No, but next to you I must look as if I could use all the help I can get." She dropped her hand to her hip, and stood back to eye Alex critically. "If you have one single blackhead on that perfect face of yours, it would take a magnifying glass to find it." With that, she turned and headed toward the house, beckoning for Alex to follow. "Come on, I'll mix up some lemonade. Tyler's asleep for a change, so we may even get to finish it."

Inside, Alex sank down on the sofa, over which was draped a granny-square afghan Leanne had crocheted when she and Chip were still together . . . before the jerk left her high and dry and pregnant, and Tyler came along to sew the net shut.

"Be right back," Leanne tossed over her shoulder as she padded into the tiny kitchen just off the living room. Alex could hear drawers and cupboards banging shut, the tinkle of a spoon against glass, followed by the refrigerator door being opened. Then, "Damn. No ice." Leanne stuck her head around the corner. "Freezer's out again. I'll run next door and get some from my neighbor. It'll only take a sec."

"Never mind, really, I mean it," Alex reassured her. "Warm lemonade is just what I feel like."

"Liar." But Leanne was smiling her old sassy smile that Alex saw so rarely these days it was like some unearthed souvenir from high school.

She'd been the prettiest girl in their class at John Muir, much prettier than Leanne would ever dare admit to herself, and even with all that had happened to her since, she'd held on to her looks. She reminded Alex of a grouping of photos she'd once come across in a gallery—of farm wives worn to a tough, sinewy beauty that had nothing to do with perfect skin or the latest hairstyle. There was something of that in her expression, too, an air of someone who's been pushed around once too often and isn't going to take it anymore. The word defeat wasn't listed in Leanne's dictionary.

"Don't forget, I tell fibs for a living," Alex joked. "While you're off saving babies' lives, it's my job to convince some poor innocent buyer that with a fresh coat of paint and some new curtains the darkest room in the world will look bright."

Leanne walked toward her, holding two tall glasses in which a pale, cloudy liquid swam. "You always were an optimist," she laughed. "Remember the time we got caught cheating on that algebra test? When Mr. Evans gave us both F's, you said it was a sign from God that we weren't meant to know algebra."

"Not if it meant going on to geometry," Alex tossed back. "Like I always say, quit while you're ahead."

"Easy for you to say. *You* can afford to sit back." An edge crept into Leanne's voice, and as she sank into the other end of the sofa, Alex thought she caught a flash of something carefully veiled in her expression.

Why hadn't she confided to Leanne about the hole she was in? Alex wasn't sure. She told herself it was because Leanne, who was forced to pinch every penny, might think less of her for being so careless. At the same time, she knew that wasn't quite true. Lately, she'd sensed a faint but discernible coolness in Leanne's attitude toward her. Nothing she could put her finger on. Just a vague sense that Leanne might be keeping secrets of her own.

Had she offended Leanne in some way? Or did it have to do with whatever was going on with their mothers? Either way, Alex wasn't leaving until she knew.

She glanced around the living room—surprisingly cheerful despite how cramped it was. Furnished with mismatched chairs you didn't have to sit on to know they were comfortable, a nice cherry table, and the cedar chest in which Leanne's photo albums and old baby clothes were stored. The outfits Tyler had outgrown were another matter; Leanne saw no point in saving them for a son who wouldn't one day look back and smile at how small and helpless he'd once been.

At least I have Nina and Lori. Jim was gone, and her daughters growing up so fast she hardly recognized them as the toddlers who'd once tugged at her hem and begged for animal crackers—the pink kind with "poka dots," Nina would crow. She smiled at the memory, feeling an unexpected tug of loss. But what was the alternative, a child that grew in size only? Poor Leanne.

"What's going on with your case? Anything new?" she remembered to ask.

Leanne sighed and leaned back, tucking one leg under her. "Nothing, except our star witness, Agnes Batchelder, is having a sudden attack of amnesia. My God, she was right there in the delivery room! She told me herself Pearce shouldn't have waited so long to do the C-section. Now she claims she's not sure what she saw." A look of disgust momentarily turned her pretty face hard and ugly. "It's only because of the pressure she's under from the hospital's lawyers. And me, well, they can't fire me, so they stick me on night shift."

"Think she'll come around?"

"If she doesn't, I'll try not to hold it against her."

"The hell you will."

"What I'd *like* to do is wring her neck," Leanne conceded with a harsh laugh. "Two years from retirement, so she hangs me out to dry." She sipped thoughtfully at her lemonade. "Dennis, my lawyer, says we can still subpoena her, but I don't see what good it would do."

"Have they set a trial date?"

"The last I heard it was the middle of August. The fifteenth, to be exact."

"That's four months away. *Anything* could happen by then."

Leanne's gaze turned inward, and once again Alex felt a cool prickle of unease skate up the back of her neck. She wondered how to bring up the party and why her mother hadn't been invited. She was on the verge of saying something when Leanne abruptly asked, "What's new with you? I don't hear from you for weeks, then you show up out of the blue looking like a million dollars. I was picturing you on your hands and knees, dragging the last load of party favors up the hill to the club."

Alex groaned. "Don't be fooled by appearances. My makeup and hair spray are the only things holding me up."

"Isn't your mother doing most of the work?"

"Sure, but there's more to it than planning the menu and ordering flowers. There're the million and one unexpected little things that keep popping up." Alex took a deep breath and forced the words out. "For instance, this stupid fight our mothers seem to be having."

"What fight?" Leanne looked genuinely puzzled.

"I'm sure it's no big deal. At least, it *wouldn't* be, except . . ." Alex felt herself grow warm in Leanne's sunless living room, with its view out the south-facing window—islands of tall reeds surrounded by glistening gray mud, over which ribbons of dried salt snaked like dirty tattered lace. "For some weird reason your mom wasn't invited to the party."

Leanne stared at her for a moment before saying, "You're kidding, right? I mean, that's just not possible. Mom would have said something." Her voice rose on a note of incredulity . . . and something else. Was Alex just imagining the furtive gleam in her friend's eyes just before they cut away? Leanne thunked her lemonade down on the coffee table, and some of it sloshed over onto a stack of mail she hadn't gotten around to opening. "What was it about? Did she *say* what it was about?"

Taken aback by the unexpected force of Leanne's response, Alex was momentarily at a loss for words. Why was Leanne getting so worked up? As if she *knew*.

A cool voice asserted itself. *Maybe she doesn't know. Maybe she only suspects.* That alone would be enough to send her into a tailspin. Not just on account of Beryl. Because of Daddy, too. Ever since they were little, Leanne had worshipped Daddy, who was far nicer to her than her own father, according to Leanne. The feeling must have been mutual because Alex's parents had invited her along on every family trip, and even on school nights Leanne often stayed for supper. She and Alex used to pretend they were sisters, and after a while it had begun to seem as if they really *were*. Daphne and Kitty had each other, and *she* had Leanne. And yet . . . if she were to be completely honest, hadn't there been an undercurrent back then as well? An uncomfortable feeling deep down that had she been given the choice, Leanne would have slipped into her place without a backward glance, leaving Alex out in the cold.

A new thought occurred to Alex, and she grabbed hold of it as eagerly as she might have a life preserver. "Maybe it was *your* mother's decision to skip the party. Maybe she didn't want you to feel bad."

"You mean because *I* can't go? I have Tyler to think of, in case you've forgotten," Leanne snapped.

Her anger seemed to come out of nowhere—out of proportion to anything Alex had said, or might have implied. She glared at Alex, her pale face twisting with a mixture of anger and despair.

"I wasn't suggesting . . ."

"I'd come if I could, you *know* that," Leanne cut her off. "But it wouldn't be fair to Beth. She does so much as it is."

Leanne's older sister had two kids of her own, but looked after Tyler the nights Leanne worked. Even with Leanne dropping him off on the way to the hospital, and picking him up in the morning, it was a lot to ask. But Beth was like that—as sweet and uncomplicated as Leanne was nervy and difficult to read.

"You don't have to explain," Alex soothed. "Leanne, this isn't about *you*."

She watched Leanne twitch out of her chair, and begin pacing the room, stacking magazines on the coffee table, scooping up one of Tyler's socks from the floor, straightening a painting on the wall over the TV—a fairly decent oil of cows grazing in a pasture.

"I don't know what's going on with our mothers," she said at last, calmer now. "Nobody's said anything to me. Probably you're right. Probably it's just some stupid fight that got out of hand."

"*We've* certainly had our share." Alex was suddenly desperate to change the subject. "Remember our senior year, the time I accused you of flirting with Jim?"

A dry chuckle escaped Leanne, and a corner of her mouth quirked in a reluctant smile. "You didn't speak to me for a week. And that was *after* you trashed my yearbook."

"I didn't trash it. I just happened to accidentally on purpose spill ink all over the page where Jim wrote, 'It's been great getting to know you these past four years.' "

"I'll bet it's what he wrote in everyone's yearbook." Leanne folded her arms over her chest, and leveled her gaze at Alex. Softly, she asked, "Alex, are you *ever* going to get over him? It's been two years."

"So I've been told," she observed wryly.

"You know, you'd be better off if you spent more time worrying about yourself than your parents."

Alex thought of the chores waiting for her at home— dinner to cook and laundry to do, and that was *before* she got around to playing triage with the stack of bills on her desk. Armed with a calculator, she would see what could be staved off another month, and how thinly she could slice the overdue notices highlighted in boldface. "There aren't enough hours in the day for *that*," she said. This time her laugh was forced.

Leanne sighed in commiseration. "Don't I know it."

Alex let a few more minutes go by, sipping at the warm, too-sweet lemonade that tasted more like cough syrup, before she allowed herself to glance at her watch. "Oops. I'd better get going." She jumped to her feet. "I promised Mother I'd drop off some stuff on my way home."

Leanne walked her to the door, and put a hand on her arm. "Sorry I couldn't help. Our mothers must be getting a little senile. They'll get over it, I'm sure. Maybe even in time for the party."

Alex wasn't so sure. But she'd said enough already. Better to let sleeping dogs lie . . .

They don't bite when they're asleep.

Her mother's standard variation on that old theme—it popped into Alex's head like some dangerous object she'd forgotten to look out for . . . a rusty nail, or a piece of broken glass.

"Why don't I give you a call later in the week? Maybe we can get together." But even to Alex's own ears, her words sounded as false as the smile she flashed her friend on the way out.

Leanne stared at her distractedly for a moment, her pale blue eyes seeming to focus on something visible only to her, then she smiled back . . . as if righting something about to tip over. Once again, Alex had the odd feeling her friend knew more than she was letting on.

"Sounds good." Leanne stared at the small wrinkled sock in her hand, as if wondering how it had gotten there. "If I'm not dead of exhaustion by then."

Her conversation with Leanne haunted Alex all the way up to Agua Fria Point. Leanne *had* seemed worn out, yes, but that didn't explain her erratic behavior. The way she'd bristled when the subject of their mothers came up. Almost as if *she'd* had something to do with their falling out.

But that was ridiculous, of course. What could Leanne be guilty of other than perhaps knowing more about the contretemps than she was letting on?

Alex's thoughts drifted to the rented candlesticks in her trunk. Five minutes, she told herself. That's all she could spare to drop them off. And this time, she wouldn't let Mother get to her; when she started in about their not being quite what she'd had in mind, Alex would refuse to play her little game. If her mother wanted to use the stupid things as an excuse not to talk about what was *really* wrong, she didn't have to go along, did she?

It was nearly dark by the time Alex turned onto Cypress Lane. She wondered if Kitty had remembered to call Daddy about his tuxedo. Probably not. Her sister had seemed unusually distracted this morning, as if something was eating at her. *Is that so far-fetched? Did you think you had the market cornered on personal problems?* Alex made a mental note to phone Kitty in the morning and apologize for the way she'd snapped at her.

She was a block from her parents' house when she spotted the police cars.

Two of them, parked in front. Accompanied by several policemen milling about, one of whom was inexplicably tying yellow police tape to the porch railing. Two more emerged from inside the house, toting what looked like garbage bags.

In the glare of her headlights it was a scene from one of those cheap horror movies she and her sisters used to stay up late to watch, just to scare themselves senseless. Somebody's idea of a joke—so silly, in fact, Alex was seized by a sudden hysterical urge to laugh.

But the laugh got stuck, and suddenly she couldn't breathe. Dizzy, she pulled over to the curb, where she sat staring in glassy wonder at the badly lit black-and-white movie stuttering in and out of focus.

When someone tapped on her window, she jumped as if struck.

A policeman was peering in at her. Alex lowered her window, while at the same time a distant part of her brain registered that there seemed to be no sensation in her hand. She fixed her gaze on the cop, a nervous young man with a wiry build to match, who would have been handsome if not for scars left by acne.

"Officer, what's going on here?" The crisp, business-like sound of her voice surprised her.

"Do you know the people who live here, ma'am?" the cop inquired.

"Of course I do. They're my parents." Alex began to tremble violently.

A troubled, almost panicky look crossed the young rookie's face. "Stay where you are, ma'am." Not so much an order as a plea. He added nervously, "You want to do what I say. Believe me, it's for your own good."

"What is it? What's happened?" Alex's voice grew shrill.

Her first thought was that her mother had suffered a heart attack. Nana had died from a massive coronary before they could get her to the hospital. Then Alex remembered the pills her father took for his blood pressure. Nothing to worry about, he'd said, but what if . . .

Alex jerked in her seat, and began scrabbling wildly to unfasten her seat belt.

"I'll get Sergeant Cooper. Just stay put." The cop looked truly panicked now, as if she were a junkie about to flip out.

"Is it Daddy? Did something happen to Daddy?" Alex screamed, but it didn't matter—the cop was already running across the lawn. Running for help she didn't want or need.

With fingers that felt frozen, she somehow managed to struggle free of her seat belt and clamber out of the car. Yet when she stood up, her knees wobbled, threatening to buckle under her. She staggered onto the lawn, crying, "Daddy! Mother! *Will somebody please tell me what's going on here?"*

In the distance, an ambulance wailed as if in faint, keening echo.

An older heavyset officer with half moons of sweat darkening his uniform jogged over to her, his heavy boots stamping a glistening trail in the damp grass. "I'm

Sergeant Cooper," he introduced himself. "Mind stepping over here so I could have a word with you?" He
gestured toward his squad car parked at an angle
blocking the driveway.

"What's going on?" she demanded.

"Ma'am, please, if you'll just come with me . . ."

Alex stared in fascination at the mustache twitching
like a caterpillar on his upper lip, as if somehow inde-
pendent of the sounds emerging from his small mean-
looking mouth. "I'm not going anywhere until you tell
me what's going on." Her voice rose on a thin, hysterical note.

The flinty-eyed officer shot her a sharp look, then his
expression softened. "There was an . . . incident. I'm
sorry to have to tell you this, ma'am, but your father's
been wounded. Badly. Gunshot wound to the chest. He's
on his way to the hospital now."

His words hit Alex like a blow, and she had to lock
her knees to keep from crumpling to the ground. A high
maddening whine started in her head, like a swarm of
angry hornets.

"Oh God. Mother. I have to see her." Alex tried to
push past him but she might as well have been trying to
chop her way through a tree trunk with her bare hands.
He stood rooted to the spot, steadying her as she flailed
wildly in protest.

"Your mother's been brought in for questioning," he
told her.

"What on earth for? It was an accident, wasn't it?"
Alex ceased her struggling and staggered backward a
step before lurching to a stop. She stared at him, a
pocket of cold forming in her solar plexus—like the cold
dark mouth of the well into which she could feel herself
starting to fall.

"Your mother's under arrest for attempted murder,"
he told her in a flat voice that sent a second jolt ringing
through her like a hammer striking an anvil.

"No . . . no . . . *nooooo*." Alex sank to her knees in
the damp grass, covering her face with her hands. This
wasn't happening. This *couldn't* be happening.

But when she looked up, the stars winking in the sky

overhead seemed to stare down at her with a blank idiot glee. A kind of numbness, like a blanket of warm air, engulfed her. The house, the squad cars, the unaccustomed shadows flitting behind the closed living-room blinds of her childhood home . . . all of it faded to a flat grainy gray as she spiraled down into darkness.

Chapter 4

United Flight 348 out of JFK touched down in San Francisco International at half past five the following morning. Daphne was the only passenger in first who wasn't pulling off a sleep mask or groggily grappling with the seat belt. She'd been wide-awake the whole way, holding herself so rigid that her neck ached, and the trick muscle just below her left shoulder, which she jokingly referred to as her "stress meter," was throbbing steadily, like a silent alarm going off. Throughout the flight, she'd refused anything to eat or drink; the very thought of food had made her sick to her stomach. But now she realized she was starving.

Your father is dead, your mother is in jail, and all you can think about is a toasted bagel with cream cheese?

A weak laugh bubbled to the surface as she sat there watching the other passengers hauling their hand luggage down from the overhead bins. A laugh that shocked her, causing her to clamp down hard enough to bite her tongue. The sweet, coppery taste of blood filled her mouth, and she was almost grateful for it. Yes, *grateful,* because it reminded her not only of why she was here, but that she could still *feel.*

The shock of Kitty's news had left her numb, and what she remembered of last night was scattered. She had no memory of packing, for instance. Only of being driven to the airport, Roger at the wheel. Or had that been the drive home from the book signing? It must have been, yes, because by the time she left for JFK their baby-sitter was long gone. Roger wouldn't have left the children alone. He would join her in a day or two, he'd promised, as soon as he could make the arrangements. He'd kissed her goodbye at the door and—

Daphne didn't remember getting *into* a taxi . . . only getting out of one at the airport, and calmly asking for a receipt.

As if nothing were wrong. As if she weren't flying off to California in the middle of the night to see about a father who was dead, and a mother in jail for his murder.

Even the fact that he *was* dead hadn't quite sunk in yet. Kitty had called back just as she was getting ready to leave, weeping but no longer hysterical, to inform her that he'd died on the way to the hospital. Massive gunshot wounds in his chest—he'd never stood a chance.

Daphne tried not to think about what must have happened next, but the images kept rudely elbowing in. The sheet-covered gurney riding the elevator down to the basement level, to the morgue where her father, through the years, had tended to generations of Miramonte's deceased. She saw him stretched out on the stainless steel table, surrounded by the instruments he'd fought for at every budget meeting, the residents he'd handpicked and trained. The very residents who would—

Stop. Stop right there.

But something told her she needed to envision the scene. If only to keep at bay the other image her mind kept wanting to insert—the one of her father waiting for her at the gate. As she started down the ramp, carryall in hand, Daphne half expected she *would* see him: standing to one side of the ticket agent's desk, not leaning on it—Daddy never *leaned* against anything, except to keep his balance on a moving train or boat—his sharp blue eyes sweeping the stream of emerging passengers like beacons.

But it was only Kitty she saw as she stepped into the terminal. Kitty, who'd driven through the dark to meet her, no doubt with the same unanswered questions beating at her like the wings of a trapped bird. She rose from the chair she'd been sitting in, tentatively almost, as if she weren't quite sure the pale, red-eyed woman Daphne had glimpsed minutes before in the airplane toi-

let (a woman she'd barely recognized as herself) was
really her sister.

"Oh, Daphne . . . you're here. Thank God," Kitty
murmured in a voice low with throttled emotion as she
clasped hold of her, hard enough to crack a rib. "I wasn't
sure I would make it if I had to wait much longer."

"Me neither," Daphne whispered back.

Clinging to her sister, she thought how good it felt,
Kitty's arms around her. Like a gulp of fresh air to
someone drowning. She hadn't realized how badly she
needed this—the touch of someone with whom she could
share her sense of loss and confusion. Not yet grief, no,
she wouldn't have described it as that—that particular
emotion was a bit farther down the road, waiting with
bared teeth to pounce—but a feeling of having misplaced something valuable. Something she needed to
find, or find out.

"Come on, let's get out of here." Kitty grabbed her
hand, pulling her along the walkway almost faster than
Daphne could keep up. "Do you have any luggage?"

"Only this." Daphne hefted the canvas carryall.

"Good. That'll save us time."

By quarter to six, safely buckled into Kitty's ancient
Honda Civic, they were emerging from the underground
parking garage into the pale light of day. Her sister
turned to her a face that glowed with a ghostly luminescence. She said weakly, "I didn't want to break down in
front of all those people. It's bad enough I spent most
of the night down at the police station, bawling my head
off. Oh God, Daph, can you *believe* this is happening?
It's like some kind of nightmare."

Daphne stared at Kitty as she drove. Her ginger-colored
hair, anchored at the back of her neck with a barrette,
flared out in a wild, uncombed mare's tail. And the
clothes she had on—a pair of jeans, a grubby old
sweatshirt—were probably the same ones she'd worn
yesterday. She was shivering, too. Uncontrollably, as if
with a fever. But Daphne had a feeling that were she to
put a hand to her sister's brow, it would be stone cold.

"Tell me," she said.

And Kitty did. But not until she'd pulled off the freeway onto Route 96, where the chances of them getting into an wreck while she wept and raged were less likely.

"At first, I thought for sure it had to be an accident," she said, knuckling away the tears that dripped from her chin. "Like the ones you're always reading about in the paper. A gun that went off while someone was cleaning it. Or Mother mistaking Daddy for an intruder. But that's not what happened."

"What *did* happen?"

"She killed him. In cold blood."

The Honda started to wander into the oncoming lane, and Daphne shrieked, "Watch out! Do you want to get us killed, too?"

Kitty yanked on the steering wheel, and the car fell back in alongside the white line. "Sorry."

Daphne touched the back of her sister's hand, as cold as the buckle on her seat belt. "Are you sure you don't want me to drive?"

"The shape you're in, I doubt we'd be any better off." Kitty flashed her a smile so black Daphne had to look away.

She stared out the window at the rising sun flashing amid the scrub pines and eucalyptus forming a dense tapestry of green along the winding mountainous road. Softly, she asked, "Do you know for a fact that's what happened, or is that just what the police told you?"

There was a beat of silence in which all she could hear was the whistling of the tires against a blacktop wet from rain that had fallen sometime during the night, and the rattling of something loose in the bowels of an engine that sounded as if it had more than the eighty thousand miles logged on its odometer. Then Kitty cleared her throat, and said, "Mother told me. That's how I know."

Daphne didn't try and disguise her shock. She dropped her head into her hands, and it was a moment before she could bring herself to croak, "Why? Did she say *why*?"

Kitty shook her head. "We didn't talk for very long. I stopped her at a certain point. The police . . . well, I didn't think it would be a good idea for her to say any more until her lawyer got there."

"What lawyer?" Until this very minute, the thought

hadn't crossed Daphne's mind that her mother would need a lawyer.

"I called Ellis Patterson," Kitty said. Ellis had been their family lawyer as long as Daphne could remember. "He recommended someone, the best in criminal law Miramonte has to offer, he said. His name is Tom Cathcart. We're meeting with him this morning, as soon as we grab a cup of coffee and something to eat."

"What about Mother?"

Kitty looked as if she was about to remind her that Mother wouldn't be joining them, but all she said was, "You can see her after we meet with Cathcart. The police will want a word with you, too. I know there isn't much you can tell them, but if it will help Mother . . ." she choked, and had to pull over for a minute or two to blow her nose into the wad of Kleenex Daphne pressed into her hand.

There, in the breakdown lane off the feeder road to Highway 1, as the sun climbed the Chihuahua pines with their branches like upraised arms, and the trickle of traffic swelled to a steady flow—the first of the morning's commuters—the sisters clung to one another and wept. Out of shock and confusion and exhaustion, and out of fear for what lay ahead.

Kitty was the first to draw back with a shaky laugh. "We'd better get going before some Good Samaritan pulls over to see if we're in trouble."

"We *are* in trouble," Daphne reminded her. "Just not the kind you can fix with a tire iron and a jack. In fact, I have a feeling we're going to need all the help we can get." She blew her nose hard into a Kleenex. "That reminds me . . . is Alex meeting us at the lawyer's?"

Kitty fell silent, and Daphne watched her expression darken as she threw the car into gear. "Alex isn't meeting us *anywhere*," she said angrily. "When I called her last night, after . . . after I'd been to see Mother, she told me she couldn't think about anything right now except Daddy. Making sure Daddy gets properly buried. No, *decently*—that was the word she used. She wasn't hysterical or anything. Just really cold and, well, dead-sounding." She winced at her poor choice of words. "Well, you know what I mean. It was just so *weird*."

Daphne felt a twisting sensation deep in her gut—some terrible grief struggling to break through the wall she'd erected around it. But she couldn't think about Daddy right now. He was dead. It was Mother who could still be saved. "I'll talk to her," she said. "We need to stick together. All three of us."

"Don't count on our little sister. If what Mother says is true, Alex will never forgive her."

"I don't care what Mother *says*. There had to have been a reason! Suppose her mind's been slipping, and we just didn't notice?" Daphne couldn't imagine her mother as senile, or just plain crazy . . . but then, weren't family members always the last to see such things?

"We'll know soon enough, I guess." Kitty sighed, and a strange sort of calm seemed to overtake her. Daphne didn't recognize it at first for what it was: a weariness so profound that even crying would require an unbearable effort.

They drove the rest of the way in silence, past windswept bluffs and the ocean glinting cold and steely along the horizon, past field after field of brussels sprouts and houses silhouetted against the rose-hued sky like lone outposts, not stopping until they reached the city limits. Only then did Daphne allow herself to fully absorb what she'd been holding at arm's length. To acknowledge what awaited her at the other end. She could actually *feel* it—the weight of it settling into her bones like the ballast necessary to keep a boat on stormy seas from being blown off course.

Not a nightmare that would be over anytime soon, she understood, but a long, bloody ordeal from which none of them would emerge unscathed.

Three hours later Daphne was seated in a cubicle facing a glass barrier, staring at the elderly woman on the other side. This *old* person with her lank yellowish-gray hair and bruised hollows for eyes wasn't her mother, she thought. Mother would have been wearing lipstick, with her hair falling in soft waves about her still-pretty face. And a nice dress.

She and her sister had met earlier that morning with Tom Cathcart in his office, situated in the recently renovated Victorian-era courthouse a few blocks away. The courtly, if somewhat avuncular, sixtyish lawyer had warned that her mother was sticking to the sworn statement she'd given the police. *Religiously,* was how he'd put it. As if Mother were merely reciting by rote what some preacher had drummed into her head. But neither he nor Kitty had prepared her for this . . . this *apparition.*

When Daphne smiled, the woman in the orange canvas jumpsuit printed with the faded block letters, MIRA-MONTE COUNTY JAIL, didn't smile back. She seemed to look right through Daphne the way a sleepwalker might, or someone under heavy medication. A gaze so devoid of life, it sent a shiver up Daphne's spine.

For the dozenth time since stepping off the plane in San Francisco a few hours ago, she felt an odd vertigo sweep over her. Like seasickness: a shifting of natural, known boundaries that left her nauseated and short of breath. If this *was* her mother, then what the hell were they dealing with here? For someone Daphne knew and loved to do something so out of character, so *unthinkable,* it meant that nothing she had ever taken for granted could be counted on.

Dizzy, she glanced about to regain her bearings. This place, too, it was all wrong—a cruel joke. Not grim and seedy like in movies, no Big Bertha casting a gimlet eye. The visitors area was plain and functional, but clean. It smelled faintly of fresh paint and new carpet. Like a cubicle in an office building, the only sounds that of a keyboard tapping in the next room and the low hum of an air-filtration system.

The jail—with its reception desk and booking area, beyond which lay the visitors' area and a dozen cells—was situated on the ground floor at the north end of the sprawling three-story building that housed the Jasper L. Whitson Justice Administration. Jasper, as it was called, was a paean to civic pride: tongue-and-groove redwood paneling, brushed-nickel doorknobs, glassed-in corridors that looked out on a Japanese rock garden. The only reminders that she *wasn't* in some fancy office building were the security door you had to be buzzed in and out of and the closed-circuit cameras in all four corners of the acoustic-tiled ceiling.

Daphne picked up the phone mounted on the wall of the cubicle in which she sat, her heart bumping about in her chest like something blindly seeking an exit. Did her mother even recognize her? Or was she *completely* out of it?

She wanted to cry out, to hammer with her fists against the barrier. Loud enough to make her mother snap out of her stupor. Loud enough to wake the *dead*. But she only sat there, waiting, her palm growing slippery against the black receiver.

It was several moments before the woman known to the world as Lydia Seagrave—devoted wife of Dr. Vernon Seagrave, chairwoman of the Ladies Garden Society and treasurer of the Miramonte chapter of the Sierra Club, not to mention an artist of some local repute— shook herself from the trance she appeared to be in, and slowly, ever so slowly, her hand trembling as if with palsy, picked up the receiver at her end.

"Hello, dear," she said.

The voice Daphne heard, though muffled and tinny, sounded so much like her mother—the mother who at this moment ought to have been standing at the stove in her large, sunny kitchen, sliding scrambled eggs onto a plate with the old wooden-handled spatula that had belonged to Nana—she began to cry.

"Mother . . ." Her voice cracked, and she brought a hand to her eyes. But it didn't stop the tears. They trickled between her fingers and splashed onto the purse clutched tightly in her lap. Through the thick plateglass, her mother wore a look of helpless sympathy . . . as if their roles were reversed and Daphne the one in need of rescuing. Ashamed to realize she did, at that moment, want nothing more than her mother's consoling arms around her, she straightened suddenly and swiped impatiently at her eyes with a loose, trembling fist. "I'm afraid I'm not handling this very well," she said.

"You're doing just fine, dear." Her mother managed a faint smile, and in that instant looked reassuringly like her old self.

"Am I? It doesn't feel like it."

"It never does." A small, knowing sigh escaped her mother.

"I met with your lawyer before coming here," Daphne plunged ahead. "He says you've been very cooperative. *Too* cooperative, in his opinion. Mother, you can't go around telling people that you . . ." She closed her eyes, and pulled in a deep breath, the words spilling out on her forced exhalation. ". . . *that you killed Daddy.*"

"Well, Daphne, it is the truth." Mother was getting that glassy look again, one that matched the peculiar flatness of her voice.

And yet . . . at the same time, Daphne sensed her mother wasn't *really* crazy, that what she was seeing was someone in a state of profound shock.

"Okay." She gripped the receiver, and licked lips that felt dry as Styrofoam. "Okay, but it was an accident, right? You didn't *mean* to kill him."

Her mother grew very still. Behind the cloudy glass, she appeared to float. Only her vivid blue-green eyes—eyes Daphne had inherited—remained rooted in the silt of her daughter's words, like the undersea plants Lydia was so fond of painting: delicate-looking sea fans and eelgrass tough enough to survive the millennia.

Then, very slowly, she brought a hand to her chest. Her pale wrist, Daphne saw, bore the bright red marks of the handcuffs shackling them. "It wasn't an accident," she protested softly.

"You mean you don't *remember.*" Daphne grasped desperately for any straw, however slender, to hold on to. If she could have, she would have grabbed her mother by the shoulders and shaken loose the words she wanted to hear. "Could it have been some sort of blackout, like when Dr. Kingston gave you the wrong prescription for your heart? You were so out of it, you didn't know what *day* it was. Maybe something happened last night to—"

"No." Mother cut her off, politely but firmly. "It was nothing like that."

Sensing this wasn't the moment to get tough, Daphne reined herself in. More would be revealed in time. The thing to do right now, she told herself, was simply keep Mother talking, keep her from drifting back into her trance. She allowed a moment of silence to go by, then asked, "Are you okay? Healthwise, that is."

"I'm feeling as well as can be expected, under the circumstances." A ghastly smile illuminated her face just then, like on Halloween when Daphne and her sisters would shine flashlights under their chins to spook each other. "It's not exactly home, is it?"

Home. Where was that exactly? The house in which Daphne had grown up, apparently without the vaguest notion of what was *really* going on under its roof? The house which, at this very minute, detectives were combing for fingerprints, bloodstains, powder traces?

Daphne, her voice cracking, urged, "Mother, please, I want to help you. We all do. But you've got to help us. If you won't tell me what happened, tell your lawyer. It's Tom's job to protect you. Let him do his job."

A puzzled crease formed in her mother's pale, smooth forehead. "I've told Mr. Cathcart what happened," she said. "I haven't denied anything."

"You're not giving him anything to work with, either." Daphne was sweating under her turtleneck. Why hadn't she thought to wear something lighter? *You weren't exactly packing for a fun weekend getaway,* a dry, cool voice reminded her.

Her mother's mouth took on that pickled look it wore when she was expected to do something she didn't want to do—as if she'd bitten into something sour. "He knows everything he *needs* to know," she insisted, a testy little edge creeping into her voice. "I was in my right mind. I knew exactly what I was doing."

Daphne was getting that seasick feeling again. Stronger this time. She gripped the ledge in front of her. "But there has to be a reason. You . . . you can't just say *nothing*."

"Why not?" Something dark flashed in her mother's

undersea eyes. "It's what I've been doing for the past
forty years."

"Is there something I should know? About Daddy?"
Daphne was sweating profusely, her too-warm clothing
like clammy hands holding her pinned to the chair. What
could her father have done that was terrible enough to
get him killed? Unless there was a side to her father
she'd never known existed. But how was that possible?

*You wouldn't have believed Mother capable of murder,
either,* the cool voice asserted.

A sigh as lonesome as the wind moaning amid the
eaves of a deserted house filled Daphne's ear.

"No more questions." Mother sagged, and only then
did Daphne realize how stiffly upright she'd been holding herself. Her voice was a dry husk of what it had
been minutes before. "I appreciate your concern, dear,
but I'm tired. So tired. I think you'd better go now."

"Should I come back later?"

"Not today. Tomorrow maybe. Are you staying with
Kitty?"

"I suppose so." Daphne hadn't given it a moment's
thought until just now. "For the time being, anyway."

"That's nice."

Daphne leaned forward to declare vehemently, "Don't
worry, Mother. Kitty and I are going to do everything
we can to get you out of here."

"I notice you haven't said anything about Alex." Before Daphne could reply, her mother held up a hand.
Her eyes were bright with some deep, labyrinthine sorrow that Daphne sensed was beyond any comprehension
she might be capable of at this moment. "It's all right,"
Lydia said without bitterness. "I understand. She's always been her daddy's little girl. I don't suppose that's
going to change now that he's gone."

"Mother, I—"

She silenced Daphne with a firm shake of her head.
"I'm sorry, dear, but I really must go. It was good of
you to come. You look as if *you* could do with a little
lie-down as well." The look of affectionate concern that
crossed her mother's smooth, relatively unlined face

gave Daphne a start; it was as if she were five again, and Mother was urging her to take a nap.

"Please. There's so much I still don't under—"

But her mother was already hanging up. Behind the barrier, she rose from her chair, looking even smaller somehow than she had sitting down: a frail, shrunken woman surrendering herself to the young female officer, a pretty dark-haired Hispanic woman, who'd appeared to escort her away.

It wasn't until she'd disappeared from sight that Daphne gave in to the exhaustion and anguish plucking at her like small greedy fingers. Not caring who might be watching, not caring if every damn one of those closed-circuit cameras was recording a different angle of her grief, she brought her head to rest on her folded arms, and wept.

Minutes went by, minutes that might have been hours. When at last she lifted her head, and blew her nose into a napkin she'd had the foresight to save from the breakfast she and Kitty had bolted, Daphne felt as if she'd been unraveled, then stuffed into a bag—a jumble of disconnected parts that no longer fit. But deep inside, a bead of resolve was forming. Something too small to call a purpose; perhaps it was merely the suggestion of what might lay in store for her—if she had the wits and courage to tackle it.

But first there was someone she needed to see. Someone in this very building. It had been a long time, sure, and maybe she'd only be stirring up more trouble. But it was worth the risk. And, anyway, she didn't really have a choice, did she?

It was like when she was writing, and her conscious mind stepped aside to let her subconscious take the helm. Just as she had very little say over what traveled through her fingers as they flew over the keyboard of her laptop, Daphne was unable now to resist the signal her id was sending. A voice that sounded as if it were being transmitted from a distant radio tower drifted in and out of a blizzard of static. It was calling out a single name, over and over: *Johnny.*

Did he go by John now? Assistant District Attorney

John Devane. It had a nice ring to it. He was married, she'd heard. Alex had kept her updated, reporting that she occasionally saw him and his wife around town. When Johnny made ADA, her sister had clipped the article from the *Mirror* and sent it to her. Daphne had saved it, tucking it under the front flap of a romantic novel Roger never in a million years would have picked up.

Time hadn't exactly stood still for her, either. Here she was, a wife and semisuccessful novelist with two kids. A woman with season tickets to Carnegie Hall, who collected vintage photographs of New York City, and every Christmas sang in a choir that performed Handel's *Messiah* at St. Bartholomew's on Park Avenue.

A lot of water under the bridge, she thought. Maybe *too* much. Or maybe not enough. Suppose he wanted nothing to do with her? Leaving aside ethical concerns of the moment (the ADA catching up on old times with the daughter of the accused—how would *that* look to the pack of reporters gathered outside the building?), there was the simple fact to consider that twenty years ago she'd broken the man's heart. That *he'd* been the one to walk out was a mere technicality.

Yet once upon a time, there was nothing Johnny wouldn't have done for her. Correction: *hadn't* done. If there was even a trace of that chivalry left, she needed to know. If nothing else, he'd provide her some sense of where the prosecution was headed.

At the same time she knew perfectly well it wasn't just her mother she was thinking of. An instinct, old as the vestigial pull toward water—water of any kind: ocean, lake, stream, pool, even a bathtub of hot water would do—was drawing Daphne toward the stairs, below which was posted a sign that read, district attorney's offices, second floor. Drawing her to the one person in the world she always, without exception, had been able to count on.

T rudging up the granite-and-glass staircase that seemed to hover in midair, anchored by a complicated network of reinforced steel to the ground floor below, Daphne found herself remembering the first time she'd exchanged more than a furtive look with Johnny Devane.

She was seventeen. Johnny, with his boxer's build and army flak jacket cut off at the shoulders was more like seventeen going on thirty. Not the kind she and her friends normally hung out with, but she *had* noticed him around campus—mostly in the parking lot behind the science building, otherwise known as the smoker's pit, slouched up against the wall with a Salem dangling from the corner of a mouth her mother would have described as "hard."

They'd had a class together, too, their junior year. Spanish III. Daphne, who'd been Señor Machado's star pupil all through Spanish I and II—the only one doing her book report on the original untranslated *Don Quixote*—had been surprised, and yes, come to think of it, not exactly pleased when it turned out Johnny had a conversational ease that put her own to shame. He'd grown up around a lot of Spanish-speaking kids, he explained to their teacher with a shrug. Daphne didn't need to be told what neighborhood he was referring to. The Flats, as the area down by the Boardwalk was known, with its collection of seedy rent-by-the-week motels, had a reputation for harboring illegal aliens, among other unsavory types. From the time Daphne and her sisters were old enough to ride bikes, the Flats had been off limits, a rule their father strictly enforced.

But if pressed to pinpoint the exact moment the lure had been cast, she would have had to say it was that day in Señor Machado's class when Johnny grinned, his eyelids heavy with lazy amusement, and said, loud enough for everyone to hear, "I know a few words that aren't in that textbook, too, but I'll save *those* for outside the classroom."

To be honest, hadn't she felt a secret thrill at the thought of it? Summer evenings in the Flats, the scent of axle grease and cotton candy drifting from the Boardwalk, the clacking of the cyclone as it swooped and reeled, accompanied by screams that faded in and out of earshot. She imagined bumping into Johnny on the sidewalk, outside some fleabag motel. He'd be shooting the shit with his buddies—guys who took shop and remedial English, and had been shaving since the ninth grade—but when he saw her, he'd peel away and slowly saunter over. *"Hey there,"* he'd drawl, his smile with its slightly overlapping front teeth gleaming unnaturally white in the harsh glare of the motel's neon sign, his shoulder-length dirty-blond hair begging to have her run her fingers through it.

Their actual meeting wasn't so much film noir as it was sophomoric. Daphne, chafing at the bonds of her reputation as class brain and budding poet laureate, had slipped out behind the science building one day to bum a cigarette off a dumbfounded Skeet Walker. Her friends would be equally shocked, she knew, but wasn't that the point? Even so, with her first puff, she realized that a practice session or two in the privacy of her bedroom might have been in order. Doubled over with a coughing fit, she'd been chagrined to find herself staring down at a pair of motorcycle boots. Black, with straps across the tops, and scuffed toes creased at an upward slant from riding with the heels cocked down.

A hand on her shoulder steadied her, and a familiar voice with a hint of laughter in it remarked, "Your first time? Here, let me show you . . ." When she straightened, she found herself looking into a pair of gray-blue eyes that made her think of cloud shadows playing over the ocean's surface on a calm day. Johnny rescued the cigarette from her fingers and took a drag from it. "See, like this. It's mainly in how you hold it, you know? I mean, if you're aiming for effect." Again, that flicker of amusement behind the heavy lids of a loner who observed much . . . and said very little. Was he making fun of her? she wondered.

Embarrassed, she'd replied huffily, "I never said I was trying to impress anyone."

"You didn't have to." He stuck out a hand that wasn't callused like she'd imagined. It was warm and dry, and most surprising of all, a bit tentative. "Don't we know each other from somewhere?"

"Spanish III," Daphne blurted.

"Yeah, that's it." A corner of his mouth flickered, and she saw at once that she'd been set up. He remembered, all right. He was just seeing if *she* did.

Daphne found herself smiling, too. At the absurdity of their meeting like this—in a parking lot littered with old cigarette butts, with Skeet Walker and Chaz Lombardi squinting at her curiously from behind a scrim of smoke, and Mr. Crane, her advanced English teacher, scowling from the half-open window of his office in the administration building across the way.

"*¿Como estás?*" she'd asked, seeing Johnny's heavy-lidded eyes register her use of the familiar "you." Glancing at the cigarette smoldering between his fingers, she'd grimaced. "It *was* pretty stupid of me, wasn't it? I have a better idea. How about you teach me some of those words?"

"Yeah? And what words might those be?" His mouth, which she saw wasn't hard at all, spread in a slow crooked grin.

"The ones you can only say outside of class," she responded with mock primness.

At which point Johnny—the same Johnny Devane who in the ninth grade was rumored to have started a fire in the trash barrels down by the bleachers, and more recently, to have been the one responsible for the chipped tooth Skeet Walker was at that moment flashing them—startled her with an uproarious laugh. "I dunno, Princess," he'd drawled. "I'll bet you could teach *me* a thing or two."

And she had. More than either of them had bargained on.

Daphne had taught him that an open heart is a broken one. And that prejudice isn't just something your parents ram down your throat every chance they get; it's also what you take away from them, and unwittingly pass on to others.

She'd loved Johnny. And he'd loved her. She'd been spared the realization of just *how* much until the passage of time had not only given her some perspective, but also made it possible for her to see it without feeling as if she would die from the pain.

Now, as she made her way down a carpeted corridor
lined with offices from which emanated snatches of
barked conversations and the buzzing of phones,
Daphne found her heart beating high and fast in her
throat. Would he recognize her? Would she see in *him*
the eighteen-year-old with whom she'd been so desperately in love? The young man with an anger as untamed
as the loving heart to which he'd allowed only one person access: a girl too stupid to realize how precious a
gift it was.

At the end of the corridor, she found the door she
was looking for. It stood partway open, and Daphne,
expecting to find some officious secretary positioned to
head her off at the pass, didn't think twice before stepping inside.

"I'm looking for—" She stopped, her eye traveling
from the corner of a desk strewn with papers and files
to the man seated behind it.

The gaze that met hers across a cluttered space designed for someone far more organized was shocking in
its familiarity. Daphne felt as if she'd stepped out of the
cold into an overheated elevator going up—a short sharp
tug in her midsection, followed by an outbreak of sweat
that seemed to crawl down from her hairline to cover
every inch of her in a fine warm mist.

"Hello, Johnny," she greeted softly.

He looked the same . . . but different. More finely
calibrated somehow. The dirty-blond hair he'd worn to
his shoulders was peppered with gray and cropped in a
way that lent him authority. He'd filled out, too, an acquired heft that creased the shoulders of his charcoal
suit jacket as he pushed himself to his feet. But it wasn't
just his muscular build; it was the air of quiet assert-
iveness he wore. As if the boy who'd used fists and a
foul mouth to pave his way in a world hostile to his kind
had discovered that real power lay in one's ability to
harness it.

Only the smoky, heavy-lidded eyes regarding her with
guarded surprise were exactly as she'd remembered—
the eyes of every man who'd promised the moon, and
delivered a broken heart instead. For in that instant it

was all she could think of: that it had been Johnny, not her, who'd walked away. The fact that she'd left him little choice didn't register as she stood there taking shallow breaths, with her heartbeat coming in short, startled bursts like a stone skipping over a still, bright surface.

"Daphne. It's been a long time." Johnny stood gazing at her several seconds longer than was polite before walking around the desk and extending his hand.

Seeing its oddly flattened knuckles, Daphne's mind flew back to the day he'd broken them—defending her against that drunken idiot, Bif DeBolt, a behemoth from whom any sane person would've run like hell. The memory was jarring in contrast to the smooth voice now remarking, "Wish I could say it was nice of you to stop by. But I know why you're here—it's not exactly social, is it?"

"No, it's not." Another thing about Johnny that hadn't changed: his habit of cutting right to the chase.

"Have a seat." He scooped an armload of files from a chair, gesturing for her to sit down. When she was comfortable—as comfortable as she *could* be, given the circumstances—he leaned back against the desk, folding his arms over his chest. "There's not much I can add to what you probably know already."

"The only thing I know is that my father's dead!" she cried in frustration. "What I don't know is *why*."

"Have you spoken with Sergeant Cooper?"

"Heavyset, gray hair?" He nodded, and she went on. "We met for a few minutes, just before they let me in to see my mother. I didn't get much, only that it was Mother who'd called 911. She said my father had been shot, and in the sworn statement she gave the police she was very clear about one thing: it was no accident. She'd *meant* to pull the trigger." Fresh tears flooded her eyes. "But that doesn't really explain anything, does it?"

Johnny twisted his upper body around to pull a sheet of paper from a file that lay open on his desk, scanning it as if he hadn't already memorized its contents. Whatever he might be feeling, it didn't show. Still the same poker face that could trick you into believing ninety miles an hour down the coast highway was no more life-

threatening than a stroll on the beach. What he couldn't
disguise, though, was the flicker of compassion she
caught when he looked up.

"Your father was shot twice in the chest at close range
with a Smith & Wesson .357 Magnum," he informed her.
"According to this report, your mother was holding the
gun, wrapped in her apron, when the police arrived."

Daphne felt the blood drain from her face. Cooper,
either out of negligence or misplaced compassion, had
kept *that* particular detail from his account. "I remember
it," she recalled in a low, stricken voice. "My father kept
it in a locked box on the top shelf of their closet. And
I *do* mean locked. He told us he'd seen too many times,
up close, what could happen to a p-person—" her voice
broke, and once more she began to cry. Tears that stung
against the raw wound of those already shed.

Johnny waited patiently until she'd regained some
measure of composure. Then, with a gentleness that
caught her by the throat, he said, "I'm sorry about your
dad, Daphne. We'll know more as soon as the police are
finished with their investigation."

"But either way, my mother stays locked up, right?"
She spoke more harshly than she'd intended.

"The arraignment is set for Monday," he told her.

"That's a whole week away!"

For the first time, Johnny appeared uneasy. His slate-
colored eyes slid away from hers. "Judge Gilchrist asked
to be recused. We're waiting on one of the district circuit judges."

The name was like a soft blow to her solar plexus.
Quent Gilchrist, one of her father's oldest friends. He
was to have been at the anniversary celebration on Sunday. Daphne sucked in her breath. *God. This isn't happening.* She would close her eyes, and when she opened
them she'd be getting off the plane, her husband and
children in tow, eagerly anticipating the weekend ahead.

In a thin, shaky voice Daphne scarcely recognized as
her own, she said, "I don't know why I came to see you.
It's as crazy as everything else that's happened. You're
supposed to be the enemy, aren't you?"

"In a manner of speaking, I suppose." He gave a faint,

mirthless smile that showed his crooked front teeth. To her chagrin, Daphne found herself thinking, *I'm glad he never got them fixed.*

She managed a smile in return, putting an end to her tears with a single decisive blow of her nose into the Kleenex she fished from her purse. *Not very ladylike,* she thought. *But I'm not here to impress anyone, am I?* "I guess I was hoping that you would somehow make it all go away," she acknowledged ruefully.

"Like when we were kids?" Some long-banked ember seemed to flare in his eyes.

She felt herself grow hot. He hadn't forgotten after all, she thought. "You were the one who broke it off," she reminded him coolly.

He startled her with an offhanded grin that didn't quite disguise the shadow of an old, reawakened pain in his eyes. "That's one way of looking at it, I guess. Another is that I rescued you from doing something you would have regretted."

"You mean eloping? I seem to recall that was my idea," Daphne shot back, surprised at the anger she still felt after all these years.

"Running away isn't the same as eloping."

Suddenly it was as if the twenty years since they'd last spoken about this had never transpired. "This is about my father, isn't it? It always boils down to that, doesn't it? Because I was afraid to stand up to him. Okay, I admit it. I was eighteen, I was scared. I thought if we were married, he'd be forced to accept you."

"And he wouldn't cut off the money for college."

"There was that, too. Is that such a terrible thing to want?"

"No." He leaned back, his expression smoothing over as suddenly as a door being shut in her face. "No, it isn't."

But they both knew it hadn't been just the money for college that had panicked her into suggesting they elope. It was her own lack of conviction as well. Her love for Johnny might have stood up to the steady onslaught of her father's disapproval. But, would it have survived four years of their being mostly apart? At the time, marriage had seemed like the safest alternative. Now, with the benefit of hindsight, she could see it from Johnny's point of view: that if she'd truly loved him, she would have waited, even fought for him.

The way he'd always fought for her.

Shaking free of those memories, Daphne released a deep sigh. "Look, let's just forget it. Whatever happened, it's history. I heard you were married, with kids." She fixed a pleasant, neutral expression in place.

"One, a son. He's fourteen. Sara and I are divorced, but J.J. is still very much in the picture. He lives with me, in fact."

No explanation necessary, she thought. If his son was anything like Johnny at that age, he'd be more than a handful for any single mom. Directing her gaze out the window, where a man in a navy bill cap astride a Lawn-Boy was mowing the grass out front in long, uneven swaths, she confided, "I got married, too. Right out of college."

"So I heard."

"His name is Roger. We have two children, a boy and a girl."

He smiled—did she detect a note of wistfulness?—and mused aloud, "All these years I've carried this picture in my head of you with a husband, two kids, nice house. Roger? Yeah, it fits." He looked her straight in the eye, the way her husband almost never did. "I guess not all nice guys finish last."

For no reason in particular, Daphne felt compelled to explain, "This was supposed to have been a family trip. To celebrate my parents' anniversary. They've been . . . they *would* have been married forty years." Her voice caught, and she had to clear her throat before she could go on. "Under the circumstances, Roger thought it best that one of us stay home with the kids until . . ." she stopped. *Until what?*

Johnny spared her any sloppy sentiment that would have caused the frayed thread of her control to snap. "I'll be honest with you, Daphne. It doesn't look good. Tom Cathcart is looking to bust this down to a lesser plea, but my boss ain't buying. He's got your mother's sworn statement, why should he?'' His eyes cut away to the open door, and he dropped his voice. "Look, I'd get strung up by the *cojones* if anyone around here heard me say this to you . . . but I'll say it anyway: if there's *anything,* anything at all that might go in her favor, now would be a good time for your mother to remember it.''

Wrapping her arms about herself and leaning forward, Daphne asked, "And if she doesn't?''

Johnny's jaw tightened. "It's our job to see that justice is done.''

Daphne fought the urge to put her hands over her face, the way she had as a child when she didn't want to confront something. Staring back at him, she replied grimly, "I can only hope that justice, in this case, serves my mother well.''

"For whatever it's worth, so do I.''

He pulled away from the desk and straightened, as if releasing her in some way. Not until then did Daphne realize how close he'd been perched . . . close enough for her to catch a faint whiff of nicotine. A memory came flooding back: the warm curve of a car hood against the small of her back, the engine ticking beneath her as it cooled; the smell of cigarettes on Johnny's breath, and on his army jacket as she pushed her hands up underneath it, her palms sticking to his hot bare skin.

In the cool of his air-conditioned office, Daphne flushed so deeply she felt sure he could see it rising like heat from baking pavement. Abruptly, she jumped to her feet. "I should be going. My sister is waiting downstairs.''

"Sorry I couldn't be more help.''

"Maybe all I needed was someone to talk to.''

She took the hand he offered, its flattened knuckles oddly reassuring. In her mind, she saw Johnny's fist—a blur of clenched, bloodied knuckles plowing one last punch into Bif DeBolt's big, stupid Holstein jaw. She saw Bif stagger backward, wide, exaggerated steps like that of a clown. Then he lay sprawled on the pavement, with Johnny standing over him, growling, "You ever lay a finger on her again, you son of a bitch, and it'll be more than just your big mouth hurting.''

Daphne gave herself a mental shake. Twenty years. A long time . . . even for someone who longed, at this moment, to bury herself in a past that held no surprises. Even Johnny breaking her heart all over again, she thought, would be preferable to what lay ahead.

He walked her to the door. "I'll call if I get wind of anything that's not strictly classified," he promised. "Is there a number where I can reach you?"

Daphne wrote Kitty's phone number on the back of a pink message slip. "I'm staying with my sister. She runs a tea room on Ocean Avenue, if you ever want to just drop by. Tea & Sympathy—emphasis on the sympathy." Frowning, she added, "Poor Kitty. God knows what this will do to her business. Have you seen the reporters out front?"

Johnny nodded. "They practically skinned me this morning on my way in." He touched her arm solicitously. "Hey, you look a little pale. Can I get you something? A glass of water?"

"How about an armored car? I have a feeling I'm going to need one." She shook her head, resisting the unwelcome impulse to lean into Johnny. "This is going to be hard on our family."

But did she even *know* her family? Or was her picture of them simply made up, like in those *Dick and Jane* readers—a figment of her wishful thinking? Whatever the reality, one thing was clear: she could no longer hide from it.

"Anything you need, just let me know," he said.

"I'll keep that in mind." She managed a small smile. "Meanwhile, we never had this conversation, right?"

"It might look better that way. For the time being," he agreed. "Off the record, though, you want my advice?"

"Shoot."

"If your mother won't talk, you and your sisters may need to do some digging of your own."

Looking into Johnny's solemn gray eyes and remembering that any show of support from him could be costly to his career, she said with more feeling than she'd intended, "Thanks. I'll remember that."

Chapter 5

There couldn't have been more than a dozen or so, but equipped with Minicams, boom mikes, and hand-held flashes, they appeared to be an army. Kitty, eyeing in alarm the reporters that swarmed over the concrete walkway and onto the lawn, seized hold of her sister's hand, gripping it tightly.

" 'The Assyrian came down like the wolf on the fold,' " muttered Daphne darkly. They were standing just outside the entrance to Jasper, beneath an overhang that partially hid them from view. Kitty, who'd gotten an eyeful of the horde gathered outside while waiting downstairs for Daphne, shot her a questioning look. Daphne clued her in. "A line from Byron. Clearly he knew a thing or two about the press—they look as if they could eat us for breakfast, and still be hungry for lunch. Any ideas?"

"If we keep our heads down and our mouths shut, we'll be okay." Kitty sounded more certain than she felt. Deep down, she wasn't at all sure of her ability to make it from here to her car without her knees, weak as an invalid's, collapsing under her.

As they headed toward the fray, she felt Daphne slip an arm through hers. "Remember, if we can get through this, we can get through anything," she whispered fiercely under her breath.

"Hey, it's the daughters!" a man's voice bellowed. *"Hold up there, ladies!"* A large man wearing an Oakland Raiders cap loomed into view, bearing a Nikon the size of a toaster anchored about his hairy neck by a rainbow-colored strap.

Someone else yelled, *"Any word on your mother?"*

"She sticking to her confession?" shouted another.

Then the questions were coming at them all at once, fast and furious, like bullets whizzing past their ears.

"Has a date been set for the arraignment?"

"She gonna plead guilty?"

"Is she sorry she did it?"

"Miss Seagrave, would you care to comment on the allegation that your mother suffered a mental breakdown?"

Kitty caught her heel on a crack in the pavement, and stumbled. She would have fallen flat on her face if Daphne, at that moment, hadn't tightened her grip on Kitty's arm. It sank home then: this was only the beginning.

A perky blonde resembling an aging cheerleader in a pink blazer and black miniskirt shoved a microphone in her face. "Cindy Kipnis from Channel Two. Is it true your parents were planning a party for their fortieth anniversary this weekend?"

It must have been the shock of a familiar face, seen nightly on the local evening news, as familiar to Kitty as those of her regulars at Tea & Sympathy. Before she knew it, she was blurting hotly. "My parents were deeply committed to each other. We don't *know* what happened. But if there's any way to make sense of this tragedy, we're not going to find it with all of you hounding us!"

Daphne urged breathlessly in her ear, "Let's make a run for it. We'll be okay once we get back to the house. They can't trespass on private property."

Kitty wanted to ask if she was *sure* about that, or if Daphne, who made her living telling stories, and who, as a kid, had spent as much time in the land of make-believe as in the here and now, was perhaps confusing real life with a Joseph Wambaugh novel. Then there was no time for any further speculation. She and her sister were charging down the walkway, heads ducked low, cutting a swath through the gauntlet of reporters with their boom mikes outstretched like spears.

The exhaustion clinging to her like a web fell away suddenly. Adrenaline sizzled in her veins. Her vision became clear and sharp, a kaleidoscope of bright shifting images. She was aware of trees flashing by, a camera lens catching the light in a fiery arc, a woman in a yellow nylon windbreaker gaping at them with her mouth open, a half-eaten doughnut delicately pincered between her thumb and forefinger.

Kitty didn't stop even when a tall balding man with a Minicam perched on his shoulder sprang into her path, tracking her with his lens like a sniper fixing her in his crosshairs. She pushed past him without missing a step.

She spotted her Honda in the parking lot up ahead, and was scrabbling in her purse for her keys when she realized she'd left it unlocked. Earlier, in the thick of her nearly catatonic exhaustion, it hadn't occurred to her that she might be robbed. What could be worse than what had already happened?

Then she was wrenching open the door and diving into the driver's seat. She watched her sister skip around a scrawny guy in a red Nike sweatshirt who darted up to snap her picture, then Daphne, too, was tumbling into the car with a breathless whoop. Seconds later, they were peeling out of the lot, the reporters rapidly dwindling in the rearview mirror until they resembled nothing more threatening than a swarm of insects.

A mile or so down the road, turning off Emerson Avenue onto Ocean, Kitty and Daphne broke into simultaneous peals of hysterical laughter. They laughed until tears streamed down their faces, and Kitty thought that if they didn't make it home within the next few minutes, she'd have an accident that didn't involve a moving violation. Yet the release it brought was nearly exquisite coming on the heels of what they'd endured . . . and would continue to endure in the weeks to come. What had happened back there, a sober voice reminded her, was only the tip of the iceberg.

Still ahead lay their father's funeral. And their mother's arraignment. And she hadn't stopped long enough to even *consider* how it was going to alter her own existence—this catastrophe that seemed to have descended out of nowhere, like a car bulleting around a blind curve.

It struck her now that Heather and Sean would have

seen it on the news, or in the morning paper. It would explain her abrupt departure in the midst of dinner last night, but naturally they'd be horrified. Who wouldn't be? They'd wonder what kind of family Kitty had been brought up in, and no doubt question her own ability to raise a child. What remained to be seen was whether or not Kitty could convince Heather that this was no reflection on her. It would be difficult, maybe even impossible. But . . .

She felt selfish for even thinking such a thing. *But if any good is to come out of this tragedy, can't it be Heather's baby?*

Then, like a sledgehammer swinging down, came the thought of her father. Daddy stretched out on a slab in the funeral home. *He's not going to step in and rescue us from this mess,* she thought as she coasted into the driveway behind her house—with a wary glance in either direction to see if any reporters had caught up to them. *He really is dead.*

"Is the coast clear?" Daphne twisted around in her seat, straining to see out the back window.

Kitty glanced about once more, but the only soul in sight was old Mrs. Landry, taking her afternoon stroll down Harbor Lane with her miniature schnauzer, Pip. The gate was still latched, she saw. And the glistening trail of footprints across the back lawn, still wet from last night's rain, belonged to none other than Willa, who'd stopped by earlier to straighten up and cancel any outstanding orders.

She gave Daphne the all-clear signal, but wasted no time nonetheless in making a dash for the back porch. Minutes later, the kitchen door was locked tight, and every window latched, even the ones upstairs. Kitty was struggling with the bolt on the front door, so seldom used it had grown balky, when the first TV news van coasted to a stop at the curb.

"Uh-oh, looks like we've got company," she announced over her shoulder to Daphne, her stomach clenching.

If Heather hadn't yet heard, she'd soon get a full report. Complete with Kitty's face on the evening news, and all the grisly details those vultures had been able to dig up. By the time the press had finished dragging her family through the mud, Kitty would be viewed as the daughter of a murderess . . . and Heather would be long gone.

The phone rang as she was taping a CLOSED UNTIL FURTHER NOTICE sign to the door's beveled glass oval.

Before Kitty could warn her sister about the reporters who'd been calling nonstop since early this morning—she seemed to recall Cindy Kipnis's voice on her answering machine at one point—Daphne yelled from the kitchen, "I'll get it!"

But it wasn't a reporter. She heard Daphne exclaim, "Oh Alex, thank goodness it's you."

When Kitty picked up the extension on the wall behind the counter, nearly knocking over a chair in her haste, she caught the tail end of their exchange. ". . . taken care of everything. The service is set for ten o'clock on Sunday, and I've arranged for viewing hours on Friday and Saturday." She sounded remote and businesslike, like a lab technician phoning with the results of a blood test. There was a pause, then she asked, suspiciously, "Kitty, is that you?"

"I'm here," Kitty piped, frowning. "How come we weren't consulted about any of this?"

There was an irritated little sigh at the other end. "If you'd checked your messages, you'd have known that I *did* phone. A couple of hours ago."

"It must have been while we were at the lawyer's," Daphne recalled.

Silence. Then a harsh, hissing intake of breath. "Well, I suppose we each have our priorities. *Mine,* as you can see, is making sure Daddy gets a proper burial."

But Daphne clearly wasn't going to be goaded into choosing sides. "Alex, look, we're all still in shock. I don't know about you, but the only thing on my mind right now is getting some sleep. Then I think we all need to sit down together and figure out where to go from here." Daphne's voice was soothing, like ointment gliding over a scraped knee. At that moment, she sounded exactly like . . .

Mother, Kitty thought. She shuddered.

"For starters, we can start calling the relatives—those who haven't already read about it in the paper or seen it on the news." A harsh, biting note crept into Alex's voice. "They'll want to know about the funeral."

It must have occurred to Daphne at the same time it did to Kitty: all those aunts and uncles and cousins en route from out of town. Coming together for an anniversary celebration that was to have taken place in just five days. She heard Daphne moan, "Oh, God. How on earth are we going to tell them?"

"You can start by telling the truth. That Daddy was murdered in cold blood." The brittle voice at the other end turned nasty and shrill. "That *is* what happened, isn't it? It's no use glossing it over. Whatever you might think, she's not crazy. She did it to get back at him."

"Get back at him for *what?*" Daphne demanded to know.

Kitty interjected hastily, "I don't think this is the time to—"

Alex cut her off at once, crying, "She can rot in jail for all I care! If she stays locked up for the rest of her life, it won't be long enough!" She was breathing hard, as if struggling to get a grip on her emotions. Finally, she seemed to gain some measure of control, adding in a low, furled voice, "I'm counting on you two to be there. For the viewing. That's not too much to ask, is it?"

"He was *our* father, too, in case you've forgotten," Daphne snapped wearily, sounding as querulous as a child kept up long past her bedtime.

Kitty sighed. "Alex, why don't you come over so we can discuss all this in person?" She was suddenly and acutely aware of the fact that she hadn't had any sleep since the night before last. Exhaustion settled over her like a thick, furry blanket.

"The last time I looked at the map," Alex reminded her coolly, "it was just as long a drive to *my* house as it is to yours. You're welcome anytime. I can't promise any homemade cookies, but I'm certainly capable of boiling water for tea."

"There's no need to get huffy. Let's not forget, we're all in this together," Kitty reminded her.

"Are we?" There was a long silence, then Alex said, "We'll here's a thought. While you two are running around in circles trying to rescue Mother, keep in mind that it's too late for Daddy. He's *dead*." She gasped, a tiny sob escaping her.

Before Kitty or Daphne could respond, the line went dead. Alex had hung up. *It's no use pretending*, Kitty thought, her mind spinning in lazy circles with exhaustion. The bullets that had taken Daddy's life had blasted a hole through their family as well. As a unit they'd managed to keep the illusion of togetherness alive. But what would become of them now? How would they cope in the days and weeks to come?

A wave of tiredness crashed over her, and she sagged into the chair that stood against the wall near the phone. The deserted tea room seemed to mock her. Would there be anything left of it when this was over? Would there be anything left of *her?*

She closed her eyes, and brought her head to rest against the wall where the flowered paper had begun to curl away from the seam between two panels. It wasn't until she felt the soft brush of fingers against her hair that she remembered Daphne. Kitty looked up to find her sister smiling down at her. The expression on Daphne's face, one stripped of all defense, naked and beseeching, like that of an uncomprehending child, pierced her to the core . . . and, at the same time, lent a measure of hope.

Together they would get through this, she thought. Somehow.

The rest of the week passed in a blur. First, there were the friends and relatives who insisted on coming over, to console and be consoled . . . then endless phone calls to make, a list that multiplied with every call. *Cousin Jack from Dayton? Oh, honey, you remember him, don't you—he's your second cousin on your mother's side, or is it once removed? I never can keep those two straight*. A few of the relatives offered to make calls on their behalf. Like her mother's eldest sister, Aunt Rose, whom they tracked down at the bed-and-breakfast on Tidewater Avenue, where she'd booked a room for the weekend. Aunt Rose Tremain had been a travel agent before she retired last year because of emphysema. Though wheezing alarmingly, she'd rasped with her usual briskness, "I'll take care of Bill and Susie and the kids. You've got your hands full as it is."

Had she been there, Kitty would have kissed her. But by the time she contacted everyone on her list, she'd forgotten all about Aunt Rose.

Then yesterday, braving the reporters camped out front, she and Daphne had driven downtown for another visit with Mother, followed by a second meeting with her lawyer. Cathcart had tried to get the arraignment pushed up, but to no avail. The hearing was scheduled for Monday, the earliest date for which a new judge could be summoned. "Look at it this way," he'd reassured them, "it'll give us more time to get our bearings." He didn't have to say what they all knew: that if her mother refused to budge, a plea of innocence, or even self-defense, would be pointless.

It wasn't until late in the afternoon on Friday that Kitty found herself with nothing left on her list of things to do. She welcomed the respite . . . but it frightened her a little, too. With the tea room closed, and Willa laid off with pay until further notice, she was at loose ends. She could no longer put off the grieving she'd kept more or less at bay, nor could she go on avoiding certain sticky subjects that had yet to be discussed. It occurred to her, as she stood in her kitchen boiling water for their afternoon tea, that it was high time she and Daphne had a little chat.

She arranged a tray and carried it into the front room, where Daphne was busy sorting through the scribbled reminders on scraps of paper and Post-its that covered most of one table. She'd already begun doing some detective work, gently questioning friends and relatives about what they knew or remembered and jotting down anything that might bear looking into. Daddy might be going to his grave . . . but Daphne was going to see to it that Mother didn't join him.

But there was something her sister needed to know first.

"Milk or lemon?" Kitty asked as she poured her sister a cup from the steaming pot. "I forget how you take it."

Daphne peered up at her. "The last time you had to ask how I liked something was when we were kids, and Mother fried those trout Daddy caught up at the lake. You wanted to know if I'd take mine plain, or with its face on."

Kitty managed a wan smile and settled into the chair across from her. "I don't know about you, but I have a thing against eating anything that's looking back at me."

She did her best to appear normal—whatever *that* was. Right now, the concept of *normal* was like some foreign country she might have visited at one time, the memory of which she had grown hazy. Humor was the only thing that kept her going. Humor so black that at times it was downright morbid. But it kept her from having to speak aloud what she and her sister were thinking: that whatever had driven their mother to do what she did, its roots were in all of them. Invisible to the naked eye, perhaps, but with careful examination they might better see the forces that had shaped them growing up.

Daphne abruptly dropped her head into her hands, as if those childhood memories were suddenly too much to bear: Faint wisps of steam from the teapot drifted up around her, and Kitty couldn't help smiling at the Post-It stuck to the back of one wrist. *If our family were a corporation, Daphne would be its majority shareholder,* she thought. It was she who had the most invested in the myth of their Ideal Childhood. Her ability to conceive of past events, not as they were, but as they *might* have been was partly what made her such a gifted writer. But it wasn't helping her understand what pushed their mother over the edge. For while stories might get better with each retelling, Kitty reflected soberly, family history only grew more tangled.

Kitty reached out to comfort her, stopping short of the exposed nape of her neck, where a dusting of baby-fine hair tapered to a sweetly attenuated point. Daphne was her favorite sister, and dearest friend . . . yet sometimes she wanted to shake her, make her stop pretending it was all so wonderful. She had to make Daphne SEE.

But as Kitty was opening her mouth to say that they needed to talk about the memories that *weren't* so amusing, Daphne seemed to sense it. "Milk," she said, with an abruptness that was all too transparent. "I take my tea with milk."

Kitty sighed. "I just hope we haven't run out." The idea of shopping—having to plow her cart through a grocery store aisle thronged with reporters and rubberneckers—was too much to even contemplate. She'd make a list this very afternoon, she promised herself, and call in an order to Ray's Market.

On her way to the kitchen, she cast a nervous glance out the front window. Through its tightly drawn lace curtains, she could see the KCBS minivan that had been parked at the curb since the day before yesterday. It wasn't the only one. The local TV crew had been joined by reporters from all over the state. Arriving home yesterday, she and her sister had been besieged from all sides as they dashed toward the house.

Today, they'd managed to lie low, but the welcome respite would soon be over. In a little while they'd have to leave for the funeral home, for their father's viewing. Kitty shuddered as she pulled open the refrigerator.

There was enough milk left to fill a small creamer, which she carried out to Daphne. "I'd offer you something to eat, but I'm afraid all that's left is what's in the pantry. I don't suppose I could interest you in a nice, hot bowl of oatmeal."

Daphne made a face. "I'm not *that* hungry. Anyway, I doubt I could eat anything if I tried. This will do me just fine." She helped herself to one of the cookies Kitty had unearthed from the freezer, and took a dainty bite.

Despite her chic wardrobe and big-city sophistication, Kitty thought, there was something oddly old-fashioned about her sister. With those wide blue-green eyes that needed no makeup, and her gentle air that seemed out of another era. An image formed in her mind of Daphne in a ruffled high-necked blouse, pouring tea from a sterling service instead of the fat ceramic pot from which she was now refilling her cup.

"Have you heard from Roger?" Kitty asked.

Daphne's expression clouded. "Not yet . . . I'll try his office again in a little while." She looked away, placing the half-eaten cookie on her saucer. "We could order take out, couldn't we? Maybe by then I'll feel up to it."

In other words, we're not discussing the fact that he hasn't called in several days. But Kitty kept her thoughts to herself.

"There's a decent Chinese restaurant not too far from here," she said, adding drily, "There's even a good chance they don't read the newspapers. None of them speak more than a few words of English."

But Daphne was already somewhere else in her head, not listening. "If this were one of my novels, I'd at least have some idea of where to begin. But this . . ." she spread her hands in a gesture of hopelessness. "It's like those stories Daddy used to read aloud to us, where an evil spell is cast over some innocent bystander. I can't help thinking of Mother that way. Like someone under a spell."

Maybe it was because Kitty hadn't slept more than a few hours here and there in the past four days, or maybe just that her patience had been stretched past its limits, and she could no longer hide her exasperation. Whatever the reason, she found herself snapping, "It must be convenient, living so far from home. You never have to take off your rose-colored glasses."

Daphne blinked in surprise, and sat back. In her dark gray turtleneck and slim black slacks, she looked prim, almost severe. "Why would you say a thing like that?"

The note of hurt in her voice found its mark, and Kitty winced inwardly. But she didn't back down. It was much too late for that. "You. All your stupid fantasies about our perfect childhood. It *wasn't* perfect, Daph. Not by a long shot." She drew in a deep breath. "Remember that essay you wrote for school when we were kids? You must have been in the fifth or sixth grade. About the time Daddy accidentally left us at the gas station?"

Daphne grew thoughtful, fingering the handle of her spoon. "He forgot we were in the bathroom," she recalled with a slow nod. "It could have happened to anyone, I suppose."

"That's not what I'm getting at." Kitty rolled her eyes with impatience. "Mother made you tear the essay up, and start over. She claimed it didn't happen the way you said it did. That Daddy hadn't forgotten us, he'd *never* do such a thing. That he must have thought we'd wandered off, and gone looking for us."

Daphne's eyes darkened, but her expression remained puzzled. "It was such a long time ago. What difference does it make now?"

Kitty wanted to seize hold of her, shake her until the pieces fell into place. "Don't you see? Mother was rewriting our past even back then. She wouldn't let you turn in that essay because *she feared the truth.* Daddy was thinking about something else, and he *forgot* us. You're right, it doesn't make him a terrible father. Just imperfect. Why couldn't Mother have accepted that?"

"I don't know."

"Maybe," Kitty said, choosing her words carefully, "she was afraid that if she acknowledged the truth, she would have had to look at other things."

Daphne stopped playing with her spoon, and folded her hands quietly in her lap. Her eyes were huge and bright as she asked, "What things?"

"Let's start with the fact that he wasn't exactly the most faithful of husbands."

Daphne stared back at her. A struggle seemed to be taking place on her face—a war between her need to know what might have caused their mother to kill him and her desire to cling to what was familiar and comforting, even if it was false. She opened her mouth as if to say something, but apparently thought better of it, her back teeth coming together with a soft but audible click.

If she could have read Daphne's mind, though, Kitty would have learned that her sister wasn't quite as stunned as she imagined her to be. Daphne was remembering something, too—the long-ago occasion of her parents' New Year's Eve party. At the time, the scene she'd witnessed had made no sense, but now it was placed in sudden, jarring context. Daphne covered her face with her hands.

"Oh God. So I *wasn't* just imagining things." Her voice emerged as a muffled croak.

Now it was Kitty's turn to be surprised. "You too?"

Daphne let her hands drop. "I wasn't sure, not at the time. I was only eight. There was a party, and we were playing hide-and-seek, you and me and Alex."

"I remember. Sort of."

"It was my turn, and I was hiding out in the closet in Mother and Daddy's room." Daphne's gaze drifted inward. "It was dark, and it smelled nice . . . like perfume. I must have fallen asleep because the next thing I knew someone was whispering on the other side of the door. It was cracked open, and even though the room was dark I could see out . . . just enough. There were *two* people, and they weren't just whispering."

"Daddy and some woman, right?"

"How did you know?"

"I saw it, too. Only about ten years later, with a different leading lady." Kitty told her about the time she'd seen their father romancing their former neighbor, Mrs. Malcolm, in a parked car behind the Masonic Lodge.

Daphne shook her head as if to clear it before fixing Kitty with a fierce, unforgiving stare. "I don't understand. How could you have kept something like that from me?"

Kitty had to look away from the hot accusation in her sister's eyes. She reached down to pat Rommie, sacked out at her feet, his gray mane springing up against her palm like the softest of porcupine quills. "I could ask you the same thing," she said.

"You were, what, fourteen?" Daphne cried in protest. "I was just a little girl! I wasn't sure if what I'd seen was real . . . or . . . or if I'd just imagined it."

Kitty straightened, and crossed her arms over her chest. "Exactly my point. We were *raised* to think that way—that if something doesn't quite fit Mother's rosy picture, it must be our imagination."

"So *that's* what Mother meant when she—" Daphne

brought a fist to her mouth, lightly grazing her teeth with its clenched knuckles. In a low, hoarse voice, she asked, "Do you think that's why . . ." She let the sentence trail off.

"She had to have been turning a blind eye to his affairs for years," Kitty guessed. "Maybe something in her just snapped. I don't know. Maybe we'll never know."

"What about Alex? Does *she* know?"

"I've always suspected she knows more than she lets on."

Daphne was quiet for a moment, her pensive face softly illuminated by a hazy shaft of sunlight sifting through the lace curtains. At last, she said with a kind of pained awareness, "So all that lovey-dovey stuff with Mother and Daddy was just an act?"

"That's the weird part," Kitty puzzled aloud. "I don't think it was. I think Daddy really loved her."

Outside, the clamoring voices seemed to have faded. Rommie's ears pricked up every so often . . . as if he were chasing in his dreams the cats that darted in and out among the thicket of table legs. For a luxurious moment Kitty wallowed in a daydream of her own—that her life as she'd known it was simply on hold—that any moment a button would be pushed that would switch everything back on again.

In a minute, she fantasized, the bell over the door would start to tinkle—the signal that her afternoon customers were arriving for their tea. The oven timer would go off, and Willa's singsong voice would call out from the kitchen. And in the midst of it all, Heather Robbins would stop by to announce that she'd made her decision. *I've thought about it, she'd say, And I can't imagine anyone who could do a better job of raising my ba—*

Kitty's reverie was interrupted by a loud jangling. The phone that had been ringing nonstop all day, but had grown oddly still in the last hour or so, had started up again. With a heavy heart, she heard her own recorded voice click on, saying, "I'm sorry I can't take your call right now. If this is in regard to the funeral, it's at ten A.M. on Sunday, at Evergreen Memorial Chapel on

Church Street. Viewing hours today are between four and six . . ."

An hour later, Kitty was pulling into the circular brick drive in front of the funeral chapel—a white-columned, neoclassical affectation plunked like a scaled-down antebellum mansion in the stucco heart of old Miramonte. She'd been dreading this—more than she'd realized. And for reasons not entirely to do with the morbid spectacle of her father stretched out in his coffin, with Alex holding vigil like a one-woman Greek chorus. On impulse, she turned to Daphne. "Don't ask me what," she said. "But there's something I need to do right now. Will you hate me if I don't come in with you?"

Daphne solemnly searched her face before breaking into an indulgent smile. "Honestly? The only time I ever hated you was in the seventh grade, when you borrowed my charm bracelet without asking. I didn't think I'd ever forgive you for losing the little Scottie dog. But I got over it." She brought a hand to Kitty's cheek. "Will you be all right?"

"Never mind about me." Kitty cut her gaze to the passenger-wide window, watching as a huddle of elderly women in nearly identical black coats slowly mounted the steps to the porticoed entrance. "*You're* the one who's going to be taking all the heat from Alex. She isn't too happy with us right now."

"Because we're not tearing our clothes and smearing ourselves with ashes? I loved Daddy, too . . . but my main concern right now is getting Mother out of jail." Daphne's eyes flashed. "Another thing," she went on with unaccustomed sharpness, "you'd think Alex didn't know the first thing about Daddy. He'd have *hated* this place." She shuddered visibly. "An open casket? My God, what could she be thinking?"

Kitty wished now she'd stood her ground when Alex insisted on making all the funeral arrangements—as if *she* were the only one for whom it mattered. But in all the shock and confusion of the moment, it hadn't occurred to her that her sister would make a Hollywood spectacle of their father's death.

"She's coping as best she can, I suppose. Same as you and I," Kitty sighed, too worn out to concern herself with Alex's motives, whatever they might be.

Not until she'd driven halfway down the street, her sister a dark speck against the white-columned facade in her rearview mirror, did Kitty give in to the grief battering at her ramparts. Daddy . . . oh God . . . he really *was* dead. No one was going to tap her elbow and say, *We're sorry, it's all been a terrible mistake.* She wasn't going to wake up and find she'd only been dreaming.

A long-ago memory surfaced: her father a fair-haired giant, swinging her up, up. Holding her high overhead, where she could look straight down into his clear blue eyes that twinkled like the lakes she'd seen from the airplane the time they'd flown to visit Nana. Eyes you could *fall* into. "How's my favorite redhead?" he'd boom, making her giggle because everyone knew she was his *only* redhead. She'd pretended to squirm away, that was part of the game, too. But when he abruptly set her down, it was as if she truly had been airborne . . . and had suddenly crashed to earth.

Why weren't we enough, Daddy? Why wasn't Mother enough? Did you love those women . . . or was it just the thrill of the chase? She was hit by the dull realization that what she *hadn't* known about her father was greater than what she had. Kitty began to tremble violently.

Just off Locust Avenue she had to turn into the parking lot behind Hair Affair and Pizza My Heart, where she doubted any reporters would be lurking, until she could pull herself together enough to drive on.

A mile or so down the road, she passed the exit for the freeway, and turned onto Bishop, where the mushroom factory—its dense, loamy odor of fertilizer causing her nose to wrinkle—sprawled over several acres, in clusters of low cinder block buildings. Several rambling turns later, she found herself in a neighborhood of small, run-down houses with overgrown yards enclosed by chainlink fences.

The sun had gone down, and twilight was setting in—

an hour when most families would be sitting down to
supper. Damn, she should have phoned ahead. Heather
might be annoyed at her for simply showing up out of
the blue . . . and right now Kitty couldn't afford any
more black marks on her record.

She continued on nonetheless, stopping only long
enough to consult the scrap of lined notepaper on which
an address was written in a large childish hand. It occurred to her, *This is how a junkie must feel.* Heart racing, every nerve on fire, knowing this was wrong, that it
might just kill her . . . but too desperate to care.

Cruising along the twilit street, its trees forming deep
pools of shadow in between street lights spaced far
enough apart to cast only a feeble glow, she peered at
mailboxes that leaned drunkenly, their numbers so worn
they were almost unreadable. She found the one she
sought at the end, facing a weed-grown vacant lot. The
house, half obscured by trees, was set a dozen or so
yards back from the sidewalk behind a tumbledown
picket fence. A rusted swing set out front was the only
sign that a family lived here. But upon closer inspection,
she saw that it wasn't unkempt. The small patch of
lawn—if you could call it that—was neatly mowed, and
the old yellow pickup in the driveway piled with tree
cuttings.

Instantly, Kitty was overcome with doubt. What did
she hope to accomplish by coming here? The other
night, Heather had seemed to warm to her. Even Sean
had begun to open up, telling her about his part-time
job trimming trees and the classes he was taking at the
university. Then, in the midst of it all, like a rock hurled
through her window, shattering not just the evening, but
everything, had come the call from Alex . . .

She ought to give it a few more days, wait until the
shock had worn off. Heather would see then that Kitty
couldn't be held responsible for what her mother had
done.

By then, it might be too late, a voice whispered.

Taking a deep breath, Kitty summoned the courage
to climb out of her car. Halfway up the darkened concrete path leading to the house, into which her feet

seemed to sink to the ankles with each step, a deep voice called from the shadows, "She's not home."

In the long shadows stretching across the driveway, the figure of a man stood silhouetted against the yellow truck. Something about his relaxed, almost insolent stance struck a familiar chord. She watched as the glowing tip of a cigarette moved in a lazy arc, then flared briefly to illuminate Sean's handsome, sharply defined features.

"Any idea when she'll be back?" Kitty asked, her heart rate picking up.

"It would've been a wasted trip either way. My sister doesn't want to see you." Sean sounded matter-of-fact, but she caught the note of contempt in his voice.

Kitty cleared her throat, speaking forcefully to show that she wasn't so easily intimidated. Not by someone young enough to be her kid brother. "I understand how she must feel," she said. "But if I could just explain—"

"You don't owe us an explanation," Sean cut her off.

Light spilled onto the driveway from the narrow alley between the garage and the fence marking their property line. As he stepped into the muted glow, his boots crunching over gravel, she saw that he was dressed the same as before, in jeans and a sweatshirt with its sleeves pushed up over his elbows. His muscular forearms were smudged with tree tar that hadn't quite come off, though it was obvious he'd showered. His dark hair stood up in damp spikes.

"Would it be okay if I came in for a minute, just to sit down?" Kitty felt suddenly too weak to stand, as if she might topple like the sawed-up tree she'd spied in the bed of Sean's pickup.

His dark eyes searched her face. Was he imagining this was some sort of trick? But she must have really looked like death warmed over because after a moment he beckoned for her to follow him.

With a mixture of relief and apprehension, Kitty tailed after Sean down a gravel path that opened onto a small yard in back. A high wooden fence partially blocked the view of the freeway that ran alongside a steep embankment directly below. But there was no way of disguising the staccato flash of headlights zipping past, or the noise—a chorus of tires against blacktop that rose and fell in accompaniment to the distant honking of horns and squealing of brakes.

An outbuilding stood off to the right, which she mistook at first for an oversize toolshed. But as Sean started toward it, Kitty realized this must be his living quarters. Of course, she thought. He wasn't a kid, after all. His remaining at home, she suspected, was more for Heather and their dad than for him.

"The former owner was some kind of artist. This used to be his studio," he informed her, a corner of his mouth hooking up in a tiny smile, as if at the irony of anything creative coming out of such barren soil. "No kitchen, but it has running water, and a john."

A chunk of driftwood was nailed to the door, from which hung a frayed rope of Tibetan brass bells. As Kitty followed Sean inside, their jingling cheered her for no reason in particular.

The room she stepped into was surprisingly tidy. Her gaze took in a double mattress on the floor neatly made up with a worn madras spread, a philodendron trailing from a paint-spattered stool, folded clothes and well-thumbed paperbacks on the homemade shelves that lined one wall.

Then she happened to look up, and was at once captivated. In the center of the roof was a skylight, offering up a transparent slice of moon on a velvet tray of sky.

Sean followed her gaze upward, nodding in shared appreciation. "I sleep under the stars, and don't need an alarm clock to wake up. Almost makes up for the rest."

Kitty was once again aware of the faint traffic sounds drifting in—a succession of low *whumps,* like hard gusts of wind buffeting the side of a building, followed by the low zippering whine of car engines nearing, then fading off into the distance. Headlights strafed the window, outlining its venetian blinds in a yellow flash that cast a rippling ladder of shadow over the bed.

But none of it mattered. For Kitty, who stood gazing up at the stars winking on like porch lights in some far-off galaxy, the world seemed to have shrunk to this one small room. She felt herself grow dizzy, and the floor begin to rock gently under her feet as if she were standing on the deck of a boat gliding slowly out to sea.

She wasn't aware of what was happening until the room abruptly tipped onto its side, dumping her unceremoniously onto the mattress at her feet. She went sprawling backward, knocking her wrist against a table leg. She yelped, but the sound she made seemed to come from behind a closed door in some distant corridor. The sharp edge of a table blurred into soft focus, and her head was filled with a high, faint buzzing.

Then Sean's concerned face loomed into view. He was crouched beside her, elbows resting on his knees, his dark eyes fixed on her with an intensity that was like a taut wire—one that seemed to be the only thing holding her tethered. "Hey, are you okay?"

"I'm not sure. I was fine one minute, and . . ." She closed her eyes against another attack of wooziness.

"When was the last time you had anything to eat?"

"Honestly? I don't remember."

Sean rose with a faint popping of his kneecaps and ambled over to a minirefrigerator tucked in one corner. He grabbed a can of soda from inside and brought it to her. "Here, drink this." He smiled with the air of someone familiar with the effects of going too long without eating. "You'll be okay in a minute, trust me."

For no reason she could think of Kitty *did* trust him. She rolled onto her side, propping her head on one elbow, and took a long swallow. She didn't particularly like Coke, but this tasted like ambrosia. It occurred to her that in addition to being famished, she was probably dehydrated as well. She could only imagine how she must appear to Sean. If she couldn't take care of herself, how was she supposed to take care of a baby?

"You're right. I shouldn't have come," she groaned.

"Stop apologizing." Sean spoke gruffly, but he didn't sound annoyed. "Whatever happened, it's not your fault."

"My father's dead. My mother's in jail. But none of it is my fault." Struck by the insanity of it all, she began to giggle weakly.

Sean dropped onto the mattress, positioning himself so that he was seated cross-legged, facing her. In the half-light, his fierce dark eyes searched her face—eyes that seemed to hold back more than they revealed. "Look, I know I came off like an asshole the other day." He sounded uncomfortable, like someone unused to making apologies. "The truth is, I've got nothing against you. You're a nice person, and I'm sure you'd make a good mom. But we've got all we can handle around here. The last thing we need is more trouble. And pardon me for saying so, but it looks like your family is in a shitload of trouble right now."

He didn't mean to be unsympathetic, she could tell. He was just being blunt. Clearly, there was no room in his life for pity, hers or anyone else's. She guessed that long before his father became crippled, Sean had been the one to shoulder the responsibility of running a household, always with an eye out for his sister. *An old soul,* she thought.

Her head was beginning to clear, and the room ceased its rocking. She mustered a faint smile. "I was just remembering when I was your age. I thought I knew what trouble was, but I didn't know a damn thing."

He snorted derisively. "You make it sound like a hundred years ago. You're not that much older than me."

"I guess not." She met his hard, unnervingly direct gaze. "How old *are* you, anyway?"

"I'll be twenty-five next month."

A ripple of unease passed through her. Why were they discussing the difference in their ages? She felt a slow warmth begin to creep into limbs gone cold with hunger and exhaustion. *It matters because of the way he's looking at me,* she thought. A frank, speculative gaze that raised the flesh along her arms and legs as it traveled over her.

"I didn't come here to try and change anyone's mind," she blurted, eager to change the subject. "I was just hoping . . ." she let the sentence trail off.

"You were hoping Heather would be broad-minded enough not to hold it against you, what happened. And, by the way, I *am* sorry about your dad—shit, I can't even begin to imagine what you must be going through," he sympathized. "But you've got to look at it from my sister's point of view. She's just a kid, and she's already bitten off more than she can chew. Any more, and she'll go under."

Kitty set her soda aside and rolled onto her back. Tears spilled down her temples and into her hair. "I know. I don't blame her. I'd probably feel the same way in her place," she confided miserably.

When Sean reached out and began to stroke her hair, Kitty wasn't aware of a line being crossed. The normal boundary between thought and action didn't seem to exist here, in this room, with this man. Each moment seemed to flow seamlessly into the next, so that she couldn't recall the exact one in which Sean stretched out beside her and drew her into his arms. Only that it felt like the most natural thing in the world.

She closed her eyes, savoring the length of him pressed up against her, and his scent—sawdust and soap, and some secret musk that was uniquely his own. His embrace was surprisingly gentle, his face warm against hers. She could feel the taut muscles in his jaw flicker beneath her fingertips as she drew them across his cheek.

He kissed her then, and she moaned softly at the warm shock of his mouth against hers. None of it seemed real . . . yet the sensations were beyond anything she'd experienced even in dreams. Rich and intense, each touch, each deepening kiss, not so much imagined as *magnified* somehow.

Kitty felt as if she'd been lost at sea, treading water for days on end, and he was the first solid thing to cling to. She lowered her head to graze his neck with her mouth, and slid her palms under his sweatshirt, hungry for his warmth, for the sweet solidness of him. He caressed her in return, smoothing a hand down the curve of her flank. She wore a sweater and slacks, but his touch burned against her flesh as though she were naked.

She offered no protest when he eased her sweater over her head.

In the lowering darkness, she could see only the outline of his head with its bristling spikes of hair. Then another strobe flash lit the window, bringing him into sudden, startling view. The eyes staring into hers were blacker than any she'd ever seen. It seemed she could fall into those eyes and never touch bottom.

With a groan, Sean caught her by the nape of the neck, and brought his mouth down on hers, hard this time. Not just a kiss, a force of nature. It seemed to grab her by the ankles, and turn her inside out. She felt something tethered pull loose inside her, followed by a hot, fierce rush.

This is wrong . . . all wrong . . .

The voice of reason . . . but she refused to listen. Kitty knew deep down that she had no business getting involved with *anyone* right now, much less the brother of the girl whose baby she hoped to adopt. But a kind of recklessness had overtaken her. As if she'd climbed into one of the cars she could hear speeding off into the night, and was unable to stop.

She was aware only of Sean, and the stars winking overhead. Then he was sitting up, tugging his sweatshirt over his head in the casual way of someone too young and beautiful to feel self-conscious in his nakedness. The outdoors had made him as hard as the trees he climbed for a living, she saw, the lean suntanned muscles in his arms and chest those of a working man, not an athlete.

She unfastened his belt. The buckle glinted in the light that careened off the walls and ceiling, and she clasped her hand about it, delighting in its coolness against her heated palm. When she reached into his jeans to hold him in the same way, he moaned. Oh, God. She'd forgotten what a twenty-five-year-old was capable of. That he could be so *ready*.

Minutes later, when he entered her, Kitty had to thrust her fingers into his hair, gripping it to keep from falling off the earth that spun in slow, lazy revolutions beneath her. She didn't want to lose herself, not completely. She wanted to experience it all, every delicious bite. Because at this moment, the heat of their two bodies coming together was the only thing in her crazy, slip-sliding universe that made perfect, irrefutable sense.

Chapter 6

The coffin was solid chestnut fitted with satin brass—
the most expensive one by far. But for once, Alex
wasn't concerned about making a good impression. She
didn't give a damn, either, that her sisters might object
to its cost. She had chosen it for the simple reason that
it reminded her of a poem.

*Under the spreading chestnut tree, the village
smithy stands . . .*

Years ago, she'd memorized it for school, and while
her classmates had stumbled over the fulsome words and
phrases, Alex had sailed through without a miss. Not
that she was so much smarter than everyone else; the
poem had simply captured her imagination. For it was
her father she'd seen standing under that chestnut tree,
tall and noble. Daddy, at the flaming forge of life . . .

*Thus on its sounding anvil shaped each burning
deed and thought . . .*

Tears stood in her eyes as she gazed at her father,
stretched out in his coffin not ten feet away—no longer
mighty, just another old man laid to rest. His profile
gleamed with a waxy luminescence of its own in the
chapel's muted light, his austere lips and Roman nose
giving him an exaggerated look of disapproval.

Daphne, seated in the plush folding chair beside hers,
seemed to feel it, too. She groped for Alex's hand,
squeezing tightly. Alex squeezed back, a quick pulse,
before pulling free. Yes, Daddy could be intimidating,

she thought. But he'd been charming and witty, too, with a passion for life that drew people like moths to a bright flame. Best of all, he'd made her feel *safe*.

An old memory surfaced. She'd been at the cove with her father and mother and sisters, wading in the surf . . . right where she could look up and see the top of their house, a dazzle of lacy white gingerbread and sunstruck shingles, peering over the cliff like a giant's brow. She couldn't have been more than four or five, just big enough to be allowed in up to her knees. She must not have been paying attention, though, because suddenly a huge wave had knocked her over. One that had *seemed* huge, at least, to a little girl who hadn't yet learned to swim.

It had been Alex's first lesson in panic. To this day, she could still recall the helpless terror she'd felt as she churned below the surface, flung about like a rag doll, her eyes and nose filling with sand and seawater. She'd felt her shoulder scrape the sandy bottom, and her bathing suit belly out.

She'd begun to choke. Then just as she was certain she was going to drown, strong arms seized hold of her, and lifted her up. She'd felt the cold water sluicing away, replaced by a sudden, solid warmth: her father. "Daddy, my daddy," she'd sobbed, clinging to him. The water couldn't have been that deep because she could feel the measured tread of his feet against the bottom, traveling up through him and into her small shivering body.

"It's okay, Daddy's here," his deep voice had soothed, *"I'll never let anything bad happen to you."*

All these years later, Alex shivered in the windowless temperature-controlled room where her father's body lay, as if clad in a wet bathing suit instead of the beautifully tailored black knit suit she'd selected for the occasion.

For Daddy, she'd chosen his double-breasted gray suit and Yale rep tie. She'd found the suit hanging on the knob of the closet in the master bedroom, shrouded in plastic, alongside the tuxedo he'd planned to wear to the party. Had he remembered to stop at the dry cleaner's, she wondered, or had Mother seen fit to attend to that

wifely chore just before she picked up a gun and murdered him?

Alex swallowed against the lump in her throat. For
two days it had sat lodged in her throat. She hadn't been
able to eat, and could barely swallow. She wondered
vaguely if she was coming down with something—strep
throat, or worse.

Slowly, she swiveled toward her sister. Daphne, she
saw, wasn't even *looking* at Daddy; she was staring down
at her lap. As if the coffin weren't six feet away. As if
she was nothing more than a casual acquaintance, biding
her time for a decent interval until she could make her
escape. Alex watched her absently rub her cheek, but it
wasn't a tear she was wiping away. Just a lipstick
smudge, no doubt from one of the mourners who'd
stopped to view the body and pay their respects.

Fury rose in Alex like a hot, dry blast from a furnace.
How could she just sit there, dry-eyed? As if Daddy had
been but a distant relative, or an old friend of the family
she hadn't seen in years. As if he hadn't raised her, put
food in her mouth, paid her way through college.

If Daphne cared so little, why hadn't she stayed home
with Kitty, where the two of them could sit around plot-
ting ways to get Mother off the hook? Already, the
wheels were turning, she knew. As her sister lifted her
head, Alex observed a newly calculating expression she
hadn't seen before. As if Daphne were wondering
whether Daddy might have brought this on himself.

Might others think so as well? Alex cast a panicked
glance about the room, at the friends and relatives who'd
been drifting in and out all afternoon. She spotted Aunt
Rose in the back row—an older, more doughty version
of her mother, sitting tall despite the recent weight loss
that had stripped her nearly to the bone. In front of her
sat Aunt June and Uncle Dave, who'd driven up from
Del Mar in their Winnebago. And Great-aunt Edith, all
the way from Maine, accompanied by her son, Cameron,
whom everyone knew was gay. Everyone but his mother,
that is, who insisted on referring to Cam as a "confirmed bachelor."

They all wore the same glassy, uncomprehending expression, one that made Alex think of passengers who've survived a plane wreck. How often, encountering the faces of those survivors on the evening news, had she reached for the remote control?

If only she could do so now: click a button that would erase the past four days. She wouldn't be sitting here, gazing in shocked disbelief at her father's body. And tomorrow, instead of attending his funeral, she'd be dancing with him up at the club. Gliding over the floor in her high heels—just the way he'd taught her when she was a little girl balancing on his shoes in her bare feet.

Alex blinked back the tears that threatened to spill over. A selfish fear crept in. How would *she* survive? Scandal might sell newspapers, but in real estate it was the kiss of death. Take the Brewster estate—a year on the market and not so much as a nibble. Its taint of suicide had scared off any serious buyers. And *this*— well, she couldn't begin to imagine what it would do to her commissions. Forget about not having the money to pay off the IRS; she'd be lucky not to be standing in line at the welfare office.

And here sat Daphne, with her rich doctor husband, and her fancy penthouse in Manhattan. Daphne, who could afford to stay home with her children and write her precious little novels that had nothing to do with real life. As soon as this ordeal was over, she would return to New York, safely removed from the hornet's nest of gossip and innuendo that Alex would have to contend with.

A kind of numb fear settled into her gut like something icy she'd swallowed. Alex was glad she was sitting up front, where no one could see her face. People might wonder about the panic she was sure was written all over it. They might wonder, too, about Daphne's dry eyes and carefully veiled expression.

"Do you need a tissue? I brought extra," Alex whispered pointedly to her sister, dabbing at her own brimming eyes.

Daphne turned to give her a cool, assessing look. "No thanks. I'm fine." Under her breath, she whispered back, just as pointedly, "Don't worry, I'm sure I won't embarrass you at the funeral."

"You could at least *act* upset."

"What makes you think I'm *not?* You're not the only one who lost a father. Just because you were closer to Daddy than Kitty or me doesn't give you exclusive rights." Daphne was keeping her voice low, but every word was steeped with outrage. "And another thing, I think it's horrible the way you're treating Mother."

Alex cast a panicked glance over her shoulder. "For God's sake, Daphne." She hissed. "Someone might hear."

"Good. Let them."

Daphne glared at her with a defiance Alex had never before seen in her sister . . . and, until this moment, wouldn't have believed her capable of. She understood now what that veiled look on Daphne's face had been hiding: her sister was furious with her.

It's just like when we were kids, she thought. *Daphne and Kitty against the world, with me out in the cold.* Dammit, where was Kitty anyway? Probably with Mother, or that fat-cat lawyer Kitty had hired to defend her. When she ought to be *here,* with Daddy.

In the perfumed stillness, with its whispering voices and the hushed murmur of air from hidden vents, Alex felt like screaming.

Then she risked another peek at the coffin, and her face crumpled. She moaned under her breath, "God, please, tell me it isn't real. Tell me that isn't our father lying there . . ." She broke off, cupping her face in her hands.

She felt Daphne lean close and slip a comforting arm about her shoulders. When she looked up, Alex saw the gleam of tears in her sister's eyes as well. "I know," Daphne whispered in a trembling voice. "It doesn't seem real to me, either."

Impulsively, Alex found herself confiding, "That night, up at the house . . ." The lump in her throat began to throb ". . . I almost passed out, right there on the lawn."

What she didn't say, and what no one other than the police who'd witnessed it knew, was that she *had* lost consciousness . . . for a minute or so, anyway. Long enough to bring a flood of shame at the memory of coming to on the lawn, her skirt soaked through with what she'd prayed was water from the freshly sprinkled grass.

Daphne closed her eyes and said, "On the plane, the whole way, I kept thinking I was going to get here and find out it'd all been a horrible mistake."

But before Alex could reply, she caught a glance out of the corner of her eye of someone walking toward them. Leanne. She looked pale and drawn, her eyes bloodshot as though she'd been crying. Trailing several yards behind was Leanne's mother.

Beryl Chapman, a gaunt wreck of the beautiful woman she'd once been, was decked in black from head to toe—as if *she* were the bereaved widow. Only she didn't exactly look grief-stricken. Though her eyes were hidden behind a pair of huge dark glasses, there was no mistaking the cold contempt on her face.

Alex watched as Beryl slid into a chair several rows behind her and Daphne. That woman had had a hand in her father's murder, she was convinced of it. Not directly, perhaps. But that didn't make her any less guilty. She and Mother must have gotten into some sort of fight, during which Beryl had spilled the beans about her and Daddy. Maybe Beryl knew about the women who'd come after her, too. Yes, that would make sense. Hearing about an affair that had happened thirty-some years ago might not have pushed her mother over the edge. But finding out that Beryl hadn't been the only one, that was another story.

The nerve of that woman, showing up here, Alex fumed. *I ought to march right over to her and—*

"Alex."

Alex started, and glanced about to find Leanne slipping into the empty chair on her right. Up close, her friend appeared even more miserable than she had from a distance. The flesh around her bloodshot eyes was pink and swollen, and her nostrils were chafed raw from Kleenex. She wore a plain white blouse and black skirt, her only jewelry a tiny gold crucifix on a chain around her neck. When Leanne hugged her, Alex was reminded of a shivering, half-starved stray.

"Oh, Alex. I haven't been able to stop crying since you called."

Leanne smelled of the Calvin Klein perfume Alex had given her last Christmas. Leanne, who couldn't afford to spend money on herself, much less on others, had crocheted her a lace table scarf. Now, in this room where death reigned and it was always sweater weather, Alex felt a surge of warmth. Leanne loved her, more than Alex's own sisters did. She'd loved Daddy, too. But the tears that were at this moment coursing down Leanne's cheeks were exclusively for *her*, Alex felt sure.

"Thanks for coming." She dabbed at Leanne's cheeks with the tissue balled in her fist. "Daddy would be glad that you're here."

Leanne averted her eyes and pulled away. She looked suddenly uncomfortable. It struck Alex: *She doesn't want to step on any toes.* When they were children, Leanne had worshipped Daddy. Alex used to wonder at times if *he* were the reason Leanne hung around so much. But as much as she'd adored him, and might have secretly wished he was her father, Leanne clearly didn't intend to overstep her role as a mere friend of the family.

Alex had never loved her more than she did at this very minute.

"I would have gotten here sooner, but Tyler was acting up," Leanne apologized. "I had to wait for Beth to feed her own two before I could leave him. Then, on our way over, of *course* Mom had to stop for cigarettes." She frowned in disgust.

Glancing over her shoulder at Beryl, Alex struggled not to let her anger show. For Leanne's sake, her father's too, she had to keep the peace. Even if it meant biting her tongue practically in two.

Sitting there, stiff-necked and quivering with outrage, she found herself remembering a time when she hadn't been so good at pretending. The truth was she'd never liked Leanne's mother. As a kid, it had always seemed as if Beryl didn't notice, much less care, how much time Leanne spent over at their house. She had Beth, her favorite. And the friends who showed up every other Tuesday for mah-jongg. She had her career, too: professional ex-wife. Leanne used to joke that her mother would shoot a man before she'd marry him and give up her alimony check.

The joke no longer seemed funny.

Then one day, when they were fourteen, Leanne's long honeymoon abruptly ended. She and Alex had been playing cards up in Alex's room—spit, and seven up. They'd just finished trying on outfits for the father-daughter dance that coming Friday night, and the bed was strewn with clothing. Leanne was excited, because she was going to the dance, too. A little while ago, she'd phoned her mom to say she'd been invited by Dr. Seagrave himself—he'd volunteered to escort *both* girls. Beryl hadn't replied, except to say that she was coming over to pick Leanne up, and they'd talk about it on the way home.

Neither Leanne nor Alex had had a clue that she might be upset. Beryl wasn't the type to yell or scream. Which was probably why she and Mother had stayed friends all these years. It wasn't until the door to Alex's room flew open, and Beryl burst in, that they knew something was wrong.

Beryl's eyes were so dark Alex couldn't see her pupils. Her lips were a vermilion slash in her pale angular face. Alex knew the exact color of the lipstick she used—she and Leanne had tried it on when Beryl wasn't home—and at that moment it had occurred to her how fitting the name was: Jungle Red. Leanne's mother looked exactly like a savage jungle beast about to pounce.

And that's exactly what she *had* done: pounced on her daughter with both claws bared. Beryl grabbed Leanne's arm and yanked her off the bed.

"You little brat. How *dare* you? Isn't it bad enough you're over here every minute of the day? Now *this*. Acting as if you don't have a family of your own. A father who would love nothing more than to take you to that dance." Bright flags of color stood out on her high curved cheekbones.

It had taken a moment for Leanne, shocked white as

the candlewick bedspread that still bore the innocently curled imprint of her body, to regain her speech. She'd glared at her mother for a long moment, her eyes glittering with unshed tears. Then she'd shrieked something Alex would never forget.

"I wish I *did* live here! At least Dad has an excuse for ignoring me. He's three thousand miles away."

Alex had found her own tongue then, as well. Jumping up off the bed, she'd cried, "Leave her alone! You just leave her alone!"

Beryl had turned and given her a long hateful look. Then seized Leanne's arm and silently marched her out the door.

After that, Leanne had come to their house far less frequently, and she seldom spent the night or accompanied them on family trips. She and Alex never spoke of the incident. Alex hadn't mentioned it to her parents, either. What would have been the point? Daddy would have thought it was old bitterness toward him resurfacing. And Mother would have defended Beryl, saying she had a perfect right to be upset, and that they should have been more sensitive to the fact that Leanne had a father of her own.

Now, staring at the spotlighted coffin before her, Alex thought, *Look who's fatherless now.* She felt something twist inside her at the irony of it.

Leanne, as if reading her mind, abruptly took her hand, squeezing it so tightly Alex could feel the pinch of her wedding band. She couldn't imagine why Leanne still wore it. Hadn't it been nearly five years since that no-good husband of hers had cleaned out their savings account on his way out of town, leaving her broke and pregnant?

"He was a wonderful man." Leanne's voice was a broken whisper.

A second or two passed before Alex realized she was talking about Daddy, not Chip. She nodded, too choked up to respond. At that moment Daphne leaned across to greet Leanne, pecking her lightly on the cheek.

"It was good of you to come," she murmured.

Alex wondered if she'd only imagined the flash of resentment in Leanne's eyes when she murmured back, "I'm so sorry for your loss. Please let me know if there's anything I can do."

Before Daphne could offer some equally polite response, all three women were distracted by a sudden stir in the room. Alex looked about just in time to see Beryl Chapman gliding toward the front of the chapel, her head held high, the light glancing off her dark glasses in sharp points like tiny daggers. Fury mounted in Alex, but she could do nothing to stop her. She merely sat there, rigid, watching Beryl jerk to a stop before the coffin.

Glancing out of the corner of her eye, she saw that Leanne looked equally horrified. No, not just horrified. *Responsible* somehow. Like someone who'd brought along a pet snake that had gotten loose from its cage and might bite someone.

Daphne and Alex exchanged a look. Her sister wore a startled expression, as if their mother's best friend— the woman with whom Mother had regularly lunched and shopped, bought Christmas gifts for, and gossiped with over the phone—had been transformed into some horrid stranger.

Their attention was brought back to the coffin by a low, guttural cry. Beryl, spectral in her dark glasses and black sheath, was staring down at Daddy as if in some sort of trance. Her bony hands curled at her sides, their long scarlet nails like claws reddened with blood. Her mouth twisted in a hideous grimace that raised the hair on the back of Alex's neck.

Softly—just loud enough for Alex, Daphne, and Leanne to hear—she hissed, *"You fucking bastard. You'll pay in hell for what you did."*

They didn't speak of it until they were getting ready to leave. The last of the visitors were drifting toward the exit when Leanne leaned close to ask, "Can I catch a ride home with you guys?" Her voice was low and fraught with some emotion Alex couldn't quite pinpoint.

Anger at her mother? Embarrassment? She would soon find out.

"No problem," she said.

She watched as Leanne made her way over to her mother, standing in back by the mahogany stand where the maroon leather guest book Alex had selected lay open for friends and relatives to sign. Their exchange was brief, but Beryl's expression, she observed, was pinched and disapproving. She nodded and said something to Leanne before turning and walking stiffly out the door.

It was Daphne who suggested they stop for coffee at the Denny's on Del Rio Boulevard, four blocks or so from Kitty's house. Leanne, to Alex's surprise, quickly took her up on it.

"God, I feel so terrible about what happened back there," she confided to the two sisters a short while later in the privacy of their booth. She sat across from Alex and Daphne, cradling a thick white mug of coffee between loosely cupped palms. "My mother . . ." Leanne reached for a packet of Sweet'n Low, "she, uh, hasn't been herself since she heard about your dad. This has really hit her hard."

"It didn't sound as if there was any love lost between the two of them," Daphne observed coolly.

Alex eyed her sister uneasily. Daphne's face held the hyperalert look of someone tuned in on every frequency, someone with a mission, a quest, for whom the truth might be secondary. She wanted Mother exonerated and would go to any lengths necessary to accomplish it. *Even if it means digging up dirt about Daddy,* Alex thought with growing apprehension.

In a stylish forest-green dress, Daphne looked out of place in the vinyl booth, with its laminated pressed-wood table. It was just after six, the restaurant at not quite half occupancy on this Friday evening in April, with the bowling league having its annual play-off at the Bowl-A-Rama and bingo night at St. Ignatius swinging into high gear. The weekend crowd would, of course, be down at the marina, dining out at the Crow's Nest or Hernando's Hideaway.

At the club in Pasoverde Estates, where they would be preparing this weekend's menu, Alex wondered if it would include the prime rib and lobster Newburg ordered for the eighty guests who would not be attending tomorrow's canceled anniversary banquet.

The thought left her faintly nauseated.

She watched Leanne's pale cheeks color as she fiddled nervously with the pink packet of sweetener. "Actually, I was thinking of your mother," she said. "What happened to Lydia. Mom feels responsible in a way."

Alex fought to keep from shouting, *Goddamn right. She all but put the gun in Mother's hand!* But all she said was, "Leanne, what do you know that you're not telling us?"

The eyes Leanne raised to her were so tortured, Alex instinctively wanted to snatch back the question. Suddenly, she knew what Leanne was going to say and didn't want to *hear* it. She didn't want to know why her friend had lied the other day. The very same day her father . . .

She swallowed hard, waiting while Leanne brought her mug to her mouth with hands that weren't quite steady. As she put it down, she said, "I'm sorry, Alex, I should have told you. That day at the house, I *did* know why my mother wasn't invited to the party. But I'd had such a lousy day, I just . . . I didn't feel like getting into it."

"Your mom had a falling out with our mother? This is the first I'm hearing of it," Daphne put in, frowning.

"Mom told me she couldn't take it anymore, seeing the way he treated her. Forty years of her eating his lies, she said. A few weeks ago, she . . . she just lost it, I guess."

A wave of heat rushed through Alex, followed by a deep, numbing cold. "You *knew*. About Daddy's . . ."

"Affairs," Daphne supplied. Her clear green gaze settled on Alex, who winced a little at the realization that her sister hadn't been so innocent after all. "I guess *I* was the last to know," Daphne went on. "I didn't find out until a couple of hours ago. Kitty told me." Something dark flickered in her eyes, as if she might not be saying everything she knew or felt. She leaned forward, asking in a low, taut voice, "My God, does the whole *town* know?"

Leanne shrugged. "I've heard a few rumors, here and there. People like to talk. I wouldn't put too much emphasis on it."

"How long have *you* known?" Alex demanded of Leanne.

"Mom told me about her and Vern," she confessed. "One night a few years ago when she'd had too much to drink. But I got the impression it was no big deal. Just one of those things."

"What?" Alex sat back, stunned. "It's the reason your parents got divorced," she blurted.

Leanne frowned with annoyance, pushing her mug aside. "I was pretty young at the time, sure, but what I've learned since is that nothing like that is ever cut and dried. Mom must have been pretty unhappy in the first place to have cheated on him. My dad's not exactly the warm and fuzzy type."

"So let me get this straight," Daphne interjected. Her head was lowered, and she rubbed one temple thoughtfully. "Thirty-odd years ago, your mother and our father had an affair. Your mom's kept it from her best friend, Lydia, all this time. Why would she suddenly decide to let the cat out of the bag? And more important, why would it push Mother off the deep end?"

Leanne shook her head, falling silent while around them diners chattered, bolted their food, and joked with waitresses. It seemed to Alex at that moment that there were two worlds traveling on parallel tracks—the one she and her sisters inhabited right now . . . and the one in which people glided along in utter complacency, foolishly believing themselves immune to the kind of tragedies they watched on the six o'clock news.

"I'm sorry, Alex, I should have told you." Leanne began at last, hesitantly, "There was some talk, at the hospital. I heard it from one of the interns in Path. Your mom was on antidepressants. I guess Vern must've said something to him."

"Even if it's true, it doesn't necessarily make her

crazy," Daphne objected. But the seed of doubt had been planted; Alex could see it in her eyes.

"I'm not saying she's crazy," Leanne was quick to agree. "I wouldn't even have mentioned it, except . . . ," She spread her hands in a helpless gesture, adding in a voice soft with regret, "None of this changes the fact that he was an exceptional man. Truly. Whatever his faults might have been." Directing her gaze at Daphne, she said, "Did you know it was your father who fought for an organ donor counselor at General? Too many precious opportunities were going by the wayside, he said, not to mention that families suffering the loss of a loved one could be shown a way to make sense of their tragedy. He was right. Since Mrs. Canfield was hired, organ donations have increased by at least thirty percent."

"I didn't know." Daphne had the decency to look slightly abashed.

It was no surprise to Alex, of course, but until now, looking into her friend's flushed face, it hadn't hit home that she wasn't the *only* one for whom Daddy had been a kind of hero.

"I guess the answer is we still don't know what killed him," she concluded miserably. The fury toward her mother that had sustained her these past few days, keeping her from the deeper and, she suspected, much darker emotions waiting in the wings, seemed to have dissipated for the moment. She leaned back in the booth, her coffee untouched.

"The question is will we *ever* know?" Daphne cried in frustration.

Several long moments passed before any of them spoke. Then with a sigh, Daphne retrieved her purse and said, "I don't know about you, but if I don't get to bed soon, I won't be good for anything more challenging than a crossword puzzle. What do you say we table this discussion until after the funeral?"

But Alex knew there wouldn't be another time. Not for her. And certainly not for Leanne, who, she could see, was already retreating into her shell. Her face closing in, her eyes carefully shuttered as she reached for her own purse.

Alex, for her part, would try not to think too hard about the fact that Leanne had lied to her the other day. She would try not to wonder what other lies Leanne might have told her . . . and what that would say about their friendship. Right now, if she had to cope with one more thing, she simply couldn't take it.

It was well past dark by the time Alex turned down her street in a gated development so new the landscaping consisted of little more than fledgling junipers and euonymus dotting naked parcels of earth tied off with string. Like the miniature bushes in the scale version of Vista-Del-Mar on display in the model house.

She'd moved here only last year, when the house she and Jim had lived in while they were married was sold. It had been a huge adjustment, not only to life without Jim . . . but for the girls, who'd had to get used to a new school, new friends. And now, short of a miracle, she might be forced to sell this place, too, move into some cheap and dreary house like Leanne's.

The thought of it brought a sudden burst of pain, like a taut wire snapping in her head. Her temples throbbed, and the swath of blacktop lit by her headlights appeared to gently undulate. In her mind she could see Beryl, standing at the coffin like a cobra about to strike. And Leanne, in the booth at Denny's, purposely not meeting her eyes. But what did it all mean?

Suppose her friend knew more than she was saying? That still didn't prove anything. Even if Daddy were seeing someone when he died, and Beryl had seen fit to enlighten her dear friend about *that* as well, it would still not explain how someone like Mother, who'd spent her whole life avoiding confrontation, would pick up a gun and . . .

Alex couldn't bring herself to finish the thought. Not with her head pounding, and a pair of distraught daughters awaiting her at home. Crying was a luxury she simply couldn't afford.

When she spied her ex-husband's silver-blue Audi in the driveway of her town house—Jim, who flew business class to Hong Kong and vacationed with his girlfriend on Maui, and who didn't have the IRS breathing down his neck—it was all suddenly too much.

Jim was only supposed to have had supper with the girls. Didn't he realize that the last thing she would need, on top of everything else, was one more headache?

To add insult to injury, he'd taken *her* spot.

Pulling in along the curb, Alex sat for a moment, gripping the steering wheel and sucking in deep greedy breaths until she felt calm enough to climb out and negotiate the quarry slate front path in her high heels.

No sooner had she let herself in the front door when she was assaulted by peals of laughter drifting down the hall from the kitchen, where Nina and Lori were obviously in pig heaven with their father—never mind the gruesome circumstances that had brought him.

Fury beat at Alex with both fists. He ought to be *ashamed.* Taking advantage of her tragedy to perform for his fan club. Oh, yes, she knew his game. Hadn't she, too, once fallen all over him in the same way? She'd been the same age as the twins, she recalled, when Jim Cardoza, with his curly dark hair and gypsy eyes, first sauntered into her homeroom like it was the Western Hemisphere, and he owned everything in it.

I would have done anything for him . . . anything but turn a blind eye like Mother. For unlike her father, Jim had had no reason to cheat on her.

Tossing her purse onto the hall bench—piled with backpacks, schoolbooks, crumpled sweatshirts—she stalked into the kitchen, where she found her daughters at the table, bent over an instruction booklet, while Jim fiddled with the cord on a brand-new popcorn maker. Three faces turned up in surprise that immediately turned to wariness.

Alex froze in her tracks. Was she really so threatening? Was the look she was seeing in her daughters' eyes the result of the temper that lately had become harder and harder to control? The last thing she wanted was for her girls to feel as if they had to—

Tiptoe around and speak in whispers like you did when a Certain Somebody was in one of his moods.

Alex was seized by an impulse to scoop them into her

arms—Nina, a dark-haired, dusky-skinned replica of her father . . . and Lori, with her angelic face and long blond hair like sunshine spilling through a window. They were fifteen, but in the past year or so Nina had grown quite busty while Lori, who was slender and small-breasted, had merely grown obsessive about undressing in private.

It was Lori who broke the tense silence. "Hey, Mom. You're back sooner than we thought."

Alex was opening her mouth to say how good it felt to be home when she caught her ex-husband looking at her with such pity the words dissolved in her throat. She didn't need his sympathy, dammit. What she'd *needed* was a husband.

"So I see." She folded her arms over her chest. Directing a cool gaze at Jim, she said, "I wasn't expecting to find you still here. Your girlfriend had other plans for the evening, I take it?"

Alex was gratified and a little ashamed to see him flush—a deepening of his naturally ruddy complexion that, maddeningly, made him even more attractive. Why did he have to be so handsome? Even better-looking than in high school, with those Michael Corleone eyes and curly dark hair threaded with silver. In his jeans and Irish fisherman's sweater, he managed to look both distinguished . . . and a tiny bit dangerous. Like someone guarding the door to an exclusive club of one.

In a carefully controlled voice, he said, "The girls and I were just about to make popcorn."

"The old popcorn maker was broken," Lori rushed to explain with her usual Jill-came-tumbling-after eagerness to please. "We had to go out and buy a new one." She offered Alex a tentative smile, holding up the cord Jim had been in the midst of unraveling. "It's awesome. You don't even need oil—it can pop with just air."

Nina poked her sister with the spoon in her hand. "You idiot. Can't you see Mom's upset? Grandpa's dead and all you can talk about is *popcorn?*" She cast a sheepish gaze at Alex. "Don't be mad, Mom. We weren't being disrespectful, or anything. It's just that Dad thought—" She bit her lip.

"We could all use a break." Jim walked over, slipping

an arm about Nina's shoulders. Directing an unflinching gaze at Alex, he said, "I'll leave if that's what you want. But wouldn't it be better if we sat down and talked this over? Maybe I can help."

Alex snorted in disgust. "Haven't you done enough already?" She marched over to the sink, where the dirty dishes from supper were still piled, and cranked on the tap. Less harshly, she added, "If you really *could* help, believe me I wouldn't turn it down. But there's nothing you or anyone can do. My father's dead. And barring a miracle my mother will spend the rest of her life in prison."

"You shouldn't talk that way." Jim's voice was cold with reproach.

"She murdered him," Alex shot back. "Doesn't she deserve to pay?"

Behind her, Lori began to cry softly.

"You girls go on upstairs," her ex-husband ordered gently, and at that moment Alex hated him most of all for being able to provide their daughters with the one thing she was incapable of right now: tenderness. He gave them each a quick hug, waiting until they were out of earshot before saying, "It doesn't look good for your mother, I agree, but I refuse to believe it's hopeless. I spoke with Kitty, and she tells me your mother's lawyer is looking to plead second degree, in light of mitigating circumstances."

"I'm not surprised. Mother isn't above milking this for all it's worth." Alex squirted soap into the water rising in the sink.

"Are you suggesting she might be *enjoying* this in some way?" Jim's coldness tipped over into anger.

Alex whirled about, soapsuds flying from her hands to spatter the gleaming white tiles at her feet. "I don't know! All I know is that my father is dead, and *she's* responsible!"

Jim stood there, staring at her. His very presence seeming to mock her. Against the cool backdrop of the kitchen she'd thought so sleek and modern, with its pale woods and stainless surfaces, he was a reminder of something unique and vibrant that had somehow slipped between her fingers. Suddenly, it wasn't just this kitchen, but her whole life that seemed devoid of any real warmth.

Jim stood his ground, eyeing her with a sad contempt that was like a rusty nail being driven into her. "Where does it end, Alex? When are you going to stop making excuses for the man? Now that he's gone, don't you think it's time?"

"How dare you lecture me!" she flung back. "What about you? Shouldn't I have figured out what *you* were doing behind my back?"

"Let's not go over all that again," he said wearily.

"Why not? Is there a statute of limitations?"

"There was more to it than that, and you know it."

"At least I never cheated on you!"

"Technically, no."

Alex grew rigid. She didn't have to ask who he meant. *Daddy.* Her hands dropped to her sides, clots of white foam dripping from her fingers.

When she summoned the strength to slap him, the sound seemed to ricochet like a gunshot in the stillness.

Jim reeled back, his face hard as packed earth, and for an instant it looked as if he meant to hit her back. Dammit, she almost wished he *would.* But in sixteen years Jim hadn't once lifted a finger to her, and as much as he might have wanted to, he wasn't about to do so now. As he turned away, she was filled with a helpless, ranting love like something banging itself to death against the bars of its cage. She watched him snag his windbreaker from the kitchen chair over which it was draped, and it took every ounce of control she possessed not to cry out.

"Say goodnight to the girls for me," he said in a low, tight voice. "And while you're at it, think about what this is doing to them." Jim stopped in the doorway to level a long hard look at her. "The old man always came first with you, and don't think they weren't aware of it. But he was still their grandpa."

Then he was gone. Alex remained rooted to the spot, as if to keep from jostling something loose. Her whole body felt strung together by the most fragile of threads, any one of which could snap with the slightest movement, scattering her bones over the floor like so much broken china.

With a low moan she dropped her head into her hands. Behind her the water faucet continued to gush—she'd neglected to shut it off, and now the sink was overflowing, spilling sudsy water over the clean white floor at her feet. She didn't care. For once in her life, instead of running for a mop or reaching for a sponge, she remained perfectly still. Allowing the soles of her high heels to grow damp, and the popcorn maker's instruction booklet, which had fluttered to the floor, to swell and buckle like some poor creature in the throes of dying.

Chapter 7

"What do you *mean,* you can't make the funeral?" Daphne cupped a hand about the receiver, though Kitty was out of earshot downstairs.

After a moment's silence she heard Roger sigh. "I'm sorry, sweetie. There's just no way I can leave Jennie right now. She's spiking a temp, and I don't like the sound of her breathing."

The familiar current of frustration starting to sizzle in Daphne was immediately short-circuited. Her baby? Sick? "I thought all she had was a little cold."

"It's probably nothing serious," he assured her. "But you can never be too careful about these things."

Daphne felt torn. Every fiber of mother instinct urged her to fly home, where she could hold her small daughter, soothe her fever with a cool cloth and the cubes of frozen fruit juice Jennie loved to suck on. At the same time, a sixth sense, or maybe something in Roger's voice, told her Jennie wasn't really all that sick. A little sniffle maybe, but not the dire picture Roger was painting. She didn't know how she knew, she just did.

Her mind picked up a thread of memory that had been all but lost in the shell-shocked confusion of this past week. Roger in the bookstore, flirting with that blond Junior Leaguer. Yes, *flirting.* At the time, unwilling to face the possibility that Roger might be cheating on her, she hadn't been able to fully acknowledge it. But now, in light of Kitty's revelations about their father—confirmed by the ugly incident with Beryl at the funeral home—she could no longer dismiss it out of hand.

"What about your mother?" she asked, tightening her

grip on the receiver. "I'm sure she wouldn't mind staying with the children for a few nights."

"Mom and Dad are in London," he reminded her patiently, as if for the third or fourth time, though this was the first she was hearing of it. "And I don't want to leave my children with just anyone. They're really upset by this." There was a pause, then in a voice that set her teeth on edge, he added, "Look, it tears me up that you're going through this alone . . . but we have to put Kyle and Jennie first."

My children. As if he alone were responsible for their welfare, and wouldn't dream of putting his own needs above theirs. And if his wife couldn't see it, well, he'd just have to be extra tolerant because wasn't he responsible for her as well?

Daphne squeezed her eyes shut. How could she argue that she needed him more? What kind of mother would make such a demand? Suppose Jennie were sick. Roger would be right to stay with the children.

So why wasn't she comforted by the image of Roger tucking them in at night and reading aloud to Jennie her favorite book, *Goodnight Moon?*

Maybe if you trusted him . . .

Roger, who was so adept at appearing to accommodate her while accommodating no one but himself. Like the winter before last, when she'd been desperately sick with the flu, and had begged him to come home early that day—to which he'd responded compassionately by showing up half an hour ahead of usual. Or their trip to Sanibel in February, when a computer glitch had cost Daphne her seat on the return flight . . . and he'd gone ahead without her, arguing persuasively that he was scheduled to operate the following morning and couldn't risk being delayed.

"When's the soonest you *can* get here?" she asked.

"Can't say. But it'll be the very first instant I can swing it, you know that, Daph." He sounded mildly surprised that she should have to ask. "Meanwhile, I've made some calls, lined up a few names."

"Names?"

"You don't think your mother should have the best lawyer money can buy? Let's get real here."

She drew in a breath to stave off the anger that slapped at her like a storm-driven tide. "From what I know," she told him with forced evenness, "Tom Cathcart is a fine attorney."

"Fine for a town the size of Miramonte, maybe," he scoffed. "I'm talking about someone who really knows the ropes."

As recently as a week ago—which, given her newly distorted sense of time, might just as well have been a year—Daphne might have felt stymied, unable to combat Roger's irrefutable logic that had, after all, only her mother's best interests at heart. But over the past few days something seemed to have shifted in her, imperceptible until now, like a bicycle chain slipping—a tiny thing that nonetheless prevented the wheels from turning.

"The size of the town in which you live doesn't necessarily equal the size of your intellect," she was quick to point out, a sharp edge in her voice. "Remember, *I'm* from here . . . and that didn't stop me from marrying you."

Roger fell silent, and from his carefully measured breathing she could tell he was struggling not to lose his temper. But instead of rushing to smooth things over as she would have done in the past, Daphne sat quietly on the iron bed in Kitty's guest room. She watched the lace curtains flutter in the damp breeze blowing in through the open window, from which she could see the ocean shimmering hazily in the distance, like some half-remembered dream. Roger was the first to break the silence.

"I was under the impression, mistakenly I can see, that you *wanted* my help," he said in a richly aggrieved tone of voice.

"What I *want* is for you to start acting like a husband."

"As opposed to what?" She imagined his large head with its shingles of graying hair reeling back, a shaggy brow arching in surprise at this new, unexpected side of her.

A father, she nearly cried. But the words caught in her

throat, and she said through gritted teeth, "Roger, just this once, do you think you could try not being so fuck-ing *reasonable?*"

"You'd rather I shouted and carried on?" He sounded as if he'd have liked to do just that. But it just wasn't in Roger's nature. Wasn't that precisely why she'd married him? He was what she'd thought she needed at the time: an anchor to steady her against the wild buffeting of a heart cut loose and set adrift. "At the risk of sounding like a doctor," he continued in that same highly injured tone, "I'm going to chalk this up to your being under an enormous strain. Daphne, I want you to get some rest. If you don't take care of yourself, you could wind up getting sick as well."

Suddenly, Daphne felt sure he was right. She was nearly sick with exhaustion. So tired, the thought of stretching out on the faded old quilt beneath her seemed the most enticing thing in the world. She looked around the room, cozily decorated as only Kitty would have—a cracked Victorian pitcher planted with scarlet geraniums on the antique washstand by the door, a dressmaker's dummy draped with a beaded scarf, a mirror in a gaudy mosaic frame hung over a simple pine dresser. In an angled recess of the pitched ceiling, she recognized one of her mother's watercolors, a lovely seascape of the cove below their house.

Admiring the delicate wash of grays and whites—an effect, she knew, that was achieved by sponging away the paint while still wet—Daphne wondered if it was possible to ever really know the mind of a loved one . . . or if it was merely the *illusion* of knowing that sustained you.

"It's been a long day. I think I will lie down," she told her husband wearily. "Give Jennie and Kyle a kiss for me. Tell them Mommy misses them and is working hard to get home just as soon as—" *When? If her mother stood trial, it could be months* "—I possibly can."

The following morning at ten o'clock, the chapel at Evergreen Memorial was filled to overflowing. As Daphne and her sisters slid into the front pew, she thought uncharitably, *Alex couldn't have asked for a better audience.* Every seat was taken, and the standing-room area in back was packed with latecomers—more than a hundred pairs of eyes, all fixed on Vernon Sea-grave's daughters as they bowed their heads in grief.

Daphne greeted Alex's ex-husband with a nod, planting a kiss on the solemnly presented cheeks of each of her nieces, seated alongside him. Jim reached across to grip her hand. Her brother-in-law. She realized she'd really never stopped thinking of him as that and was glad he'd come. In his custom-made dark-blue suit and twill tie, he struck a note of refinement that would have pleased Daddy, she thought. And it was Jim who'd thoughtfully greeted the mourners at the door while she and her sisters had met with the minister to discuss last-minute arrangements.

At the moment, however, his focus was on Alex. He kept glancing out of the corner of his eye, as if not quite sure what to make of his ex-wife. He was right to be concerned, Daphne thought. She'd never seen her sister so out of it. In the sepia-tinted sunlight filtering in through the amber windows, her black straw hat cast a faint pattern over her pale face that made Daphne think of scattered ashes. She was staring at the coffin, but her eyes were somewhere else. Softly, as if to herself, Alex remarked, "Aren't the flowers lovely? I helped Mother pick them out."

Kitty, seated between her two sisters on Daphne's right, let out a low gasp. Under her breath she whispered, "Oh, God, please tell me those aren't the ones for the party."

"No point in letting them go to waste." Alex went on gazing serenely at the floral arrangements that enveloped the burnished coffin like a rich tapestry, overflowing onto the platform below.

Daphne didn't speak. It required every ounce of her control just to keep from bursting into tears. And the flowers *were* lovely—yet another example of Mother's impeccable taste. The only off-key note was the orange tiger lilies. They seemed rowdy somehow against the polished dark wood of the coffin. But how on earth could she have known?

Daphne fought to hold back the sob rising in her throat.

Then the Reverend Thomas Buckhorst stood up to read a psalm, followed by Uncle Spence, who'd asked to deliver the eulogy. Seeing him at the podium—her least favorite of Daddy's two brothers—she was struck by the monumental unfairness of it, this bad Xerox of her father, as arrogant as he was undistinguished in every respect—from the slope of his weak chin to his overstuffed beggar's purse of a belly. She recalled with disdain the faux wood paneling on the wall of his office at Seagrave's Chrysler City. How could *he* have survived Daddy?

She listened to him spin tales of their boyhood, reminiscing about her grandfather, who'd died before Daphne was born, in a tone that was almost reverential—when, according to Mother, Grandfather Seagrave had been one of the meanest, stingiest men alive. To hear her uncle describe it, you'd have thought he and his brothers had been raised in a home where voices were seldom raised, and the only time their father had laid a hand on them was in blessing.

More eulogies followed: a doctor who'd interned under her father; Will Henley, a boyhood friend. And last, a man Daphne didn't immediately recognize rose and began making his way to the podium. He was tall and slightly stooped, with a bald spot like a monk's tonsure on the back of his graying head. His ill-fitting suit, from which his rawboned wrists poked, brought to mind a country preacher sporting his Sunday best.

"I didn't know Dr. Seagrave," he began in the low, tentative voice of someone unused to speaking before an audience, "but I guess I didn't have to. You see, twenty-five years ago he saved my boy's life . . ."

It all came rushing back. They'd been driving home from Del Mar after a visit with Uncle Dave and Aunt June. It was the second day of their trip, Daphne recalled, and they'd been on the road since early that morning. Darkness had abruptly fallen, as it tended to do in those cow towns that ran in an unbroken string along Highway 5 between LA and Sacramento—like a tarp being rolled down and buttoned to the horizon at all four corners.

Daddy had pulled off in one of those little burgs, the name of which escaped her. They were on their way to the Frosty Freeze, where they'd been promised all the burgers and fries they could eat, when Daphne caught sight of the pickup angled on its side in a ditch, taillights flashing. She must have been twelve, thirteen—old enough to know that the man standing beside the overturned truck, wildly scissoring his arms to get their attention, was hurt. Not badly, as it turned out. A broken rib, some bumps and bruises. The real victim lay stretched out in the ditch—a small crumpled figure in bib overalls, with fair hair that glowed white as the moon overhead in the shaft of a cockeyed headlight.

Daddy pulled over to the side of the road and leaped out.

"It's my boy, Benjie," the man gasped. "He's hurt bad."

"I'm a doctor," Daddy told him. "Let me see if I can help."

The boy, who looked to be six or seven, was unconscious, and as Daphne and her sisters and mother watched, speechless with a mixture of horror and awe, Daddy lifted him from the grassy ditch and carried him to their station wagon. Folding a blanket over the dropped hatch, he fashioned a makeshift examining table. Mother shone the flashlight over the boy while Daddy gently poked and prodded.

Except for a knot on his forehead, he appeared unhurt. But his face was oddly swollen and his breathing shallow. Daddy glanced up at the boy's father, who looked like a scarecrow—all arms and legs and strawlike hair, with an elongated shadow that seemed to stretch forever across the potholed blacktop. The man took a shuffling step toward Daddy, his arms held out as if beseeching him to perform a miracle. Which in a way, was exactly what her father *had* done.

Daddy asked, "Is your son allergic to bee stings?"

The man drew back to eye him warily, then shook his head. "Not that I know of."

"Well, he appears to be suffering from anaphylactic shock. In layman's terms, an allergic reaction to bee venom."

A light seemed to go on in the man's dull, glazed eyes. "Was a wasp that made me go off the road. Buzzing 'round like a banshee. I was swattin' at it, and I . . . I guess I must've lost control. Is Benjie gonna be okay?"

"He will be once I give him this." From the black doctor's bag Mother had retrieved from behind the front seat, he produced a hypodermic needle. Within minutes of the shot, the boy was breathing normally, and the swelling had begun to go down.

They drove the boy and his father to the nearest hospital, twenty minutes away, where Daddy refused the crumpled bills the man tried to press into his hand—gas money, he muttered, as if embarrassed it couldn't be more. "Send us a Christmas card," Daddy had said, giving the man their address. "Let us know how you and your son are doing. That's all the thanks I need."

The man, whose name was Dawson, *had* sent them a card—faithfully, every Christmas for the past twenty-five years.

As Daphne sat in the overflowing chapel, listening to him tell his story, she thought that if there had been a remedy for the searing pain in her heart she would have welcomed it. Her father had had his faults, yes . . . but he'd been smart and kind, too. Above all, he'd loved them. His family. She was sure of it.

Even if he did drive Johnny away. For decades, she'd held that against him. But now, at long last, she allowed forgiveness to flow through her, rinsing her clean of old resentments. Even the tears coursing down her cheeks felt good and pure, healing somehow.

More than an hour had passed by the time Mr. Buckhorst, a portly clergyman whose untidy comb-over gave him the look of an overgrown Gerber baby, rose once again to take the microphone.

"In a town the size of ours, it isn't difficult to stand out in some way," he began. "What's exceptional is being able to make a name for yourself without blowing any trumpets. To lend a hand in a way that isn't proud or boastful. Dr. Vernon Seagrave was such a man . . .''

Daphne closed her eyes, letting his words pour over her like balm: praise for Daddy's efforts in raising money to furnish the hospital with the latest in diagnostic equipment and his passion for preserving Miramonte's historic buildings. There was even a mention of the first-aid instruction he'd instituted years ago in both the elementary and high schools.

But all she could see in her mind was her father, in the unsteady beam of a flashlight, bent over a little boy stretched out on the open hatch of their station wagon.

I won't think about the other Daddy. Not until I have to. Today is just for the father I looked up to, who didn't deserve to die. Who, in his sixty-seven years on this earth, surely did more right than wrong.

Near the end, the minister paused to remove his glasses, wiping them on a voluminous handkerchief before concluding with ''I ask you all to pray for his wife, Lydia, as well. For just as we cannot know the mysteries of God or the universe, neither can we begin to judge the actions of our fellow human beings. Those of you who might rush to condemn, I urge you to keep in mind that God not only knows all, He forgives all. We must try to do the same.'' His head bobbed low. ''In the name of Jesus Christ. Amen.''

Daphne glanced over her shoulder and saw heads shaking in dismay and bewilderment, faces shiny with tears. Mother's younger sister, Aunt Ginny, grown stout with age, wept quietly into a handkerchief beside Aunt Rose, who'd brought along a small, portable oxygen tank and looked near death's door. Uncle Spence's second wife, young enough to be his daughter, clung possessively to his arm as if to advertise her devotion. And there was poor old Edith, Mother's cousin on their grandfather's side, frowning as she fiddled with her hearing aid. Was this how it would be from now on, Daphne thought, everyone wondering aloud, or to themselves: *What made her do it?*

Had Mother gone crazy? Based on the two brief visits

they'd had so far, Daphne would have said no. But after what Leanne had divulged, she wasn't so sure. The fact that her mother had been taking medication—if it was true—didn't prove anything other than the obvious: that she'd been depressed. But what if she'd used a prescription to mask something deeper, and far more disturbing? Something that had been eating at her for a long time— long before Beryl Chapman, under the guise of friendship, had served up her little dose of venom.

Thinking of Beryl, she felt her stomach tighten. Fearful of a scene like the one at the viewing, she'd been tense throughout the service. But if Beryl was here, she was keeping a low profile. Only her daughters had come to pay their respects. Leanne, seated a few rows back with that poor little boy of hers draped over her lap like an overgrown infant. And her older sister, Beth, with her dark-red hair, as plump as Leanne was slender. Beth was wiping the drool from her nephew's chin with a handkerchief, as efficiently as someone who does it so often she barely notices.

As Daphne surveyed the crowded chapel, a familiar face leaped out at her. *Johnny.*

What was *he* doing here?

Isn't that obvious? a voice mocked. *He's here for you. The old king is dead, and the beggar who's really a prince in disguise has come to take you away.* She nearly laughed out loud at the narcissistic idiocy of it, her thinking that Johnny could have no other motive in coming than to feast his eyes on her, his aging Rapunzel.

Practically everyone who knew my father is here, she reasoned. *Why* not *Johnny? If he wasn't exactly a friend, he'd certainly known Daddy. In some ways, all too well.*

Her heart began to race nonetheless. As if Johnny were only a few feet away, instead of all the way in back. He stood with his arms crossed over his chest, the memorial card that had been handed out at the door curled in one flat-knuckled fist. He was wearing a double-breasted gray suit and dark-blue tie, and like several others—those loath to put their emotion on display—a pair of dark glasses.

As she watched, he slipped them off, and Daphne saw

that she wasn't imagining things: he *had* come for her. He was looking straight at her, *staring* almost. As if to let her know he hadn't forgotten their conversation in his office, and that he was on *her* side, if not her mother's. Yes, she thought, that was just like Johnny. Still reckless. Still thinking with his heart as much as with his head.

She turned quickly, before the heat in her face could give her away. Her own heart was no longer just racing, it had crossed the finish line and was heading for the bandstand to claim its prize. *Johnny* . . .

Seeing him forced her to confront her father's darker side. Suddenly, she was viewing Daddy as Johnny surely must—not as a kind philanthropist and Good Samaritan . . . but as an ironfisted despot guilty of the worst kind of snobbery. If it hadn't been for Daddy, would she and Johnny be married today?

Who was to say? Four years away at college was a long time. That alone might have changed how she felt about him, though she doubted it. Daphne recognized it now as merely the rationalization she'd been using all these years, as old as the way to Rome, and about as viable. Unhindered by Daddy's fierce disapproval, she felt sure she would have gone on seeing Johnny every chance she got. The long separations between holidays and semester breaks would only have fanned the flame.

An old, banked memory flickered to life—the night of their senior prom, when she'd gotten tipsy from drinking too much of the spiked punch. Arriving back at her house, Johnny had insisted, like the gentleman he was, on escorting her to the front door . . . though he couldn't have missed her father's shadow looming in the etched-glass sidelight. As soon as she'd let herself in, Daddy had taken one look at her disheveled hair and bleary eyes, and the high heels she'd slipped off in order to better negotiate the porch steps, and with a low cry had gone charging after Johnny. As Daphne stood by helplessly, too scared and inebriated even to yell out a warning, her father raced down the front path and grabbed him by the shoulder, spinning him about.

Now in the coolness of the chapel, Daphne closed her

eyes, but the long-ago scene continued to play out behind her eyelids. She saw her father seize Johnny's lapels and begin shaking him violently, calling him names Daphne had never before heard him utter. While Johnny just stood there in his rented tuxedo jacket that was now torn—a jacket he'd have to pay for with money he didn't have—fighting the toughest battle of his life: with his own pride. In Johnny's clenched white face, she saw every curse he was biting back, every punch deliberately not thrown. She'd known then that he loved her. Not the way other boys loved . . . but as deeply and profoundly as Romeo had loved Juliet. For had it been anyone else that night he'd have been lying on the walk, wearing the mark of Johnny's fists.

Maybe it had been that look on Johnny's face, or her own outraged sense of justice finally kicking in . . . but something in Daphne's mild-mannered soul had risen up in protest. Tossing aside the satin pumps clutched in one hand, she'd raced down the steps and onto the lawn. In her stocking feet, reeling from the punch Johnny had warned her against, she'd grabbed a rake lying near the path and done something she never in a million years could have imagined herself doing: whacked her father across the back of his knees.

She cringed at the memory even now. At the same time, it brought a tiny smile of triumph to her lips.

The music was playing now—a Bach organ cantata, lovely and elegiac, yet unsentimental. Her father would have approved, she thought. She watched as the pallbearers—Daddy's two brothers; along with Uncle Ned, from her mother's side; Will Harding; and Alex's ex-husband, Jim—hoisted the coffin and began the slow procession out to the hearse.

Her throat tightened, and she felt a stab of guilt for having thought ill of Daddy on this day, if only for a moment. Guilt that instantly turned to sorrow. The sob she'd been holding back burst forth, and she clamped a fist against her mouth to stifle it. All around her, people were rising and shuffling toward the exit. Some were coughing, and discreetly blowing their noses in handkerchiefs. But when Daphne stood, her knees buckled, and she had to clutch the back of the pew in front of her to keep from sinking back down. It was several minutes before she felt strong enough to join her sisters, already making their way out to the limousine that waited to take them to the cemetery.

When she reached the parking lot, Kitty and Alex were nowhere in sight, and the mourners were already making their way to their cars. Someone tapped her elbow. She turned to find Johnny eyeing her with sympathy. It was obvious he'd waited for her; they were the only ones left on the chapel steps.

"I'm sorry about your dad," he said.

She appreciated the fact that he'd come, and that he wasn't larding on any false sentiments. What Daphne *didn't* like was the way he was making her feel. Or the heat generated by his steady gaze that traveled through her in lazy rolling waves.

"It was good of you to come," she said, keeping her eyes averted from the limousine idling at the curb below, in which her sisters and nieces were no doubt growing impatient.

"Good isn't a word your dad would've used in connection with me." A corner of Johnny's mouth lifted in a crooked smile. "One thing we had in common, though— wasn't a damn thing either of us wouldn't have done for you."

She gave a short ironic laugh. "Well, as you can see, I've managed to survive quite nicely on my own." Thinking of Roger, she shifted from one foot to the other, growing uncomfortable.

Johnny's smile widened as he took her in with an appreciative glance. "No one could argue that."

Uncertain about where this was leading, and beginning to grow a little nervous, she found herself blurting, "Why *did* you come, Johnny? You had every reason to hate my father. And now you and your cronies are going to do your best to see that my mother goes to prison. Doesn't it seem strange to you—the two us standing here, chatting like old friends?"

"That's what I wanted to talk to you about—where we stand in all this. But not here." He tightened his grip on her elbow. "Could we meet later on? I was thinking of Plunkett's Lagoon. We used to go there a lot, remember?"

Daphne stared at him. Remember? Their first time had been at Plunkett's Lagoon—on a blanket by a driftwood fire, under stars that were like sparks thrown from their naked bodies. Even now, sometimes late at night, in that slow, drifting space just below the rim of conscious thought, she could recall each sensation as precisely as if retracing her footprints on the sand. The heartbreaking care with which Johnny had moved in her, the taste of her own swallowed cries like salt on the back of her tongue. The smell of smoke in his hair, and the sand furrowed beneath the blanket. Dear God, *remembering* wasn't her problem. It was learning how to forget.

"I'll be at Kitty's most of the afternoon," she told him. "She's having everyone over when we get back from the cemetery." Daphne swallowed hard, unable to picture her father being lowered into the ground. "But maybe I could get away later on, just for an hour or so."

"I'll be waiting," he told her. "Whenever you get there."

She shook her head. "I wouldn't want to keep you. Why don't I call instead, and let you know if I can make it?"

But she could see from the stubborn set of his mouth and the tilt of his head that his mind was made up. "I've waited this long," he said . . . as if either of them needed reminding of that fact, his heavy-lidded eyes more blue than gray in the bright sunlight skimming off the cars of departing mourners. "I guess it wouldn't hurt to wait a little longer."

Over the years, the dirt road to Plunkett's Lagoon had been paved by thousands of tires to the packed hardness of asphalt. Mostly by those of the teenaged lovers who parked out at the end, where the marsh grass grew high enough to block them from view by anyone who might be walking on the beach. At night, when no one was around, the kids built fires on the sand with driftwood gathered from along the high tide line. Here, on the windward side of the bay, the dunes were higher than in the more sheltered coves, and the cooler temperatures worked in favor of young lovers. The mothers and fathers who flocked to the warmer state beaches didn't have to know what went on behind those dunes, under old tartan blankets their teenaged sons and daughters had played on as children.

As Johnny's '65 Thunderbird bumped its way over the road he'd traveled many times since high school with his wife and son, and more recently on his own, he was nevertheless struck by the oddest feeling—that it had been years since he'd made the journey.

He was thinking of the night he and Daphne had driven out here in his old Pontiac after their junior class spring dance. Its windows filmed with their heat on the inside and the fog pressing in from outside. Like always, they'd done everything except the one thing he wanted the most . . . but had held back from until she was ready. Then without warning—as if it had just that minute occurred to her—she'd tugged her dress over her head and tossed it over the front seat, as naturally and unselfconsciously as if it weren't her virginity but a slice of some delicious fruit she was offering him.

Making love to Daphne was practically all he'd thought about since the day they'd met, when he came across her making a grand show of smoking a cigarette in the smoker's pit behind the science building. A pretty sleek-haired girl with Agua Fria Point written all over her. He'd remembered her from Spanish class and was surprised that she remembered him. He wouldn't have thought he was her type. But he'd been wrong . . . about that, and so many other things.

The only thing he *was* certain of that day, and had been ever since, was that whatever he'd been looking for, he'd found it.

He could see her in his mind as clearly as he had that long-ago night, naked under the blanket she'd wrapped about herself, laughing as he chased her over the dunes. And later, after they'd found a spot to build a fire, the way the light had played over her naked limbs, making them glow as if with a heat of their own.

Now, as he pulled to a stop in the rutted turnabout, the thirty-eight-year-old man in khakis and a canvas windbreaker who these days answered either to John or Mr. Devane, never Johnny, wondered if she'd known the true depth of his love for her . . . or if what Daphne had been able to see was like the ocean spread out beyond the lagoon: vast to the eye, with nine-tenths below the surface. Would it surprise her to learn his decision to leave her had been among the hardest of his entire life? Within days of walking out that door, he'd hit the road with just twenty dollars and a bone-handled penknife in his pocket headed nowhere in particular, bumming rides and cigarettes, drinking bad coffee and too many beers in countless roadside stops.

You're scum, nothing but SCUM, not good enough to shine my shoes. The immortal words of Daphne's old man. But they could just as easily have been uttered by his own father. In many ways, though neither would have been pleased to hear it, the two men were very much alike—both narrow in their thinking and fiercely committed to the Gospel According to St. Know-It-All. But while the good Dr. Seagrave's flock had apparently been legion, Frank Devane, with his view from the bottom of a shot glass—where everything looked pretty damn profound—had held forth to no one but his cronies down at the Surfside Tavern.

Johnny stepped from his T-bird, a Brittany-blue landau convertible he'd spent the better part of a year and a good deal of his salary restoring. Leaning against the warm hood, he lit a cigarette, cupping his hand around the flame to keep it from being put out by the wind. The turnabout was empty of other cars, and there was no sign of anyone around. Still too early for the lovers' lane crowd, he supposed. And too cold for beachgoers.

Strolling out onto the sand, he climbed the nearest dune and stood squinting out at the waves rising up to snatch at the sun now descending in plump red-robed majesty toward the horizon.

Knowing Daphne, she'd have had her fill by now of

weepy relatives and sandwiches with the crusts cut off. She'd be thinking that if one more insensitive clod pumped her for an explanation for this tragedy, she'd jump out the nearest window. But she was far too polite to make her exit the way Johnny would have: by walking out the door.

The years he'd spent on the road, getting by on his thumb, his wits, and whatever work he could pick up in auto shops along the way, Daphne had been at Wellesley—studying Chaucer and Hegel, and marching in protest against a war no one seemed to have paid much attention to until it became fashionable to do so. By the time Johnny had burned out, or wised up enough—he wasn't quite sure which had come first—to wrest from the jaws of defeat a scholarship to UCLA, she'd been in grad school, setting up house with her new husband.

The one constant through the years had been the voice in his head whispering, *Bet that guy doesn't have a scar on him with her teethmarks.* That last time, knowing he was leaving her, Daphne had been so furious and at the same time so crazed with wanting, that when she came, weeping all the while, she'd bitten down on his arm, hard enough to draw blood. The scar had faded to white over the years, but you could still see it: the faint imprint of her teeth, just below his shoulder, where he was touching it now.

Johnny squinted hard, and the horizon dwindled to a long strip of hammered silver. His eyes were watering from the cold, and he could taste the salt in the air gusting off the ocean. Though dimly aware of a car door slamming shut, he was so lost in his thoughts he didn't pay much heed until he heard her call out *"Johnny!"*

He turned to find her standing a short distance behind him. Her face tilted up to him, catching the last gilded rays of the sun. Daphne had changed into jeans, and wore a nylon windbreaker over a red sweater that brought out the color in her cheeks. Her green eyes were narrowed against the glare—eyes that had seen more than their fair share of grief lately, but which he was glad to see hadn't lost their light.

He could feel his heart thumping against his ribcage like an unanswered knock.

"They tore down all the signs," she remarked, cupping a hand over her eyes as she scouted the broken-down fence that ran parallel to the beach like a poorly stitched seam. It marked the property lines of the houses up on the bluff, whose owners had been at war with beachgoers ever since Daphne could remember.

"Kids," he said. "They use the wood to build fires."

Johnny smiled, remembering when it'd been he and Daphne ignoring those signs warning against trespassing, dogs, overnight camping, you name it—courtesy of the folks living in those fancy homes up on the bluff. The fact that Daphne's folks were among those who could afford to lay claim to what was God-given and open all year round seemed not to have occurred to her.

"Those signs never stopped anyone from doing as they damn well pleased," she recalled, her eyes sparkling with amusement in the narrow band of shade cast by her hand.

"You and I are living proof of that."

"I wasn't thinking about us."

"You're lying," he teased. "I can always tell."

Daphne's hand dropped to her side, and she squinted up at him. "*You're* the one who's lying, Johnny Devane. I used to fall for it . . . because I thought you were so much smarter. Now I know better—you're only trying to throw me off balance."

Johnny ignored the faint smile flickering at her mouth, which for some reason made him think it had been a long while since she'd been properly kissed. "Smarter? Jesus. That's rich, coming from you."

"You think because I got A's in English, that made me some kind of genius? I'm not talking about report cards, or SAT scores. You knew stuff about *life*. You didn't automatically look up to people just because they happened to be older. You drove too fast, but always seemed to know where you were going. You could change a flat tire with your eyes closed."

"I probably still could. Unfortunately, it hasn't left me any more enlightened about the meaning of man's existence." He smiled and said, "Come on, let's take that walk before it gets too dark." Johnny reached to take her hand, but Daphne hesitated. Sensing her confusion, he returned his to his pocket, casually, as if it were no big deal. They hadn't gone more than a hundred yards when he said, "Remember that reading you gave at UC Berkeley a couple years ago? I was there, in the back row."

She came to an abrupt halt, turning to stare at him. "The one time more than fifteen people showed up?" Shaking her head, she demanded, "Why on earth didn't you come up and say hello?"

Johnny fished around for a moment, then decided on the truth. "Too intimidated, I guess. I had no idea you were so talented. It crossed my mind that maybe you wouldn't want to admit you'd known me."

She startled him with a bitter laugh. "My life isn't as glamorous as you think." In the last fiery rays of the setting sun, her face seemed to glow with a light of its own—so beautiful it took his breath away. "I wish you'd at least come up and shaken my hand." Smiling, she added, "You wouldn't even have had to buy a book."

"I have all your books anyway. And I wouldn't have stopped at shaking your hand."

He watched the red in her cheeks deepen. "You could have at least said hello," she chided softly.

"Hello, then." He put his hand out, and this time she took it, wrapping her fingers tightly about his and not letting go.

Johnny no longer bothered to hide the hunger tearing at him, stripping him to the bone, reducing him to the man who stood before her now: one lacking in all pretense and driven by pure need. What would be the point in pretending? This wasn't a class reunion—all of which he'd skipped for the simple reason that Daphne wouldn't be there. Nor was this a chance meeting. Lives hung in the balance. And maybe his and Daphne's were among them.

"Johnny."

Just that, his name, but he found himself snatching it like a tossed coin from midair, tucking it away in his

pocket. The way she'd spoken it, drawing out the vowel
as if it were something she possessed, which was worn
down with caressing.

He hadn't planned on kissing her. It wasn't until she
turned her head toward the light, and he caught the flash
of tears in her eyes, that it suddenly seemed the most
natural thing in the world to take her in his arms and
do what he'd wanted to do from the moment she'd
barged into his office the other day.

At first, Daphne seemed more startled than anything.
Not resisting him, but not exactly melting. He felt the
tip of her tongue, as if sampling something she hadn't
tasted in a while. Then with a moan, she was opening
her mouth to him, like when they were sixteen and
hadn't yet learned that not every kiss felt this good, not
every lover left you hungry for more.

As she clung to him, he could feel the waves lapping
up to lick the heels of his battered old Weejuns. But
the cold seeping through his canvas jacket only made
Daphne's body against his seem warmer—bringing to
mind the driftwood fire the night they'd made love for
the first time, not far from where they now stood.

When he could finally stand to pull away, he found
himself looking down into the haunted face of a woman
who'd traveled some hard roads of her own, who'd married and borne children but who hadn't forgotten what
it had felt like to be in love that long-ago night. He saw,
too, a wife who wasn't cherished nearly enough, someone who'd grown cautious in her gestures and in her
expectations.

He shook a sudden desire to plow his fist into the jaw
of a man he'd never even met. Johnny chose his words
carefully. "I spent three years blaming you for not having the guts to stand up to your old man," he told her.
"And a couple of decades kicking myself."

"You were only doing what you thought was best for
me." She sounded angry, but he sensed it wasn't at him.

"That didn't make it hurt any less, did it?"

"No."

He cupped her chin in one hand, and kissed her again,
more deeply this time. The salt on her lips—was it

tears?—stung against his own, and drove a sharp blade of longing through his groin. He found himself thinking of his ex-wife. Poor Sara. No wonder she'd divorced him. Every time they'd made love, there had been two women in the bed: the one lying beneath him and the woman tucked away in his heart.

"If we had more time, I'd build us a fire," he murmured into Daphne's hair.

Daphne shivered against him, but managed a brave laugh nonetheless. "Without a single no trespassing sign?"

"If we looked hard enough, I'm sure we could find one."

"I'm afraid I have more pressing business at the moment. Of which you seem to be very much a part." She spoke with a quaint formality he recognized as Daphne at her most vulnerable. Only when he leaned to kiss her forehead did he see the fear in her eyes. In a low trembling voice, she asked, "Johnny, what's happening to us?"

Same as before, and your old man is still coming between us—even from his grave, he felt like saying. Then Johnny remembered there were a few other obstacles in their path, like the fact that she was married.

"Nothing that hasn't happened before," he told her, pulling her close again, and this time holding tight. "But maybe we learned something from the past. Maybe we're *both* smarter than we gave ourselves credit for."

"Tomorrow, after the hearing, will we still feel the same way about each other?" Daphne's mournful voice seemed to float up to him from the surf hissing into shore.

"I have a job to do. I won't lie to you about that," he replied grimly, refusing to let go even as he felt her grow tense. "But I *can* promise you one thing. I'll do everything within my power to see that your mother gets a fair trial."

"Even if it's at *your* expense?"

"Even if it's at my expense."

"Johnny, I can't ask you to—"

"Sssh." He muffled her protest with his mouth, brushing it softly against hers in the dying golden light. At that moment he would have given her the moon, if she had asked for it. "You're not asking me to do anything. Call it a debt to myself that's come due. Whatever we can salvage out of this mess, don't you think we owe it to ourselves to at least try?"

The only other time Daphne had been inside a courtroom was years before, when she'd sat on a jury—a case involving a woman who'd been struck down by a taxi and was suing for the chronic pain and suffering caused by her injuries. After several days of testimony, the jury had found in the woman's favor. On this particular day, however, the Monday morning following her father's funeral, as she sat in the packed gallery of Miramonte County District Court No. 2, Daphne had to steel herself against the very real prospect of another decision that ultimately might not be so favorable.

Today's hearing, her mother's lawyer had explained, would accomplish two things: a plea would be entered and bail set. In the absence of a grand jury indictment, the judge would then rule on whether or not there was enough evidence for the case to merit a trial. "A formality," Cathcart warned. There would be a trial, no question about it. *More like a public hanging,* Daphne thought, grimly recalling the tabloid headline she'd spotted the other day while standing in line at the supermarket: KILLER GRANNY TO COPS: "I DID IT!"

Was Mother sticking to her story? she wondered. Or had Cathcart succeeded in persuading her to enter a lesser plea? The last time she and her mother had spoken, the day before yesterday, Mother had been adamant. It was neither an accident nor self-defense, she'd insisted. Why would she say something that wasn't true?

Daphne had argued that strictly speaking it didn't have to be true. The important thing was that they find a way out. If it meant building a case around mental anguish, or even an implied threat, so be it. Daddy was dead. Nothing could hurt him now.

But Mother would have none of it. "I'd like to go

home, if Mr. Cathcart can arrange for me to be released on bail," she'd said, her lips tightening as she added, "but as far as my freedom is concerned, you have to understand something, dear: I'll never be free. Even if I were to be found innocent."

Now, seated beside her sister in the front row of the crowded courtroom, Daphne exchanged a worried glanced with Kitty. She wore a distracted look, as if her mind were elsewhere. Was she thinking of the young man who'd dropped by after the funeral to pay his condolences? There had been so many people milling about, Daphne might not have noticed him . . . except for the way her sister had tracked him with her gaze. A leanly muscular young man with dark hair and dark eyes—the kind their mother would have called "bedroom eyes."

At one point, he'd taken Kitty aside for what appeared to be an intimate exchange. No one else would have noticed except the older sister who knew her better than anyone. When Kitty tilted her head slightly, letting her hair fall over her face in a springy curtain, Daphne didn't have to see it to know she was blushing. Perhaps when the time was right, Kitty would tell her about him. At the moment they each had more important things to concentrate on.

Daphne's gaze was drawn to her mother, seated at the defendant's table not eight feet away. Mother was flanked by her attorney and Cathcart's paralegal, a waifish woman with a cap of Peter Pan-like blond hair and who, though in her late-twenties, looked too young to be babysitting Daphne's children much less defending her mother against a charge of murder.

Tom Cathcart, on the other hand, she was pleased to note, inspired confidence through his very appearance alone. A hackneyed line from literature came to mind: *he cut a fine figure.* Indeed, she thought. Tall, with silver hair that gleamed like burnished sterling, and wearing a pinstriped gray suit and tie rescued from being too conservative by a colorful pair of suspenders, he came dangerously close to dashing.

Even Mother looked her best. Her hair was neatly coiffed, and she wore a touch of lipstick. She had on the suit Kitty had brought her, which Daphne recognized as the one she'd worn at her most recent gallery showing last summer—light blue with navy piping around the lapels and cuffs. It was at least a size too big for her now.

That little detail was what pushed Daphne over the edge. She reached for the tissues she kept on hand these days—tucked in her purse—as vital as her wallet or key ring.

Maybe that was why she'd purposely kept her gaze averted from Johnny. She'd caught a glimpse of him on her way in, seated at the prosecutor's table with a large Asian man she took to be the DA. But to connect with him now, if only through eye contact, would be a kind of torture. Since their walk on the beach yesterday, she hadn't been able to stop thinking about him: his words, his touch, the memories he had evoked. Would it all vanish like a dream under the harsh glare of reality?

The ever-vigilant voice of reason whispered, *Forget the fact that you're married, and that you're both old enough to know better. How will you feel when he cross-examines you on the witness stand? Could you love a man who might send your mother to prison?*

She didn't know. Or maybe she just didn't want to face what to some would be painfully obvious. But there was nothing new about that, was there? Hadn't she spent a good deal of her life running from hard truths?

Daphne sneaked another glance at Kitty out of the corner of her eye. How was it possible, she wondered, for them to have grown up under the same roof and yet have emerged from childhood with entirely different sets of memories? The household she remembered had been warm and noisy, and full of homey little pleasures as worn and comforting as the stuffed animals that had lined her bed. Yes, there were times they'd had to tiptoe around, when Daddy was tired and short-tempered after a long day at the hospital. But for the most part, she and her sisters had enjoyed a freedom that wasn't overly restricted by rules and planned activities. Summers they'd practically lived in their bathing suits, with the cove below the house as their front yard. Their friends came and went like members of the family, many of whom, like Leanne, seemed to prefer the huge old white elephant on Cypress Lane to their own houses.

Her mother, too, was different from other mothers. In an era when Wonder Bread and the Jolly Green Giant had ruled, she'd baked her own bread and grown her own vegetables. In spring, she would drive Daphne and her sisters out to a farm in Pearsonville, two hours inland, where they would pick Kirby cucumbers straight from the field for the pickles she would spend the following day canning. Each season was marked by such an excursion. In summer, they traveled to orchards to buy apricots, peaches, plums, and in the fall, field boxes of apples. And no Christmas was complete without a blue spruce felled by their own hands, at a nearby Christmas tree farm.

The only things that were solely for Mother, and no one else, were the hours she carved out for her painting, and her morning ritual in warm-weather months of taking a swim across the cove—nearly half a mile, counting both ways. She used to say it was the only thing she truly looked forward to all winter long, when the wind blew cold and storms sent the waves pluming up over the rocks. And the first reasonably mild day in April or May would find her on the steep wooden stairs that zigzagged down the face of the cliff below their house, a towel tossed jauntily over her shoulder and a spring in her step. No matter if the water was cold enough to send the rest of them skittering for the safety of the shore and a warm sweatshirt, there would be Mother heading out to sea with strong, sure strokes.

Now Daphne found herself wondering if the exercise had masked a need her mother had had to lose herself in something requiring no thought, no rationalizations. Had she used those taxing swims to scour her mind of the niggling doubts and suspicions that must have crept in? Doubts about her husband, whom she'd loved above all else. Enough to . . .

Kill him to keep him from leaving her.

The thought caused Daphne to jerk upright—a movement that delivered a sharp twinge to her shoulder. Suppose Daddy had asked for a divorce. Something Daphne would have believed impossible until a week ago, but which she now turned over in her mind, as delicately as a fallen leaf, lest it crumble.

Perhaps, she thought, what she'd mistaken for serenity in her mother had been nothing more than a quiet abdication of her spirit. The relinquishing of one's own reality that comes from forever turning a blind eye. She felt a chill pass through her.

Is that what I've been doing with Roger? Pretending? Allowing wishful thinking to take the place of cold hard facts?

Like the fact that she wasn't in love with Roger. Oh, she *loved* him. He was the father of her children, the man she'd slept alongside for the past fifteen years. They shared so much—memories of idyllic spots they'd visited, along with vacations where everything had gone wrong; of their sweet babies rosy from the bath, and of bouts of colic and measles and croup that had kept them up all night; of friends they adored spending time with, and those they secretly poked fun at. In short, the accumulated history of a marriage. But it wasn't the same as shared passion, she acknowledged sadly.

And what of Roger? He wasn't being entirely honest with her, either. All his excuses—weren't they just hostility in disguise? And if that woman he'd been flirting with at the book signing was any indication, he'd been lying all those times he assured her he'd never looked at anyone but her.

Look who's talking, an inner voice mocked. *Yesterday at the beach, you and Johnny weren't exactly building sand castles.*

Daphne's gaze strayed to Johnny. He was bent over the briefcase that stood open in front of him. She couldn't see much more than the back of his head, where the barbered line of his graying hair grazed his starched shirt collar. But it was enough to remind her of the days when he'd worn it longer. When he would lie on his back after they'd made love, smoking a cigarette and squinting up at her fixedly through a lazily drifting scrim of smoke while she ran her fingers through the dirty-blond hair that fanned over the pillow.

She looked away quickly, her eyes stinging.

At the moment, the bailiff, an older woman with frizzy henna hair and gobs of bright blue eye shadow that gave her eyes the startled look of peacock feathers, stepped to the front of the courtroom to bark, "All rise for the Honorable Judge Harry Kendall . . ."

The gallery erupted in a shuffling of feet and the rustling of jackets and briefcases being rearranged. *So many people!* Daphne thought. Most of them were reporters, though earlier she'd spied a number of blessedly familiar faces among the crowd. Her mother's sisters, Aunt Ginny and Aunt Rose, sat several rows back. As did Mrs. Langley, who owned the gallery where Mother's paintings were displayed. Several women from her mother's church had come to show their support as well.

Yet Mother seemed unaware of the stir she'd created. As she rose quietly to her feet, her gaze fixed on the bronze plaque depicting the blindfolded Lady Justice that was mounted on the wall above the judge's bench.

Daphne caught the nervous glance Cathcart darted at his client, and Roger's words returned to haunt her. Was this lawyer as good as he was reputed to be? Good enough to hold his own against that bruiser of a DA? They would soon see.

Bruce Cho, who stood six feet and was a mixture of black, Chinese and Samoan heritage, was clearly out for blood. Daphne recalled Kitty telling her about the last sensational case Cho had prosecuted—a drunk driver who'd struck and killed a mother and her two children. It hadn't mattered that the driver was a respected dentist and town councilman, the district attorney had hammered home a conviction of second-degree murder, which carried a sentence of up to twenty years.

Now, she watched him lean over and whisper something to Johnny. As Johnny turned toward Cho, she caught a glimpse of his expression. Grim was the only word to describe it, the set of his jaw like case-hardened steel. *He's not enjoying this,* she thought as she rose dutifully to her feet.

Daphne brought her gaze to the bench, where the judge was settling in. A large man who looked to be in his early fifties, a good thirty or forty pounds overweight, with a fleshy face and small eyes that narrowed in displeasure as he scanned the thronged gallery.

But the mighty pronouncement from on high that Daphne braced herself for never came.

"Am I the only one who finds it cold enough in here to hang meat?" Kendall boomed. "I would appreciate it if someone would be good enough to turn down the air-conditioning." He glared pointedly at the bailiff, who scurried over to the wall to adjust the thermostat.

If the room was cold, Daphne hadn't noticed. With the stakes so high—and Johnny so close at hand—she felt as though she were burning up.

The judge waited a moment before clearing his throat, a sound, amplified by the microphone in front of him, that resonated like the rumble of distant thunder. "Court is now in session. Will everyone please be seated. Mr. Cathcart, are we ready to proceed?"

The lawyer remained standing. "We are, Your Honor."

Cho, glowering like a giant in a Grimm's tale, didn't wait for an invitation to jump in. "Your Honor, the people are prepared to demonstrate that the accused, Lydia Seagrave, in blatant disregard for the life of her late husband—"

Kendall silenced him with a curt wave. "This isn't a trial, Mr. Cho. I think we're all familiar with the particulars in this matter. In fact, I'm going to waive a formal reading of the charging document." He folded his arms, the sleeves of his black robe puddling on the polished surface before him. Directing a stern gaze at Daphne's mother, he inquired, "Mrs. Seagrave, do you understand the nature of this proceeding?"

Lydia glanced nervously at her lawyer, as if not quite sure how to respond. Hesitantly, she replied, "Yes, Your Honor, I believe I do."

"You understand that the sworn statement you gave the police can and will be used against you?"

Watching her mother nod in assent, Daphne's chest tightened.

"Let the record show the accused has answered in the affirmative." Kendall leaned forward, his small pursed mouth nearly hidden by the fleshy jowls bracketing it like bookends. "Mrs. Seagrave, you're charged with first-degree murder in the death of your husband. Are you aware that a guilty verdict would carry a maximum penalty of life imprisonment?" He sounded impatient, as if Lydia were a not-very-bright pupil who wasn't quite grasping his meaning.

But she understood, all right. She began to tremble, remaining silent as she once again nodded.

Cathcart, who'd returned to his seat, jumped up to protest, "Your Honor, my client has been under a great deal of duress—"

Kendall gestured for him to shut up while continuing to hold Lydia's gaze. "Mrs. Seagrave, this is a free country. You have a right to plead however you like." Casting a warning glance at her lawyer, he added, "You have the right to ignore the advice of your counsel if you so choose. But for my own peace of mind, if nothing else, I'd like the record set straight on this matter. Were you acting of your own free will when you signed the statement I have here before me?" He fingered a document withdrawn from the file in front of him.

Daphne felt her sister reach over and grip her hand.

As if from a distance, Daphne heard Cathcart interject, "Your Honor, I move that formal charges be suspended until my client has undergone a full psychiatric evaluation."

Ignoring him, the judge demanded, "Mrs. Seagrave, do you believe yourself to be of sound mind?"

A ghost of a smile flitted at her lips. "I should hope so, Your Honor."

"So you were perfectly aware of your actions on the night in question?"

"Yes, Your Honor."

He sat back, frowning like a teacher being given the wrong answer. Wearily, he replied, "Motion denied, Mr. Cathcart. Let's get on with it. How does your client wish to plead?"

Daphne fought an impulse to leap over the guardrail and grab her mother and shake her to her senses. Kitty must have sensed it because her hand convulsed suddenly about Daphne's, squeezing so tightly she almost yelped in pain.

She shot a glance at Johnny, and he turned just in time to catch it. For a split second their eyes met and his expression softened, beseeching her almost—to what? Forgive him for being helpless to prevent this from happening to her mother? Or was he offering silent apology for kissing her yesterday on the beach? A kiss that had reopened a door she'd believed forever shut, and which she now must agonize over whether or not to walk through.

A hush fell over the courtroom. Then, in the lilting voice with which she might have responded to a request for a charitable donation or an invitation to a social event, Lydia replied, "Your Honor, I wish to plead guilty."

Chapter 8

Below the printed sign on the front door of Kitty's house that read SORRY, WE'RE CLOSED! was taped a smaller, handwritten one: *Death in the family. Thanks for your patience.*

Two weeks had passed since the funeral. It was now the beginning of May, a time of year when the winds gusted hard off the ocean, lashing its surface into a billion sparkling points of light and scouring the sky to a clear cold shine. The pussy willows that grew along Watley's Creek, in the hills just off Highway 9, were starting to show up on windowsills and porch railings, bunched in jars and canisters and old pottery jugs. And the Ladies' Garden Club was putting the finishing touches on plans for their annual Memorial Day begonia festival.

Tea & Sympathy had been closed since the middle of April. But that, as it turned out, hadn't proved much of a deterrent to Kitty's regulars. It had begun with Josie Hendricks. The Tuesday morning following Lydia's hearing, at exactly 7:05, the retired schoolteacher had commenced banging with her cane on Kitty's locked door. Josie had been in a near state of collapse, frightened half to death by the reporters camped out front on the sidewalk. Gracious, she'd only come to pay her respects! But since she was here, would it be too much trouble for Kitty to fetch her a cup of that nice Darjeeling tea?

The following day, it had been Father Sebastian offering to say a mass for her father. Kitty had been touched. And when she offered him a slice of marzipan coffee cake, just out of the oven, the priest had been only too happy to accept.

Since then, word had spread that Tea & Sympathy,

while officially closed for business, might make an exception—if you knocked hard enough and showed the proper amount of appreciation. Or, in some instances, *desperation*. Like Joe Donelley, from the tannery, who'd shown up looking as sheepish as a third-grader as he shifted from one foot to the other, the porch boards creaking in protest. It was terrible what had happened to her dad, he'd said, and what all those stinking rags were saying about her mother. Kitty had the full support of every man on his crew. If she needed a hand with anything, anything at all, she had only to ask. No disrespect to the dead, but the sooner things got back to normal, the quicker she'd be able to put all this behind her. And while they were on the subject, things hadn't been running too smoothly at work without her cinnamon sticky buns.

Kitty had thanked him and packed up the rest of the muffins from breakfast, sending him off to work with a bulging sack, and a huge grin.

The truth was, she didn't mind. In a world that had slipped its axis, the pleasure her baking brought to others seemed the only sane thing left. Here, away from the rapacious press and lurid headlines, Kitty could find a small measure of serenity. When Gloria Concepción asked timidly if she might have the recipe for Kitty's lemon cake—just until Kitty was up to baking it herself—she was flattered. And when Gladys Honeick asked in a hushed voice if what she'd heard was true—that poor Lydia had been denied bail—Kitty didn't feel as if Gladys was prying, only that she had one more sturdy shoulder to lean on.

Any worries she might have had about reopening so soon, if only on an informal basis, had been dispelled by the overwhelming support of her patrons. Even Daphne seemed to welcome the activity, pitching in with her usual helpfulness. And though her sister's sponge cake wouldn't win any prizes, self-styled psychic Serena Featherstone, Tea & Sympathy's toughest critic, had generously asked for seconds.

On this particular morning, the first Monday in May, Kitty was in the throes of a thorough cleaning of her pantry. She'd discovered a canister of flour infested with mealybugs, and now the entire kitchen needed to be emptied of its dry goods and swept clean. Experience had taught her that you had to nip these things in the bud. One mealy batch of muffins might accomplish what even her family's scandal had been unable to: it could close her doors for good.

She'd gone through every shelf and was sweeping the spilled remains from the floor when Willa ambled in through the back door.

Kitty looked up in surprise, smiling at the faint greenish trail of lawn cuttings that wound its way from the front door to where her helper was tossing her denim jacket over the back of a kitchen chair.

"Hey," Willa greeted her, waggling her fingers in an awkward little wave. Though the weather was on the chilly side, she wore a flowered sundress that was tight in all the wrong places and wedgies that showed off bright-red toenail polish.

"Hey, yourself."

"I just stopped by to see how you're doing. Looks like you could use some help." Willa glanced about the disordered kitchen, with its rolled up rugs and the emptied canisters piled in the sink, waiting to be washed. "It doesn't have to be waiting tables. I'm pretty good around the house, too. Like, you know, with laundry and stuff . . . long as you show me what's not supposed to go in the dryer. This one sweater of my mom's? It got shrunk so bad, she said next time why don't I toss *her* in the dryer, so for once in her life she could feel what it's like to be a size six." She risked a cautious smile.

Kitty was unexpectedly moved to tears, and had to look away so Willa wouldn't see. "Oh, Willa, it's sweet of you to offer . . . but trust me, you don't want to be around me right now."

Out of the corner of her eye, she watched Willa's sweet face, round and plump as dough rising in a bowl, grow thoughtful. Softly, Willa said, "My uncle Eddie? This one time, he got drunk, and took a knife to some guy in a bar. When me and my brothers were little, Mami used to take us to visit him down in Lompoc. I never cried or nothing." She shrugged, not needing to spell it out—that in her community, things that might seem extraordinary in Kitty's were fairly commonplace.

Kitty cleared her throat and said briskly, "Well, now that you're here, why don't you give me a hand with this floor? I haven't even had time to check my answering machine."

More calls from reporters, no doubt. Yesterday's messages had included a stringer for *People* and an elderly neighbor who'd wanted to know if it was true what she'd read in the *Globe*, if the reason her mother had been denied bail was because she was the ring leader of a secret satanic cult.

There had been none from either Sean or Heather. But if simple good-hearted Willa could take all this craziness in stride . . . maybe it wasn't too much to hope that Heather might do the same. As for Sean . . .

The day of the funeral, she'd been startled when he showed up at the house. Their little interlude earlier that week had already begun to seem like a dream, spun of moonbeams and whatever fine madness had brought them together for that single magical moment. She hadn't expected to hear from him again.

But Sean clearly had other ideas. Though respectful of the occasion, he'd left no doubt as to his intentions. He wanted to see her again, he'd stated flat out. Embarrassed, and at the same time flattered, Kitty had laughed nervously, saying she didn't know if that would be wise, given the circumstances. But if she'd expected Sean to retreat, she'd miscalculated his stubbornness . . . or perhaps his degree of interest. And truth be told, wasn't she more than a little tempted as well? Like an aftertaste of something sweet on her tongue, she could still remember the heat of his hard young body and the urgency in his muscled shanks as he moved inside her.

In the end, she'd promised him she'd think about it, but not until this whole ugly affair was resolved. For the time being, she needed to concentrate solely on her mother. The DA had been adamant in insisting that she be denied bail. And the judge, clearly baffled by Mother's calm refusal to submit a lesser plea, and perhaps mistaking her refusal to gloss over her crime for something more insidious, had gone along. For the foreseeable future, Lydia Seagrave would remain a guest of the Jasper L. Whitson Justice Administration.

Daphne had been crushed. More than Kitty, she'd been counting on their mother coming home. But all it had done was turn up the flame under her determination to set Mother free, one way or another. At this very moment, she was out canvassing the neighborhood, knocking on the doors of everyone who would agree to talk to her. Not that she'd come up with much so far. No one, it seemed, had noticed anything unusual in Lydia's behavior prior to the shooting. But Daphne wouldn't rest until she'd gone through every name in their mother's red spiral-bound address book.

Last on the list was Beryl Chapman. Daphne had filled her in on Beryl's creepy behavior at the viewing, and Leanne's explanation for it. At first, Kitty had wanted to march right over to Beryl's and twist her arm into telling them everything. But she'd since thought better of it. An affidavit from Beryl would no doubt be instrumental in building a case around Mother as the betrayed wife. So it would have to be handled carefully. Better that they butter her up first, as they had when she unexpectedly showed up here after the funeral. Daphne, smiling through gritted teeth, and she herself thanking the woman graciously for the covered casserole she'd brought . . . which had gone straight down the garbage disposal the minute she left. Later, they could use the excuse of returning the empty dish to gently pry information about their parents out of her. If she refused to comply, Cathcart would subpoena her. But only as a last resort.

Meanwhile, Kitty and Daphne had decided to play it by ear. They would stay in touch with Beryl, and when the right moment presented itself, they would pounce.

When Kitty returned from checking her messages— blessedly, there were none—Willa was busily mopping the kitchen floor. "Any calls?" she asked over the slapping of the string mop against the wet tiles.

"Just the usual hang-ups." Kitty shook her head in weariness. "You don't want to know what it's been like around here. The God squadders are the least of it, believe me."

"God squadders?"

"Oh, you know, your usual fire and brimstone types. The other day I had an old lady scream that my mother was going to burn in hell. The rest seem to think it's their personal mission to redeem her with religious tracts. They've been arriving in the mail by the bushel. Daphne says I should open my own recycling center."

Willa plunged her mop into the overfull bucket, sloshing water onto the floor. "I like your sister; she's nice. I'm glad for you that she's here. But I'll bet she misses her kids. Me? I'd be going crazy without mine."

"The children are with her husband."

Willa looked up in bewilderment. "Husband?"

"His name is Roger." No wonder Willa didn't remember that Daphne was married, Kitty thought. Her sister's husband hadn't exactly made his presence known around here of late.

Willa went back to her mopping. "Well, this really sucks for *everybody,* don't it?" Her long silky black hair whipped back and forth as she pushed the mop across the floor with uncharasteristic fervor. "Your mom, like, she could really get screwed. Get sent to prison like my uncle Eddie. Bet if somebody knew something that might help . . . you know, like a secret they never told nobody . . . it'd be a good thing, right?"

It was a moment before it dawned on Kitty: the girl knew something. Something that had to do with her mother. A tiny ping, like the timer on her oven, went off inside her head.

With a casualness that masked her thumping heart Kitty asked, "What kind of secret would that be?"

Willa's eyes cut away. "Yeah, well . . . it's probably nothing."

"Why don't you tell me anyway?"

Willa stopped her frenzied mopping and leaned into the broom handle, clutching it to her ample bosom as if it were her dance partner and this the last waltz of the evening. Quietly, she said, "It's Mami, she's the one who saw."

"Saw what?"

"It wasn't none of our business, Mami said. Anyway,

who'd believe us?" A defensive note crept into Willa's voice, and her round face was uncharacteristically furrowed. "I know I shoulda told you, but I kept thinking about how bad you'd feel . . ." She bit her lip, a tear sliding down one plump cheek.

Kitty waited in tense silence.

"Your dad," Willa finally blurted. "He was one of our regulars . . . at the motel. Usually he'd come in the afternoon when I wasn't around. Him and his . . . his friend. They never made no trouble, Mami says. But, well, with your mom in this mess, I just thought you should know."

Kitty began to laugh softly. A woman. Of course. Noting the shocked expression on her helper's face, she quickly explained, "Oh, Willa, I'm sorry. I don't mean to make light of it, but this friend of my father's, well, let's just say she wasn't the first." She ran a thumb under eyes wet with tears of her own. "Who was she? Anyone I might know?"

Willa shook her head. "Mami didn't say what she looked like, 'cept she was younger than him and kinda pretty. But," her eyes narrowed with unexpected cunning, "she might remember more if it was you asking."

Kitty hesitated only an instant before wresting the mop from Willa's clutch. "Well, what are we waiting for? Come on." If there was even a slim chance this mystery woman could shed light on Daddy's murder, she had to follow through on it. "Call your mother and let her know we're on our way. I'll meet you out at the car."

Kitty was halfway down the back porch steps when she saw a familiar yellow pickup coast to a stop along the curb just short of her driveway. She froze, her heart bumping to a stop.

Sean. She watched him swing down out of the cab, slamming its door with a hollow thunk that seemed to rattle the leaves of the huge old catalpa shading the sidewalk where he stood.

He spotted her and waved.

Kitty didn't wave back. She remained rooted to the step as he emerged from the shade into a patch of bright sunlight. He looked as if he'd come straight from work.

Even from this distance, she could see the tar smudging his jeans and the rolled-up sleeves of his chambray shirt, the sawdust sprinkled over his spiky dark hair. His eyes, in the bright light spangling the grass at his feet, were the rich brown of steeped tea.

He's younger than I am. So why, dear God, am I the one standing here speechless as a love-struck kid?

She needed to *do* something. March over there and tell him she'd given it some thought and decided there was no point in their continuing to see one another. No future in it, for one thing. And what would Heather think if she found out?

Whatever had happened that night—and no use kidding herself, it *had* been wonderful—it was a onetime thing: like being hit by lightning.

But Kitty never got the chance to tell him. Before she could make a single move, Sean was striding though the gate and across the yard. He paused at the bottom of the staircase, his eyes flicking from the jacket folded over her arm to the car keys clutched in one hand before coming to rest on Kitty's face. The expression he wore wasn't hard or wary, merely questioning.

Kitty, her heart racing even as she stood frozen in place, was acutely aware of several things at once: the heat rising in her cheeks; the patch of suntanned skin poking through the torn knee of his jeans; the sight of Rommie, who normally kept his distance with strangers, wandering over to lick Sean's hand.

He patted her dog's head. Then, as if he'd been given the answer to whatever he'd wanted to know, he hitched a tar-blackened Red Wing boot onto the bottom step and climbed to meet her.

Prying the keys from Kitty's hand, Sean said gruffly, "Wherever you're going, the way you look you could just as easily end up in a ditch. Better let me do the driving."

They took the coast highway to Barranco. It was the long way around, but the back roads were so winding and potholed Willa had insisted it would take an hour or more to travel the short distance from town.

As Kitty stared out at the dusky green fields of brussels sprouts unfurling on her right and the ocean on her left, tarnished by an overcast sky to the dull sheen of blackened silver, she wondered what in God's name she could have been thinking. It was one thing to have slept with Sean in a weak moment, another thing altogether to be tooling out to Barranco with him, Willa in tow. And telling him of her mission?—pure insanity. She scarcely knew the man. What would prevent him from turning around and selling this juicy tidbit about her father's infidelity to one of those sleazy tabloids? God knows he and his sister could use the money. And, really, what did he owe *her?*

Yet for reasons she couldn't quite put her finger on, Kitty trusted Sean. She sensed he would sell everything he owned before he'd sell another person down the river. More than that, there *was* something between them—a bond, a connection, or maybe a mere spark of what could develop in time. Whatever, she remained silent as Sean turned down the rutted road on which Willa lived, making no effort to extract any promise of confidentiality. There was no need to.

It had begun to rain by the time they reached the shabby motel managed by Willa's mother—two stories of faded-pink cinder block trimmed in peeling turquoise. Climbing out of the car, Kitty felt her heart sink. She'd never heard a single complaint out of Willa, but God, this was truly dismal. Sean was right. She *didn't* know what it was like to be this kind of poor.

Stepping over a large puddle that had gathered in one of the potholes dotting the cracked asphalt parking lot like craters on a battlefield, she instinctively reached for Sean's hand. His palm felt warm and callused against her own, igniting a tiny thrill of the forbidden. She glanced nervously over her shoulder. But who was there to judge her? Willa? Kitty smiled at the thought. The sweet-tempered come-what-may single mom tromping ahead of them, oblivious of the dirty water that had soaked her shoes and splashed onto the hem of her flowered dress, wouldn't say boo if she walked in on them naked, swinging from a chandelier.

At that moment, though, Willa clearly wasn't thinking about Kitty or even her own impressive array of boy-friends. The door to the manager's unit stood open, and as she ducked under the dripping overhang, two dark-haired, brown-limbed little boys hurled themselves at her—the younger one wrapping around one leg while the older, taller boy took a flying leap into her out-stretched arms.

"Tonio, Walker, you minding Mamita? You take your naps like good boys? Eat everything on your plate?" Willa showered them with kisses as if she'd been gone for weeks instead of just a few hours.

Kitty felt a familiar pang. She'd once attended a meet-ing of a group of single adoptive parents in which an angry woman had railed, "It's not fair! All those brain-less teenagers living on Coke and potato chips, they don't deserve to be mothers!" But watching Willa with her boys, Kitty knew that wasn't true; good mothers came in all shapes and sizes . . . and ages.

She felt Sean's fingers tighten about her own and glanced over at him, a nervous flutter making her queasy all of a sudden. "I have a feeling that whatever I'm about to find out, I may only end up making things worse," she muttered. "Promise you won't hold it against *me* that my dad was cheating on my mother in a cheap motel."

"What's worse, the cheap motel . . . or the fact that he was cheating?"

She caught the mocking gleam in his eyes, and shot him a dirty look. "I'll pretend I didn't hear that."

As they walked in, Mrs. Aquino, as heavyset as her daughter with none of Willa's bouncy appeal, heaved herself from a worn, seat-sprung Naugahyde recliner. Stepping forward to greet her with a handshake, Kitty tried not to notice the trampled shag carpet littered with toys and the bad religious art decorating the walls along with cheaply framed K-mart photos of Willa's children in every stage of babyhood.

"Thanks for making the time to see us, Mrs. Aquino," she said. "This is my . . . uh, friend, Sean Robbins. We

won't take too much of your time. I know how busy
you are."

The large woman with a broad brown face as heavily
grooved as the back roads to Barranco treated her to
the throaty laugh of a heavy smoker. "Busy? Yeah, I'm
busy, all right . . . with these two monkeys on my hands."
She cast a weary but affectionate glance at her grand-
sons. "Have a seat. You take diet or regular?"

Disoriented, Kitty didn't quite know what was being
offered. Luckily Sean sensed her confusion and spoke
for both of them. "Make that two Diet Cokes."

It wasn't until they were seated on the lumpy sofa
with their sodas, opposite Willa's mother, that the woman
grew evasive. "I don't like to say nothing bad about the
dead," she began, her gaze shifting to a framed photo on
a shelf above the TV, a garishly tinted black-and-white
studio portrait of a mustachioed man with slicked-back
hair wearing an unmistakably cocky expression. Willa's father, who'd walked out on her when she was a baby?
Come to think of it, there *was* a resemblance. Before she
could speculate any further, Kitty's attention was drawn
back to Willa's mother, who was saying, "It's not my business what people do, long as they're paid up. But when I
saw on the news what happened . . ." her voice trailed off.

"Mrs. Aquino, please, *anything* you remember would
be helpful." Kitty started to add that she knew most of
it anyway, that it wouldn't kill her to hear the sordid
details, when she was silenced by a quick squeeze to
her arm.

She watched Sean fish a cigarette from the pocket of
his chambray shirt and offer it to Mrs. Aquino, who
nodded in thanks, a Bic lighter materializing from the
depths of the voluminous apron she wore over her
housecoat.

The woman's small, fleshy-lidded eyes narrowed as
lazy tendrils of smoke drifted up around her lined face.
It occurred to Kitty with a mild shock that judging from
Willa's age, she couldn't have been much older than
Kitty herself.

"I don't need nobody coming around, asking a bunch

of nosy questions," Mrs. Aquino grunted. "I got enough to worry about as it is."

"Nobody's going to make any trouble for you," Sean was quick to assure her. "Your name won't even have to come up."

"I run a clean place here. It's not much, but it's a living." Willa's mother heaved a deeply put-upon sigh before sucking greedily on her cigarette.

"I promise there won't be any—" Kitty began.

"No police," Sean interrupted. "Swear to God." He sealed it with the sign of the cross, one good Catholic to another, warning Kitty with his eyes to let him do the talking. "We just need you to tell us what you saw. It doesn't have to go any further than this room."

Kitty glanced at him in surprise, and more than a small degree of admiration. She'd nearly blown it, but Sean, who must have endured his own share of small-town injustice where the police were concerned, had known exactly how to put this woman's fears to rest.

After a brief contemplation, punctuated by forced exhalations that sent garlands of smoke upward to festoon the ceiling in undulating wreaths, Mrs. Aquino relented. "I only seen her once, from a distance. Kinda young. Not as young as Willa—thirty, maybe thirty-five. Blond hair. To here." She touched her shoulder.

"Anything else?" Sean probed.

"Well, there's *this*." The woman rose to retrieve something from the shelf above the TV. Something that glinted in the fleshy palm she held out to Kitty. "Marites found this when she was cleaning the room."

An earring. Gold, in the shape of a small knot. From a pair that could have been purchased in any one of a hundred department stores. It certainly wasn't going to lead her to this woman, whoever she was. Kitty tried not to show her disappointment.

Fingering the earring, she asked, "Mind if I take it with me?"

You never know, she thought.

Mrs. Aquino hesitated so long that Willa, observing the exchange from her cross-legged position on the carpet, a little boy perched on each of her plump knees, wailed in protest, "Ma-mi!"

Her mother shot her a frowning glance, but nevertheless relinquished the earring to Kitty. "Jus' no cops, okay?"

"No cops," Kitty promised.

It wasn't until she and Sean were saying their good-byes at the door that Mrs. Aquino remarked out of the blue, "A nurse like that, you'd think she didn't have sick people to take care of."

Kitty's heart quickened. "What nurse?"

The woman shrugged indifferently, as if it had only just occurred to her and probably wasn't all that important anyway. "The lady, in the car with your dad. She had on a nurse's uniform."

It was late afternoon by the time they got back to the house. Kitty had been mostly silent on the trip back, mulling things over. So Daddy had been having an affair with a nurse. Why didn't that surprise her? He'd worked in a hospital full of nurses. It could have been any one of dozens. The odds of Kitty learning her identity based on little more than a nondescript earring were roughly the same, she thought dismally, as finding a fit for Cinderella's glass slipper.

And the woman was clearly no Cinderella.

As Sean pulled into the driveway, Kitty was so lost in her thoughts she didn't at first spot the girl seated in the cab of his pickup. A girl with dark hair that swung away from her shoulders as her head jerked about, revealing a sullen mouth and narrowed eyes. Oh, God. Heather. And she looked upset. No, not just upset . . . *mad*. Kitty felt a jolt of alarm.

"Shit, I forgot I was supposed to pick her up from school." Sean cursed under his breath, braking too hard and causing them to lurch forward. He cut the engine, tossing Kitty the keys as he jumped out.

Heather climbed down from the cab to meet him, awkwardly, like someone cradling a carton of eggs. Her pregnancy was more noticeable than before, Kitty observed with a pang. She took in Heather's bright yellow leggings and a hot-pink sweatshirt with a teddy bear appliquéd to the front. At that moment, she didn't look sixteen; more like a pouty six-year-old on the verge of a tantrum.

"Heather! What a nice surprise." Kitty strolled over to greet her as if nothing were out of the ordinary while inside her thoughts careened wildly. *How did she get here? Does she know about me and Sean?*

Apparently not, because though Heather flicked her a cursory glance, all her anger appeared to be focused on her brother. "You were supposed to *be* there! I had a doctor's appointment, remember? If Misty hadn't offered me a ride home from school, I wouldn't have known what happened to you. We were going to stop at Misty's first, to tell her mom she'd be late, and what do I see? Your stupid truck parked in the last place I would have expected!"

"Hey, Sis, I'm sorry." Sean raised his arms in mock surrender. "Ninety-nine times out of a hundred, don't I keep my promises?"

"That still doesn't make it all right." Her mouth turned down, and her lower lip began to quiver. "Sean, you know how I get. You *know* I hate to be left."

"I didn't *leave* you. I just forgot." Sean sounded a bit irritated even as he draped a comforting arm about his sister's shoulders. Watching them, Kitty had the sudden and somewhat chilling feeling that she was intruding.

At the same time, she'd never felt more drawn to Sean. Not like the other night, when he could have confessed to her that he robbed banks for a living, and even then, wild horses couldn't have stopped her from making love to him. This was different—something as elemental and inevitable as a rising tide, yet at the same time more frightening than if she had discovered he was a bank robber. *Oh, God, I think I'm falling in love with him.*

If Kitty could have prevented it from happening, she would have. Right then and there. She didn't need this. She didn't even *want* it. All she wanted was the baby that was being cruelly withheld from her.

"Look, why don't we go inside?" she suggested with

a calm that was like a mockery of her wildly tumbling emotions. "I'll make us a pot of tea. Heather, you look as if you could use some." It had stopped raining, but a damp chill clung nonetheless, and she could see that the poor girl was shivering.

"No, thank you." Heather flashed her an annoyed look.

"It's no trouble, really."

"I *said* no thank you."

Kitty took a step back, her cheeks flooding with heat. The anger that had been leveled at Sean was now directed at her. Heather's pouty lower lip pushed out even further, and her dark eyes regarded Kitty with the instinctive wariness of a threatened animal.

Before Kitty could reply, Sean leaped to her defense. "Give her a break. She's just trying to help. You want to take it out on someone, take it out on me. I'm the one who screwed up."

He spoke gently, as if all too familiar with what too harsh a scolding could trigger, but Kitty was nonetheless acutely aware that he was defending her. As she stood there, surrounded by all that was ordinary and everyday—the lengthening afternoon shadows, the distant growl of a power mower, the faint tinkling of the antique calliope two streets away outside the Old Courthouse Street mall—she was engulfed by a peculiar sense of being drawn into something against her will.

Heather looked in confusion from Sean to Kitty, as if it had just that moment occurred to her to wonder what Sean had been doing there in the first place. Petulantly, she demanded, "What's going on, Sean? I thought you were against the whole idea of me giving the baby up."

Sean shifted uncomfortably, dropping his arm from around her shoulders to fish his keys from the front pocket of his jeans. "Who says I changed my mind?"

"Well, why else would you be here?"

Kitty jumped in before he could answer. "Heather, *I* haven't changed my mind. If you'll give me a chance, I'll show you what a good mother I'd make."

Heather gave her a long measuring look. "You've got to be kidding, right? I mean, after what *your* mother did, I'm gonna let you within a hundred yards of my kid?" Suddenly, she didn't seem so young anymore. She looked and sounded old beyond her years, with a coarseness that hadn't been apparent in their first meeting.

Kitty wrapped her arms about herself. She was shivering, but the cold she felt seemed to be coming from inside her. *You knew it was a long shot,* she reminded herself. But that hadn't prepared her for the dull ache that spread through her.

Sean drew back to scowl at his sister. "Jesus, Heather, you don't have to be so nasty. A simple *no* would have done it."

The anger in his voice caused something in Heather to snap. She buried her face in her hands and began to sob noisily. When Kitty hesitantly touched her shoulder, she only cried harder. *Like a child,* Kitty thought. A lost little girl in need of her own mother. Heather cast her a sheepish glance, one wet eye peeking up at Kitty from between spread fingers. "I'm sorry," she muttered, gulping back a sob. "I didn't mean to take it out on you. Sean's right. This isn't your fault."

"It's okay," Kitty said.

"I'm sure you'd make a good mother. Maybe . . ." Heather stopped to wipe her nose with the sleeve of her pink teddy bear sweatshirt.

Kitty felt the air leave her lungs—not in a rush but as if she'd been scooped out, left as hollow as a cored apple. She waited, every nerve alert, not daring to move, or even breathe, lest it break the spell.

But when Heather spoke again, it was to her brother. She seemed to have forgotten all about Kitty. "Sean, can we go now? I don't feel so good."

Kitty fought the urge to shout, *"No, wait! At least tell me if I have even half a chance . . ."*

But before she could utter a word, Sean once more slipped his arm about his sister's shoulders, saying with weary patience, "You'll feel better once we get you home."

Heather docilely allowed him to guide her over to the pickup, where he helped her back into the cab. As he was walking around to the driver's side, he shot Kitty a relieved look, as if to say, *That was a close call.*

But for Kitty it was more than just a close call. It was torture. Instead of having her hopes laid to rest, she'd been placed in agonizing limbo. For wasn't there an outside chance that Heather might come around? *If she learned to trust me . . .*

Watching Sean's pickup disappear around the corner onto Ocean, Kitty longed to run after it. Instead, in the reflected glow of the sun glancing off the windows of her solid clapboard house, turning them to shimmery fun-house mirrors, she prayed that she might one day hold in her arms the baby that was hers now only in dreams, dreams from which she awoke aching and empty.

Chapter 9

"The view from the third floor is stunning. Would you like to see it?" Alex turned to smile at the well-dressed fortyish man, a new client on his first walk-through with her, who'd lingered to admire the intricate design of the parquet floor at the foot of the stairs.

She always made it a point to ask, even when a client seemed enthusiastic. Though with a property like this one—a mint-condition Queen Anne with an ocean view, a few blocks from where Alex had grown up—who wouldn't be? At this price, it was sure to be snapped up in a matter of days, if not hours. The only fly in the ointment was that she didn't have an exclusive. This afternoon alone, six other realtors were lined up to show it, and if she didn't bag it first, someone else would be pocketing the commission.

Please, God, don't let me blow this by seeming too desperate.

She *needed* this. Badly. It was May already—incredibly, more than two weeks since her father was laid to rest. But if lately time had a habit of folding in on her, the stack of late notices on her desk at home were an ever-present reminder that the rest of the world hadn't stood still. Notices that had grown increasingly demanding, like the one from Fog City Motors, to whom she owed three thousand in back lease payments on her BMW. If her account wasn't settled in full by the tenth of this month—just a week away!—her car would be repossessed. And without transportation, Alex thought bleakly, how would she earn a living? She couldn't expect her clients to ferry themselves and her from house to house; the only job left for her would be as some office drone, scraping by on minimum wage.

And there was still the IRS. Her accountant had phoned last week with bad news: the deal he'd attempted to negotiate had fallen through. The federal agent, a hateful little man, had come down even harder than either of them had expected. It was as if her mother's criminal behavior had left a taint on *her;* as if he worried that she might grab the next flight to Brazil.

Which was laughable, really. She barely had enough money for bus fare, much less a ticket to Rio. Her sales were way down from this time last month. And it wasn't just the days she'd missed in the first shell-shocked aftermath of her father's death. People were uncomfortable around her, she'd found, wary even. Those who knew of her family's tragedy—and, let's face it, who didn't?— avoided her as if it might be catching . . . or she herself a threat.

At the office, it was even worse. Fellow brokers mouthed their sickly sweet condolences, but she hadn't missed the opportunistic gleam in their eyes. "I'd be glad to cover your clients for a few days . . . if you need some time with your, uh, family," Mimi Romero had offered cloyingly just the other day. *I'll just bet you would,* Alex had answered silently while mouthing her appreciation of the offer, *and rob me of every last cent of my commissions, too.* The minute she dropped her guard, they'd *all* be snapping at her heels.

What no one knew was that Alex, despite all the pains she took to hide it, felt herself to be a little less in control with each passing day. *Maybe if I could cry,* she thought. At her father's grave, she'd watched in dry-eyed anguish as his coffin was lowered into the ground, feeling like frozen water in a pipe about to burst. Daddy was dead . . . and, in a way, so was her mother. How the hell do you cry over a thing like *that?* If she ever got started, she wouldn't be able to stop.

Now, as she climbed the oak staircase, with its turned spindles and hand-carved posts, Alex calculated what her commission would be. Six percent of eight hundred fifty thousand—just enough to get the more demanding of her creditors off her back. The others she'd worry about when the time came. What she had to do now was simply hang on . . .

Alex paused only briefly on the second-floor landing before continuing on up. Once this guy, who was obviously well off without being a show-off—pressed chinos, navy blazer over dark-blue Lacoste shirt, his blond hair styled just so—had gotten a good look at the spectacular view from the top floor, she could risk showing him the one below, with its cramped bathrooms and master bedroom that let in only a trickle of light. By then, he'd be so smitten he wouldn't notice.

"Everything was restored by hand," she continued, her practiced spiel like a well-oiled machine, so smooth only she was aware of its gears meshing. "The owners did a lot of the work themselves—like stripping and refinishing all the woodwork and laying the tiles in the entry hall. That lovely dentil cornice in the dining room? It's all new, made to look original."

It was important to do your homework, she'd learned. Interested buyers asked questions and not knowing the answers might be perceived as a lack of enthusiasm. Either that, or some flaw you were attempting to hide.

She was rewarded now by the look of bright interest on the man's face. Lawrence Godwin—even the name had a monied sound to it. He was being transferred by his company, he'd said, though he hadn't mentioned what line of work he was in. Lawyer, she'd guessed earlier, from his firm handshake and confidence that bordered on arrogance. Not bad-looking, either. Tall, over six feet, with even white teeth that made up for a slightly weak chin. The trouble was, she couldn't look at other men without comparing them to Jim—usually to their disadvantage.

On the third and uppermost floor, he admired the view from the sun-drenched cupola, which, on this sparkling clear day in May, took in the entire bay, as far south as the Monterey Peninsula. Far below, racing sloops the size of toy sailboats zigzagged over the ocean's bright crimped surface, and the public wharf seemed to beckon like an outstretched arm. If she'd ordered it up, custom-made and wrapped in a bright red bow, Alex couldn't have asked for a better day to show-case this property.

Beside her, Lawrence Godwin gave a low whistle. "You weren't kidding. This is fantastic! Honestly, I just don't see how anyone could let this place go."

"Mr. Rudman was offered a professorship at the Rhode Island School of Design," Alex explained. "But they're absolutely brokenhearted about having to sell this house." She saw no need to point out that the Rud-mans would make a hefty profit in doing so.

"I see." Lawrence—or was it Larry?—turned to her. "What can you tell me about the neighborhood?"

Alex felt a familiar tingle start in her fingertips and begin working its way up her arms and the back of her neck—her own personal weather vane. Once they started asking about the neighborhood, she knew, you were three quarters of the way home.

Please, let him make an offer.

She tried not to sound too eager when she replied, "Agua Fria Point is the oldest and most exclusive one in the area. I think you can see why. It has its own beach, too. Small but private—we call it Smuggler's Cove." Alex tipped him a coy smile, as if to suggest buried treasure . . . though as far as she knew, the only thing buried there was the pearl necklace she'd lost in the sand her junior year in high school while making out with Jim.

"I wouldn't mind speaking with one or two of the neighbors," he remarked casually. "You know, sort of get a feel for the area—schools, the kind of people I'd be socializing with, that kind of thing." She caught an avid gleam in his eyes that she hadn't noticed earlier. For some reason, it made her uncomfortable.

"I guess I'm the one to ask then. I grew up in this neighborhood," Alex volunteered, giving a little laugh to hide her uneasiness. With clients, she made it a point to offer as little information about herself as possible. Who cared whether she listened to AM or FM, or liked her carrots diced or julienned? But if it would help move things along, hell, she'd shine the man's shoes if he asked.

He pivoted around to face her, smiling warmly. With his back to the window, the lines in his face that had been smoothed by the light looked harsh and suddenly not at all well bred. "Well, then, maybe you can tell me if it's true what I've been reading in the papers?"

Alex blinked in confusion, then felt herself stiffen. A tiny alarm pulsed in the back of her head. But she told herself: *I'm being paranoid.* "The real estate section *does* exaggerate some," she agreed.

"I wasn't referring to the real estate section."

A chill traveled down her spine. She stared back at him, deeply shaken. Did he know who she was? Or was he just being nosy?

"I take it you're referring to the unfortunate tragedy on Cypress Lane," she replied stiffly. "It's no reflection on the neighborhood, I can assure you."

"Did you know him? Dr. Seagrave."

It was more than curiosity. That gleam in his eyes she'd mistaken for interest was something else altogether, she realized too late. Something almost . . . sharklike. She shivered, noticing the thin gold chain peeking from the open-necked collar of his Lacoste shirt. No one *she* would associate with would be caught dead wearing such a thing.

Pretending not to have heard, she turned and headed for the door, suggesting briskly, "Why don't I show you around downstairs? They combined two rooms for the master bedroom—it's quite something. With a *huge* walk-in closet you won't believe."

She was stopped dead in her tracks by Godwin's smooth voice behind her. "I'll be honest with you—I'm not really interested in buying this or any house. I'm a reporter from the *Banner.*"

Alex felt something inside her shift downward, like a heavy bag of groceries she'd been juggling that was now splitting open—cans and bottles and bright globes of fruit rolling in every direction. The *Banner* was the worst of the bloodthirsty tabloids, she recalled. No story was too sensational . . . or too gory.

She whirled about to face him, blood mounting in her cheeks.

"How dare you." Her voice was a hoarse rasp.

He shrugged, seeming unfazed. "Just doing my job, ma'am. Same as you. But if it means anything, I'm sorry."

He smiled, his perfectly even teeth—which she now saw were capped—reviving an old memory she hadn't thought of since the seventh grade: the creepy man who'd offered her a ride home from school one day. Just as she'd been backing away, he'd whipped open his coat . . . under which he'd been stark naked. Alex had caught no more than a glimpse of the nasty purple thing between his legs, just enough to leave her sick to her stomach. Lawrence Godwin—if that was even his name—made her sick in the same way.

"Get out," she ordered.

He spread his hands in a conciliatory gesture. "Look," he said, "you can despise me all you like . . . but as long as I'm here, you might as well give me *your* version. With all the garbage that's being printed, don't you want to set the record straight?"

Alex felt something inside her snap. "You—all of you newshounds—you make me sick!" She jabbed a finger in his direction. "Dragging my family through the mud. Making us all look like . . . like . . ."

"What?" he prompted with undisguised eagerness.

"Trash," she blurted. "No better than those awful people on *Sally Jessy*. My father was worth ten of you. Everybody looked up to him. That's why you're here, isn't it? You can't find a single person with a bad word to say about him."

"Yeah? I can think of at least one person who must've had a beef with him. Your mother."

She gaped at him, not certain she'd heard correctly. In her family, politeness had been strictly enforced, the word "please" expected to accompany every request, however small. Now here was this reporter, this . . . this *bully* . . . shoving his way in, raking up all the hurt she'd tried so hard to bury. As if her family's tragedy weren't *real*, just something out of a cheap detective novel.

And it was all her mother's fault.

Suddenly, Alex felt like shrieking, *Hasn't she done enough? Am I going to have to pay for what she did the rest of my life, too?*

Shocked by her near outburst, she rocked back on her heels. Oh God, what if she *had* said it? However much she might hate her mother for what she'd done, to betray her would be unthinkable.

But isn't that what you've been doing all these years? Keeping Daddy's secrets at her expense, mocked a voice in her head. And who ended up paying for it? Maybe if she hadn't been such a willing accomplice, her father would still be alive.

The realization slammed home, momentarily knocking the wind out of her. Then with a gasp, Alex was lurching out the cupola's quaintly rounded door and stumbling down the steep narrow staircase. Halfway to the floor below, her heel caught on the corrugated rubber runner . . . and only by tightening her grasp on the banister did she manage to keep from being pitched headlong onto the landing below. For a terrifying split second, as she clung to the railing struggling to regain her footing, she was afforded a dizzying bird's-eye view . . . all the way down the stairwell to the parqueted vestibule three stories below. It was like peering into the throat of a monster about to swallow her.

Alex couldn't have said what possessed her. Later, she would have no clear memory of actually getting there. One minute, it seemed, she stood poised in the driveway staring at the FOR SALE sign tilted at an angle on the front lawn, which seemed to mock her . . . and the very next thing she knew, as if in the blink of an eye, she was two blocks away, stepping out of her car onto a *different* driveway, that of her childhood home.

Time wasn't the only thing that had folded in on her. It was as if she'd entered some murky zone where rational thought held no sway. She was aware only of being *pulled* somehow, like a boat being carried by a current along a narrow channel. What thoughts she did have were distorted, like voices heard underwater. In some submerged part of her brain, she had a vague sense of needing to see for herself if it was true, if Daddy really *was* gone, because part of her still didn't believe it. Part of her was convinced that when she let herself in the front door, her father would be sitting in his favorite chair by the fireplace, with his briefcase at his side and an open file in his lap.

As if in a dream, she gazed up at the house—a rambling three-story Victorian the dusty pink of candy hearts trimmed in lacy white gingerbread. It sat perched atop a slope of lawn edged in neat flower beds, in which the first of the roses were just now beginning to bloom.

Home, she thought.

She and Jim had owned a nice split-level, in which they'd been happy—or so she'd thought—but home, in her mind, would always be the old house in which she'd grown up. Strange, wasn't it? Her senior year in high school, she couldn't *wait* to move out. She was so eager to escape the dark hallways reeking of furniture polish, the ancient toilets that ran, the pipes that thumped and rattled in the walls that she'd snatched at early admission to UCSB as if it were the last chopper out of Saigon.

Now she found herself wondering if what she'd really been escaping was herself: the person she'd grown to dislike. The keeper of secrets . . . not all of them her father's. What would Daddy have thought had she told *him* about Kenny Rath? How she'd gotten knocked up after just that one time in the backseat of his father's Impala.

She'd been fifteen. And already she'd known more about her father's affairs than anyone alive. *My gal,* he would say, always with a twinkle in his eye, reserved especially for her. Yet somehow she'd sensed that it wouldn't be a good idea for Daddy to know about Kenny. She could tell him anything, of course, anything at all. But not *that.*

Oddly, it was the one time she'd felt closer to her mother. The memory, long shut out, flooded back to her now. She'd been about six weeks pregnant, according to the Planned Parenthood doctor who'd examined her . . .

and about nine-tenths desperate enough to do something that might have turned out to be really stupid. There was a clinic in Berkeley that she'd heard about through a friend—cash up front, no questions asked. All perfectly legal, of course. But who knew what kind of doctors ran it? Worse, she'd have no one to see her home safely afterward.

Kenny? He'd been so drunk that night he probably didn't remember what they'd done. Since then, whenever she passed him in the halls at school, he barely acknowledged her. She couldn't confide in her sisters, either; Daphne and Kitty were, and always would be, a closed corporation. She could have told Leanne, she supposed. But her best friend, though sure to be sympathetic, had never gone further than making out. Leanne would be shocked to learn that she was no longer a virgin.

To this day, Alex wasn't quite sure how her mother had guessed. Woman's intuition, maybe. But wasn't it peculiar, then, that that same intuition hadn't applied to Daddy? Whatever the reason, the night before her planned trip to the clinic, Mother had unexpectedly walked into her room and sat down on the bed. After a few minutes of awkward conversation, she'd asked, bluntly but not unkindly, "Alex, is there something you need to tell me?"

The only thing Alex had told her was that she'd be baby-sitting all day for the Myersons—chosen as an excuse because they lived on the other side of town. Had Mother somehow gotten wind of her plan? Maybe she'd spoken with Carole Myerson, who as far as Alex knew had absolutely no intention of going anywhere that day. Alex opened her mouth to assure her mother that everything was perfectly fine—what in the world could have made her think otherwise?—when, without warning, she'd burst into tears.

The story had come spilling out, and she remembered being shocked at herself for so easily confiding in her mother. But the most surprising part was that Mother had been sympathetic. "Don't cry, honey," she'd soothed as she awkwardly patted Alex's heaving back.

"We all make mistakes. The only ones you have to worry about are the ones you can't fix."

Seated on the end of the bed in her powder-blue quilted robe, with her hair done up in curlers, she'd looked so much like an old maid—the kind who lives with an elderly mother and plays bridge every other Tuesday with her friends, and would blush at the thought of a man taking advantage of her—that if Alex hadn't been so utterly miserable, she'd have smiled.

"You must hate me. *I* hate myself," she'd sobbed, inconsolable.

Mother had drawn back and given her a startled look, saying sternly, "I could never hate you, Alex. And you mustn't hate yourself. You'll get through this, don't worry. We'll get through it together."

And so they did. The following day, telling Daddy that the Myersons had canceled their plans and she was taking Alex shopping instead, Mother had borrowed his roomier late-model Chrysler—which would be more comfortable for Alex on the drive back—and they'd struck out for the freeway, headed north. At the clinic in Berkeley, her mother, who normally went along with everything, no questions asked, had grilled the nurse extensively before she would allow Alex to be taken into one of the procedure rooms in back.

When it was all over, Alex had been too worn out, and in too much discomfort, to be properly grateful. And in the weeks and months that followed, the memory had faded. Maybe because she'd allowed it to fade. She hadn't wanted to view her mother in any light other than the one that had suited Alex: as someone more married to her rose-colored version of the world than to Daddy.

But the fact was, Alex realized now with a dull sense of shame, her mother hadn't been wearing rose-colored glasses that long-ago day. She'd been *there* for her . . . in the way that counted most.

And when she needed you, you let her down. The thought sneaked in before she could stop it. And the vague sense of shame she felt deepened into true remorse. But only for an instant. Angrily, Alex started toward the house as if pursued by demons that could be outdistanced . . . if only she could run fast enough.

As she made her way up the front walk, she concentrated all her thoughts on Daddy instead.

In her mind, Alex could see him clearly—handsome and vibrant, even in his later years. There were photos in the family album of when he was younger, a dashing officer in his World War II uniform . . . but the father she knew had cut an even more striking figure, reminding her of a wonderful old Gary Cooper movie.

As she mounted the porch steps a lump formed in her throat, as hard and sour as the crab apples that had littered their lawn every summer. The first thing she noticed was the weeds sprouting up in the flowerbeds alongside the foundation. Then, like a rabbit punch to her gut, she saw it: the yellow police tape wound about the railing, blocking her path, on which was stamped: CRIME SCENE—DO NOT CROSS.

Alex gave a low cry and began yanking at it, tearing it free in great snaggled fistfuls. She didn't care if it was illegal. This was her *home,* dammit.

Using the spare key on her key ring, Alex unlocked the vestibule door and stepped inside. Even with the faint glow from the etched-glass transom and sidelights, it was a moment or two before her eyes adjusted to the gloom. It was much cooler than outside, too, with a dry grassy scent like the inside of her mother's herb cupboard.

On the small oak table against the wall to her left, her mother's mail was neatly stacked—no doubt by the investigators, after they'd first combed through it to see if it contained anything incriminating. "How thoughtful," she muttered sourly, stepping around the scattering of brown leaves on the Oriental runner, left by a Boston fern that looked more dead than alive. Apparently, no one had thought to water it.

Her heart began to beat with ponderous heaviness, like the grandfather clock still ticking away in the hallway at the foot of the stairs. She thought of a line from a bad western, *No one gets out of here alive.* And that's how it felt as she slowly approached the parlor, just ahead on her right—as if whatever she was about to find would leave her altered in some profound way. The Alex who walked out of this house, she felt dreadfully certain, wouldn't be the same one who'd walked in.

The pocket doors had been pushed into the walls on either side, leaving the arched doorway wide open. She braced herself as she stepped into the large darkened room. But at first glance, in the thin light that had found its way through the drawn velvet drapes, the parlor didn't look as if it had been disturbed.

Then she saw the evidence of the police investigation: tables and chairs pushed up against the wall, the tall Chinese vases on either side of the fireplace shoved into one corner, the antique tea caddy containing her mother's crewelwork spilling bright loops of yarn.

A sudden movement across the room made her jump, and she drew in a quick startled breath. But it was only her reflection in the gilt-framed mirror over the mantel. In the stillness of the deserted parlor, Alex gave a shaky laugh that reverberated with shocking loudness.

At that precise moment, her gaze fell on her mother's prized Turkish carpet, and the laugh shriveled in her throat. Oh, dear God. *That's where Daddy . . .*

She took an unsteady step backward . . . and bumped up against a small table that teetered, then righted itself. There was a crash, and she looked down to find the little Dresden candy dish she'd given her mother for Christmas last year in jagged shards at her feet. A tiny mewing cry escaped her. But she didn't dare avert her eyes from it. If she did, she would have to see the . . .

. . . blood.

A huge kidney-shaped stain that for a fleeting moment made her think of a country on a map. Greenland, or Africa . . . some vast, far-off place she never in a million years could imagine visiting. She gazed at it in horror, while beneath her the floor seemed to tilt slowly to one side. Then with a low moan, Alex collapsed into the brocade chair opposite the sofa.

Daddy's blood . . . that's Daddy's *blood,* babbled a hysterical voice. There, on the faded carpet on which she and her sisters had played as children. Oh, sweet Jesus.

What had been going through her mother's head at the time? Had she *meant* to shoot Daddy? Or, in her jealous rage, had the gun gone off by accident?

No, that's not how it happened, a calm voice disagreed. In her whole life Mother had never lost her temper to such a degree. At least not that Alex had ever witnessed. *This was deliberate,* she thought.

She could see it in her mind, playing out like a badly scratched print of an old black-and-white movie . . .

It's been a few weeks since Beryl's bombshell . . . enough time for Mother to absorb it and maybe begin to piece together all the lies he's told over the years. They've eaten at her like a slow-acting poison until she can no longer bear it. Until the thought of all those people at the party, all those endless champagne toasts, has become intolerable. She climbs the stairs to the second floor as if in a trance, planting both feet on each step before mounting the next.

In their bedroom she has to drag the chair from her dressing table over to the closet, where the top shelf is too high for her to reach. Standing on tiptoe, wobbling a bit on the plump cushioned seat, she gropes for the metal box wedged between a dusty crocodile train case monogrammed with Nana's initials and the pile of old New Yorker *magazines Daddy refuses to throw out.*

The box is heavier than she expected. Who would have guessed a gun could weigh so much? Had the starter gun she'd once fired, as captain of her swim team in college, been this heavy? She can't remember, and it doesn't really matter. She allows such thoughts to roam freely only because they keep her from focusing on what she's about to do.

The gun is loaded, she discovers. As she tucks it into the deep pocket of her apron, she can feel its cold snout grazing the top of her thigh. She toys with the idea of using it on herself and thinks how convenient it would be. No one to foot the bill, as Vernon would have said. She's not scared to die. Only that won't make it stop— the women. Soon, one of them would be moving into her house. A second wife who would eat off her plates and sleep in the bed where her children had been conceived. And that was unthinkable.

Even so, when she hears a door slam shut downstairs she almost loses her nerve. Her husband, home from the hospital. He calls up to her, sounding a bit impatient. And she shouts down that she'll only be a sec. Because a second is all it takes for her to release the safety. Then slowly, almost as if she were floating, she walks out onto the landing, and begins to descend the stairs . . .

Alex didn't know how long she'd been sitting there, staring vacantly into space while the scene from her imagination flickered to its inevitable end. Only a minute or two seemed to have elapsed before she stirred and looked around her . . . mildly surprised to note that it had grown dark.

What had roused her was a loud insistent hammering against the front door. A sound that seemed to be coming from a distance, muffled by a series of long passageways. Alex rubbed her eyes, as if she'd been awakened from a nap.

Whoever it was, he or she wasn't going away. Vaguely, it occurred to her that it might be the police. She knew it was against the law to tamper with a crime scene, but who had more right to be here than she?

"It's not locked!" she called weakly, too exhausted even to pull herself to her feet.

There was the sound of the door opening cautiously, then muffled footsteps on the hall runner. A moment later, Alex found herself looking up into a familiar face. One that startled her and at the same time sent a surge of relief through her.

"Leanne." She stared up at her friend, blinking stupidly. "What are *you* doing here?"

Leanne's cheeks were flushed and her hair disheveled, as if she'd dashed over here on foot. "I could ask you the same thing," she said. "Alex, have you completely lost it?" She sounded both angry and scared, like a mother who has caught her child doing something dangerous.

"I . . . I came by to check up on things," Alex stammered lamely.

"Well, it was a stupid thing to do. For one thing, you're breaking the law. And for another, you . . ." she stopped, as if to catch her breath, finishing weakly, "you just shouldn't be here, that's all."

"I had to come," Alex insisted dully. Tears stood in her eyes, making the room seem to dance in shimmery facets, as if seen through a prism. "I had to *see*."

Leanne followed her gaze to the bloodstained carpet and gasped, clapping a hand over her mouth. In a small voice muffled by her fingers, she cried, "Oh, my God. Oh, Alex. We have to get out of here. *Now*."

She grabbed Alex's hand and dragged her to her feet. But the suddenness of the movement caused Alex to lose her balance, and she lurched against Leanne, who reached to steady her. Something hard poked Alex in the chest, and she looked down at the laminated ID badge clipped to the front pocket of her friend's uniform. She must have been on her way to work when she—

But no, that didn't make sense. Agua Fria Point was miles from Leanne's route to the hospital. Which meant she'd gone out of her way. Why? What had *she* been hoping to find?

Alex drew back to look at her. "You never answered my question. What brought *you* here?"

Something flickered in Leanne's eyes . . . then was gone. Something dark and unreadable. She took hold of Alex's arm and began pulling her toward the door. "I had the same idea as you," she said, her voice high and breathless. "Only I wasn't planning on going inside. Until I saw your Beamer parked out front."

"What idea was that?"

Leanne paused to look at Alex, her blue eyes filling with tears. "I still have trouble believing it. I guess I wanted to make it real somehow."

In that moment, Alex was struck by the realization that she wasn't alone in all this. There *was* someone who understood exactly how she felt. Someone who knew her better than anyone. She'd been foolish to doubt Leanne's motives, if only for an instant.

"Is it as bad as you expected?" All at once, she needed desperately to share her sense of horror.

"Worse." In the darkened vestibule, Leanne's face glowed as ghostly white as the frosted sidelights at her back.

"Do . . . do you think she planned it . . . or that it just *happened?*"

Leanne hesitated, as if not sure how much more Alex could take, then in a forced attempt at briskness, she replied, "What I *think* is that we could both use a drink." She glanced at her watch. "Unfortunately, I'll have to make mine coffee. But there's still half an hour before I have to be at work. We could stop somewhere along the way."

Then they were out the door and dashing down the steps. It wasn't until she was safely behind the wheel of her BMW, guided by the winking taillights of Leanne's tan Taurus, that something that hadn't fully registered at the time clicked into place. Leanne had said she was just driving by, that she hadn't planned on going inside. As if such a thing were even possible. Because for that she would've had to have . . .

. . . a key.

Alex quickly dismissed the thought. Why would Leanne have a key to her parents' house? It didn't make any sense.

A figure of speech, she told herself. That's all it was. Just a stupid figure of speech.

Several hours and four gin and tonics later, Alex was back home, safe but not quite sound. Kneeling on the bathroom floor with her head in the toilet and, the remote phone clutched in one hand, she thought if she could only stop throwing up long enough to call her sisters help would soon be on its way. The twins were old enough to look after themselves. But they were scared, she knew. *Scared of what's become of their mother.* Having their aunts here would calm them, for the moment at least.

God, if only she hadn't had so much to drink. What

could she have been thinking, hanging around that bar long after Leanne had left for work? Now, on top of the fare home, tomorrow she'd have to call for another taxi to take her across town to pick up her car, still parked in the lot behind Hernando's Hideaway. Not to mention she'd have a wicked hangover to boot.

Alex was retching up nothing more than a thin, acid-tasting bile when she heard a tap on the bathroom door.

She moaned. "Go away. I'm sick."

It had to be one of the twins, worried half to death. And no wonder. She hadn't even called to say she'd be late. And, God, seeing her arrive home in this state . . .

It all came flooding back in a blinding rush. *The blood. Daddy's blood. Oh Jesus Christ . . .*

She felt her face break out in a clammy sweat as she heaved. But nothing more came up. She'd thrown up everything already, including what felt like most of her internal organs. Now the bathroom she'd decorated in a Santa Fe motif—wrought-iron towel racks, a Brett Weston print of Thumb Butte framed in barnwood—tipped and whirled like a carnival ride.

Tap tap. Louder this time.

"Alex, it's me. Jim. Can I come in?"

Jim? Christ, what was *he* doing here? Panic settled into the scooped-out cavity where her stomach had been. She couldn't let him see her like this. He'd know what a lousy mother she was, that she didn't deserve such sweet loving daughters. Daughters who'd cared enough to phone for help . . . and whose precious necks she'd like to wring. Why *Jim*, of all people?

"Go away," she muttered again, louder this time.

But either he hadn't heard or was simply ignoring her. Because the very next thing she knew her ex-husband was standing there, looking down at her with his arms crossed over his chest. From her vantage point, huddled on the floor at his feet, he resembled nothing so much as a reproachful giant. If this were a commercial on TV, she thought, he'd be advertising toilet bowl cleaner. Her head spun, and a weak laugh bubbled up her throat.

Before she could utter a protest, Jim was unceremoniously scooping her up off the bathroom floor and carrying her into the adjoining bedroom. As he set her down on the bed, none too gently for that matter, she felt the bed tilt sideways like an overladen raft.

Alex tried to sit up . . . and instantly felt as if she were going to slide off the raft. She plopped onto her back with a groan. "The girls. Oh, God. I don't want them to see me like this."

"Don't worry about them. They're fine," he said. "I brought over some takeout. They're downstairs in front of the TV, scarfing up Chinese food." He grinned. "I told them you probably had some kind of bug. Lucky for you they're not used to seeing you drunk."

The thought of food—greasy Chinese takeout in particular—caused her stomach to roll once more. She clutched her middle, fighting the urge to retch. "I am not drunk." She enunciated each word with elaborate care.

Jim gave a wry chuckle as he tugged off her shoes. "If you're not drunk, then you must be dying."

"You wish."

He grinned. "That's what I love about you, Alex. Even flat on your back, you never give in."

She groaned and curled onto her side, holding a pillow mashed against her roiling belly. "I don't need your sermonizing. Not tonight," she muttered thickly. "Find one of your girlfriends to preach to."

"Jesus, Alex. Does it always have to get back to *that?*"

"Isn't that where it all started? With your coming home at night smelling of Jean Naté?" She sat up abruptly, the sudden motion driving an ice pick through one temple. "For God's sake, Jim, couldn't you have at least picked someone with a little *class?* Not some stupid little secretary who shops for perfume at Rexall's?"

"Okay, you win. I'm a shit," he agreed. "What I did was unforgivable, and you have every reason to hate me for it. But can we give it a rest? Just for tonight? I'm not here to dig up old bones." He sat down next to her on the bed, laying a hand on her shoulder.

Alex rolled onto her back to glare up at him. "Why *are* you here?"

She wanted to hate him, but in the darkened bedroom, with his dark head haloed in the lambent light spilling through the doorway, he looked so warmly familiar all she wanted to do was weep for what she'd lost.

Then she *was* crying, great gasping sobs torn from her as brutally as what she'd vomited up into the toilet a short while ago. Clutching at him, she retched up her grief . . . over Daddy . . . and Mother . . . and Jim himself. With her anger momentarily stripped away, she could remember and mourn for what they'd had. All the good times . . .

Jim was the only person on earth besides her mother who knew about her abortion. And who had understood, when her first pregnancy with him ended in a miscarriage, why she'd felt so guilty . . . as if she were being punished. When she told him, she'd expected him to be shocked, disgusted even. She'd thought he might blame her in some way. But he hadn't. He'd simply held her while she cried her heart out. Just as he was doing now.

"Oh, Jim," she sobbed drunkenly. "Why did it have to end? Why in God's name did it have to end?"

Chapter 10

"In the thirty-two years I've been practicing law, I've never seen a case like it." Tom Cathcart sipped thoughtfully at his Virgin Mary, the club sandwich on his plate only half eaten. "We'd have gotten bail if she'd pled to a lesser charge, I'm certain of it. The judge was practically offering it to her on a silver platter. She knew what he wanted her to say . . . but she damn well wasn't going to say it."

Daphne sighed, poking listlessly with her fork at her shrimp salad. She felt frustrated, nothing new there. What *was* new, disturbingly so, was the seed of hopelessness that had taken root inside her and was growing by the day.

"There was a time I thought I knew her," she said. "When I could have predicted her every move—what she'd say about something one of my sisters was up to, or how I ought to be raising my kids. Even what she'd order in a restaurant." Her gaze fell on the stack of menus on the waiters' station catty-corner to their table and her mouth twisted up in a rueful smile. "But now I think only how arrogant I was. No one should ever think they can predict a hundred percent what someone else will do."

They were having lunch in a sun-drenched café on Old Courthouse Street and Main, a block from Cathcart's office. He'd suggested this place, where they'd be more relaxed, away from the buzzing of phones and whirring of fax machines. Between the steady stream of calls from reporters and the influx of clients brought by his new notoriety, Daphne couldn't help noticing that recently business had gotten a lot livelier for the firm of Cathcart, Jenkins & Holt.

For his infamous client, though, nothing much had changed. Mother was entering her fourth week as a "guest" of the Miramonte County Jail. The cold winds of early May had given way to milder breezes heralding the onset of summer, and along the brick-paved pedestrians-only Old Courthouse Street mall tubs and hanging baskets of sweet alyssum, ivy-leafed geranium, and rose moss bloomed in bold disregard for the suffering of those unable to fully appreciate their glory.

She wished Kitty had been able to join them, but her sister had had other, equally important business to attend to. She was hosting a small gathering at Tea & Sympathy for their mother's garden club. Its members were organizing a drive to collect signatures for a petition calling for Mother's release pending trial, and Kitty was hoping to persuade them that affidavits testifying to her sterling character and countless good deeds would be even more helpful. But so far only a few, like Mrs. Holliman and old Mrs. Carter, had agreed to be deposed. The others were frightened of the publicity it might engender . . . as well as, let's face it, any possible taint on themselves.

Kitty was more understanding than Daphne, who had dismissed them all as spineless. It had been her idea that Daphne's time might be better spent this afternoon strategizing with Cathcart. Her sister didn't have to add that the last thing she needed was a bristling presence frightening off any of the ladies who might be leaning in their direction.

Now her attention was brought back to Cathcart, who sat shaking his silver head, his own frustration all too evident. "I've done what I can to work around it, but she's blocked me at every turn. It's as if she *wants* to be punished."

A good man, Daphne thought. Starchy, a bit full of himself . . . but essentially decent. His frustration seemed to stem as much from a true desire to help her mother as from any personal ambition. His pale blue eyes were troubled as he ran a thumb along the inside of one suspender.

Never trust a man in suspenders. One of Mother's more curious prejudices. And it had to be one of the most curious ironies in all this, Daphne thought, that on every one of the half dozen occasions he'd met with her and Kitty, their mother's attorney had been sporting a pair of suspenders. Today's were particularly fanciful: saffron yellow with a bold black pattern of clock faces. But after a steady diet of monogrammed French cuffs and Gucci loafers (Roger's wardrobe tended toward the pompous), she found Cathcart's whimsy a refreshing change.

Daphne didn't waste any time in getting to the point. "For the time being let's stick with what we *can* control. For starters, what about getting the trial date pushed up? August fourteenth seems awfully far away, and as you know my mother's not a young woman. Four months could end up being a life sentence."

At some level, yes, she was aware it could be longer. That it could be *years.* But if she allowed herself to dwell on that very real possibility, she wouldn't be able to go on. The growing despair she felt would become paralyzing. She had to concentrate instead on what was within her grasp—like making sure her mother had the best legal representation money could buy.

Cathcart's good . . . but what if he isn't the best man for the job? The thought niggled at her as she toyed with the straw in her iced tea. She hated to think Roger might be right. What if she'd been acting out of knee-jerk defensiveness, not her mother's best interests, when she dismissed his offer to find a more high-profile attorney? There was no doubt Cathcart was experienced, but what was needed here was clout: someone familiar with the ropes and who wasn't afraid to go head to head with Bruce Cho.

Now, in this quintessentially Californian restaurant, with its hanging ferns and tanned blond waitresses in striped gardeners' smocks, Daphne waited for Cathcart to show his hand. He was smart, sure, and best of all, he didn't condescend. But at the slightest hint of waffling, he'd be gone. She'd fire him without a qualm.

The silver-haired lawyer from Central Casting cleared his throat and sat back, hooking a thumb under one suspender. "I'm aware of the risks, Daphne, but I have to weigh that against what I see as being in your mother's best interests long-term. Right now, we need all the time we can get. In the meantime, I'm still fighting for bail. For some reason Cho is determined to block the motion—the guy's a real showboater, but I'm hoping the judge will see his way clear to granting it. What's even *more* essential is that we continue to pursue every angle we can, even the ones that don't require Lydia's"—his pale blue eyes narrowed, "—well, shall we say, her full cooperation." Suddenly, he wasn't a polished gentleman of the old school . . . but a wily cardsharp in suspenders, one, Daphne hoped, with an ace up his sleeve.

Daphne perked up at the thought of something new and previously undiscussed. "What exactly did you have in mind?" The discovery process was well under way, but with the exception of a handful of her mother's closest friends, who'd agreed to act as character witnesses, it was thin soup indeed. Anything that might help her mother's case was worth considering, however far-fetched.

Like this mysterious nurse Kitty had uncovered. As of yet, they had no way of learning her identity, much less of tracking her down, but even a slim lead was better than none. As soon as they could get Beryl to open up—and Alex to return their calls—maybe they would know more.

"I'd like to play up your mother's psychiatric history," Cathcart replied firmly.

Daphne stared at him in confusion. "Her psychiatric history? My mother's never been to a psychiatrist in her life. She doesn't even *believe* in them." Then she remembered what Leanne had told her. "Though I *did* hear that she was on some sort of antidepressant, around the time of my father's death, which I'm not even sure is true."

"If it is, we'll know soon enough."

"How will you know if Mother won't admit to it?"

"She's seeing a psychotherapist. Starting tomorrow."

"How did you—?"

"You mean without your mother's cooperation? Simple. It's court ordered," he informed her with a sly wink. "Kendall granted the motion just this morning. And he's agreed to reconsider the matter of bail based on the doctor's recommendations. Avery Scheiner, maybe you've heard of him? I've worked with him in the past—he's decent, not the best, but at least he's not pimping for the DA."

Thinking of Cho brought to mind Johnny, and her heart quickened. Should she say anything? No, she decided. At this point, there was nothing *to* say. Not really . . . unless you counted one kiss and the hours of sleep he'd cost her.

She pushed those thoughts to the back of her mind, where they belonged. "Are you saying that's my mother's best chance of getting off? Not guilty by reason of insanity?"

"No, not exactly. You see, that has its own risks." He unhooked his thumb with a faint little snap of elastic popping back into place, and brought his hand to the table. She watched it curl about his knife, one elegantly tapered forefinger tapping its blade for emphasis as he spoke. "For one thing, courts nowadays are much less lenient in their interpretation of temporary insanity. She might not go to prison, but she'd spend the rest of her life in a psychiatric facility, which could be worse. What I'm suggesting is something a lot subtler. We show your mother to be a reasonably sane person who was pushed beyond her limits. She knows the difference between right and wrong. Fact is, she's so overcome by remorse she insists on being punished for what she's done. In short, she's acting *against* her own best interests. And therefore not getting her constitutional right to a fair trial."

Daphne sat back to consider the ramifications of what he was saying. Any attempt to prove that her mother had been pushed past her limits would show her father to be a monster . . . or at the very least, immoral. Would that be fair to Daddy? And did *any* of them need the extra publicity this would rake up?

Whatever it takes, the voice of reason whispered in her ear. And suddenly she knew that it didn't matter in the least that her father's reputation would be tarnished. This was her mother's *life* they were talking about.

"What exactly are you proposing?" she asked.

Cathcart leveled his gaze across the table at her. "I'd like your permission to file for conservatorship. In effect, what that means is that until such time as your mother is capable of looking after herself, you and your sister will be in charge of her welfare."

"Which means we can try to negotiate a lesser plea?"

"Exactly."

Daphne nodded in respectful appreciation. Cathcart might not be Clarence Darrow, she thought, but he was nobody's fool. Kitty had done the right thing in hiring him after all.

Finally, she said, "I'll be honest with you, Tom. I *hate* the idea of having to declare my mother incompetent. On the other hand, I guess we're sort of running out of options." She sighed deeply and pushed her plate aside. "I'll talk it over with Kitty and let you know. Will you be in your office later this afternoon?"

He glanced at his watch. "Until seven-thirty or eight— if my wife doesn't send over a goon squad to drag me home before then." He gave her a small smile that flickered, then died. "By the way, don't forget I'm seeing your mother on my way back to the office."

She fell silent, reflecting on what they'd discussed. After a long moment, she said softly, "You know, it's ironic because in a way I think she sees things more clearly now than she ever has."

Cathcart blinked, and a neatly trimmed silver eyebrow shot up. "Would you care to elaborate on that?"

Daphne pondered how best to explain it. Or should she say nothing at all? She settled on putting it in the simplest terms possible. "She adored him," she began, choosing her words carefully. "I know you might find that hard to believe in light of what happened. But the way I've come to see it, my mother's problem wasn't that she didn't love him enough, or even that she secretly resented him. She loved him *too* much. And it came at a great cost."

"How do you mean?"

"I didn't think it was possible to love someone too much," she said, closing her eyes for a moment and seeing Johnny's face. "But what if you'd do anything to keep that perfect love from getting tarnished? Lie to yourself, turn a blind eye. Even kill."

In the silence that followed Daphne was aware of each clinking fork, each voice raised in merriment. Her gaze took in the relaxed-looking lunch crowd, with their breezy hair and open tanned faces. Not like New York, where no one bothered to hide it when they were having a bad day. What went on behind some of those smiles? What hidden despair would one day erupt into full-blown calamity?

"A lot of husbands cheat on their wives. They aren't all killed for it." Cathcart lowered his voice so the chipper blond waitress approaching their table wouldn't overhear.

Daphne shook her head. "It doesn't make sense, I know, but . . ." she struggled to come up with an analogy. "Say you own a beautiful vase that you prize more than any other possession. One day you notice a crack in it. The vase might still hold water, but it's no longer of any value. And every time you see that crack, your heart breaks a little, too. So you throw the vase out. But first you smash it up so no one else can have it."

"That's quite a theory," he said.

Daphne waited impatiently for the waitress to finish clearing away their plates. She'd barely touched her shrimp salad. It wasn't just today. Lately, her appetite had shrunk to almost nothing.

"I'm only guessing," she replied with a shrug.

What she didn't tell Cathcart was that her guess was probably better than most. She knew what obsessive love could do, even to a reasonably sane person. How it could force you to act against your better judgment . . . and risk everything you held dear. Because, to a lesser degree, wasn't that exactly where she was heading with Johnny?

She thought of last weekend when he'd dropped by Tea & Sympathy—just as she was getting off the phone with Roger. She'd been so frustrated with her husband she could have screamed. His latest excuse? Some crisis with the practice, which he didn't want to go into over the phone. "I'm shooting for next weekend," Roger had said. "Don't worry about the kids—Mom and Dad are going to watch them. Oh, by the way, they send their love."

He'd hung up before she could ask whose love was being sent—his parents' or her children's. She opted for the latter.

Then there had been Johnny striding in the door, as welcome a sight as any she'd ever seen. In his jeans and a scuffed leather jacket, she'd been reminded at once of the *old* Johnny, the young man with whom she'd nearly eloped on a similarly blustery day in May some twenty years earlier. A day when she'd been as frustrated with her father as she was now at her husband.

"Johnny! Don't tell me—you're dying for a cup of tea and one of my sister's scones, right?" She'd spoken more heartily than usual, not wanting Gladys Honeick or Mac MacArthur, seated at tables nearby, to get the idea that they were anything more than friends. Though if anyone had taken her blood pressure just then, it would have been an instant tipoff.

"Thanks, but I'll have to take a rain check. I just came by to give you this." He handed her a sealed envelope. Noting the anxious glance she cast over her shoulder, he added in a low voice, "You don't have to open it right now."

They'd chatted briefly. About Johnny's son, a sophomore at their old high school. And how much Daphne missed her kids. She didn't say anything about Roger; she didn't have to. Johnny could tell she was upset. And she would never be more grateful to him than she had been at that moment, when she could see in his troubled eyes that he desperately wanted to ask what was wrong . . . and chose not to. Instinctively, he'd understood. It wasn't the time or the place.

Not until after he was gone, when Daphne was safely ensconced in the guest room upstairs, did she tear open the envelope with trembling fingers. It wasn't a letter, as she'd expected, but a brochure. For a quaint bed and breakfast a few miles up the coast. No note attached to it. There was no need for one. Johnny's offer was clear.

It was only when she unfolded the brochure that she saw what else had been tucked in the envelope: a pair of ancient creased tickets. They fluttered to the floor, and when she picked them up she saw that the bus for which they'd been issued had long since left the depot. Twenty-one years ago, to be exact. The night she and Johnny were to have eloped. All this time, he'd saved them.

As she'd sat there on the bed, tears sliding down her cheeks and dripping off her chin, she'd understood what he was saying to her: *it's not too late. We can still catch that bus.*

But what if they were just kidding themselves? Daphne thought now. What if what she felt for Johnny was as irrational and insane in its own way as the obsessive love that had ended up killing her father?

She looked across the table at the lawyer in whose hands her mother's fate rested. He appeared to be pondering what she'd said, as if struggling to see a way to make it work for them. When their waitress asked if they'd like coffee and dessert, he was so preoccupied he didn't wait for Daphne to reply before requesting briskly, "Just the check, please." At last he turned his attention to Daphne. "You've certainly given me food for thought. Nothing new, really . . . just a new spin on what I already know. If nothing else, it'll help me in understanding where your mother is coming from."

That reminded Daphne. She reached for the shopping bag stowed beneath the table—something her sister had sent for him to give their mother. Handing it to the lawyer, she said, "Tell her it's from Kitty."

He peered into the bag at the pink cardboard box

wrapped in string. "Anything I should know about?" he asked, only half teasing.

"Like a file or a hacksaw, you mean?" Daphne indulged in a brittle laugh. "No, I'm afraid not. It's a cake. My sister baked her a cake. Mother's favorite kind."

"What kind is that?"

"Lady Baltimore," she said.

Daphne didn't add that it was the same kind her mother had planned on serving at the party for her fortieth wedding anniversary.

On her way home, Daphne decided on a whim to stop at the local bookstore. The Bookworm, where as a teenager she'd hung out for hours on end, was a Miramonte institution of sorts—the survivor of several earthquakes, the flood in '76 that had destroyed half the shops along Old Courthouse, and more recently, the Highstreet & Bowers superstore that had opened a mile down the road, in the Harbor Lights Mall.

She found it exactly where it had always been, on the corner by the old Buster Brown shoe store that was now Mud, Sweat & Tears, a cutsey pottery shop that featured the usual array of chunky handmade earthenware in the window. Beside it, The Bookworm was a welcome shout of authenticity—yellow stucco faded to a shade resembling parchment and colorful Mexican tiles webbed with age framing a window in which piles of books were artfully displayed.

As she pushed her way in through the Dutch door, Daphne felt as if she were coming home. No coffee bar, no color scheme, no airheaded clerks—just books, books, and more books—crammed onto shelves and towering precariously atop tables, in some spots even spilling onto the floor. Popular fiction and nonfiction rubbed elbows comfortably alongside titles by lesser-known authors, and a rack of *Cliffs Notes* made no apology to the rows of literary classics on the wall behind it. The same worn, seat-sprung chairs and sofas she remembered from her last visit were still there providing a haven for the devout—bibliophiles of all ages, with their

noses buried in books, taking shelter from the cold winds
of commercialization.

The cork message board on the wall by the counter
held the same crazy quilt of index cards, too. The usual
assortment of giveaways and services—everything from
kittens to gardening services and classes in vegan cook-
ery. The only new addition that she could see was the
rack of aromatherapy oils next to the register, a different
scent for every mood. She imagined the startled look on
the bearded clerk's face were she to ask, *What do you
have for a woman contemplating an affair?*

For the truth was, though she knew she ought to, she
hadn't tossed out Johnny's brochure. She'd tucked it in
the bottom drawer of the bureau instead. *Just in case.*

Of what? Daphne wondered now. In case she decided
to throw every last bit of caution to the winds? Even if
she weren't a married woman with children, didn't she
have enough to cope with just trying to get her mother
out of jail?

Nevertheless, images of Johnny lingered—that sunset
walk on the beach, their shadows stretching across the
wet sand, the look in his eyes just before he kissed her.
Memories that, as she stood here surrounded by books,
reminded her of an earlier time long before she'd known
Johnny, when all her heroes had been fictional ones.
Ivanhoe. Mr. Rochester. Heathcliff. The passions of a
dreamy child who spent every spare minute, when her
nose wasn't buried in a book, scribbling in her spiral-
bound journal.

Daphne clearly remembered the day she'd made up
her mind to be a writer. She'd been thirteen and with a
wistful sigh had just turned the last page of *Gone With
the Wind.* She'd thought, *If I had written it, I'd know,
wouldn't I? What happened to Rhett and Scarlett.*

That was it in a nutshell, she thought wryly, the need
to know. Another way of putting it, she supposed, was
nosiness made respectable. A good portion of what
prompted her to write was the irresistible impulse to get
under the skins of people she saw passing on the street
or seated in front of her in buses. To create imagined
existences for them over which she had total control.

They could stumble, they could even fall . . . but in the end, they would find a way to redeem themselves.

When she was fifteen, after two years and numerous short stories featuring damsels in distress, she'd attempted a novel of her own—a truly terrible gothic romance in which the villain had fallen off a horse into a patch of poison ivy and broken his neck. A brilliant touch of irony, or so she'd thought, until the publishing house to which she'd sent it returned the manuscript three months later with a scribbled notation on the bottom of the printed rejection letter: *Didn't know you could die from poison ivy?*

Daphne lingered at a table near the register on which stacks of current releases were displayed. Some years back she'd given one of her first readings here, to a respectable turnout. So it came as a pleasant but not entirely unexpected surprise to find her most recent novel, *Walking After Midnight*, arranged in a pile with the uppermost copy face out on a stand atop it.

Smiling, she traced a finger over the dust jacket—a pastel drawing of the moon reflected in a pool of water. Only if you looked closely could you see that the reflection resembled a woman's face. The idea for this particular story had come to her while vacationing with Roger in Barbados a few winters ago. A woman staying at their hotel had drowned while swimming in the ocean one moonlit night. No one knew why—a heart attack, someone had suggested. But according to the woman's husband, she'd been in good health and was a strong swimmer. Daphne had returned home with the tragedy still unexplained. But it occurred to her now that perhaps some mysteries weren't meant to be solved, that in her attempts to follow the convoluted back alleys of the past, reinvent them if need be, she might have been avoiding her own more treacherous present.

"It's one of our hottest titles at the moment."

Daphne turned toward the clerk who'd spoken, a chubby young woman in a shapeless smock, her glossy brown hair braided in a thick plait that was slung over one shoulder. "The author's from around here," she continued, blissfully ignorant of the blood draining from

Daphne's face. "Maybe you've heard of her? Daphne Seagrave. The old lady who killed her husband—that's her mother."

She stopped to peer curiously at Daphne, who for a panicky instant was certain the girl had recognized her. Then Daphne caught a glimpse of her own stricken face in the gilt-framed mirror on the wall. She was as white as a ghost. Who *wouldn't* stare?

"I, uh, yes . . . I've heard of it," she stammered.

"I haven't read it yet myself, but I can't *wait*," the girl jabbered on, apparently clueless. "Ever since it hit the *Chronicle*'s best-seller list, we haven't been able to keep it in stock. This just came in." She indicated the stack Daphne had been admiring just moments before . . . but from which she now found herself backing away in horror.

She had to get out of here. Now. Before this girl *did* recognize her.

Be careful what you wish for . . .

Another of her mother's axioms, and now it was coming home to roost in a particularly gruesome way. How often had she fantasized about having one of her novels plucked from obscurity? Yet she never would have imagined it would come at such a price.

As she was pushing her way out the door, she remembered Roger's having mentioned several urgent messages from her editor on their answering machine. She'd been meaning to give Claire a call. But deep down hadn't she been a little bit annoyed as well? Apparently, her editor hadn't stopped to consider that she might have more pressing things on her mind than wondering whether or not her publisher was going back to press for another three thousand copies or had decided to run an add in the *Putnam County Register*.

Now she realized why Claire had been so eager to reach her. If the *San Francisco Chronicle* was any indication, her book must be selling like hotcakes all across the country. Until now, none of her titles had netted more than fifteen thousand in hardcover. She could see why her editor would be overjoyed, but what Claire had clearly failed to grasp was how *she* would feel about profiting from her father's death. Right now, Daphne felt as if she'd just bit down on something rotten.

She walked quickly past the older stucco buildings lining either side of the brick-paved mall. It was only two blocks to Kitty's tea shop, but it felt like a mile. Blood thumped a steady drumbeat in her head, and though the day was clear and pleasantly cool, she was sweating in her cotton skirt and linen blazer. In front of the original beaux art courthouse, which had been converted into offices—one of them Cathcart's—a juggler in clown makeup was entertaining a group of laughing children. She thought of her own children and ached with longing for them. One day when Kyle and Jennie asked how she'd become famous, what would she tell them?

Be careful what you wish for . . . you just might get it.

What she wished for now was that none of this had ever happened. She wished she were back in New York, safely if not exactly blissfully ensconced in her Park Avenue penthouse. She wished she'd never met Tom Cathcart. Or been thrown back in with Johnny. *Especially* Johnny. For if she hadn't seen him again, she wouldn't *know,* would she?—what it would have been like if, on that long-ago night, they *had* boarded that bus.

B y the time she reached her sister's house, Daphne was out of breath and nearly doubled over from a stitch in her side. Coming in through the back door, she sank down at the kitchen table, mildly astonished to find she'd made it here in one piece. She couldn't recall having stopped at a crosswalk. It was probably pure luck that she hadn't been run over.

Kitty, who'd been sliding a cake from the oven when she walked in, paused to look at her. Gloved in the lobster-claw oven mitts Daphne had given her as a gag last Christmas, her curly ginger hair pushed up in a disheveled topknot, she looked so comical that Daphne found herself smiling even as she winced at the pain in her side.

She watched as Kitty gently eased the cake onto the butcher block. It smelled heavenly—like nutmeg and candied orange peel. Daphne's mouth began to water, and she nearly laughed out loud at the wonder of it: her appetite rising from the dead like Lazarus.

"As soon as it cools a bit, I'll cut you a piece," Kitty said.

"Make it two. You're even skinnier than me."

Kitty took the kettle from the back burner and poured boiling water into a teapot. While the tea was steeping, she pried the cake from the pan and cut two thick wedges. "*You* look as if you've been beat up," she said. "Was it something Tom Cathcart said?"

"Worse." Daphne tugged off her loafers—she could feel a blister forming on one heel—and dropped them under the table, where one of the cats was snoozing. "I stopped at the bookstore on my way home. Thanks to all the press we've been getting, it appears my book is an overnight success."

Kitty understood at once and glanced reflexively out the window. But the voracious pack that had swarmed outside in the days after their mother's arrest had, for the time being, gone on to other fresher kills. There was no one out there now, just her big gray Samoyed mix, parked on his haunches staring up at a treed cat. She looked back at Daphne and sighed. "Oh, Daph, I know how you must feel. But it's not as if you had any control over it."

"Easy for you to say. *You're* not the one making a profit from our family's horror show." Immediately regretting her outburst, Daphne was quick to apologize. "I'm sorry, that wasn't fair. It's just . . . well, it feels sometimes like *we're* the ones on trial. Don't tell me you haven't felt it, too."

Her sister's delicate face clouded. She carried the tea tray over to the table and set a plate down in front of Daphne. Blue Willow, she recognized, from an old set of their mother's. "I've had my moments," Kitty said quietly.

"How did it go with the garden club ladies?" Daphne remembered to ask.

Kitty was frowning as she sat down across from her. "Well, let's see. Mrs. Underwood wanted the recipe for my lemon squares. And Ardelia Spivak offered to send someone over to mow mother's lawn and do some weeding. And, oh, before I forget, so far they've collected almost two hundred signatures."

"In other words, nobody's offering to stick her neck out."

"That's one way of putting it."

Daphne took a bite of the warm cake. Heavenly. "There's an old Chinese saying," she said. "True friends are like evergreens—you don't know them until winter comes."

"I'll be sure to remember that one." Kitty offered her a pained smile and went about pouring them each a cup of tea from the familiar flowered pot with the chipped spout. "How did the lunch go?"

"Nothing new in terms of Mother. But wait till you hear what Cathcart's come up with."

She explained to Kitty the attorney's suggestion that they file for conservatorship. Daphne still wasn't sure she liked the idea, but Cathcart was right about one thing: they were running out of options.

Kitty, though, was firmly opposed. "If we make the case that she's not competent to handle her own affairs, isn't that the same as saying she's crazy?" she argued. "I don't know about you, Daph, but I wouldn't feel comfortable doing that unless it truly is our last resort."

"Do you have a better idea?"

Kitty blew on her tea, setting in motion the wisps of hair that corkscrewed down around her temples. At the same time, her fine-boned face, with its delicate, almost elfin features, grew still with concentration. When she spoke, her voice was firm and clear.

"I think it's time," she said, "that we pay a visit to Beryl Chapman."

B eryl Chapman lived several miles across town, in a neighborhood that years ago had been fairly affluent but was now struggling to keep up appearances. Once a quiet street just east of John Muir High and the old public library, Rio De Campo had suffered from the widening of adjoining Seacrest Drive into a four-lane boulevard providing access to the freeway. Property values had plummeted practically overnight, and in the decade since, despite creative attempts at remodeling and landscaping, they hadn't gone up appreciably.

Beryl's house was a flat-roofed split-level with a freckling of mildew along the front where a dense border of pyracanthas had recently been cut back. There was something sad about it, Daphne thought as she and her sister pulled up in front: it wasn't so much a sense of neglect but rather one of failure radiating from every patched-over crack and cheap home "improvement"— like the faux brick siding and tiny glassed-in sun porch off the kitchen. Even the rose bushes along the front walk, uniformly trimmed and staked, looked bleak somehow.

Over the phone, Beryl had been friendly, if cautiously so. She had an appointment later that afternoon, she'd said, but why didn't they drop by for a cup of coffee?

Now, she met them at the door in her usual full-dress armature: perfectly coiffed platinum hair, and makeup that must have taken an hour to apply, complete with false eyelashes. She was wearing a silky caftan of some kind, which Daphne saw was nothing other than a housecoat attempting to pass as fashionable. The only things missing that would have completed the *Sunset Boulevard* illusion, she thought, were the turban and cigarette holder.

"Girls," she greeted, letting the word hover as if to underline some sense of authority that she imagined would give her an edge over them. "You're looking well. Please, come in."

Stepping inside, Daphne was at once assaulted by more attempts at home improvement: a glass-brick partition separating the entry from the living room, mirrored tiles spanning the wall behind the cream-colored sofa, a scaled-down chandelier with teardrop-shaped prisms that threw a cold spangled light over the white carpet.

"Why don't we take our coffee in here?" Beryl said with a sweep of one caftaned arm that took in the glass coffee table, which appeared to float above the carpet on a cluster of polished chrome strips bunched to resemble a water fountain.

"None for me, thank you," Kitty declined.

Noting Beryl's frown of displeasure, Daphne was quick to reply, "I take mine black, no sugar."

Beryl, as she swished off toward the kitchen, reminded her more than ever of Norma Desmond—an aging movie queen in desperate need of a starring role. But if she and Kitty weren't exactly Cecil B. DeMille, they'd be more than happy to give Beryl her close-up.

The woman purporting to be Mother's friend returned a few minutes later carrying two steaming mugs, with a snow-white miniature poodle trotting at her heels. As soon as the dog spotted Daphne and Kitty, it began to yap. "Muffie, be a good girl," Beryl scolded, setting the mugs down on the table before scooping it up under one arm. She cast them a glance of mock contriteness. "I had her locked up in the laundry room—she can be such a pest with company. But she looked so unhappy. Didn't you, Muffie girl?" She rubbed her nose against the dog's thimble-size snout before setting it back down. "Now," she said as she settled onto the sofa and helped herself to a cigarette from the enamel box on the Chinese end table, "What can I do for you girls?"

You can address us by our names, for one thing, Daphne felt like snapping.

But before she could open her mouth, Kitty piped, "We're really here for Mother." In a yellowish top and dark-red drawstring trousers, seated in an easy chair across from the sofa, she looked like a bright-eyed robin that had mistakenly flown in the window.

"Your poor mother, yes." Beryl drew down her garishly painted mouth in an attempt to look heartbroken that only made her appear clownish. "How is Lydia? Not an hour goes by when I don't think of what that woman must be going through. I'm just *sick* about what happened."

But not enough to help her, Daphne thought disgustedly. Aloud, she said, "She's well. As well as can be expected, that is. Have you been to visit her yet?"

The click of Beryl's cigarette lighter in the stillness of

the latter-day *Sunset Boulevard* living room sounded harsh and contemptuous somehow. Beryl sucked deeply on her cigarette before shaking her head, mouthing amid a plume of smoke, "You have no idea how many times I've headed out the door to do just that. But always at the last minute, I just can't face it. The sight of poor Lydia locked up in that place." She gave a visible shudder, pressing a bony arm to her chest. "But, of course," she added, "if there's anything I can do to help. Anything at all . . ." she let the sentence trail off.

"There *is* something actually," Kitty said. "The last time we spoke you told us it'd been weeks since you'd talked to Mother. Before the . . . the shooting, that is. But there's something I still don't understand."

"What might that be?" An edge had crept into Beryl's gravelly voice.

"It's about the fight you and Mother had," Daphne plunged in. "The one Leanne told me about."

Beryl frowned in annoyance even as she feigned innocence. "Fight? I wouldn't go that far. We had *words,* yes. But your mother and I have known each other for almost forty years. We're not about to let a silly little argument get in the way of our friendship."

"But something else got in the way, didn't it?" Against the backdrop of the all-white room, Kitty's bright blue eyes seemed to glow the deep purple of twilight.

Beryl stared back at Kitty through slitted eyes, like a cornered cat. "I'm not sure I know what you're getting at," she said.

"Let me refresh your memory." Daphne leaned forward in her chair. "You and Daddy were lovers at one time. We know all about it, Beryl. Ancient history as far as you're concerned, but for Mother, hearing it for the first time, it must have felt as though it had just happened."

The flash of displeasure Daphne had seen earlier blossomed into a full-blown scowl. Clearly, Beryl realized the game was up. Or maybe her conscience—whatever little there was of it—had finally gotten the best of her.

"What do you want from me?" she rasped. "All right,

I told her. I couldn't take it anymore. I knew about the others. I knew how he'd been making a fool of her all these years. She was my *friend,* dammit. She deserved to know."

Kitty stared at her without blinking. "Did she? Did she *really?*"

Daphne, sensing they were finally getting somewhere, felt her heart quicken. "You didn't do it for Mother's sake—it was really your own. You were jealous of her, weren't you? She had everything you didn't. Husband, money. She was about to celebrate her fortieth anniversary . . . and you had nothing."

"That's a lie!" Beryl jumped up so suddenly that Muffie, curled up at her feet, began yapping manically. "If you're trying to pin this horrible tragedy on me, you can just—"

"We're not trying to pin anything on you," Kitty broke in, her tone gentle but firm. "We need your help, that's all."

"We need you to testify on Mother's behalf," Daphne explained.

The miniature poodle was now dancing around on her hind legs in frenzied little circles, barking furiously. Beryl clapped her hands over her ears and shouted, "Will you shut up? *Will you just shut up?*"

It was a moment before Daphne realized it was Muffie she was shouting at, not them. Kitty, scooting off her chair onto her haunches, coaxed the frantic dog over to her and pulled it shivering into her lap.

Beryl glared down at her as if she'd kidnapped her only child. "I can't help you." Her voice was cold. "I know you think it's cowardly of me, but I just can't," she added more pitiably. "Your mother had Vern, yes. But *I* have my reputation. Without it, I *would* be nothing."

Her voice broke, and she dropped back onto the sofa. In that instant she appeared to melt, not like Norma Desmond after all but the wicked witch in *The Wizard of Oz*, her face sagging and her bony chest seeming to sink in on itself.

Daphne forced herself to press on despite the compas-

sion that took her unawares. "You're her only hope."
She spoke softly, hating herself for having to cajole but
knowing it was the only way. "No one else knows what
it was like for her. Finding out after all those years that
the husband to whom she'd devoted her life had been
unfaithful throughout their marriage. It must have
been devastating."

With a harsh gasp, Beryl dropped her head into her
hands. "I didn't expect her to kill him!"

"No, you couldn't have known that," Kitty agreed,
rising to her feet with the still-shivering poodle cradled
in her arms. "But it happened. And now the only decent
thing for you to do is to come forward with the truth."

For a moment it looked as if Beryl were about to
crack. Then she shook her head violently. A fat tear
rolled down one gaunt cheek, trailing a thin ribbon of
mascara. "It wouldn't help. Lydia herself admits she's
guilty. Nothing *I* say is going to change that. Why should
we both pay?"

Daphne felt an urge to slap her. Beryl was like Roger.
Weak, and full of excuses. Unwilling to face up to the
consequences of her bad behavior. God, what could her
mother ever have seen in this woman?

"It *might* help," Kitty argued. "If the jury sees there
were mitigating circumstances . . ."

She didn't get a chance to finish. Because at that very
moment, Beryl shot to her feet. Marching over to Kitty,
she snatched Muffie from her arms. As her crimson tal-
ons closed about it, Daphne saw the poodle's lips wrinkle back over its tiny pointed teeth, and was almost
certain she heard a low growl.

"I'm afraid I'm going to have to ask you to leave."
Beryl's voice dripped with poisoned courtesy. "As I believe I mentioned earlier, I have an appointment with
one of my accounts. I can't afford to be late."

She was reminding them that she was the sole Bay
area distributor of Désirée—a line of floral fragrances
sold in gift shops and clothing stores catering to older
women. What kind of business would she have left with
her name linked to a murderess and splashed across
every newspaper in the country?

Whatever sympathy Daphne had felt dried up in that instant. She stood up alongside Kitty. "Thanks," she said coldly, waiting until they were almost at the door before turning to add, "for the coffee."

There was a single message on Kitty's machine when they got back. From Johnny. Playing it back, Daphne felt the chill that had caused her to shiver all the way home in her sister's car turn to instant heat.

"I was walking on the beach, and I found this sign. It says NO TRESPASSING, but it looks dry enough." There was a low chuckle. "What do you say we build a fire?"

Overhearing the message, Kitty shook her head as she hung her coat in the closet. "God knows I'm not one to tell you what to do. But Daph, don't you think you have enough to deal with as it is?"

They were in the hallway outside the kitchen, by the back stairs used by maids in the days when even a modestly successful homeowner could afford household help. Daphne knew her sister was only speaking out of concern and that they were both tense from the encounter with Beryl, but she bristled nonetheless.

"I haven't noticed you barring the door against the boyfriend who slips up your stairs at night when he thinks I'm asleep," she shot back.

The color flooding her sister's face told her she'd hit a nerve. Kitty brought her hands to her cheeks as if to cool them, but she couldn't hide her tiny smile of chagrin. "Oh, dear. And we thought we were being so quiet."

Daphne rolled her eyes. "Come on, I wasn't born yesterday. It's the same guy who stopped by after the funeral, isn't it?"

"How . . . how did you know?" Kitty stammered.

"It was written all over your face. Just like it is now." She walked over and slipped an arm around her sister's shoulders. "Look, it's okay. We're human, for God's sake. And at least *you're* not married."

When Kitty drew back, her expression was troubled. "I wasn't thinking of Roger—only of you. Daph, I don't

want to see you get hurt. If you let yourself fall in love
with Johnny all over again—"

"I never *stopped*," Daphne interrupted. "Don't you
see? That's the problem." There. She'd said it—the thing
she'd kept locked inside all these years. But instead of
shame or remorse she felt a profound sense of relief.

Kitty smiled ruefully. "I had a little crush on him, too,
you know. When I was thirteen, for about five minutes."
Softly, she said, "It's funny, isn't it? I used to envy you
because of Johnny . . . and now I envy you your kids."

Daphne wanted to rush in with assurances—Kitty was
still young, she could have a child of her own. If it didn't
happen on its own, one of the adoption agencies to
which she'd applied was sure to come through. But that
would have been the *old* Daphne . . . the woman she'd
left behind in New York, who was quick to smooth
things over, to avoid conflict at any cost. She decided
instead to say exactly what was on her mind.

"I miss them," she sighed. "There hasn't been a day
since I got here that I haven't wanted to fly home to
my children."

Holding on to the banister, Kitty lowered herself gingerly onto the bottom step. She wore a faraway look
Daphne couldn't quite decipher. "His name is Sean. And
he's not just a boyfriend. His little sister is pregnant, and
she's looking for someone to adopt her baby. That's how
we met."

Daphne was all at once flooded with guilt. Here she'd
been so wrapped up in her own problems, she hadn't
given a thought to what her sister's might be. Now she
sank down next to Kitty. "Why didn't you tell me?"

Her sister's mouth twisted up in a humorless smile.
"With everything else that was going on? I don't know.
I guess I thought it would seem selfish somehow."

"It's not selfish. It's . . ." she grasped for the right
word ". . . your life."

"My life?" Kitty turned a mournful face up to her. In
the half light of the stairwell, it seemed stripped of flesh,
nothing but bone in which a pair of brilliant eyes glimmered with an almost feverish despair. "Yeah, I guess
you could say that. But you know something? Deep

down I'm really no better than Beryl. Because if I'd been given the choice, I would have done exactly what she's doing. For this baby, yes. I would have turned my back on Mother, pretended I didn't even know her. What kind of person does that make *me?*"

"Someone who isn't perfect," Daphne replied softly, tears welling in her eyes. She knew exactly how Kitty felt. Because hadn't she, too, made up her mind, the instant she'd heard Johnny's voice, that wild horses couldn't stop her from going to him?

The old Hudson's Bay blanket on which they lay nestled in the crook of a dune, a mile south of Plunkett's Lagoon, had come out of the trunk of Johnny's Thunderbird. In the flickering firelight, Daphne could see in one corner a charred hole the size of a dime—a souvenir from some family outing, no doubt. She thought of all the memories he'd accumulated over the years, of which she wasn't a part, and felt her chest constrict.

She brought a hand to his heart, feeling its sure, steady beat even through the thickness of his sweater. "Did your son always live with you?" she asked.

"Not at first. J. J. was twelve when Sara and I got divorced," he told her, his expression clouding. "Custody wasn't an issue. As much as I wanted him with me, I wouldn't have done that to my son. Besides, I can't fault Sara. She's a good mother."

"When did things change?"

"Six months ago. He and his mom weren't getting along. Frankly, I don't blame her for booting him out. He's a handful at times . . . like his old man." Johnny laughed ruefully, plucking at a tough stalk poking up through the sand. "What about you? You told me awhile back how much you miss your kids. It must be tough being so far away from them."

"It is." She thought of the last time she'd spoken with Kyle and Jennie over the phone. Her son had chattered briefly about some Nintendo game his dad had bought him before rushing off to play. Jennie, on the other hand, had seemed shy . . . the way she got with strangers. Hanging up, Daphne had thought her heart would break.

Johnny tipped his head in a way that illuminated only one side of his face. The rest was lost in shadow, one blue-gray eye looking out at her as if through a cracked door. "Why not have them come out then?"

"I wish it were as easy as that," she sighed. "But Roger is having trouble getting away. Some crisis with the practice. Or so he says." A note of bitterness crept into her voice, which she didn't bother to hide.

Johnny cocked his head in wry amusement. "I wasn't referring to your husband."

He'd made it sound so simple that for a moment Daphne almost believed it *was* possible. Then reality came flooding back.

"I can't just pull them out of school." Kyle was in first grade at St. David's, and Jennie just starting Montessori. What she didn't add was that Roger would never allow it.

"What's worse—changing school for a few months or being without their mother?" he reasoned.

"Months?" Daphne felt a flutter of alarm.

"It'll be at least that long . . . if you plan on sticking around through the trial."

"Did you think I wouldn't?"

"The thought crossed my mind."

Daphne rolled over onto her back. "I'm not leaving, not until this is resolved one way or another." She stared at a shower of sparks funneling up into the dark, unable to meet his gaze. "But there are other things at stake here besides my mother."

He surprised her with a bitter laugh. "Nothing ever changes, does it? Hell, look at us . . . pushing forty and still sneaking around."

"Twenty years is a long time," she reminded him. "A lot *has* changed."

"Not how I feel about you."

His words were like a soft blow to her midsection. She sat upright, hugging her knees. "Oh, Johnny, why does this have to be so hard?"

A sudden fierce gust off the ocean flattened their fire,

then scooped it upward in a long spit of flame. Overhead, stars peeked through a thin layer of fog like the flecks of mica winking in the furrowed sand at her feet—sand that felt warm against her soles, but cool underneath as she thrust in deeper with her toes.

The beach was deserted—too cold for lovers. At first, it had seemed so to her as well, but the fire built out of driftwood gathered from along the high tide line had warmed her. Now, in its crackling glow, she felt as if they were the only two people left in this world: a man and a woman old enough to know better, digging up shipwrecked memories near where they'd made love as teenagers.

"What's *hard*," he said, "is always doing what's good for everybody but us." His voice behind her was low and tight. "Haven't you ever stopped to wonder what our lives would've been like if we'd done what *we* wanted all those years ago?"

Daphne smiled into the restless flames. "At least once a day."

"I married Sara thinking a lousy piece of paper was going to erase you from my mind." He was silent a moment, then said, "It seemed like a good idea at the time."

She swung around to face him. "I never told Roger about you. Not in any detail. I didn't have to."

Johnny gazed at her in silence, firelight dancing over his strong uneven-featured face. When he sat up to take her hand, slowly drawing her back down beside him, she felt the shock of the cooler air just a few inches from where she'd lain . . . chased by Johnny's warm mouth closing over hers.

His kiss deepened, and Daphne felt something shift inside her, like the sand beneath their blanket as she settled in next to him. She was all at once flooded with memories. The two of them, naked under a clear sky in which the stars had wheeled and flashed like a vast game of roulette on which their entire futures hung. The taste of salt on his skin . . . and the tenderness with which he'd eased into her. Afterward, he'd cradled her while she wept, not with regret, but with an overwhelming sense of relief. At sixteen, he'd known exactly what she'd needed. In a way her husband of nearly twenty years never had.

Now, on this windy night in May, years later, his hands didn't hesitate as they once had. He unzipped her jacket, and slipped her sweater over her head. She shivered as the damp salt-laced wind struck her bare flesh . . . then Johnny was wrapping her in his arms, kissing the base of her throat before moving lower. His mouth left a trail of goose bumps between her breasts and down her belly to where he was now thumbing open the button of her jeans.

I can't do this, she thought in some distant part of her mind. *I'm married.* But it didn't feel sinful, or even wrong. All these years with Roger, it was *Johnny* to whom she'd been unfaithful. Johnny for whom she'd yearned while straining to enjoy Roger's boisterous, and often clumsy, attempts at passion.

And now, poised over her was the face she'd so often tried to imagine—this grown-up version of the boy she'd loved, with the wind blowing the hair she used to delight in running her fingers through. Older, and yes, wiser . . . but wanting her no less than he had back then. If anything, the desire in his eyes, banked through the years, burned all the brighter.

She watched him undress before wriggling out of her own jeans and tossing them onto the growing heap at one end of the blanket. A handful of change from Johnny's pocket had spilled onto the sand, where it sparkled like unearthed treasure. In the firelight that polished his bare torso, still lean and muscular, she saw the faint scar in the shape of a crescent, barely visible on his right shoulder. If she closed her teeth over it, she knew, it would fit exactly. The thought excited her deeply.

Not since she'd last lain with Johnny, when she was seventeen, had she felt such urgency, such a wild craving to be filled by him.

He cupped a breast and gently ran a tongue over her nipple. When he drew back, it stung deliciously with the cold. She clutched at him, pulling him back over her like a blanket, smothering herself with his warmth.

He tasted . . . oh, like no one, like nothing else. Like Johnny. How she'd missed him. How she'd missed *this*.

"Are we doing the right thing?" she whispered.

He looked down at her with a solemnness she found touching. In his hooded gray eyes pinpoints of reflected light danced. "Do you want to stop?"

"No." She didn't have to think it over. She couldn't have stopped if she'd wanted to.

He slipped a hand between her legs, stroking her gently until she thought she would die from the sweetness of it. "Jesus," he whispered, "you have no idea how much I've wanted this. Ever since that day you walked into my office."

As he entered her, the tiny cry she gave was muffled by his mouth. He fit inside her as perfectly as she remembered, but with age and experience she was able to move as she hadn't known how to back then—finding her rhythm, knowing to pause as Johnny's quickened. And when his control began to slip, and he moved down to satisfy her first with his mouth, she readily opened herself to the delicious sensation of his tongue amid the cold air slipping along the insides of her thighs.

Daphne arched, and let out a shout, the milky sky seeming to lap over her like the waves whispering somewhere out in the darkness. *Lord. Dear Lord. I don't care if you're up there watching. Because if it's a sin to feel this good, there's no hope for anyone in this world.*

Then he was inside her again, once more bringing her to climax, even before the sweet fluttering from the first one had stopped. *Oh, God. God . . .*

She tipped her hips up, knowing instinctively when and how to meet his last quivering thrust. Not until Johnny had collapsed and rolled onto his side did she stop to marvel at the exquisite sense of release that flowed from every corner of her being.

Daphne drew in against him, huddling close, not wanting to let go of those feelings or allow in the cold. Grains of wind-driven sand landed against her like sparks from the fire that heated her flank while the rest of her grew chilled. Only where her bare flesh met Johnny's was she perfectly warmed.

"I love you," he said.

"I know." She brought her hand to his cheek, where she could feel a muscle working . . . as if he were struggling not to cry. "You're the only man I ever wanted."

"I wish . . ."

"What?"

"Never mind. I don't want to think about the past."

"Or the future." She shivered, and drew in more tightly against him.

After a few minutes, he murmured, "I should throw another log on the fire."

"We should get dressed," she protested sleepily, making no move to get up.

He laughed. "Why bother? We'll only get undressed again."

"Because there's a chance someone might see us . . . and then you won't want to know what tomorrow's headline will be." Now Daphne did sit up, thinking, *Anyone could have spotted us. And then Roger would know.*

Strangely, the idea appealed to her. She imagined Roger snapping open his morning paper and getting the shock of his life.

Then a wave of guilt washed over her, and she remembered the night, some years back, when she'd been caught in a blizzard driving home from a speaking engagement in New Haven. By the time she'd staggered in the door, hours late, Roger was beside himself. He'd hugged her until she thought her ribs would crack, then followed her from room to room as if determined to never again let her out of his sight.

Pulling away from Johnny, she began shoving her legs into jeans gritty with sand, a sweater that felt clammy against her skin. Johnny regarded her in amusement, waiting until she was fully clothed before languidly slipping on his shirt.

"Last time, you were scared your dad would catch us," he recalled teasingly. "Who are you scared of this time?"

"Me," she told him. "If we let this go any further, I'm afraid of what *I* might do." She didn't know what the future would hold, but whatever had been lost, she'd regained it tonight, in Johnny's arms. Now the only question was, could she keep it?

The only thing Daphne knew for certain as she trudged up the dune, leaning into Johnny to escape the wind that snatched at her hair and pushed the collar of her jacket up around her neck, was that if she let him go a second time, there would be no more chances.

The knowledge pooled about her heart like the tide she could see faintly below, rushing in to shore.

Tomorrow, she thought, *I'll arrange for Roger to put the children on a plane. I won't say anything about when we're coming home. If he gets tired of waiting, he'll know where to find me.*

Chapter 11

Thursday morning of the following week, Kitty drove her sister to the airport in San Francisco to pick up Roger and the children. But the flight was delayed, and more than an hour had passed by the time he ambled through the gate with Kyle and Jennie in tow. Kitty hung back, watching her brother-in-law crush Daphne in a jaws-of-life hug while the children flung themselves at her knees hard enough to send her sprawling back with a whoop of laughter into a conveniently positioned chair.

Daphne's changed, she thought. Kitty marveled that her sister had managed to persuade Roger, despite his initial objections, into letting her enroll the kids at Miramonte Elementary for the remainder of the school year. A short time ago, she wouldn't have been able to stand up to him, but now, instead of shrinking back, Daphne was quietly taking charge.

"I need them with me. And they need their mother," she'd told Roger over the phone. Waiting patiently until he'd had his say, she'd continued, "If it's not convenient for you to bring them right now, fine. I'll come get them. I'm afraid this time I'm going to have to insist, Roger."

Kitty had wanted to cheer.

Roger seemed to sense the change in her as well. Throughout the drive back to Miramonte he kept flicking uncertain glances at Daphne while the children chattered on uninterrupted, peppering Kitty with questions about which rooms they would sleep in, if they could make cookies like last time, and whether or not they could watch TV upstairs.

Jennie, adorable in a ruffled blouse and pink bib overalls, pale-blond pigtails sprouting from her head, reached shyly into her Barbie backpack. "Lookit, Aunt Kitty. It's *The Little Mermaid*." She held up the videocassette so Kitty could see, confiding earnestly, "Daddy says there's no such things as mermaids. What do *you* think?"

Kitty hesitated, then said, "Well, I've never *seen* one . . . but I've never seen a kangaroo, either. And I know there's such a thing as kangaroos."

She ignored the irritated glance Roger darted at her.

Her brother-in-law could stay only through the weekend, as it turned out. But it was long enough to swell the house with his presence and cause her sister to shrink a little more with each passing day. Hearing his heavy and somehow proprietary tread on the stairs, Kitty couldn't help cringing a little herself. Observing his attempts to calm Daphne's fears about their mother—the same jollying tone he used with Kyle and Jennie—she'd feel her own muscles tighten in resistance. Her brother-in-law wasn't a *mean* person, Kitty knew. Though a bit too strict with the children, in her opinion, he clearly adored them. And in his own way, Roger was trying to make it up to her sister for not coming sooner. Nevertheless, when he left for the airport bright and early Monday morning, even the house seemed to breathe a sigh of relief.

Like mice creeping cautiously out into the open, the children played quietly at first, then grew more rambunctious as it sank in that their father wasn't there to scold them. Daphne, seated cross-legged in her pajamas on the braided rug by the fireplace, watching Kyle and Jennie build a fort out of Lincoln Logs, looked relieved as well. An hour later, when everyone was showered and dressed, they trooped downstairs to the kitchen, where the dough Kitty had gotten up early to start had risen to a great floury dome in its bowl.

Kitty gave each of the children a grapefruit-size lump to knead, and while they gleefully pummeled away—tow-headed miniatures of Daphne with heart-shaped faces and wide gray-green eyes—Kitty set water on to boil for tea.

She was slicing bananas for cereal when the sun, cloaked in fog all weekend, made a sudden and dramatic appearance. A brilliant shaft aimed like a spotlight over the pair of sleeping calicoes twined in a single furry ball on the rug. Over the kettle's whistling, Kitty could hear the merry tinkling of music upstairs. The theme song to *Sesame Street*. Kyle and Jennie must have left the TV on. She smiled, and for the first time in weeks felt blessed.

It came to her like a quarter dropping into its slot, a familiar axiom buffed to a shine by hard fate, *Whatever doesn't kill me will make me stronger*. In the midst of her family's ordeal, and the ruins of her own expectations, Kitty had discovered an amazing truth: that things can grow, even in barren soil watered by tears.

It was Sean who'd taught her that. Kitty looked upon each night that he let himself in the back door and tiptoed up the stairs to her room as a precious gift, to be unwrapped and savored. She didn't always know when he would come. Between school and work, and looking after things at home, there wasn't much time left over for himself. Often, by the time he slipped into Kitty's bed, she was fast asleep, and he would become wrapped up in whatever dream she was having. When he crept away in the early hours of the morning, she was left shivering, as if deprived of a necessary source of heat.

For the rest of the day, Kitty would go weak at the mere thought of him. She'd feel the imprint of his hands burning beneath her clothes and grow almost uncomfortably aware of her panties, damp from last night's lovemaking. It was no good trying to distract herself. Even when she shut the door on those memories, they slipped out along the floor and around the jamb in sweet bursts of longing.

At the same time, Kitty carried a checklist in her head of every reason *not* to fall in love with Sean. There was no future in it, she told herself. But most of all, there was Heather. She still believed there was a chance Heather would decide in her favor. No other adoptive parents were being considered; she knew for a fact because Sean had told her.

Yes, but that was days ago, a cautious voice reminded her. *Suppose she's found someone by now.*

Kitty resisted the urge to put her hands to her head,

to literally *drive* that thought from her brain. Yet she knew perfectly well why lately she hadn't asked Sean about Heather. *You're afraid of what you might find out.*

There was just one subject on which they strongly disagreed. Kitty felt that Heather ought to be told about *them*. But Sean argued that his sister had enough to deal with right now. Finding out that he was involved with Kitty would only upset her. The other night, as they lay talking in bed, Sean had struggled to put it into words.

"My sister's a little . . . well, you've seen how she can get." He'd been lying on his back, staring up at the ceiling, his profile sharply outlined in the moonlight. "It's been like that with her since our mom took off. Heather gets a little crazy when she thinks someone might be leaving her—even if it's just in her mind. You know what I mean?"

Kitty had nodded. In the darkness, with the moon rippling behind the lace curtains like something caught in a net and slowly drowning, she'd understood that all the reasons she was in love with Sean were the same ones for why he couldn't be with her the way she wanted him to.

Kitty knew, too, what Sean was secretly hoping: that his sister would decide to keep the baby. *Would that be so terrible?* she thought: *At least I'd get to see it, hold it. And once Heather gets used to the idea of Sean and me as a couple, maybe . . .*

Standing in her sun-struck kitchen, surrounded by Daphne and her children, Kitty felt suddenly sure that *nothing* was impossible. Who knew? They might even find a way to set their mother free.

She shuddered then, as if a cloud had passed over the sun.

So far Daphne's and her efforts had turned up very little. Detective work, she'd learned, was like archaeology—a lot of work for a few old bones. Since last week's fruitless showdown with Beryl, she and her sister had spent the better part of a day digging through old letters of their mother's and several more hours on the phone with friends and relatives. Most were eager to help but couldn't think of a single reason why Mother would have wanted to leave their father, much less harm him.

Starchy Aunt Rose had said it best, "I'd have bet cash money on my sister doing just the opposite—lying down in the road herself if it would keep Vern from getting run over." She'd paused to suck in an emphysematic breath that made her sound like a drowning woman gasping for air. "Never quite understood it myself. But *this* . . . well, it makes even less sense."

One thing was clear: if Mother had known about Daddy's affairs, she hadn't confided in Aunt Rose. Nevertheless, Kitty was determined to find a way to force the truth out of its cave and into the light. Their best hope at this point, the way she saw it, was to get their mother to testify on her own behalf. But first Mother had to want to save herself. So far she'd stubbornly refused to discuss it beyond the fact that she was guilty and deserved to be punished. But what about what this was doing to her daughters and to *their* children? It wasn't just Mother's health and welfare at stake, it was the whole family's. *If she can't see that for herself, well then, I'll just have to make her see.*

Today, she was meeting with Mother and her attorney while Daphne enrolled the children in school. And this time, Kitty intended to get somewhere . . .

Poised at the sink, she felt her normal sense of direction, which somewhere along the line had become as disengaged as a fly wheel spinning aimlessly inside a broken watch, slip back into groove. Yes, she mourned her father and would go on doing everything in her power to save Mother. But meanwhile, she had her own life to live. Wasn't that the real lesson in all this: that the strength of a family as a whole is only as good as that of its individual members?

"Cornflakes are in the pantry, and oatmeal is in the cupboard over the stove," she told her sister, who was busy setting out bowls and spoons. "I'll be right back."

Without further ado, Kitty marched through the doorway into the front room beyond, whose empty tables had come to remind her of a stage set during intermission, and flipped the sign on the door to the side that read COME IN, WE'RE OPEN!

*   *   *

Shortly past ten o'clock that morning, Kitty found her-self seated at a metal table bolted to the floor of a secured room in the Miramonte County Jail. The temperature outside had remained cool, but inside it was sweltering. Tom Cathcart, seated to her left, had removed the jacket of his dark gray suit and draped it over his chair. Kitty fanned herself with an envelope fished from the wastebasket.

On previous visits, a glass barrier had somewhat obscured her view of her mother, but this time Kitty could see just how frail she'd become. The skin stretched over her now-prominent cheekbones was the yellowish hue of old acid-eaten paper, and her sunken eyes under the harsh fluorescents were flat and lifeless. Even the erect posture she'd so rigorously maintained had given way, though not without a fight. Seated across from Kitty, she had the look of an ancient monument, rounded at the shoulders and listing slightly to one side.

Kitty's heart sank as she struggled to reconcile this shockingly reduced version of her mother with images from childhood—Mother in white gloves and a wide-brimmed hat, shepherding them into a church pew, and in the yard, puttering about in her old grass-stained dungarees. Their house had always been full of fresh-cut flowers: asters and snapdragons and gladioli.

In her mind a clear picture formed: her mother emerging from the surf, sleek and dripping from her morning swim. The sun was newly risen, its light glancing off the ocean in bright starpoints and transforming her white bathing cap into a shining halo. She was rosy and smiling, as if newly baptized. Her footsteps glimmered briefly in the wet sand before being washed away.

Oh, Mother, think of all you used to love to do. Think of walking on the beach . . . and sprinkling packets of seeds over freshly turned earth. Think of peeling onions for soup—the way you taught me, by holding them under running water so you don't cry. Think of Sunday suppers, all of us around the table. Think of me, *your daughter.*

A knot formed in her throat, and as Kitty reached over to squeeze her mother's manacled hand, she found herself struggling not to cry. Glancing about, she took in the drab cinder block walls and windows reinforced with wire. On the table's gunmetal surface someone had crudely scratched JESUS SAVES. But at the moment, it didn't look as if anything could save her mother—a grim outlook she saw reflected in Cathcart's firm-jawed patrician face.

"Daphne sends her love," she said. "Oh, and you should see her children! They're each at least two inches taller and bright as can be. Jennie's like a little parrot, repeating everything she hears. And Kyle," she smiled, "yesterday he wanted to know if sand was the same as rocks, only much littler, as he put it."

Mother's halting smile was like a cracked reflection of her own. "Please, give them my love. I only wish . . ." she bit her lip and straightened a bit, bringing her listing shoulders to port.

"You wish what?" Kitty prompted softly.

"Nothing. How's Roger?" she inquired with forced brightness. Whatever Mother had been about to say, she'd clearly decided against it.

"He couldn't stay—some urgent business back home," Kitty told her. "But he wants you to know he'll do everything he can."

"I don't expect that will be much." Her mother's mouth stretched in a thin, humorless smile. Her tone was curt, almost harsh. "Forgive me for saying so, but I never much liked the man. I tried, for Daphne's sake . . . but I suppose that was part of the problem. I've set rather a poor example, haven't I?"

"Roger *is* like Daddy in some ways." Kitty had never thought of it until now, but realized that except for Daddy being smarter and far more charming, Daphne had, in some ways, married her father.

"She should leave him."

Kitty sat back, startled. She couldn't believe what she was hearing. Hadn't Mother put up with far more from Daddy? Perhaps it simply hadn't occurred to her that she'd had as much right to happiness as her daughters.

"Daphne can take care of herself," Kitty assured her.

"Oh, I don't doubt that. She's stronger than she knows."

"If you mean Roger, I . . ."

"It's not just Roger I'm thinking of." Her mother's smile remained wan, but a spark of light had crept into her eyes. "Of the three of you, Daphne was usually the last to get in line for whatever treat was being handed out. But she never hesitated to jump in when it came to making sure someone *else* got what was due them."

Kitty felt a pang of old jealousy. *Daphne . . . always Daphne. Her cherished favorite.* But she shook herself free of those thoughts as she would have brushed away the clinging strands of a cobweb.

She leaned forward to tightly grip her mother's hands, swallowing hard at the *chink* of the manacles against the metal tabletop. "Daphne's strong, yes. But not strong enough to save you if you won't even try to save yourself. Mother, you've got to tell us what happened. *Everything.*"

Her mother's hands in hers were limp and clammy, like something dead washed ashore by a storm. "I've told you everything you need to know," she said in a voice equally dead.

Kitty bit down on her frustration. "If you think you're protecting us from the truth about Daddy, I know most of it already. I've known since I was fifteen." Tears filled her eyes, and she blinked them back angrily. "I kept it to myself because I didn't want to hurt you. But, Mother, the time for keeping secrets is past."

Her mother drew back, her face closing against Kitty. Coldly, she said, "I don't see the point in raking all that up."

Kitty felt her patience bump to a sudden, unceremonious stop. "What about your family? Don't you care what this is doing to *us?*"

Mother gave a startled blink and seemed to see Kitty, really *see* her, maybe for the first time. "Of course, I care," she said softly. "It's because of you girls that I'm not dragging this family through the mud."

"If you think you're protecting us, you've got it all wrong. We're . . ." Kitty wanted to say that they were *all* perfectly able to take care of themselves, but at the moment, she wasn't so sure about Alex. ". . . we don't need your mothering. What we *need* is a mother," she finished.

Lydia glanced at Cathcart, clearly uncertain about how much she dared say in his presence. Then just as quickly, as if recognizing the irony of such concerns, one side of her mouth twisted upward in a ghastly parody of a smile. "I guess I *have* failed you. Not just Daphne. You and Alex, too. I'm sorry. I didn't mean to."

"It's not too late," Kitty urged. "You still have us. If you let us help you, we—"

"Shhh," Mother hushed gently. "Enough."

The sigh she gave was so mournful, so *lost* somehow, that Kitty nearly let her sympathy get the better of her. Steeling herself against it, she said in a hard quivering voice, "It's Daddy, isn't it? You're protecting him, just like you always did. You knew about those other women, you *had* to know. But you never confronted him. Why? Was it the picture of us as one big happy family that you didn't want to lose . . . or were you afraid Daddy would leave you?"

Kitty wasn't aware she was practically shouting until a beefy red face with close-set eyes appeared in the grated security window—the officer guarding their door. But she didn't regret her outburst. *Someone* needed to shake some sense into Mother. As panic gripped her, Kitty thought, *She's going on trial for murder, and we've all been tiptoeing around like the reputation of a dead man counts for more. It's insane.* It has to stop.

But Lydia wasn't budging. More forcefully this time, she repeated, "That's enough, Kitty." A scolding note crept into her voice. "I don't want to listen to any more of this."

"You don't have a choice. For once in your life, you're going to hear what *I* have to say!" Kitty was halfway out of her chair when she felt a large firm hand lightly clamp her forearm. Cathcart's pale blue eyes flashed her a gentle warning, but Kitty ignored it. "Don't you see? Daddy is *dead* because we were all too afraid to open our mouths."

"He's dead because of me." Her mother's pinched mouth began to tremble. "No one else is responsible."

"*Why,* Mother? Why did you do it?"

Kitty strained forward, catching the faint sour smell of her mother's sweat. Was her mother frightened for herself . . . or of what she might have to reveal? Kitty, nearly weeping with frustration, wished suddenly that Sean were here. In his world, survival was about watching your back, looking to see what was around the next corner. In hers, family honor came first—even if it killed you.

And then a small choked cry caused the hair on Kitty's neck to stand on end. She watched her mother bring her manacled hands to her face, and in a queer muffled voice, cry, "I needed to stop it from going any further."

Kitty cringed inside, realizing that a part of her was as terrified of the truth as her mother. At the same time, she felt a quickening of excitement. Finally, finally, they were getting somewhere. Even if it was only a tiny crack in the door. All she had to do was keep that door open, keep her mother talking . . .

"It must have hurt," she consoled softly.

Mother shook her head. "Not me. I was used to it. All those years . . ." She looked off into the distance, suddenly lost in thought. When her gaze returned to Kitty, eyes that had been dead glowed with sudden fervid passion. "This was different. It was . . . *evil.*"

Kitty, her heart racing, seized the opportunity to pounce. Breathlessly, she said, "You know who she was, don't you? The woman Daddy was seeing before he died."

But the fire that had flared in her mother was just as quickly extinguished. She stared back at Kitty without comprehension, her vacant eyes fixed on people long gone and events since passed.

Even so, Kitty pressed on, frantic. "Mother, please. Tell me who she is. That's all I ask."

Cathcart chose this moment to interject, "It's crucial that we find this woman before the DA gets to her." In the grainy gray light, his wavy hair made Kitty think of old family silver rubbed to a fine sheen. When her mother didn't respond, he urged, "Lydia, all along you've insisted on telling the truth. Now let's get the *whole* truth told."

After an interminable silence, Kitty's mother shook herself from her stupor and recalled in a low, dreamy voice, "I knew . . . deep down. About Beryl. Funny, isn't it? Something that happened more than thirty years ago, and I remember like it was yesterday. In here, there's lots of time to remember. All I *do* is remember."

"Mother, we are not talking about something from thirty years ago," Kitty shot back, feeling as if she were being sandbagged. "We need to know about *now*."

"Oh, Kitty." Her mother shook her head in exasperation, as if Kitty were a child. "You girls, all you see is what's in front of you. You can't know what it was like in my day, the expectations we had about marriage. Even if I'd wanted to . . . and it never crossed my mind, believe me . . . people didn't get divorced back then. Not *nice* people."

"Beryl Chapman did," Kitty reminded her.

"How could I forget? It was all anyone talked about for months. And if there were rumors . . . well, I didn't have to listen, did I?" Mother straightened, seeming to pull about her the tattered remnants of her dignity. "I was raised to believe a lady rises above such things."

"So you never confronted either of them—Daddy *or* Beryl?"

"What would have been the point?" Her mother's expression darkened suddenly, and she seemed to be struggling with herself, her mouth opening and closing in broken little exhalations. Then, as if coming to a decision, her face smoothed over again. It occurred to Kitty, not for the first time, *She loved him. Right up to the very end.*

"Maybe if you had, none of this would have happened!" she cried nonetheless.

Her mother cupped a hand over her eyes, as if to shield them from sudden bright light. "No more. I've said enough."

"You haven't *told* me anything!"

But her mother wasn't listening. She rose abruptly— a prisoner in a county-issued orange jumpsuit who nonetheless retained the gracious air of someone excusing herself from the dinner table. "Talk to Alex," she said with a parting glance over her shoulder, a glance so fraught with a mixture of pain and love and longing it tore at Kitty's heart. "She knows it all. She's the only one who can tell you what you want to know."

Instead of heading straight home, Kitty took the long way around, down Kingston Avenue, where she stopped at a white-shingled cottage trimmed in dark green, with a sign out front that read, SHORELINE REALTY, LEADERS IN EXCLUSIVE COASTAL PROPERTIES SINCE 1961. But Alex wasn't at her desk. Not only that, no one had seen her in days. A skinny blond woman in suede slacks observed with a brittle laugh, "If she's out showing properties, there must be more on the market than *I* know about."

Kitty thanked her and left. Her sister *had* been working harder than usual these days. Whenever Kitty or Daphne called her at home, Alex was never around. She hadn't returned any of their messages either. Was she purposely avoiding them?

Haunted by her mother's words, Kitty's thoughts lingered on Alex as she drove home. When they were little, her sister had *worshiped* their father, trotting after him everywhere like a puppy. When she was older, it was Daddy who seemed to seek Alex out. They'd go for a drive or a long after-dinner walk. Kitty had been too young at the time to understand it, but she'd sensed something strange about their closeness. Almost as if they'd been . . . *conspirators*. She shuddered now as she turned into her driveway.

Walking into the house, the last person she expected to find, perched on a stepladder in the front room was Sean. He was in the midst of dismantling the old brass ceiling fixture, overseen by Josie Hendriks, leaning into her cane as she peered upward like an inquisitive parrot. He grinned down at Kitty, and for a moment, in his torn jeans and oversize T-shirt, he looked like a kid. Then she took note of the lean, taut muscles in his suntanned arms and neck, the kind that are forged only one way: through a man's tough manual labor.

"One of the bulbs kept flickering even after I changed it. Mrs. Hendricks was scared you'd have a fire on your hands," he explained, brandishing a screwdriver.

"Faulty wiring was what burned down the old schoolhouse," Josie added with a sage nod, thumping her cane against the floor for emphasis. Her wiry gray hair, coiled haphazardly atop her head, reminded Kitty of a lopsided bird's nest. She refrained from pointing out that the fire that had claimed the original building where Miramonte Elementary now stood had occurred in 1955.

At that moment, Willa, in bib overalls and ruffled peasant blouse—like a larger and somewhat comical version of little Jennie—trundled out of the kitchen carrying a tray of tea and cookies for Serena Featherstone, who sat at a table near the window with her nose buried in a paperback novel. Willa glanced down at the cookies with a sheepish smile, color rising in her plump cheeks. "They're chocolate chip, from the recipe on the back of the bag. We ran out of what was in the freezer. I didn't think you'd mind."

Kitty merely smiled, too choked up to speak. Earlier, on her way downtown to visit her mother, she'd wondered what on earth she could have been thinking—officially reopening before she'd had time to properly stock the pantry even. She was still picking up pieces of her family's wreckage. How would she cope with a sudden flood of customers?

Instead, she'd discovered something wonderful: she wasn't alone in all this. At a time when one more apple would have tipped over her cart, she had friends and family picking up the slack. Now she could only stand there, smiling up at Sean like an idiot at the moon.

"A fire?" She gave a shaky laugh. "Then I'd know for sure, wouldn't I? That there's a biblical curse on my family."

"Nothing a new fuse won't fix," responded Josie, who on top of being arthritic was hard of hearing.

Even Sean chuckled. He located the frayed wire, wrapping it in electrical tape before climbing down to where Kitty's dog stood poised to slather him with kisses. Sean dropped to his haunches to roughhouse with Rommie while Kitty waited, a pulse beating in her throat, for the inevitable moment when they could no longer avoid making eye contact. If there was a threat of fire, she thought, it wasn't from some loose wire or blown fuse.

Then, as always when she was with Sean, her thoughts turned to Heather's baby. Was Heather any closer to making a decision? she wondered. Later, when they were alone, she would ask Sean. She'd insist, too, that they stop sneaking around . . . before Heather found out on her own. Once everything was out in the open, Sean's sister might even start to see her not as the enemy, but as someone who could be a friend.

Kitty's pulse quickened as she thought about the money she'd put aside—her nest egg for the baby she'd hoped to adopt. With some careful investing, she'd so far managed to save a little over twenty thousand. Yet, she would hand it all over to Sean's sister in a heartbeat, every cent. The only thing holding her back was her fear that Heather might think of it as a bribe.

Kitty watched Sean straighten, rocking onto the balls of his feet as if poised for flight. His dark eyes searched her face, and he seemed to be waiting for her to make a move.

Kitty placed a hand on his arm and felt the heat that seemed to rise from him like sun-warmed resin. "Thanks," she said softly. "You didn't have to do that."

He shrugged. "No big deal."

Kitty was suddenly and acutely aware of everyone looking at them. Josie's head was cocked in bright interest, and Willa wore a knowing smile. At the table in the window, Serena Featherstone's dark gypsy eyes peered curiously over her paperback novel, something by D. H. Lawrence.

The awkward moment spun out, then Josie piped innocently, "I'm sure this nice young man could use something cold to drink. And while you're in the kitchen, dear, I wouldn't say no to a cup of tea."

Kitty flushed, and started toward the kitchen. She

wasn't aware that Sean was following her until she'd stepped through the doorway and felt him seize her from behind. She whirled about, conscious of their being seen. But as if he'd read her mind, he pushed the door shut with the heel of a tar-stained boot before muffling her tiny cry of protest with his mouth. She felt a flicker of alarm nonetheless.

"Someone could come in," she whispered, grabbing his wrist and pulling him into the pantry—the only spot that afforded any privacy.

In the close, fragrant semidarkness, she kissed him back. Sean pressed against her, and she could feel the edge of a shelf biting into the small of her back. She could feel him, too—every ridge and snap of his jeans through the flimsy cotton of her drawstring trousers. Overhead, a row of Mason jars winked dully in the half-light, and she caught the lambent gleam of peaches floating in syrup.

He was *hers.* Her lover. Whose warm breath against her lips was enough to make her whole body open like a morning glory to sunlight. Even now, with voices in the next room, she could feel herself unfurling, her innermost recesses parting to let down a trickle of moisture.

"I missed you," he whispered into her hair. "Last couple of nights—Christ, I thought I'd go crazy." He pushed his hands up under her cotton sweater, underneath which she was braless, his thumbs lightly circling her nipples.

Kitty moaned, arching with pleasure as several sensations converged into a single, exquisite point—his calluses catching on her taut skin in tiny delicious pinpricks, the pantry's aromatic closeness, the curved warmth of jars stroking her back.

"I missed you, too, but it wouldn't have been a good idea for you to come. Not with my brother-in-law around," she whispered back. "He's gone now, thank God."

"Tonight then, or I *will* go crazy: bare-assed, baying at the moon psycho." He grinned—a flash of white teeth in the darkness.

"Tonight," she whispered back. Suddenly, she couldn't wait.

"We're going to take it slow this time," he promised.

Kitty laughed softly. "You say that every time." Usually, Sean was inside her almost as soon as he had his boots unlaced. The first time. Then minutes later, he'd be ready all over again. And they'd take it slower, like an underwater ballet, each movement and sensation melting into the next. The thought of it now caused Kitty's legs to grow weak.

"I'm not unbuttoning my shirt until you're stark naked," he told her.

"Then what?"

"You get to undress me." He dropped his head to run the tip of his tongue along her neck.

Kitty closed her eyes and allowed herself to savor the moment. Sean's heat, his outdoorsy scent, mingling now with the fragrance of nutmeg and cloves, almonds and walnuts, dried apples gone winy with age. She felt as if the earth had swallowed them whole, like a seed that would sink its roots into rich soil and grow into something that one day would be harvested. All they'd need was a little luck . . . and a lot of honesty.

"Sean, we have to talk."

"I can think of better things to do." He nuzzled her hair, and she could feel his warm breath along her scalp like the delicious sensation of sinking into her deep claw-footed tub upstairs.

"I mean about Heather."

He pulled back to eye her warily. "I thought we decided."

"*You* decided," she reminded him.

"Look, this isn't such a great time . . ."

"There *is* no great time." Kitty folded her arms over her chest. "Sean, even if she decides to keep the baby, she has a right to know about us."

But Sean was looking at her in a way she didn't like. A brief silence fell, then he let out a ragged breath. "Look, Kitty, something's come up."

"What?" A buzzing began in Kitty's ears, faint and

ominous, like insects swarming outside under the eaves—the nasty, biting kind.

"Heather," he said. "She's made up her mind about the baby. I just found out. She's giving it to some yuppie couple she met through an ad in the paper. They're from Kansas or Minnesota . . . one of those in-between states. I can't remember which."

Kitty was flooded with a curious mixture of resignation and fierce disappointment. The rich embryonic glow of peaches and apricots floating behind glass faded to a uniform sepia. She felt not only light-headed but very nearly weightless, as if every drop of blood had been drained from her. *I should have known. I should have expected this. Who* wouldn't *choose a nice couple from the Midwest?*

And yet . . .

It didn't stop the terrible sense of loss that ripped through her as she realized the aching void inside her would never be filled.

"I see." Kitty was amazed at how calm she sounded. "Is her mind made up then?"

Sean eyed her cautiously, as if not quite sure whether to take her apparent calm at face value. "Seems to be. But maybe it's for the best. I mean, think of it—living in the same town as your kid, never knowing when you might run into him."

"Is that the only reason?"

Sean shifted awkwardly and said, "Would things have turned out differently if your mom wasn't splashed all over every newspaper? Yeah, maybe. But we'll never know for sure, will we?" He sounded angry—the kind of anger that comes not from a lack of caring . . . but from caring *too* much.

"No. I suppose not." Kitty sagged back against the shelves.

"There are other kids you can adopt, aren't there?" he asked.

Sean's expression was so earnest Kitty didn't have the heart to point out that she *had* looked into every possibility. Besides, what did he know of this kind of heartache? *No more than I do of what* he's *endured.* She began to laugh weakly.

She laughed until she could no longer stand and had to sink down onto the floor amid sacks of bulk flour and sugar, where she buried her head in her hands, and her laughter turned to gasping sobs . . . until Sean, after what seemed like hours, gave up trying to console her, and she heard the pantry door squeal open on hinges she'd been meaning to oil, and which poor childless Josie Hendricks had yet to seize upon.

Chapter 12

The alarm on Alex's clock radio was set for six a.m. Every Saturday and Sunday, without fail, she was ushered awake at exactly the same time as on weekdays by the ripe cushiony strains of KWST Lite FM. Rising early gave her a jump start on the day, she liked to boast—a cup of coffee and the *Mirror*'s headlines under her belt before the rest of the world had rubbed the sleep from its eyes.

The truth was she longed to sleep in but was worried it might prove habit forming. And she simply couldn't afford to slack off. An hour might make the difference between a deal that was clinched and one that slipped through her fingers. Another thing: deep down, she rationalized that she was narrowing the odds of being snatched awake by something other than her alarm. An intruder, say. Or what insurance companies so charmingly referred to in fine print as "an act of God"—like an earthquake, or landslide. Sleep was the only time she was utterly defenseless . . . when anything, anything at all, could sneak up like a mean little boy to poke a stick at her.

At five thirty-eight on the Saturday morning following her unfortunate lapse of the week before (which had resulted in a hangover necessitating a dozen Tylenols and half a bottle of Pepto-Bismal just to get through the day), when she was startled awake by agitated cries from downstairs, Alex's first barely formed thought was: *I knew it.* She hadn't the vaguest idea why Nina and Lori were yelling for her, merely that the other shoe—whatever it was—had finally dropped.

She tumbled out of bed, her heart knocking in her

chest and her mouth filled with an unpleasant medicinal taste, like cotton balls dipped in rubbing alcohol. Glancing out the window that overlooked her back yard, she saw that it was still dark, with only the barest hint of a blush above the rooftops. Inside, it was even darker, and she began to shiver as she groped for the light switch. The Weather Channel had predicted sunny skies for the entire weekend—unbelievably, they were coming up on the last week of May, with summer just around the corner—but for Alex it might have been the dead of winter.

Downstairs in the living room, Nina and Lori, wearing identical light-blue Pacific Rim T-shirts that bagged down around their knees, were peering anxiously out the front window. The sodium arc lamps along the curb were still on, Alex saw, their bluish glare blending with the lightening sky to coax thin, sparse shadows from the junipers and boxwood dotting her newly seeded lawn.

"Mom!" Nina cried. "Somebody's stealing your car!"

That's when Alex saw it—the dark figure of a man pulling away from the shadows of the tall fence that separated her driveway from the one next door. But he didn't seem in any way fearful of getting caught. In horror, she watched him amble around to the rear end of her BMW and stoop to feel under the bumper. A big man from the looks of it, who appeared in no particular hurry.

Alex froze, invisible fingers gripping her throat.

"Quick, *do* something!" Lori grabbed Alex's sleeve, her blue eyes wide and panicky, her long blond hair tangled with sleep. In that instant, her daughter might have been Alice fleeing the Red Queen. *Curiouser and curiouser . . . yes, that about sums it up,* Alex thought as her mind slipped gears in an odd, free-associative tumble. She wondered if she might still be dreaming. It was Lori's next words that brought it all into sudden, jarring context. "Mom, look, he's chaining it to his tow truck!"

"Duh, car thieves don't use tow trucks, you dork," Nina shot back. Her dark eyes—so like her father's—were full of bewilderment, coupled with a dark gleam of suspicion. "We were asleep, and we heard a noise," she explained. "It sounded like a chain rattling. Mom, what's going on?"

To Alex, the answer was now painfully obvious: her car was being repossessed. And yet for a frantic moment she almost wished it was a theft. Then she could call the police, scream for help, *something*.

Instead, she could only stand here as if buried to her knees in wet sand, shame rising up around her in a cold relentless tide. Alex had done her best to keep it from the girls, how close to the edge they'd been living, but this was more than even *she* could cover up.

She felt the blood drain from her head with a suddenness that left her faint. Fumbling for something to anchor her, she seized hold of a bronze finial in the shape of an elephant's ear on the floor lamp she'd paid too much for at Pier 1 Imports, just last summer. *Oh God, what now?* Every credit card was maxed out. Even her checking account was close to being overdrawn. And she'd *die* before revealing to Jim just how bad things were.

Might as well face it: she had no one to turn to.

Nowhere to run . . . nowhere to hide.

The room dissolved into a grainy blur, and she became aware of a high shrill whine in her head, like that of a sawmill somewhere off in the distance. As if through layers of foam baffling, she heard Lori calling her name.

"Mom? *Mom!*"

The panic in her daughter's voice was like an electrical current traveling up through the lamp to galvanize Alex into action. She stepped back to rub her eyes, and the gray blur around her began to sharpen into focus. The whining in her head faded to a low hum.

However badly she'd failed her daughters, she reminded herself, she was still their mother. They depended on her. She couldn't let them down. Not this time. Not without a fight.

Alex had never been able to picture someone pulling himself up by the boot straps, as the old saying went, but that's exactly how she felt now—as if she were being physically lifted; yet, at the same time, *she* was the one doing the lifting. Straightening, she marched over to the front door, pausing only long enough in front of the mirrored hall stand to be reminded that she was still dressed in her nightgown.

She grabbed the first thing she saw, off the nearest hook—a red vinyl rain slicker. *What the well-dressed executive woman wears in a shit storm.* Alex gave a dry snort of derision, not stopping to think, until she'd thrown it on and stepped outside, that it would only make her stand out more. In her bare feet, picking her way across the yard, she was certain she stuck out like a traffic light. She prayed none of her neighbors were early risers.

Against a pale sky, the watery pink of blood-tinged gauze, the man looping a chain to the rear axle of her BMW cast a long curved shadow. Hearing the hollow rattle of metal on metal that rang out like machine-gun fire in the predawn stillness, she winced. Expertly, he hooked the chain to the winch on the tow truck idling behind her car. As he straightened and turned toward her, she noticed he was chewing on something, his jaws working in a lazy circular rhythm. *Please let it be gum,* she thought. *If it's tobacco, I'll be sick to my stomach, I just know it.*

He cast a disinterested glance at her, as if she were a mere passerby, and went back to fiddling with the chain. Alex opened her mouth to protest . . . but no words came. It felt as if the chain were wrapped around her throat instead. She just stood there, struggling to find her voice while thinking of the ludicrous picture she must make, standing in the driveway in her bare feet and red vinyl slicker, with her hair probably standing on end. *He must think I'm insane,* she thought. And for a moment, she felt certain she *had* lost her mind.

Then the man walked over to his truck and leaned inside to push something on the dash. With a grinding thunk the winch began its ascent . . . and sanity reasserted itself. She stepped forward, tightening the belt on her slicker as if to bolster herself.

"This is private property," Alex informed him. "If you don't unhook that thing from my car this very instant,

I'm calling the police." She aimed for an outraged tone, but her voice was trembling too hard.

The burly man paused to eye her up and down—dispassionately, as if she herself were soon to be repossessed. "You go ahead and do that, ma'am. I got all the paperwork right here. This vehicle is now officially in the possession of Fog City Motors." He reached into the pocket of his canvas jacket, pulling out a wad of crinkly blue and pink duplicates, all of it perfectly legal, no doubt.

Cold seeped up through the soles of Alex's feet, but her face felt as if it were on fire. Oh God, how would she *live* through this? Being treated as if she were no better than trailer trash. What if her neighbors should happen to glance out their windows? What would they think?

What, she wondered, *would Daddy have thought?*

More important, what would her father have *done?* He'd have fought back, she told herself. He wouldn't have stood here like some mealymouthed idiot afraid to speak out because the neighbors might hear.

She opened her mouth to remind this . . . this *Bluto* . . . just who he was dealing with here, but the voice that emerged was thin and cracked. To her horrified dismay, she found herself begging, "Please, don't do this. I'll straighten it out with Mr. DeAngelis. Give me an hour, just one lousy *hour* . . . that's all I ask." She swallowed hard and heard a dry clicking sound in her ears. "I have kids. I won't have any way of getting to work."

He shot her a coolly unsympathetic look, but she'd gotten his attention. He stopped chewing and shifted the wad of gum—yes, that's what it was—to his cheek. "Bus stop is right down the street," he said.

"You don't understand. I'm a real estate agent."

He gave a low rumble of laughter. "Yeah? Well, it don't look like the house business is exactly booming. You might want to think about a career change."

Alex wanted to crumple the sheaf of papers in her hand and shove it down his throat. Give him something to *really* chew on. But what would it accomplish? *You're wasting your time with this guy,* she thought, her eyes filling with tears of hot impotent rage.

It wasn't until Bluto had hoisted himself into the cab of his truck that Alex darted over and hopped nimbly onto the running board, grabbing hold of the open door to keep from losing her balance. He wasn't even all the way inside yet, and one of her bare feet brushed up against the grimy toe of his work boot. It flashed through her mind that they must make an incredibly ridiculous picture: Bluto perched high in the cab with one meaty leg dangling over the edge of the seat, and she like some sort of supplicant at the foot of a throne.

"Just five minutes," she pleaded. "Give me five minutes to make a phone call. That isn't too much to ask, is it?"

The night was in its last throes. Brushstrokes of orange and gold had appeared on the horizon, and in the pale morning light, she saw that the man staring down at her wasn't out to get her. His weary expression was simply that of a working stiff whose only interest was getting to where he could wrap his red-knuckled paw around a mug of coffee.

"Give me one good reason why I should," he growled.

"Do you have kids?" she asked in desperation.

He nodded, his eyes showing the first flicker of humanity she'd seen so far. "Little boy. Just turned two."

"I have twin girls. They go to Muir High." She glanced over her shoulder and saw the blurred white faces of her daughters in the window with their noses pressed to the glass. Her heart felt as if it were being squeezed. "If this were to get out . . . well, you know how cruel kids that age can be."

He remained motionless, his blank stare unnerving— like a mean drunk lying in wait to heckle a floundering nightclub act.

Alex was shivering but forced herself to speak calmly. "I have Mr. DeAngelis's home number. I'll call him now, while you wait. I'm sure we can work something out. Please," she added in a whisper. "For my girls."

Bluto heaved a sigh. "Okay, but I'm warning you. Mr. DeAngelis don't like being bothered at home." He peered suspiciously at her. "How'd you get his number, anyway?"

"His house. I was the broker for it." Alex managed a small tight smile as she stepped down off the running board. The cold rising off the concrete driveway slithered about her ankles and crept in under her slicker. It had been only last summer, but that day in the lawyer's office—the closing for the DeAngelises' tidy Cape Cod in Pasoverde Estates—seemed like a hundred years ago.

She caught Bluto eyeing her curiously and it suddenly occurred to Alex he might recognize her from the newspapers. She broke out in a cold sweat. Christ. That was the last thing she needed right now. Before he could get a closer look and maybe change his mind, she spun on her heel, calling breathlessly over her shoulder, "Five minutes. I promise."

Back inside, she felt a little steadier, but her heart was pounding hard enough to crack a rib. Could she pull this off? She *had* to. *Honey, you could sell ice cubes to an Eskimo*—idle praise from a long-ago client, but she clutched at it now. The trick was to appear confident, in control. She'd ask for twenty-four hours, no more. It would sound definite. She'd worry later about where she was going to drum up the four thousand dollars in back payments.

"Mom, he's still out there! Why isn't he leaving?" Lori tagged after her as Alex dashed over to the remote phone on the end table by the sofa. Her daughter sounded on the verge of tears, like a little kid wanting to be told there really *is* a Santa Claus. Nina must have shared her suspicions with Lori.

"Don't worry, honey. I'll explain everything as soon as I'm off the phone," Alex assured her breathlessly as she began punching in Steve DeAngelis's number, which she'd had the good sense to enter into her Sharp Wizard.

It rang four times before a man's groggy voice answered, "Lo. Whossit?"

DeAngelis, and she'd clearly woken him from a sound sleep. *Oh, God,* she thought, *Talk about getting off to a good start.* He'd bite her head off when he found out why she was calling . . . and it wouldn't be the first time.

She recalled that twice, when the seller balked during the negotiations for his house, DeAngelis had taken it out on her.

A tough customer, that's how she'd have described the guy. In every sense of the word. A Bronx native who some years ago had migrated to California, bringing his New Yorkese along for the ride.

She glanced from Lori to Nina, who were seated stiffly on the sofa in front of the TV. The look of cool reproach Nina leveled at her from across the room was like an oar splashing down amid the waves of panic rippling through Alex. Though it frightened her to think that at least one of her daughters might be on to her, it helped steady her, too.

"Steve? Hi. It's Alex Cardoza. Sorry to call so early, but I'm in a bit of a bind here." She struck a businesslike tone, as if this were nothing more than a minor problem between two colleagues.

"Who?" the voice growled.

Pockets of sweat were forming in the folds and creases of the vinyl slicker, but she forced herself to speak calmly. "Alex Cardoza," she repeated. "The realtor who sold you your house? I also happen to lease a car from Fog City Motors, a '98 BMW."

"Oh, yeah. Right." He yawned, asking none too kindly, "What's so important you gotta call me at home at—" he paused, and she could hear him fumbling about, then the faint click of a bedside lamp switching on. "Jesus," he swore. "It's frigging quarter past six. You couldn't wait 'til office hours?"

Alex's heart was pounding, each thud like a dull blow to her temples. She licked lips that felt dry as the cotton stuffing she could see poking from a tiny tear in one of the couch cushions.

"Steve, my dad passed away last month," she told him. "This isn't a vote for sympathy, believe me. Just an explanation for why I've fallen a bit behind on my payments." She closed her eyes tightly. "Now the thing is, there's this gentleman outside with a tow truck who says he works for you. I'm sure it's just an oversight in the accounting department. I told him *you* wouldn't repossess my car without so much as a courtesy call. Not the Steve DeAngelis I know."

There was a long silence in which she could hear him breathing heavily into the phone. Finally, he said, "You've got one helluva nerve, lady."

Incredibly, despite the gruffness of his tone she caught a note of admiration. Much as he might be disgusted with her, DeAngelis, who'd come up the hard way, could obviously relate to someone with the balls to sweet-talk him at six-fifteen in the morning.

"I know it's early," Alex apologized again. "But I'm afraid this just couldn't wait."

"Shit," he swore, pulling the phone away from his mouth to murmur, presumably to his wife, "It's okay, cookie. Go back to sleep. This'll only take a minute."

"How . . . how's everything with the house?" Alex inquired politely before he could bark at her again, or worse, hang up.

"Great, just great," he said. "Now, look . . ."

"I can have the money to you by the close of business today," she hastened to interject.

But DeAngelis went on as if he hadn't heard. "Let's get one thing straight. This problem you're having? Whatever it is, it's *yours* not mine. *Capiche?*" He waited a beat before continuing, as if to let his words sink in. "Now, because I'm a nice guy, but mainly because my wife here, who's been up all night with our youngest, could use the extra sleep, I'm gonna cut you some slack. I don't know how far behind you are, Ms. Cardoza, but it must be plenty. The boys in accounting don't send Eddie out to collect on nickel-and-dime balances. So listen up good. We close at six. Have the money on my desk by five. Now put Eddie on, so I can get off this friggin' phone and let Nancy get some sleep."

Rivulets of sweat were trickling from her armpits to paste her nightgown against her rib cage, but Alex forced herself to answer sweetly, "Thanks, Steve. I really appreciate this."

Then she was dashing back outside, where Eddie-Bluto was waiting in the cab of his tow truck, drumming impatiently on the steering wheel. When she handed him the phone, he listened for a moment before answering in a jocular tone she wouldn't have believed him capable of. "No problem. You got it, boss."

Moments later, the winch was grinding, and he was unhooking her BMW from the chain. But not until she had watched him back out of the driveway and roar off down the street did she release a shuddering sigh.

Back inside, Alex had to take several deep breaths before she felt steady enough to speak. "Everything's okay. All taken care of," she assured the twins. "Why don't we go in the kitchen and make ourselves some hot cocoa? I don't know about you, but I could sure use something to warm me up."

Lori, curled on the sofa, turned a plaintive face up at her. "Was it some kind of mistake?" she wanted to know. "Like that time Daddy's check got lost in the mail?"

"Something like that." Alex opened her mouth to add that it was nothing to worry about. She'd have the whole thing straightened out by this afternoon. Then she once again caught Nina's reproachful expression and felt something inside her shrivel. *You're no better than Mother,* a voice admonished. *Pretending everything is hunky-dory when it clearly is anything but.* Swallowing hard, she forced herself to admit, "The truth is, I . . . I've gotten behind on some of our household payments. Quite a bit behind, as a matter of fact. But I'm working on getting it together. The main thing is, I don't want either of you to worry. One way or another, I promise I'll take care of it."

The silence that followed her words seemed to hang over the room like a cloud, then slowly Lori unfolded her long legs and stood up to hug her. After a minute, she was joined by Nina, who came up behind them to twine her arms about her sister's, which were tightly clasped around their mother's waist.

"I know you'll take care of it, Mom. You always do." With her face pressed against Alex's shoulder, Nina's voice was muffled, and Alex was reminded of when the girls were babies being toted around papooselike, in their carriers. Her throat tightened.

"Do I?" she asked in a small choked voice.

"I second the motion," Lori said.

Alex drew back to wipe her eyes. "In that case, I say we adjourn to the kitchen for that cocoa."

She ought to be tearing her hair out, she knew. The reprieve she'd gotten was only a stopgap. If she didn't scrape up that money somehow, by tomorrow the twins would be phoning friends to bum rides to school, and she . . . well, she might as well kiss her job good-bye. But instead of panicking, she felt a strange peace stealing over her. For the moment at least, everything she needed was right here in front of her.

Alex was in the kitchen with the twins, stirring a packet of Swiss Miss into a mug of steaming water, when the phone rang.

"Hi," Kitty's voice greeted her, annoyingly chipper as always. "Did I wake you?"

Alex had to bite her lip to keep from laughing out loud at just *how* wide-awake she was. But all she said was, "Hardly. The girls and I have been up for a while." It was the one thing she and Kitty had in common— both were early risers.

"Good. Because I was afraid if I waited, I'd miss you." Kitty hesitated before asking, "Alex, why haven't you returned any of my calls? Is something wrong?"

What could possibly be wrong? Alex wanted to snap. *Daddy's dead, Mother's behind bars, and I'm on the brink of financial ruin . . . but other than that, things are just peachy.*

"I've been busy, that's all," she said, a note of defensiveness creeping into her voice.

"Well, I was just wondering." Kitty sounded dubious. "Is this about Mother?"

"Does everything have to have an ulterior motive? I just called to see how you're doing." Softening, Kitty added, "And to invite you and the girls over."

"What's the occasion?" Alex reached into the box for another packet of Swiss Miss.

"None, really," her sister said. "I just thought it'd be nice if you stopped by for breakfast. You haven't seen

Daphne's kids yet, and they're eager to visit with you and the girls."

Alex glanced at the twins. Lori sat hunched over the table blowing on her cocoa while Nina stood at the counter shaking cornflakes into a bowl. "The girls won't be able to make it. Jim's picking them up at nine." Then she surprised herself by adding, "But I could probably come, just for an hour or so."

It was true that in the last month she'd been avoiding her sisters. But even if she'd been dying to see them, it should be the last thing on today's agenda. Far more pressing was the question of how she was going to come up with four thousand dollars by this afternoon.

She could have asked to borrow the money from her sisters, she supposed. But what would be the point? Kitty had to be operating on a wing and a prayer with every penny going back into the business. And Daphne? Three guesses as to who held the purse strings in *that* marriage.

"Great. I'll make Nana's famous blueberry waffles." Kitty's voice seemed to come from a distance. "Remember how you used to love those when we were kids?"

"Before I started putting on weight, you mean." Alex laughed to cover a sudden spasm of nervousness.

Kitty's reminding her of their childhood might very well be innocent, but even so, Alex had the distinctly uncomfortable feeling she was being set up. Whatever was waiting for her over at her sister's house, she suspected the main attraction wasn't going to be blueberry waffles.

She arrived just shy of eight-thirty, with the sun still hovering atop the canopy of trees shading Kitty's street and the clanking of the garbage truck faintly audible in the distance, surprised to find her sister out back, pruning the honeysuckle. Its vines covered most of the boxwood hedge that separated her sister's property from the one next door, cascading as fragrantly as spilled perfume onto the grass below. As Alex walked over to greet her, Kitty waved a pair of green-stained secateurs.

"I didn't expect you so soon," she said, as if mildly relieved that Alex had shown up at all.

"And *I* expected to find you in the kitchen, slaving away." Alex slipped off her loafers—J. P. Tod, in a butter yellow that would showcase the slightest grass stain—and hooked them with her thumb.

"Everything's ready. Daphne's just setting the table. Have a seat."

Kitty gestured toward an aluminum lawn chair on the grass a few yards away. In soft cotton trousers and a loose top the color of cinnamon, her springy hair clipped back with a barrette, she looked exactly as she had when she was fourteen. It was only when her sister turned toward her, facing directly into the light, that Alex saw the faint grooves bracketing her mouth and the freckles standing out against skin more pale now than creamy. Only her smile was exactly the same. Sweet and welcoming, it seemed to float upward, catching in the net of fine lines radiating from the corners of her vivid blue eyes.

Alex felt as if she'd wandered in from the cold to find a fire warming her hearth. At that moment she wanted nothing more than to sink to her knees in the soft grass and drink in the scent of honeysuckle. She remembered when she and her sisters were kids, and they used to suck on the blossoms, eeking out the fleeting drop of sweetness contained in each one. How could she have lost so much of what was simple and good in life?

Her eyes filled with tears, and everything around her—the hedge, the dilapidated doghouse with its rusty chain snaking out to touch the twisted roots of the old loquat tree, the hammock slung from its stout branches—was suddenly haloed in brightness, as if she were looking through a prism.

Gratefully, she dropped into the lawn chair, feeling it settle into the loamy earth with her weight. "Sure you don't need any help with that?"

"Oh, I think I can manage."

Kitty went back to clipping, the secateurs in her hand making Alex think of a hungry beak. *Snap . . . snap . . . snap.* Under the golden sun setting fire to the treetops, Alex shuddered, reminded of all the debtors snapping at her heels—Fog City Motors the most pressing one of the moment. Where on earth was she going to get all that money? Four thousand dollars might as well be a million. And even if she could somehow scrape it up, what about the rest of what she owed?

With her stomach in knots, she struggled to make conversation. "How have you been?" She resisted the temptation to ask about their mother. It would've made her feel too guilty, and that was the last thing she needed right now.

"Okay. I'm managing." Kitty laughed a little, as if to suggest it was just the opposite, but Alex didn't press the matter.

"It must be a lot of extra work with Daphne's kids underfoot," she remarked casually.

Kitty turned to give her a perplexed look. "Oh no, the best part of all is having Kyle and Jennie here. If it weren't for them, I don't know that I could face . . ." she squinted suddenly, cupping a hand over her eyes as if to shade them from the sun.

Alex felt a pang of guilt for not having stopped by sooner to see her niece and nephew. "I should go through those boxes of old clothes in my storage closet," she said. "Some of them would probably fit Jennie."

"I'm sure Daph would appreciate it." Kitty brushed a gnat from one freckled cheek, but her gaze remained fixed on Alex.

Impaled by those unnervingly blue eyes, Alex felt herself begin to squirm. After a moment she was compelled to blurt, "I know, it's not what you *want*. You and Daphne would prefer it if I helped with Mother's case. But I just can't. I can't forgive her."

"I didn't ask you over to twist your arm." Kitty went back to her pruning. *Snip . . . snip . . . snip.* Strands of honeysuckle gathered in loose wreaths about her bare feet.

It was the first morning in months without fog, and the sun rode the sky like a cocky warrior strutting before the vanquished enemy. Leafy shade spangled the grass, and birds called to one another from the treetops. Yet Alex felt as if a storm were about to break. Alongside the garage, Kitty's big gray dog was furiously digging away. She imagined it to be the hole she had dug for herself, bit by bit, until it was now deep enough to bury her.

"Why *did* you invite me then?" she asked.

With a sigh, Kitty tucked the secateurs into a pocket of her trousers. Turning once more to face Alex, she said quietly, "I'm not asking you to do the right thing by Mother. That's between you and your conscience. But *I* could certainly use your help."

"What did you have in mind?" Alex asked, suddenly wary.

"Tell me what you know about Daddy's affairs."

Alex shivered, as if a cloud had passed over the sun. "What do you mean?"

Kitty shot her a disgusted look. "Come on, Alex. Don't play innocent with me."

Alex dropped her eyes, unable to meet the fire blazing in Kitty's. Had she known all along? Or was she merely guessing? Either way, it didn't matter. Softly, she cried, "Can't you leave it be? For God's sake, Kitty, he's *dead.*"

"But Mother isn't." Those eyes. They seemed to scorch her, like sunlight through the magnifying glass with which they'd once burned their names into scraps of wood. "Alex, if you know anything, anything at all that might help her, now is the time to tell it."

"Whatever mistakes Daddy might've made, he didn't deserve to be *killed* because of them!" Alex cried.

Under the bright blue sky, she felt absurdly cornered. Watching a magpie swoop down from a high branch to dive-bomb a cat slinking across the yard, she thought, *I've got to get away. Now. Before I say something I'll regret.*

"Just before he died, he was seeing one of the nurses at the hospital, that much I *do* know," Kitty pressed on. "But it would help if we could talk to this woman, find out what she knows. If Daddy had been planning on leaving Mother, that might have been what pushed her over the edge."

Alex tried not to let her surprise show. A nurse? Daddy hadn't mentioned any nurse. And as for his *leaving* Mother, that was . . . well, it was preposterous. "He didn't tell me everything," she replied stiffly.

A memory rushed in. Her father standing over her, his steely eyes seeming to pierce her to the very bone. *"You mustn't tell. Not ever. It would kill your mother if she ever found out."*

But it hadn't. It had killed Daddy instead.

She shook her head, as if to clear it. Through a low buzzing in her ears, she heard her sister say, "Apparently, he told you enough."

Something in Alex snapped, and she cried, "Who else would have understood? Anyway, it wasn't his fault. Mother . . . well, she loved him, I suppose, but not *that* way. What was he supposed to do?"

"Is that what he told you? That Mother wasn't interested in sex?" Kitty wore an expression so incredulous its impact was more powerful than any argument.

Angrily, Alex said, "Okay, so maybe he exaggerated a little. But it couldn't have been a total fabrication. Who would lie about a thing like that?"

"The kind of person," Kitty said, with deliberate emphasis on each word, "who would say such things to a young, impressionable girl, even if they *were* true."

Alex felt as if she'd stepped over some invisible ledge and was tumbling in a dizzying free fall. She'd never questioned Daddy; never once wondered if there might be another side to his story. She'd merely accepted it at face value—the wistful look in her father's eyes when he reminisced about his and Mother's courtship, and how everything had changed after Daphne was born.

But now a seed of doubt had been planted. It wasn't what Kitty was saying so much as the horrified expression on her face, as if Daddy had been some sort of monster.

Her stomach executed a slow twisting half gainer. "This . . . this nurse. What do you know about her?" she barely managed to croak.

"Not much," Kitty said. "Except she's younger than

he was—around our age. And she's missing a gold ear-ring." She smiled in grim amusement. "It seems our fa-ther was in the habit of sneaking off to motels. Guess he didn't realize the manager of the one up in Barranco was Willa's mom. After he checked out last time, she found an earring his girlfriend had left behind."

Alex's head spun. So many women. But Daddy had always been discreet, hadn't he? In spite of how it might have seemed, he had loved Mother.

"It's not what you think," she insisted. "He wasn't in love with any of those women. It was just . . . well, he had certain needs."

"And you bought that? Oh, Alex." Kitty sounded al-most pitying.

"You're just jealous!" Alex flung back. "Because I was his favorite, and you . . . you . . ."

"I was nobody's." Kitty shrugged. "If I cared at one time, I don't anymore. I made peace with all that a long time ago." She cocked her head, studying Alex with a curious expression on her pretty freckled face. "What I'm wondering now is why Daddy shared all his secrets with you. I mean, if he wasn't to blame . . . why the need to unburden himself?"

Alex buried her head in her hands, feeling as if she might be sick right here on the grass. "Stop it. Just *stop*."

She was aware of a sudden coolness, as if a shadow had fallen over her. When she looked up, Kitty was kneeling in front of her. "What is it, Alex? Is there something else you're not telling me?"

Her voice was so kind and forgiving that without stop-ping to think, Alex lurched forward into Kitty's arms—Kitty, from whom she'd always felt somewhat estranged but who now seemed to care very much about what be-came of her. She smelled faintly of honeysuckle and cinnamon . . . and, oh, everything that was good and pure and decent. Alex began to weep softly.

"I'm in trouble," Alex confided in a hoarse whisper. "In debt up to my eyeballs. Uncle Sam, Visa, Mas-tercard, Pacific Gas & Electric, you name it. This morn-ing, Fog City Motors almost repossessed my car. If I don't come up with four thousand dollars in cash by five

o'clock this afternoon, I'll be hoofing it from now on."
She paused to suck in a breath, but instead of the shame
she'd expected to feel, she was left with only a queer
sense of relief.

When she finally dragged her gaze up to meet Kitty's,
she saw that the expression her sister wore wasn't judg-
mental, nor was it pitying. Incredibly, Alex saw only
compassion. "Oh, Alex," Kitty said. "Why didn't you
come to me sooner?"

"What good would it have done?" Alex dabbed at
her eyes with the tail of her silk shirt, which had come
untucked from her jeans. Her mascara was running, and
the shirt would probably be ruined, but what did such
things matter anymore?

For a moment, her sister appeared lost in thought.
Kitty stared out over the hedge for what seemed the
longest time, her expression tinged with sadness. When
her gaze drifted back to Alex, she was smiling, but the
sense of melancholy remained. "I have some money
saved up," she said. "A little over twenty thousand. It's
yours. You can pay me back any time."

Alex felt a wild surge of joy . . . followed immediately
by the cold weight of conscience. She shook her head.
"No, Kitty, I couldn't do that. You might need it."

Kitty shook her head. "Maybe someday. Not right
now. And I'd feel better knowing it was doing some
good, at least."

A heavy layer of guilt settled over Alex. How could
she have believed Kitty didn't love her? And how could
she not have cherished this sister? It was as if everything
Alex had taken for granted all her life had been torn to
pieces, and now all the little scraps were being put together in a way that didn't fit. She didn't know what to
say. How to *act,* even.

In the quiet shelter of Kitty's yard, with birds chirping
overhead and the merry sounds of children drifting from
an open window of the house she'd thought too plain—
but which she now saw to be lovely—Alex had to mouth
the words silently several times before she could get
them out.

"Thank you," she whispered, bowing her head as if in prayer.

Blueberry waffles had never tasted so good. In fact, Alex couldn't remember the last time she'd eaten so much. At the table in Kitty's sunny kitchen, she felt the tight band around her chest ease. Daphne's children were even more adorable than last time, she thought, and so well behaved. Even Daphne seemed easier with herself, as if whatever burden she'd been carrying on her shoulders had lifted somewhat.

After the dishes had been cleared away, Kitty went to help Willa with the tables out front. "You wash, I'll dry," Daphne said, reaching for the dish towel.

"You *always* got to dry," Alex complained with a laugh. "I was the only girl in seventh grade with dishpan hands."

"At least it wasn't your fault when something broke."

"You never broke anything in your life!"

"Well, that just goes to show how well you know me."

Daphne, looking especially pretty with her hair tied back, wearing a pair of chinos and a striped cotton shirt, turned to look at her. The laughter in her eyes faded, and she reached out to place a hand on Alex's arm.

"Kitty told me about the trouble you're in," she said softly. "I want to help, too."

A painful flush crawled up Alex's neck and into her cheeks. Did the whole *world* have to know? Then, just as quickly, she realized Daphne wasn't judging her any more than Kitty had. They *all* had their troubles, Daphne's expression seemed to say.

Alex glanced over her shoulder at the children, still seated at the table, absorbed in coloring with crayons on big sheets of butcher paper. In a low voice, she said, "Thanks, Daph, but I can't. I swear, if I accept any more charity from either of you, I won't be able to live with myself." She dispelled the awkwardness of the moment with a weak laugh. "Isn't it bad enough you're both skinnier than me? And after those waffles, you can tack on an extra five pounds at least."

"This isn't charity," her sister said. Color rose in her cheeks. "I . . . well, let's just say that recently I've come into some money of my own. According to my editor, my next royalty check should be in the five-digit range." She didn't have to add at what cost to herself; it was written all over her face. "You'd be doing me a favor, honestly."

Alex had to look away so Daphne wouldn't see the tears in her eyes. Tears partly of shame, and partly of gratitude . . . but mostly from the sudden shaft of love that pierced her. "I . . . I don't know what to say."

But Daphne made it easy. She didn't argue, or persuade. She merely looked at Alex as if there could be no other choice, for either of them. Softly, she prompted, "Just say yes."

In Kitty's car, her two sisters followed Alex to the bank, where Kitty added to the check Daphne had made out by withdrawing four thousand in cash, with a promise of more to follow if need be. Thanking them both with a lump in her throat, Alex drove straight over to Fog City Motors. Armed with a crisp envelope, on which PERSONAL was underlined in felt pen, she sailed past the front desk and dropped it on the desk of a startled-looking Steve DeAngelis. Inside was a check for the full amount she owed.

"Don't worry. It's certified," she told him.

A dark-complected man in his late forties, with hairy wrists that peeked from the French cuffs of his monogrammed shirt, DeAngelis tossed the envelope to one side without opening it. "I trust you," he responded with a jovial bark of laughter, as if to say, *No hard feelings, eh?*

It wasn't until she was pushing her way back through the front door that Alex was brought up short by a sobering realization. Okay, her account was paid up—so what? By this time next month, she'd be back to square one: owing another fat lease payment on a car she couldn't afford.

Slowly, with a resolution akin to some invisible pres-

ence literally *forcing* her, she turned and retraced her
steps to the front desk. The frizzy-haired blond receptionist paused in the midst of sorting through a stack of
pink message slips to look up at her.

Alex cleared her throat. "Excuse me? I was just noticing those Toyotas out front. Is there someone I could
speak to about a trade-in on my BMW?"

The receptionist, who couldn't have been much older
than the twins, but whose flammable-looking platinum
perm belonged on a sixty-year-old, punched a button on
her phone. Minutes later, Alex found herself seated in
the office—well, cubicle, really—of an equally young
salesman who seemed only too happy to arrange for a
trade-in. The least expensive of their Toyotas, he informed her, was a "preowned" Tercel . . . as if "used"
were a four-letter word. Alex, biting back her disappointment, agreed to take it.

Her clients might not know the difference, she
thought, making a right turn off the lot in her newly
acquired three-year-old green Tercel, but *she* knew.
After the airborne glide of her BMW, this crappy little
car rode like a horse-drawn buggy. She felt like crying.

Then she thought of all the money she'd be saving
and how lucky she was to have *any* car. Best of all, she
had two caring sisters who, despite all the years of bick-
ering and resentment, had come through in the end.
Blood was thicker than water, after all.

The thought of her mother flickered briefly to life, but
she quickly extinguished it. *There's a limit to what you
can forgive,* she told herself. In the far reaches of her
mind, a voice whispered that if the situation had been
reversed, Mother would have found a way to forgive *her.*
But that voice was faint. And anyway, it didn't count
because there was no way in the world Alex would ever
have committed such a horrible crime.

As she drove along Thirty-third Street, with its car
lots and strip malls, she recalled her earlier conversation
with Kitty. According to her sister, Daddy had been
seeing someone when he died. *Why didn't he tell me?*
she wondered. Alex had known about his other mis-

tresses. What had been different about this one? *Had* he been in love with her?

Unless this woman came forward on her own, they would never know. Anyway, she had more urgent things to worry about right now. Like how she was going to get the IRS off her back. Kitty and Daphne had been generous, yes, but their loans weren't enough to cover *all* her debts.

Alex was driving past the Kmart Plaza when she was suddenly reminded that she hadn't gotten around to buying a present for Leanne's son. Tyler's birthday was the day after tomorrow, and though *he* surely wouldn't notice, Leanne would be touched that she'd remembered. It didn't have to be expensive, she told herself. Just something to let her friend know she was thinking of her.

She pulled into the parking lot and ten minutes later was standing in line at the checkout stand with a set of plastic stacking rings. A heart-shaped jar of bubble bath caught her eye—something the twins would like, she thought. Mentally, she was calculating whether or not she'd have enough left over from the fifteen dollars allotted for Tyler's present, when all at once she was struck by the irony of it—standing here in Kmart, wondering if she could afford to spend four dollars on bubble bath, when just months ago she wouldn't have hesitated to drop more than a hundred on a facial and manicure at Elizabeth Arden's.

It occurred to Alex then that she'd spent the better part of her life chasing success and all that came with it, starting out as president of the local Jaycees, at sixteen, then on to college, where she'd graduated magna cum laude. And during each of her ten years at Shoreline Realty, there had been not just the goal, but the driving *need* to win the annual prize—an engraved brass plaque—for the highest sales quota. The one year it had gone by a narrow margin to Marjorie Belknap, she'd felt like an utter failure.

Only somewhere along the line she'd lost her bearings. Healthy ambition had been replaced by a lust for more material rewards, and look where that had led. The

things that had seemed to matter so much no longer
held any value. Her house, her car, her closetful of designer suits—which she didn't even fully own—were like
foreign coins dug from the pocket of a coat that hadn't
been worn since last year's trip to Europe: quaint, but
useless.

Her sisters, it turned out, had had the right idea all
along. They'd put the emphasis on what counted: doing
what they loved best, merely for the sake of doing it.

And what about Daddy? Where did *he* fit into this
newly reassembled family portrait? Disturbing thoughts
teased at Alex's mind like fretful fingers prying at the
sealed flap of an unmarked envelope. Kitty had suggested there was more to their deep bond than what
appeared, that Daddy had *used* her somehow.

But to what end? Surely not to turn her against
Mother. He'd never spoken ill of her, not once. And if
he'd gained some peace of mind by confiding his secrets
to someone he could trust, what was so terrible about
that?

Even so, that sense of unease continued to nag at Alex
as she paid for the toy—at the last minute, she decided
against the bubble bath—and hurried back out to the
parking lot. Driving to Leanne's in her used Tercel—
preowned, my ass—she felt a headache burrow into one
temple and begin to fan out like a Rorschach inkblot.

Her entire head was pounding by the time she pulled
up in front of Leanne's. She parked the car just short of
the driveway, behind a huge oleander bush, where it
wouldn't be seen from the house. Leanne would want
to know what had happened to her Beamer. And Alex
felt too exhausted to explain.

*It's not that she wouldn't understand. It's just . . . well,
I'm not sure a part of her wouldn't secretly gloat.*

The thought seemed to come out of nowhere, startling
Alex. What could have prompted it? Nothing Leanne
had done or said, that was for sure. Leanne was her best
friend. It was just that lately . . .

*I've caught her looking at me a certain way. As if deep
down she might resent me just the tiniest bit.* And maybe
a part of Alex had always resented her, starting way

back when they were children. Because *she'd* had what Leanne wanted most. A real home, with a mother *and* a father, and . . . and . . .

A key. Somewhere along the line, she must have somehow gotten hold of a key to the house. Why else would she have stopped by that night?

Alex pushed the thought from her head. She was imagining things at her friend's expense. Poor Leanne. Between working the night shift at the hospital and taking care of Tyler during the day, she deserved all this armchair psychoanalyzing like a hole in the head. As Alex waited on the doorstep for Leanne to answer her knock, she resolved then and there to stop being such a paranoid idiot.

The door swung open, and Leanne stood blinking at her with puffy red-rimmed eyes. Her pale reddish hair was rumpled, and her clothes—jeans and a long-sleeved jersey—looked as if she'd slept in them. Had she been napping? *Maybe I should have phoned . . .*

"Oh God, Lee, I'm sorry. Did I get you up?" she rushed to apologize. "I just came by to drop this off." Alex thrust the shopping bag at Leanne. "It's for Tyler." The toy inside was marked for babies six to twelve months. It wasn't gift wrapped, either. What would have been the point?

Leanne barely glanced at the bag. "Thanks," she said, as if too tired to care what might be in inside. "Come in. You didn't wake me. I've had a rough morning with Tyler is all."

As soon as she walked in, Alex could see just *how* rough. The room was a disaster—clothes strewn over the carpet, the coffee table cluttered with dirty cups and cereal bowls. Tyler's toys were everywhere, and she caught the unmistakable odor of a diaper in need of changing.

Leanne's hopelessly brain-damaged son lay on his back on a blanket in the middle of the living room floor. He was small for his age, with pale legs that looked absurdly sticklike poking from his toddler-size diaper. But the saddest thing of all was that with his big blue eyes and curly blond hair, he would have been beautiful.

Alex stared down in pity at the perfectly formed head with its lush golden curls lolling like an infant's.

Right now, an *angry* infant. His mouth was pursed, and his face a crumpled red as he thrashed from side to side, uttering horrid mewling sounds. Alex hung back, feeling faintly sick to her stomach. The sight of him never seemed to get any easier—his crabbed hands that flopped like fish at the ends of his oddly articulated wrists, his eyes that rolled about without ever seeming to register anything. She *wanted* to care about him, truly she did. But all she felt was a terrible pity mixed with disgust.

It's nothing you haven't seen a hundred times before, she reminded herself. Even so, she remained standing as Leanne kneeled down on the cluttered carpet beside her son. Somehow, amid all that flailing, she managed to change his diaper, then heave him onto her lap—an infant the size of a sickly preschooler. *How does she do it?* Alex wondered. *Caring for all those preemies in the neonatal intensive care unit, then coming home to* this.

Tyler squirmed against Leanne as she rocked him, his hands flapping, his cries growing louder. It was several long minutes before she could quiet him. Gradually, he curled into a fetal position, his cries dwindling to a soft sucking noise.

When he was at last asleep, the face Leanne tilted up to her was so blurred with exhaustion that Alex was struck by a guilty sense of relief at the relative insignificance of her own problems. However terrible, they weren't insurmountable, she knew. But Leanne's might as well be a life sentence.

"I could use some help getting him into his crib." Leanne spoke softly so as not to wake him. "He's harder and harder to lift these days."

When they'd gotten him settled into his crib in the tiny bedroom across from Leanne's, the shades drawn and his Busy Box tinkling softly, Alex and Leanne tip-toed back out into the living room.

Leanne dropped into the recliner with a sigh. "I don't know what to do. It's not just how big he's getting. He's had two seizures this past week alone. And don't ask about the expense, you don't even *want* to know. My health insurance doesn't cover baby-sitting costs or his physical therapist." She spread her fingers over her knees, clutching them as if for support. "I wouldn't worry so much if this suit weren't still dragging on. Would you believe the hospital's lawyers got another continuance? Their third. The trial has been moved to the end of September."

Alex felt a stab of remorse. In the midst of her own predicament, she hadn't given much thought to Leanne's. Now she leaned forward with exaggerated interest. "Did they give a reason?"

Leanne scrubbed her face with an open hand. "Some expert witness who can't make it until then, I think. It doesn't matter. Their plan is to keep stalling as long as possible. Until I'm dead of exhaustion." She looked up at Alex. "Speaking of trial dates, have they set one for your mother?"

"August fourteenth." Alex was too embarrassed to admit that she herself had only just found out, from her sisters at breakfast.

"What are her chances, do you think?" Her friend's curiosity wasn't just idle, Alex could see. Leanne was eyeing her with sharp interest.

"I wouldn't know. I haven't seen or spoken to her since my father died." Alex struck a hard tone that did nothing to stem her growing sense of guilt. Her headache, which had slacked off some, kicked up with renewed vigor—velvet hammers that pounded at her temples.

"Maybe you *should* go see her."

Alex stiffened, staring back at her friend in shocked silence. Why should Leanne feel any pity for the woman who'd taken Daddy's life? A man she'd claimed to revere. Was it because Leanne herself, alone and strapped down by a child who would never be able to take care of himself, knew what it was like to feel as if you've run out of options? Whatever her reasons, Alex didn't need anyone to remind her of her filial duties. Not even Leanne.

"You know what I wish?" she said. "That everyone would stop telling me what to do."

"I just thought, you know, maybe you'd feel better if you got it off your chest." Leanne dropped her gaze and began picking at a loose thread on her chair.

"Got *what* off my chest exactly?"

Leanne shrugged. "I don't know. Look, I shouldn't have said anything. I'm just tired, is all. Maybe I was thinking of my own mother. How if anything happened to her I'd probably regret all the stuff we never said to each other."

"Like what?" Alex was reminded suddenly of the *stuff* Leanne had kept from her. Like the fact that Leanne had known all along about the affair Daddy had had with her mother. What other secrets might her friend be harboring?

"The usual, I guess. Like the fact that Mom always seemed to care more about Beth than me. I suppose it doesn't really matter anymore. I mean, we're all grown-ups, right? But it still hurts."

Alex recalled her conversation with Kitty this morning. "I guess there are some things we never get over."

At the same time, another thought was flickering in the back of her mind, one that hadn't fully taken shape. When it finally materialized, she was taken aback by the clear voice that asserted, *She's lying.* Oh, the part about Beryl was true enough, but she sensed Leanne had only thrown that in to cover up something she'd been feeling about . . .

Mother. The voice spoke up louder this time.

Leanne seemed to sense her discomfort. In a sudden burst of nervous energy, she jumped up and started for the kitchen. "You had lunch yet? I could make us a sandwich."

"No, thanks. I'm not hungry," Alex told her. She hadn't eaten since breakfast, but suddenly the thought of food sickened her.

At that precise moment her gaze fell on the nurse's uniform hanging on the door to Leanne's bedroom, shrouded in plastic. Kitty's words came rushing back to her: *She's a nurse . . . around our age . . .*

Alex reeled as if she'd been struck. Dear God. *Was* it possible? At the same time, she couldn't believe what she was thinking. Her best friend. To whom Daddy had been like a father. It was beyond unimaginable.

It was . . .

Perverted.

Yet she couldn't banish the notion from her mind. Alex's head seemed to have shrunk, each constricted pulse beat like something being strangled inside her skull. She wouldn't rest, she knew, until she'd gotten rid of this preposterous notion, once and for all.

With an exaggerated casualness, Alex rose to her feet. Glancing at her watch, she said, "I'd better go. I promised the twins I'd be back in time to take them to a movie." On her way out the door, almost as an after-thought, she said, "Oh, by the way, I was vacuuming behind the sofa the other day and came across an ear-ring. Looks like real gold. Neither of the girls is claiming it. I thought it might be yours."

Leanne frowned in thought, absently fingering an ear-lobe. Alex didn't realize she was holding her breath until she heard her friend reply, "As a matter of fact, I *am* missing an earring. From my favorite pair. I couldn't think where it might've come off. You wouldn't happen to have it with you, by any chance?"

Alex felt the air leave her lungs in a dizzying rush. "Sorry." She was mildly surprised by how easy it was to sound normal with her head about to implode . . . and a thirty-year friendship possibly in ruins. "I'll bring it with me next time."

A *coincidence,* a childish voice argued against all rea-son, a voice uncannily like Lori's this morning when she'd been so scared. *Anybody could lose an earring. And Daddy had been surrounded by dozens of nurses.*

It hit her then, a delayed reaction carrying the full force of a blow: If Leanne and Daddy were lovers . . .

. . . *that* must be why Leanne just happened to be driving by her parents' house that night. And if she had a key, it might be one that Daddy had given her. Could she have gone there to look for something—a note, a letter, a credit card receipt—that would incriminate her?

Alex stood frozen with her hand on the doorknob, watching her friend's warped reflection flicker in the pebbled-glass sidelight. When Leanne spoke, her voice was muffled by the roaring in Alex's ears.

"I'm glad you found it," she said, following Alex out onto the stoop. "I was going crazy looking for that thing. You know how it is to lose something you can't replace."

"Absolutely." Alex gave a soft little laugh that stopped short of hysteria as she negotiated the driveway the way a sick person might a hospital corridor. She no longer cared that Leanne might think it odd to see her climbing into a green Toyota instead of her BMW.

Curiouser and curiouser, she thought again amid the dull roar inside her head. She had stepped into a hole, but it wasn't the grave she'd dug for herself after all. She was in Wonderland, a dark and twisted Wonderland where anything, anything at all, might rear up to snatch at her.

Chapter 13

The woman seated across from Johnny Devane in his office was what his mother would have called well preserved. *More like embalmed,* he thought. At sixty-nine—he'd culled her birth date from one of the files that covered his desk and spilled over onto the bookshelves, the window ledge, even the carpet—every detail of her appearance was as scrupulously attended to as if she feared actual decay might set in otherwise. Makeup, each platinum hair perfectly in place—and her outfit; Jesus, she reminded him of a paint brochure from Sherwin Williams, everything coordinated in complementary shades of pink and mauve.

Beryl Chapman faced him squarely, like a woman with nothing to hide, when everything he knew about her suggested exactly the opposite.

"Go ahead. Subpoena me all you like. It won't do you any good," she said, finding a chink of polished desk amid the welter of files against which to tick a long manicured fingernail. Behind thick false lashes, her narrowed eyes made him think of slits in a gun turret. "I'll let you in on a little secret. Besides being my oldest and dearest friend, Lydia Seagrave was the best *wife* any man could ask for."

"I'm sure you can understand why some people might have difficulty seeing it that way. Under the circumstances," he observed mildly.

Johnny leaned back in the chromed swivel chair that had replaced his sturdy oak one when the DA's offices had moved from their old address on White Street. An arty Scandinavian design molded to fit the rear end of an anorectic ballerina, its contours rode up in all the wrong places on his, making it a symbol of everything he disliked about the new building—a sleek soaring cathedral to the unholy mess people made of their lives.

"I don't give a damn what anyone thinks." Beryl leaned forward, holding tightly to the arms of her chair, her bony elbows angled upward as if to keep from falling out of it. In the throaty, overripe voice of a lifelong chain-smoker, she confided, "That man had everyone fooled . . . even Lydia. Everyone but *me*. Yes, he was charming. And quite the family man, if you believe everything you hear. But look up the definition of evil in the dictionary, and you'll find Vernon Seagrave's name next to it."

"Are you saying that Mrs. Seagrave's actions toward her husband were justified?" Johnny kept his voice neutral, agreeable even.

Beryl abruptly sat back, her scarlet mouth crimping shut. "Oh no, I'm not falling for any of your tricks. And don't think you can scare me with your threat of a subpoena." From the unyielding papier-mâché mask of too many face lifts, her eyes regarded him coldly. "If I were to testify, it wouldn't look good for the prosecution, believe me."

"Fair enough . . . but there's something I still don't get. That's why I asked you here. The thing is, I've gone over the witness list submitted by Mrs. Seagrave's attorney, and I don't see your name on it." He thumbed through the sheaf of documents on his desk, adding with mock innocence, "Hell, call me old-fashioned, but in a tight spot I'd like to think I could count on my friends. Unless," he added with a long measuring look, "you and Mrs. Seagrave aren't such good friends after all."

Slashes of bright color appeared on the heavily made-up cheeks of a woman who suddenly looked every minute of her age. "What exactly are you implying, young man?"

Johnny cut right to the chase. "Let's try on for size the fact that you were once, shall we say, *intimate* with Dr. Seagrave." He shrugged and spread his hands, as if to say, *Hey, I'm not one to judge.* "A long time ago, I know. But this is a small town. Things that happened twenty, thirty years ago people talk about like it was yesterday." He ought to know. In some circles, he had yet to live down his own rep as drunken Pete Devane's no-good son.

She glared at him, bristling. Then all at once, she appeared to crumple, her crisp pink jacket sinking in on itself like the air going out of an inflatable raft. In a trembling voice, she replied, "If I have any regrets about certain mistakes I may have made, it was, as you say, a long time ago. I don't see what it has to do with *now*."

Johnny didn't know, either. The woman was right about one thing—any testimony she gave would surely prove damaging to their case. In truth, this meeting was nothing more than a fishing expedition to see what nasty little surprises might be waiting down the line.

What might have surprised Beryl Chapman, as well as given his boss serious pause, was that Johnny's special interest in the case centered, not around Lydia Seagrave, but her eldest daughter: the only woman he'd ever loved. For that reason, for Daphne, he couldn't lose sight of the slender line between merely doing his job and the execution of a higher purpose: justice.

Whatever *that* might be in the case of the *People v. Lydia Seagrave.*

For Daphne, it was clear. Justice would be a verdict of not guilty. Nothing less would do, not even the plea bargain for which he'd campaigned rigorously behind the scenes—at the risk of permanently pissing off a DA with his sights set for reelection in the fall.

What Daphne didn't know was that Cho was gunning for a maximum-penalty conviction. Johnny had done what he could, but his hands were more or less tied. However deep his desire to help Daphne, his respect for the law, flawed and cumbersome though it might be, ran even deeper. But if there was a way both to serve justice and do right by Daphne, he'd find it.

Right now, with this woman, he had to bear down hard on his natural-born impatience, hold onto it with whatever slight edge he might have gained the way he would have a hairpin curve on a one-lane gravel road.

Johnny leaned forward. "For starters," he said, "I'd

be interested to know why finding out about something that happened more than thirty years ago would cause a loving wife to blow her husband off the map."

He observed Beryl carefully as she crossed one bony leg over the other, twitching her skirt down over her knees. It was burning a hole in her, that much was clear—she was dying to ask who had given him the fill on her and Dr. Seagrave.

What if he told her it was Daphne?

Here was something else Johnny knew: when a husband cheated, it was seldom confined to one woman. And unlike wives—who, either by luck or blind trust, were usually in the dark—mistresses made it their business to learn everything they could about the competition: past, present, and future. Beryl, he suspected, knew more about her ex-lover's affairs than she was revealing.

Johnny remained silent, letting her sweat it out. Somewhere down the hall, voices rose and fell. Outside, the gardener was mowing the lawn, and the snoring drone of a power mower drifted through his open window. In the office next door, a phone buzzed on and on unanswered.

After an eternity, Beryl heaved a deep sigh of resignation. "If Lydia suspected anything, she never breathed a word. Even when I was getting divorced. It wasn't until . . ." She stopped, her gaze turning inward. Then as if arriving at some sort of decision, she straightened her shoulders and looked him in the eye. "When Lydia told me about the party she was throwing for their anniversary, something in me just . . . snapped. I couldn't let her go another minute without knowing."

"The way Mrs. Seagrave snapped when she went for the gun?"

There was undoubtedly some truth to what she was saying, but for the most part he didn't buy it. After thirty-odd years of playing the two-faced friend, why would Beryl suddenly let the cat out of the bag? Something had to have triggered her confession. Something a lot bigger than an anniversary party.

The question was, whose ass was she covering? Not her own, he suspected. And clearly not her good friend Lydia's. If she'd had Lydia's best interests at heart, as she claimed to, right now she'd be sitting in Cathcart's office, not his.

Beryl eyed him the way a wary dog might eye a strange man attempting to coax it into a kennel. "The only one who could possibly know what was going through her mind is Lydia herself." He caught the flick of one wrist as she started to reach for her handbag—the unmistakable reflex of a longtime smoker. Apparently she thought better of it, clasping her hands in her lap instead.

"And she isn't saying. Depending on who's looking at it, that could be pretty convenient." Johnny leaned back in his chair, supporting his head with one hand while he regarded her thoughtfully.

"If you mean some other woman, you're barking up the wrong tree. There were *lots,* too many to keep track." One side of her mouth twisted in a ghastly parody of a smile. "Vern was the model senior citizen—active until the very end."

"Any guess as to who he might've been fucking?"

She stiffened, her nostrils flaring in outrage at his crude attempts to provoke her. "Whatever you might think of me, Mr. Devane, I don't go around spying on people."

"There are other ways of finding things out."

"One of these days I'd be fascinated to hear all your little theories." She glanced pointedly at her watch. "But I'm afraid I have to run. My hairdresser doesn't like to be kept waiting."

The sun sluicing through the blinds at his back caught her full in the face as she stood up, underscoring every wrinkle and line and giving her carefully applied mask the faintly orangy cast of the crocodile bag clutched under one arm.

"I appreciate your coming, Mrs. Chapman." Johnny rose to usher her out.

"Next time," she told him, her tone making it crystal

clear she didn't expect there to *be* a next time, "I'll send my lawyer."

An idle threat, Johnny knew. If she'd had nothing to hide, she wouldn't have agreed to come in the first place. The truth was, as much as he'd hoped to gain something from this meeting, she'd been just as eager to find out what *he* knew.

Beryl was almost out the door when she turned to him with a nasty glint in her eye, and said, "Johnny Devane. I remember when you used to sneak around with Daphne Seagrave behind her father's back. You haven't changed a bit."

Johnny grinned—his first genuine smile of the day. "Christ, I hope not."

Though the possibility that he and Daphne might not be the same people who'd been so crazy in love all those years ago *had* crossed his mind—if only fleetingly—it was a relief to learn that at least one person saw it differently.

But the real question—one he could feel his stomach clenching around like the sour green apples mothers warned against eating—was whether or not the life he'd for so long envisioned with Daphne would ever come to pass.

He hadn't heard from her since that night on the beach. She'd said nothing about the brochure for the inn he'd hoped they could slip away to ... or the pair of bus tickets that had been tucked inside like a reminder of an unpaid debt at long last come due. Did she fully understand what he was offering? Was it as plain to her as it was to him: that they had to *seize* this opportunity? Now. There might never be another chance.

The night before last, he'd called her—ostensibly to see how she was holding up, but at the same time secretly hoping she would respond in some way to his offer. She hadn't.

It's not too late, he'd wanted to tell her. There was still time. The bus might be long gone, but *he* hadn't left. Without Daphne, where would he go? Once, long ago, he'd learned the hard way: What you run from is usually what you end up taking with you. He wouldn't make that mistake again. This time he had to stay and *fight* for what he wanted, and for the woman he loved.

At two o'clock that afternoon, Johnny was still at his desk, with his sleeves rolled up and a sandwich from the cafeteria sitting untouched at his elbow. He was drafting a motion in a case going to trial next week—two counts of armed robbery that had left a convenience store clerk with minor injuries and a DA with a major score to settle. The accused, a loser with two priors, was being represented by an even slimier character named Hank Dreiser, known in local judicial circles as Hang-'em-out-to-dry Hank because of a less than impressive record of getting his clients acquitted. Dreiser was angling to have the counts of robbery and assault with a deadly weapon busted down to robbery alone, claiming the injury sustained by the victim had occurred during the scuffle that ensued when the defendant tried to escape. But Johnny wasn't buying it. And it was his job to make sure the judge didn't, either.

When the phone buzzed, he was so lost in concentration, he wasn't aware of it at first. Not until his secretary's voice crackled over the intercom, "Mr. Devane? It's your son's principal. Line two."

Startled, but not yet alarmed—though he could feel the vague stirrings of foreboding already, like something itching below the skin—Johnny snatched up the phone and punched the blinking line button.

Mr. Glenn was cordial but got straight to the point. J.J. had been in a fight. Nothing serious, and no weapons were involved. He was letting the boys off easy *this* time, he went out of his way to emphasize. J.J., who was waiting outside his office to be picked up, would be suspended only for a few days.

The pinched judgment in the principal's voice was unmistakable and instantly set Johnny on edge. He recognized it from his own time served on the bench outside the principal's office at Muir. His crimes? Mostly fights picked by bigger kids too boneheaded to realize that stacked up against Johnny's pride, size meant nothing.

But no one had ever seemed interested in hearing his side, and by the eighth grade he'd stopped giving it. In school, there was an unwritten rule: any trouble without a clear instigator was pinned on the kid with the "attitude problem." Guilty until proven innocent.

It had taken years of running, and miles more of twisting roads that had eventually led back home, to arrive at a point where he no longer felt the need to prove himself. And until all the facts had been laid out in front of him, he'd be damned if he'd make excuses for his son.

"I'll be right over," he said tersely into the phone.

Driving across town and up the tree-lined hill to his old high school, Johnny was flooded with memories. That night he and Daphne were caught in flagrante delicto in the maintenance shed—Christ, what a picture they must have made: Dr. Seagrave's oldest girl, looking pure as the driven snow even with her jeans down around her ankles and her T-shirt up to her armpits . . . and Pete Devane's no-account kid, with his dirty-blond hair past his shoulders and the pack of Camels in his shirt pocket not the only thing forming a bulge. Johnny had been sure the cops would book him, not only for picking the shed's padlock—but also for rape. They probably would have, too, if the older of the two hadn't remembered Johnny from the countless visits to his house through the years. The cop had let him off with a gruff warning instead.

Now Johnny found himself wondering if the guy had merely been taking pity on him . . . or if there had been another reason. A grown man who'd walked away from doing right by a couple of defenseless kids might have built up a fairly sizable guilty conscience, he reflected bitterly.

Yet over the years hadn't he, too, tried to block out as much as he could? Thinking of his childhood, it wasn't so much a single incident he recalled as a series of jarring impressions—voices raised in anger, the sound of glass smashing, drops of blood spattered over old scratched linoleum—and fear, yes, the sour stink of fear: when he was younger, from wetting himself in terror, and when in years hence, from the sweat of holding himself clenched like a fist, biding his time until he was big enough to defend himself.

The cops had visited often, yes, but not often enough. Daily life in the Devane household had been made up of dodging parents whose only recreation, aside from getting drunk, was to go at each other—Johnny and his brother, too—with both fists and everything that wasn't nailed down. His only recourse had been silence, constantly reinforced by horror stories of what would happen should he or Freddie breathe so much as a word of what was *really* going on. To the cops, Johnny would say instead that he'd fallen off his bike or gotten into a fight at school, believing a bloody nose and bruises were better than being shipped off to a foster home.

He didn't know whether or not he'd made the right choice, but it *had* made him tough. The only time he'd come close to knuckling under was when Freddie was shipped off to Vietnam at the invitation of the United States Army. The war was nearly over by then, his older brother one of its last casualties. After the body was shipped home, Johnny had gone through a period of blaming everyone in sight, while hurting no one but himself. But drinking too hard, staying out late, getting into trouble at school—it was expected of him, right? Why not give people what they wanted: an easy target that would keep them from having to look too hard at themselves.

The turning point had come shortly after his sixteenth birthday, and several months shy of his fateful encounter with Daphne in the smoking pit behind the science building. Around the time every other guy his age was showing off brand-new cars bought for them by their parents—while he had merely lusted after the mint-condition midnight-blue Ford Thunderbird displayed in the showroom of County Classic Motors—Johnny was given the greatest gift of all: the upper hand.

The shift was so sudden the old man never even saw it coming. He'd been drinking that night, a six-pack of tall boys chased by a quart of good Irish whiskey, and was meaner than a wet cat. He'd started in first on Mom, complaining about the casserole she'd burned. Pretty soon he was shoving her up against the kitchen cabinets and slapping her around while she cowered, her hands fluttering around her head like a bird trapped indoors, beating itself to death against a window. Johnny had yelled at his father to stop, *just stop it,* and the old man swung clumsily around to face him with blood in his eye. That's when it happened. Like a train switching tracks, one minute he was looming over Johnny—a huge beer-bellied man in a stained undershirt and dark green janitor's pants that hung below his paunch—and the next, the old man was looking down at the twin barrels of Johnny's fully loaded fists.

"You ever touch her or me again, I swear I'll bust your face in," Johnny had threatened, his every muscle and tendon quivering like a high-tension cable about to snap.

His dad never again lifted a hand to him. But on that day Johnny had understood, in some vital way, what seven years of college and law school couldn't teach: that like God, justice was in the details. There'd been no righteous thunderbolt out of the blue. Not even the satisfaction of plowing a fist into the old man's stubbled jaw—only the seed of self-respect that had taken root in him that day.

Johnny made a hard right into the parking lot and killed the engine. Muir High had changed little in the years since he'd graduated—still the same ruts scalloping the edges of the lawn, where each week at least one novice driver got a little overzealous with the accelerator, and the zigzag crack in the stucco over the arched entrance, a souvenir of some long-forgotten earthquake, patched over so many times it resembled a badly healed scar. Even the kids milling around in front looked the same. The fashions and hairstyles were different, sure, but the expressions hadn't changed: animation that could switch off in the blink of an eye, cool blankness masking emotions too hot to handle.

How was it possible that he had a son the age he'd been only a few years ago? A line from a Dylan song drifted into his head, *I was so much older then, I'm younger than that now . . .*

He found fourteen-year-old J.J. in the outer office, slouched in a chair by the secretary's desk, and half expected to see Miss Wickersham eyeing him sourly over the half rims of her glasses. Then he remembered—old Wickersham had been put out to pasture the year after he graduated. The pleasant middle-aged woman looking up at him now, with her ruffled blouse and embroidered cardigan vest, would inspire no epitaphs, he predicted, and be forgotten within six months of retirement.

Johnny clapped his son on the shoulder, and J.J. jerked upright. Out of a swollen eye the shade of a tropical sunset deepening into twilight, his son shot him a guarded look tinged with defiance—one that reminded Johnny so much of himself at that age it caught him unexpectedly by the throat, forcing him to swallow twice before he was able to speak.

"Somebody told me you might need a lawyer," he remarked drily.

J.J.'s mouth quivered, but he didn't smile. "Dad . . ."

"We'll talk about it on the way home. You all signed out?"

The tension went out of his son's neck, and his head drooped. "I'm suspended for the rest of the week. No after-school practice, even." Big for his age, with his grandfather's wide shoulders and deep chest, J.J. had made the junior varsity football team his first year out, and now despair shone on his handsome bruised face.

They joined the noisy throng in the corridor, kids racing to make their last class before the bell. Not until they were heading down the front steps did Johnny turn to his son and ask casually, "Want to tell me what happened?"

J.J. shrugged. A gesture that might have been interpreted any one of a dozen ways . . . or mean nothing at all. Johnny tried a different approach. "From what I heard, your friend is in even worse shape than you. Either you've been practicing that right hook I showed you on Stu, or you and he had a falling out. Which one is it?"

J.J. flushed, patches of irritated pink from a recent bout of acne standing out on his cheeks. "I don't feel like talking about it." He was careful to tack on, "Later, okay?"

Johnny weighed his options. He could press the issue, and wind up with a scene that would have done the Johnny Devane of yore proud, or table it until tonight and risk playing into the boy's hands. In the eight months since J.J. had come to live with him, he and his son—incorrigible, according to his ex-wife, who'd hinted it was somehow due to his father's own miscreant past—had been engaged in a power struggle that made those dished up at the office seem minor league by comparison. Like last weekend: his son was supposed to have been staying over at his mother's, but when Johnny called he wasn't there. It turned out J.J. was pulling an all-nighter with his friends—a stunt that had him grounded until the end of the month.

But Johnny sensed this was different. J.J. was clearly hurting . . . and not just where his jaw resembled a bad case of the mumps.

"It'll keep until dinner, I guess," he relented. "But let's get one thing straight—any differences you and Stu need to work out, there's always a better way. Take it from someone who's gotten his skull cracked often enough to know."

"It won't happen again." His son's flat tone let it be known he wasn't so much promising as merely stating a fact.

Johnny indulged in a tiny smile. "Fourteen, and the kid has it all figured out. Don't tell me you have the 'Bhagavad Gita' memorized, too."

"The what?"

"Never mind." They passed under an acacia tree that in his absence had baptized the T-bird with a sprinkling of powdery gold. He was unlocking the door to the driver's side when Johnny thought to ask, "This new look you're sporting wouldn't have anything to do with a certain girl named Kate, would it?"

J.J.'s flush deepened, and his one good eye narrowed. "Kate Winter?"

"I don't know another Kate."

Again, the all-purpose shrug. "She can go to hell for all I care."

"We're talking about the same Kate Winter you were on the phone with for three solid hours the other night? I thought I was going to have to have the damn thing surgically removed from your ear."

"Cut it out, Dad," his son growled. "I'm not in the mood."

"Okay." Johnny dropped his joking tone. "A word of advice then—next time, before you go rearranging your best friend's orthodonture, ask yourself if a girl you won't remember a year from now is worth permanently pissing off someone who's been your best friend since the first grade."

J.J. eyed him narrowly over the roof of the car. Three or four more inches, Johnny thought, and the kid would be as tall as his old man. Now *there* was something to chew on.

"You're one to talk," he shot back. "That lady I heard *you* on the phone with the other night, whoever she is, it sounded like you two are a lot more than just friends. Did you plan on telling me about her, or was I supposed to just figure it out for myself?"

Now it was Johnny's turn to grow heated. J. J. was a lot more perceptive than he'd given him credit for. Though his conversation with Daphne had been brief, his son had sensed something in Johnny's tone that let him know that *this* woman was different from the three or four he'd dated since the divorce.

"I didn't realize it was that obvious." Johnny gave a rueful chuckle.

"She anyone I might know?"

"Her name's Daphne. We went to high school together."

J.J. cocked his head, the light of comprehension dawning in his one good eye. "Oh yeah, *her*. Must be the one Mom told me about."

"What did your Mom say?" A band of guilt formed around Johnny's heart.

"That *she's* the one you should've married. But Mom was pretty pissed at the time. It was right after the divorce." He treated Johnny to a lopsided smile. "She said a lot of things she probably didn't mean."

"I almost *did* marry Daphne," Johnny confessed.

J.J. eyed him with new interest. "What stopped you?"

"Her old man mostly. He was a real tough customer. Didn't think much of *me*, that's for sure," Johnny recalled with a wintry smile. "Looking back, I can't help thinking we could've made it work, Daphne and I, if we'd been a little older and a lot wiser. But," he added, fixing his gaze on his son, "then I wouldn't have had you."

J.J. brightened. *Score one for the old man*, Johnny thought. Occasionally, he *did* manage to get it right. But his son wasn't giving it up that easily. With as much of a grin as he could manage, he cracked, "So you think it'll be different this time, Dad? You're not gonna make the same dumb mistakes all over again?"

No, Johnny thought. He wouldn't let go of her a second time. But unfortunately, it wasn't a decision that was his to make. The ball was in Daphne's court. She had to make up her mind if this was what she wanted and whether or not it was worth the risk. All he could do was wait, and hope.

"I guess some mistakes we have to keep on repeating until we get it right." Johnny reached into his pocket for his key ring and came up with his Swiss Army knife instead—a present from Daphne on his seventeenth birthday. He gazed down at it as if seeing it for the first time: its folded blades glinting in the sun, its red handle worn smooth as glass. For a long moment, he stood lost in thought. The box had been tied with a blue bow, he remembered, and Daphne had insisted on using the knife to cut him a piece of the chocolate cake she'd made him, laughing herself silly at the mess it ended up making. Afterward, he'd wiped it clean on the wrapping paper and slipped it into the pocket of his jeans so he could kiss her. It had been with him ever since.

On impulse, Johnny tossed it over the roof of the car to his son, who fumbled and nearly dropped it before closing his fingers around the unexpected gift with a look of bewildered pleasure. "It's yours," Johnny told him. "Hang on to it, you might need it someday."

"For what? Next time I get into a fight?" J. J. grinned.

Johnny smiled, and shook his head. "For luck. It was given to me when I was around your age. By someone I cared about—the lady you mentioned just now. I'll tell you all about it sometime."

"What's wrong with right now?"

"I was under the impression you didn't feel like talking." As he climbed into the driver's seat, Johnny caught a glimpse of his small ironic smile in the side-view mirror.

"Yeah, well." J.J. dropped into his seat, shoving his hands into the pockets of his jacket. Johnny saw him wince, then gingerly withdraw the hand that had landed him in all this trouble. He examined its raw, brusied knuckles with interest, as he might a specimen in biology. When he looked up, he was smiling his old sweet smile—one Johnny hadn't seen in a while. "I guess it can wait until you get home from work."

"Isn't that where we're headed now?"

J.J.'s eyes cut away. "Do me a favor, Dad? Drop me at Stu's instead? There's some stuff him and me need to go over."

"Homework?" Johnny arranged his features in a deadpan expression.

"Something like that."

"Just be home in time for supper. And while you're at Stu's, do me a favor and put some ice on that eye. You're starting to remind me of Edward G. Robinson."

"Who?"

"Never mind."

Johnny fired up the engine and pulled out of the lot. It wasn't until they were a mile or so up the road, driving up Church Street near the turnoff for Our Lady of the Wayside, that J.J. cleared his throat and muttered, "Thanks, Dad."

Johnny kept his eyes on the white cross gleaming atop the church up ahead. "You're welcome," he grunted. "Feet off the dash, please. And no messing with the dials."

"Aye, aye, captain."

Johnny smiled to himself. *Captain's log. Star date nineteen-ninety-nine. We are due east of enemy territory, heading into deep space . . .*

Daphne's image floated into range. She'd have picked her kids up from school by now. This time of day, he thought, she'd probably be upstairs, banging away on her laptop. In the days and weeks since she'd come home to Miramonte, she'd told him, she'd been keeping a journal of everything that went on.

Johnny wondered what, if anything, she'd written about him, whether their story would have an ending like one of her novels—all of them ambiguous and unhappy in some way—or if it would be something he could grow into, build a life around, cherish as he did this miserable half-grown excuse for a son.

He knew only one thing for certain: he had to see her. To touch her.

If nothing more, just that.

Squinting against the sunlight, his throat tight with too many things left unsaid, Johnny pictured her hands: supple and long-fingered, their bones more clearly defined now than they'd been when she was younger—hands that could write a book, tend to a child, fight for a mother . . . and, maybe, just maybe, pick up the thread of something irreplaceable lost along the way.

The worst of it, Daphne thought, was that she'd grown used to seeing her mother this way: an image behind smudged glass, like the faded snapshots in their family album. The sadness she felt looking across at her now was more wistful than anguished, a vague longing for times long past and a place she'd once called home.

Daphne realized that she might never again embrace those once-vital arms. That despite her best efforts, the mother she'd looked up to and depended on as a child, was gone forever. What was left was a drab-looking woman in an orange prison jumpsuit, old before her time, the once-firm flesh of her face sliding from her bones like the sandstone slowly eroding from the cliff below their house.

"We've spoken with all your friends and most of the relatives. But . . ." Daphne sighed into the heavy black receiver secured to the wall by a stiff cable that snaked and twisted with her every move. She'd grown to loathe this most of all; it made her think of a pay phone, calling for help in the middle of the night with her car broken down miles from nowhere. "It's not that they have anything *bad* to say—just the opposite, in fact. They all send their best and want you to know you're in their prayers. Oh, and Millie Landry, at the gallery? She's sold every one of your paintings and wants to know if you're allowed any art supplies in here. She's sure it would take your mind off things. And, by the way, she's had any number of requests for more paintings . . . when you feel up to it."

Daphne thought of her own newfound success—*Walking After Midnight* had just gone back for a fourth printing, her editor had informed her the other day—and drew a tiny degree of comfort from the cynical expression on her mother's face. It was obvious that she wasn't alone in her sense of irony.

"Millie Landry never spied an opportunity she didn't grab hold of with both fists," Lydia sniffed. "I'm surprised she doesn't have a sign out front advertising me as a limited edition." Behind the thick glass, she shook her head in disdain, and Daphne was heartened to see that some of her old spirit had resurfaced, if only for the moment.

She felt compelled to defend Millie nonetheless. "I think she meant well. She really did seem concerned."

"I'm sure she is. I just don't seem to care one way or the other." Lydia sighed. "One thing I've begun to realize in here is how little it mattered, really. All those friends and committees and drives. They were just a way of keeping busy, of staying one step ahead of my thoughts."

"What were you so afraid of discovering?" Daphne's heart quickened. Deep down, she knew what her mother was going to say. Wasn't it the same thing she'd been running from in her own marriage?

Her mother's expression turned thoughtful. "Well, *me,*" she replied softly into the receiver clutched to her ear. "The woman who'd gotten swallowed up by all that white noise. After so many years, I suppose I was afraid that if I ever came face-to-face with her, I wouldn't like what I saw."

Daphne winced in recognition of her mother's words. "Was it Daddy, too? Were you afraid you'd feel differently toward *him?*"

The sagging flesh on her mother's face grew suddenly taut, like something blurred sharpening into focus. "No," she said, quite firmly. "Nothing could ever have changed how I felt about your father. You must understand, Daphne, it's *important* that you understand." With the perfect posture of a mother who'd schooled her young daughters in etiquette the way another might have taught them to balance a checkbook or prepare a résumé—as if the basic tools of survival included knowing the proper way to address one's superiors and which fork to use at the dinner table—she leaned forward from the waist, holding her spine yardstick straight. "We can't choose whom we love, or why. We can't just shut it off, either . . . even when we want to. It doesn't work that way. What happened, what I did . . . it was *because* I loved him."

Daphne began to tremble. She thought of Johnny, all the lost years without him, years marked with spells of loneliness and longing that had not been without their share of rewards—her career, her children, and, yes, at times, even Roger—years that in retrospect were like stunted fruit from a tree denied its full share of sunshine. Maybe things would have turned out differently had she never known Johnny. But she *had.* She'd tasted love at its sweetest; she'd bitten into it and felt its juice running down her chin. And having consumed it, she'd been doomed to a lifetime of wanting more.

Mother must have felt that way about Daddy, she thought. It shouldn't have come as a revelation, but somehow it did. She'd known what an adoring wife her mother had been. It just hadn't sunk in, until just now, that what Mother had felt for Daddy was as real as the passion *she* had experienced with Johnny.

Her hand cupped about the receiver, Daphne spoke the words no one else had dared to say—the irony would have been too ghastly. "You miss him, don't you?"

"More than life itself." Her mother's chin lifted and her mouth quivered, as if she were struggling not to cry. There was no irony in her voice, just sorrow.

"Oh, Mother . . ." Daphne blinked back tears of her own, which these days were never far from the surface.

"Don't feel sorry for me," Lydia was quick to admonish. "I couldn't bear it. Anyway, you have your own life to live. You've got to let go of this. You've got to let it *be.*"

What was Mother asking of her? Daphne wondered. That she and Kitty stop doing everything they could to free her? Fretfully, *angrily* almost, she demanded, "What *do* you want then?"

A light flickered in her mother's eyes. "I'd like to go home," she said. "Just for a few weeks, until the trial. I'd like to see my flowers bloom and feel my own pillow under my head. I . . . I'd like to go for one last swim in the bay."

Daphne was unexpectedly moved by the simplicity of her mother's request. She wasn't asking for an acquittal, or even a plea bargain. She merely wanted . . .

One last swim in the bay. An image formed in Daphne's mind of her mother stroking far out beyond the waves, an arm lifting and falling, her white bathing cap bobbing in and out of view. As a child, she used to watch from shore with a little knot in her stomach. A tiny part of her had been afraid . . .

That Mother wouldn't be coming back.

Daphne quickly shrugged off the thought. "I'll speak to Tom," she said. "There *has* to be a way to get you out on bail, at least." Renewed determination pulsed through her.

Clearly, though, her mother didn't share her optimism. "Poor Mr. Cathcart," she sighed. "He's done what he could, I'm afraid."

Daphne felt her own sense of defeat start to close in once again, but this time she fought it. *Johnny,* she thought. *I'll talk to Johnny.* With his hands tied, she didn't know what, if anything, he could do, only that he wouldn't let her down, not if he could help it.

"There's someone else I can speak to," she said, "someone who might be able to help. I'll call him as soon as I get back to Kitty's. Don't worry, Mother, we'll get you out of here. One way or another you'll have your swim."

She saw him walking briskly toward her along the wharf, a distant figure against the brilliant sky and warped old railing that didn't quite meet at the seams. But even if she hadn't been looking out for him, she'd have recognized him at once. The familiar swing of his shoulders and his easy, hip-slung stride. *Johnny . . .*

She watched him pause to cup a hand over his eyes, tracking a flock of gulls that swirled upward like bits of torn newspaper in his path. To a stranger, Daphne thought, he might appear in no hurry—someone merely out for a stroll—but she knew better. In every measured step, she sensed an urgency about where he was headed and what it might hold.

He caught up with her near Louie's Catch, an ancient outpost with salt-streaked windows and tables covered in red-checked oilcloth, which served the best clam chowder anywhere along this stretch of coast. He was dressed in plain khakis and a fresh-from-the-drawer shirt he'd taken the time to change into after work—a man who could brew a decent cup of coffee, build a fire out of wet driftwood . . . and make a name for himself in a town that had once rejected him. She watched as the breeze snatched up handfuls of his thick graying hair. His cheeks were ruddy from the cold, but his eyes, when they fell on her, were warm.

"Hey." He wanted to kiss her, she could tell. Badly. But not where anyone might see. Instead, he reached up to free a strand of hair caught against her mouth by the wind. "Fancy meeting you here."

"It was my idea, remember?" she reminded him with mock seriousness. Part of her wished he *would* kiss her, damn the consequences, but at the same time she knew better.

He glanced at his watch. "You're also five minutes early. See, the idea was for me to get here ahead of you so I could sweep you off your feet."

Daphne wasn't exactly in the mood for jokes, but she laughed anyway. "Sure, that's all we'd need—everybody on this pier gossiping about us." She cast an anxious glance in the direction of Louie's Catch. Somewhat primly she added, "And both you and I know perfectly well it wouldn't end there. Before we knew it, we'd be heading off to some motel."

"Would that be so terrible?" Johnny's gaze remained fixed on her with all the intensity of the sunlight turning the silvery ends of his hair to a fiery corona.

"No," she admitted, wanting him so badly at that moment it was all she could do to keep from throwing herself into his arms.

Daphne looked past him, squinting against the sun that rode low on the horizon. At the end of the pier, an old man in a plaid shirt was fishing, and seagulls sat still as ornaments on sawed-off posts joined by lengths of rusty chain. When she brought her gaze back to Johnny, he was smiling down at her expectantly.

"You never responded to my invitation," he said. "The offer is still open, in case you're wondering."

A weekend away. God, how many times had she imagined it? Just the two of them. Sleeping in late, and making love all day, with no one to disturb them. But it just wasn't possible.

She bit her lip against the cry of frustration that rose in her. "Oh, Johnny . . . I can't."

"Because of your mother?"

"That's not the only reason," she told him. "There's Roger, too. And the children. Johnny, if we start something now, I don't know if I'd be able to stop." She cut her gaze away, unable to meet his eyes. But she couldn't escape the fierce challenge in his voice.

"What was that night on the beach?"

"I don't know." She smiled sadly. What exactly *had* it been? An overdue payment come due, maybe. A closing of old wounds. "All I know is that it was wonderful. Magical. And I don't regret a minute of it."

"But?"

She sensed him grow still, and when she dared look up, his face was hard, a muscle working in his jaw. "But it can't happen again. Please, Johnny," she begged, "for my sake, don't make it any harder than it already is."

"I'm not the one making it hard for you, Daphne."

She winced. This wasn't how she'd expected their meeting to go. She'd planned to discuss her mother's future, not her own. But, oh God, when he looked at her like that, how could she even *think* straight? It was as if every good intention had been obliterated by the voice in her head calling for him.

Daphne crossed her arms over her chest, wanting to block the yearning that was stealing its way into her heart. Her marriage of eighteen years, she thought, might not stack up against the hallowed memory of her first love, but she wasn't prepared to simply toss it out like yesterday's paper.

"I have responsibilities, Johnny. Family I can't just turn my back on."

"I'm not asking for anything we haven't *both* wanted."

She thought of the bus tickets tucked in a drawer back at Kitty's, and her eyes filled with tears that stung like the salty air blowing in off the ocean. "I meant what I said," she told him. "That night on the beach? I wouldn't have changed a single thing. But real life can't ever be that perfect. If we let this go any further, it could get messy. People would get hurt. And that would hurt us."

She watched his jaw clench in reflex, as if against a lifetime of such blows. Then he reached into the front pocket of his shirt for a cigarette. His eyes were hot against the cold blue sky at his back, like the match now flaring in his cupped palm. With a casualness that served only to betray the depth of his hurt, he asked, "Are you saying we should stop seeing each other?"

"For now, at least."

"Is that really what you want?" He sucked in a deep drag that made the tip of his cigarette glow fierce as a dragon's eye.

"Right now, I'm not sure I'd know what I wanted if it landed in my lap." She gave a hollow laugh, hugging herself against the sudden chill that gripped her.

"Let's start with what you *don't* want then."

She thought of her parents and shuddered. "I don't want to lose any more than I already have."

"Maybe what you're most afraid of losing is that perfect memory," he suggested, a note of bitterness creeping into his voice. "Memories might not keep you warm at night, but on the other hand, there's no risk involved."

She could see him in a courtroom, one by one eliminating every argument put forth by the opposition, using words the way he'd once used his fists. But this time he couldn't escape the facts. "I'm married, Johnny. I'm responsible for two small children."

"Which comes first—marriage or responsibility?"

She ducked her head, pulling her collar up around her chin. "You're not playing fair."

"This isn't a game." Tossing his cigarette onto the weathered planks at his feet, he seized her shoulders so tightly she could feel the heat of his grip through the layers of her coat. "I'm willing to fight for you, Daphne. Do whatever it takes. Risk everything I own. Does your husband feel that way about you? Because that's not how it looks. What I see is a guy sitting on his ass in New York while his wife is going through hell out here."

Stung by the truth in what he was saying, Daphne cried, "Look, I'm not going to argue that my marriage is wonderful. We have our share of problems. Who doesn't? And anyway, what I need right now, Roger can't give me. *That's* why I asked you here, Johnny. I didn't mean for us to . . ." She swallowed hard. ". . . to get into all that other stuff. I really just came to ask for your help."

He relaxed his grip but didn't let go. "What do you need?"

"Help me get my mother out on bail." Breathlessly, she

added, "I know it's unfair to put you in this position. If your boss even knew we were having this discussion . . ." she faltered a bit, then picked up. "I'm not asking you to do anything illegal. I would never do that. But if there's any way you could . . ."

"I'll do what I can." Johnny's reply was immediate and terse. But his gray-blue eyes shone bright with unshed tears. "Just promise me one thing."

"What?" She felt herself stiffen. He'd want some sort of assurance, of course. A promise that Mother wouldn't do anything stupid. Like—what? Run for the hills? Daphne almost smiled at the absurdity of the thought.

But the lawyer came second to the man, it seemed. Because when Johnny opened his mouth it wasn't to ask for assurances, but to say, "Promise me you won't make any decisions about us. Not yet."

She stood there, regarding him gravely through a film of tears in which light spun and flashed. The scent of the ocean mingled with smoke from his cigarette, reminding her once again of that night on the beach. Longing swept in, rising steadily until it filled every part of her, until there was no room left for reason, or even fear, leaving her no choice, when he brought his hands to her face, running a calloused thumb over her lower lip, but to kiss him. Right out in the open, under the watchful eye of God, and for anyone who might have been strolling by to see.

W̲alking in the door to her sister's house—which, in the weeks since she'd arrived had come to seem more like home than her penthouse in New York, and where the last customers of the day lingered over cups of tea and glasses of lemonade—Daphne was stunned to find Roger seated at a table in the window, as if her conscience had somehow summoned him there. She couldn't believe it. After all her cajoling and berating, he'd chosen *now* to show up out of the blue? It could only mean one thing: he'd sensed her withdrawing and come to investigate.

She hung back, observing him from the kitchen doorway, just outside his line of sight. He was helping Kyle put together his brand-new set of Robo Force Legos, Jennie perched on one knee. "Here, try the green one . . . it should fit." Roger waited patiently as their son struggled to snap the two pieces together. When Jennie reached for the pile of loose Legos, he was quick to avert a battle by distracting her with his pocket watch. It was sterling, with a handsome engraved case, and had been handed down from his great-grandfather. And though Daphne secretly thought his wearing it a bit of an affectation, now, in the soft brilliance of the setting sun, cupped reverently in their daughter's small hands, the watch seemed to hold an almost mythic significance.

Observing them, Daphne felt something start to unravel inside her—like the sleeve of a favorite sweater neglected longer than it ought to have been—longer than someone more careful would have permitted. Her face prickled with heat, and she imagined her stolen hour with Johnny to be written there: a scarlet "A" proclaiming her faithlessness.

Then sanity asserted itself, and a small voice whispered, *He doesn't know you've been with Johnny. Any more than you know who he might have been with.*

But had her doubts about Roger truly been a result of his actions, she wondered now—the scene in the bookstore flashing through her mind, Roger cozying up to that blond woman he'd claimed he hardly knew—or merely a projection of her own guilty thoughts about Johnny?

Before she could follow through on the thought, Jennie caught sight of her and squealed in delight, prompting Roger to lift his leonine head and turn in Daphne's direction. As she stepped forward, Daphne remembered to smile, as if pleasantly surprised. "Roger! Why didn't you tell me you were coming?"

"I didn't know myself, right up until the last minute," he said. Lowering Jennie to the floor, he stood up to give Daphne a peck on the cheek. "You *are* happy to see me, I hope."

She was saved from having to respond by Jennie exclaiming, "Look what Daddy brought me!" From a shopping bag under the table, she pulled a doll still enshrined in its molded plastic packaging. "It's Sleeping Beauty Barbie. See, she gots sparkles, and I can fix her hair."

"Doofus. You have to take her out of the box first." Kyle shot Daphne a long-suffering look, as one grownup to another, explaining, "She doesn't want it to get all messed up before our trip."

"We're going on an airplane!" Jennie crowed.

Daphne's heart sank. Trip? *Oh, God,* she thought, *he's going to insist on taking the kids home with him.* Then she remembered that school wasn't out until the end of June, almost a month away. She still had time.

And Roger, if he sensed she was anything but glad to see him, wasn't showing it. When he took her in his arms, it was with surprising gentleness. "I told them I'd talk it over with you," he said. "See how you'd feel about all of us flying down to Disneyland for a few days while I'm here."

In his light-blue cardigan with the woven leather buttons that reminded her of acorns, he smelled of their closet back home—the little muslin sacks of cedar chips tucked amid the woolens to ward off moths. Daphne was caught unawares by a pang of longing for everything that was solid and safe . . . and as far as possible from the shifting sand on which her fate—and her mother's—balanced so precariously.

"Goodness, I haven't even had a chance to catch my breath," she hedged with a laugh. "I wish you'd at least phoned from the airport."

"I did. You were out. Kitty didn't say where." He gave her a long measuring look.

He *knows,* she thought, and was in that instant struck by a wild, unreasoning panic. Then once again, reason asserted itself. How could he know unless Kitty had told him? And her sister would never betray a confidence. Daphne met his gaze, resisting the urge to run her tongue over lips still tender and swollen from Johnny's kisses.

"I was visiting Mother," she said, annoyed suddenly that *she* was the one on the defensive. Why should she have waited around when she hadn't even been expecting him? Coolly, she reminded her husband, "This isn't exactly a vacation for me, you know."

"So I gather," he observed mildly. "Seems like lately, whenever I call, you're either out or too busy to talk."

The old Daphne would have rushed in with an explanation or an apology. But she saw things more clearly now. Being apart from Roger had made her realize she wasn't one of his patients to be babied and cajoled. She didn't need to account to him for every minute of her time, either.

She lifted her chin. "Frankly, I'm surprised you noticed."

Roger jerked in surprise, and his high statesmanlike brow creased with annoyance. Then he caught himself, and with a sheepish little grimace admitted, "Yeah, I know—I've been pretty scarce myself lately. Believe it or not, I also know what a prize asshole I can be. This time was different, though. There was a reason I couldn't come sooner."

Wasn't there always a reason? she thought disgustedly. Besides, she didn't buy his self-effacing act. She'd heard it before. Whenever Roger sensed he'd pushed her too far, out came the requisite apology. But in the end, nothing ever changed.

At the same time, Daphne realized she was angry at him for more than the way he was manipulating her. Quite simply, she was angry because he wasn't Johnny. And *that*, she told herself, wasn't fair. Whatever Roger might have done, either directly or behind her back, she couldn't blame him for standing between her and Johnny.

"Something to do with that situation you mentioned over the phone?" she asked, with more concern than she might have otherwise.

Roger opened his mouth to say something but was stopped by a wail of outrage from Kyle. His sister, Daphne saw, was at the moment delicately inserting a Lego up one nostril.

"Stop it!" Kyle yelled. "You're getting boogers all over it!"

"Am not!" Jennie extracted the Lego to examine it intently.

"Booger! Boogery boog!" Kyle was really getting into it now, rolling back and forth in his chair for maximum dramatic effect. "Oh, yuck! Gross! My sister's a booger!"

"*You're* the booger," Jennie piped indignantly.

"*Gimme* that." Kyle lunged across the table at her.

"Nooooooo . . ." Jennie shrieked, jumping to the floor to bury her face in the folds of Roger's coat, still draped over his chair.

Her brother snatched up the partially assembled Robo Force gun and aimed it at the shrouded shape moving under Roger's coat, growling. "Better watch out, or I'll shoot you dead. Just like Grandma shot Grandpa!"

Daphne reeled in horror. And suddenly it wasn't her son she was seeing . . . but a miniature version of her husband, eyes round with exaggerated innocence, mouth twitching with a barely suppressed smirk. Rage swept through her like a scorching desert wind, gritty with sand that stung like flecks of broken glass. Only marginally was she aware of her hand flying out, palm extended.

Not once had she ever struck either of her children—so determined was she never to see in their little faces the fear she herself had felt growing up when her father was in one of his moods—but in that instant she would have done just that: smacked her son's face. Her sweet little boy, now staring up at her in shocked silence, his gray-green eyes huge and stricken.

It was Roger who stopped her. Lightning quick, he snatched her hand from midair.

"You know better than that, Kyle." With his fingers lightly encircling Daphne's wrist, he scowled down at their son, adding more gently, "It was terrible what happened to your grandfather. And maybe someday we'll understand why he got killed. Until then, we just have to pray for Grandma to get better."

Jennie peeked out from behind his coat, her forehead wrinkled with concern. "Is Grandma sick? Like when I had chicken pops?"

"Chicken pox, you mean." He smiled, dropping

Daphne's hand to squat down next to Jennie. "No, sweetheart. But people get sick in the head sometimes." He tapped a graying temple. "In here, where it doesn't show. It can make them do funny things."

Both children nodded, absorbing this as they would any new concept: with unquestioning acceptance. Looking into their small trusting faces, like daisies turned up to the sun, Daphne fought back tears. For once, Roger had known exactly what to say, in a single stroke succeeding where the reams of explanations she'd given them had failed.

"Why don't you guys go see if Aunt Kitty needs a hand in the kitchen?" Roger eyed the children in a way that let them know it wasn't an idle suggestion, then added with a wink, "I'll bet there's something in it for you—something sweet, just out of the oven."

Daphne watched them scamper off, none the worse for the wear, and the blanket of coldness that had settled about her heart lifted somewhat. She glanced about the tea room, oddly deserted at this hour except for Father Sebastian sipping lemonade at a table in back, absorbed in a folded-over section of newspaper disguising what she guessed to be a racing form. A harmless vice, she knew, since he never actually bet money. It was certainly nothing as terrible as what *she'd* come so close to doing.

With a sigh, Daphne sank down across from her husband and brought a trembling hand to her cheek. "I don't know what came over me." The shame she felt overlapped with an image of Johnny flashing in her head like something cheap and tawdry.

Unexpectedly, Roger's large warm hand closed over hers. "You've been under a tremendous strain. Anyone would have snapped long before this."

Seeing the genuine concern in his broad scrubbed face, Daphne wanted to cry in frustration. *Why now?* All these long harrowing weeks, where had he been?

"Maybe it wouldn't have been so hard if you'd come sooner," she said.

Roger winced, and squeezed her hand. "I know. It must seem like I abandoned you just when you needed me most."

"It's not just *this* time, Roger."

He went on as if she hadn't spoken. "That problem I mentioned? Well, it's actually more of a crisis." Roger dropped his eyes, looking embarrassed—an emotion she was so unaccustomed to seeing in him, she found herself leaning forward attentively. He cleared his throat and said, "Larry and Kurt want to sign on with an HMO. And they've asked me to bow out."

Daphne sat back, stunned. "Out of the practice? My God, Roger, *why?*"

No sooner were the words out when it occurred to her: *I'm not the only one.* His partners—they had to have borne the brunt of Roger's arrogance as well. A my-way-or-the-highway attitude wouldn't set too well with an HMO review board. There was his bedside manner, too. She hadn't questioned it before, but however good his doctoring, might the mothers of his small patients have suffered some of the same condescension as she had?

She waited for Roger's trumped-up explanations and blustering denials—from which he would surely emerge the injured party—but he surprised her by admitting, "I guess I had it coming."

Daphne eyed him with new wariness—as if the man to whom she'd been married for eighteen years had been replaced by someone she didn't even know. Was this for real? Or some kind of act?

"What are you going to do?" she asked.

He shook his head. "I don't know yet. We've agreed to try to work things out, but Larry and Kurt insisted on calling in a mediator. Some touchy-feely trouble-shooter with a degree in psychobabble." The old arrogance surfaced, and he took on a beleaguered expression. "You want to know what this is? I'll tell you. It's goddamn embarrassing. If they think they can just push me—" he stopped, as if catching a glimpse of something in her eyes. With a sigh, he lifted her hand to his mouth and in a curiously absent way, kissed it. "I know. I'm not the easiest guy to get along with. You probably feel as if I let you down, too."

"You *have* let me down, Roger."

How easy that was, she thought. All the times she'd held her tongue, feeling she lacked solid proof, she'd ignored the most compelling evidence of all: the growing distance between them.

Now, though, instead of a smugly self-centered martinet, what she saw was a large man whose ego wasn't as big as it had seemed and whose broad shoulders now sagged in defeat. He dropped her hand to fork his fingers through his hedge of thick, tweedy hair, which sprang back in disheveled clumps.

"I guess I had *that* coming, too." He managed a sheepish smile. "Would it do any good to say I'm sorry?"

Daphne hardened herself against the memories that crept in—Roger, hours after their wedding, swooping her over the threshold of the roadside motel where they'd been stranded when their car broke down en route to Baja. And when she was pregnant with Kyle, how he'd once trudged ten blocks in the pouring rain to buy her kumquats. She saw him in the delivery room, too, holding his son for the first time, as shy and overcome with emotion as any new father. No one would have guessed he was a doctor.

"It isn't about being sorry," she told him, not unkindly. "It's about doing the right thing to begin with."

Roger gave a dry laugh. "The right thing? What would that have been, I wonder. Is there *anything* I could have done that would have made you love me more?" He gave her a knowing look, his face furrowed with a mixture of longing and bitterness. "You think I don't know I was second choice? That right up to the very last minute, you'd have married that other guy if he'd come back? I may be shortsighted at times, Daphne, but I'm not *blind*."

Daphne burned at the truth in his words, coming at a time when she was most vulnerable to them. "I married *you*, Roger," she cried. "That's what you've lost sight of."

He scooped up a handful of Kyle's Legos, rattling them in his palm as if they were dice. *Double or nothing,* she thought absurdly. What kind of odds would Father

Sebastian give their marriage? A hollow laugh inched its way up her throat, but Roger's next words squelched it.

"Maybe you're right," he said. "But I'd like a chance to make it up to you." Stripped of his defenses, he looked almost beaten.

Daphne was at once resentful and oddly moved. It was true what he was saying: Roger *had* come second. In a heart filled with longing for Johnny there hadn't been room for much else, and to an ego the size of Roger's it must have seemed cramped indeed.

Much as she resisted it, Daphne knew what she had to do. She had to offer her husband what she'd denied him all these years—not a second chance so much as a new beginning. It wouldn't be easy. It wouldn't necessarily be a prescription for saving their marriage, either. But she had to at least *try.* Didn't she owe her family that much, at least?

Daphne put a hand over her eyes, shutting out the last rays of the sun slanting through the curtains. But instead of the happy family she tried to envision, what came to her instead, in the dark theater of her mind, was the image of Johnny, of his leaning into the warped old railing at the end of the wharf with the sea spread out like shining wings on either side of him—as he'd watched her walk away.

Chapter 14

From the kitchen, Kitty could hear her sister and brother-in-law arguing. She couldn't make out the words, only their low urgent tones. Whatever it was, it obviously couldn't wait. Or maybe it had been building to a head for quite some time and had waited long enough. Was Daphne finally giving that pompous know-it-all the boot in the rear he so richly deserved?

Kitty sincerely hoped so.

Immediately, she was struck with remorse. Turning away from the stove, where she was boiling Mason jars for jam, she gazed at her niece and nephew, seated at the table. She'd given them the job of pulling the stems from the strawberries—the season's first—and now their mouths and hands were the ruby of the stained dish towels tucked under their chins. If Roger and Daphne were to get divorced, she thought, the children's lives would be turned upside down, possibly scarred forever. How could she wish for that?

There are worse things, a mournful voice whispered. Like being unable to bring a child into a world that offered as much in wonderment as it did misfortune. Like waking up to the reality that your last ace has been played, and the odds are against another shot at adopting.

Sean? Gone, too. It had been two weeks since they'd last spoken. The reason she'd given him was that she needed time to herself, time to recover from the blow of his sister's decision. For the truth was she couldn't be with Sean without thinking of the baby that might have been hers. And the prospect of lying under him, feeling like an empty vessel that would never be filled, was simply too painful.

She'd tried to explain it to him—this sense of having been, well, *cheated*, not just by Heather but by fate. But Sean hadn't understood. There are lots of children out there, he'd argued. Why didn't she adopt an older kid, someone who really *needed* a mother?

Sean and his sister had been such children, she knew. Wasn't that what he'd been thinking of when he'd made that suggestion? At the same time he was reminding her of the fact that they came from two very separate places and would never see eye to eye.

"It's hard enough dealing with this on my own," she'd told him. "I don't expect you to understand, Sean. The way I feel about adopting a newborn . . . well, it doesn't make sense to *me* even. And the fact that you can't see what I'm going through just makes it harder. I need to be alone for a while, to think things over."

They'd been sitting in his truck, parked outside her house. It was early evening, the weather unseasonably warm for the first week in June. He'd stopped by to see her, but she wouldn't let him inside the house. That would have been too risky, for she'd have wanted him to stay the night.

"Don't take too long," he'd warned, attempting to strike a light tone that fell flat. In his dark eyes she'd seen a flash of fear, and something else. Anger? Was he angry at her for pushing him away . . . or for wanting something he didn't—or perhaps couldn't—understand?

But if Sean was angry at her, Kitty thought, she was no less angry at herself, for she should have seen this coming. She should have nipped it in the bud. He was all wrong for her—too young in some ways, too old in others. And maybe, in the end, she wasn't meant to be with *anyone,* not just Sean. Wasn't that the real reason she'd never married? Not because she hadn't found the right person . . . but because she hadn't really been looking.

Yet the solace she sought in her solitary bed was slow in coming. Lately, she'd had trouble sleeping, and the thought of food left her faintly nauseated. Everywhere she turned, everything she did, thoughts of Sean, wrapped up with those of the baby, went with her—an ache in the hollow just below her breastbone that seemed only to grow with the passage of time.

Once when she was little, Kitty had accidentally swallowed a cherry pit, after which Daphne had informed her with a perfectly straight face that seeds could grow in stomachs the same as in dirt. Kitty had believed her, for didn't her big sister read zillions of books and know more than most grown-ups? For days afterward, she had tiptoed about as if on eggshells, lifting her shirt every so often to examine her navel, from which she'd half expected to see a curly green tendril poking. When she'd finally asked her mother about it, she'd smiled and said that Daphne had only been *teasing*. Still, the image lingered. Now, all these years later, Kitty could see it in her mind's eye—a tree studded with the hard green fruit of every mistake she'd made, every heartache she had known. The rustling of its leaves filled her head like every whispered warning she had ignored.

As if in faint, echoing tandem, her sister's voice in the next room continued to rise and fall. But instead of the concern Kitty normally would have felt, her stomach tightened with a hard little twist of annoyance. The *last* thing she needed right now, she thought, was a family squabble.

Your mother's on trial for murder, and you're afraid of a little scene?

A pebble of amusement shook loose from the grip of her misery, and Kitty smiled a little as she slipped on an oven mitt and carefully lifted the rack of jars from the steaming kettle. What harm would there be in a little yelling? In the long run, it might even do some good. Maybe what this family needed right now was the very thing she'd wished on Roger: a swift kick in the ass.

Anything would be better than this awful sense of . . . *stagnation*. Her mother's lawyer had cautioned them against getting their hopes up, warning that the pretrial discovery would be tedious and probably not amount to anything too dramatic, but what Cathcart *hadn't* prepared her for was the crawling dread that mounted with each passing day. Kitty had long since given up hope of a deus ex machina and would have settled for *any* straw, however slender, to grasp—a legal technicality, a friend willing to testify to the strain her mother had been under, a former mistress with an ax to grind against her father. Anything.

Even at the hospital, when she'd gone to clean out her father's desk, her subtle inquiries about a special friendship he might have had with one of the nurses had been met with a stone wall. His colleagues either didn't know . . . or they weren't telling. And among her father's files and papers, there had been no evidence of anything but hard work and a dedication to his craft.

Her conversation with Alex the week before was the last time Kitty had felt she might be getting somewhere. But whatever Alex might have been on the verge of revealing, she must have thought better of it. Except for the thank you notes that had arrived in the mail—written on heavy monogrammed stationery—neither she nor Daphne had heard from her sister since. Was Alex ashamed of needing help? Or was there another, more insidious reason?

Her sister was hiding something, no doubt about it. Suspicions of her own? Or did Alex know something that could provide the missing piece to the puzzle? *It's time I paid her a visit*, she thought. Willa was off today, but Daphne could hold down the fort for another hour or so, until closing time. It wouldn't hurt Roger to pitch in, either.

Kitty switched off the burner under the kettle and tossed a clean dish towel over the jars cooling on the counter. Over her shoulder, she cautioned the children, "They're hot, so don't touch. And, guys, if it's not too much to ask, would you mind leaving some of those strawberries for the jam?"

Kyle grinned mischievously, then popped another strawberry into his red-stained mouth. His sister, for reasons known only to a four-year-old, found this incredibly hilarious and began giggling so hard she nearly fell out of her chair. Even Kitty had to smile. As she made her way upstairs, a selfish thought crept in, *If Daphne were to move out here permanently, I'd get to see them all the time instead of just once or twice a year. I'd be a part of their lives, their traditions.*

She pictured them gathered around the tree on Christmas morning—Kyle and Jennie in their footie pajamas, tearing into their presents while she and Daphne sat curled on the sofa, sipping hot cocoa and nibbling on cranberry bread. Or coloring Easter eggs with crayons, and rolling them in Pyrex dishes of dye. To look across the table on Thanksgiving and see the faces of her loved ones shining in the candlelight—oh, how lovely that would be! Kitty had to pause on the stairs to suck in her breath against a sudden dizzying rush of yearning.

In her room, instead of reaching for the phone, she stretched out on the bed—early nineteenth-century Victorian, its burled walnut frame in the shape of a sleigh. Browsing in an antique store one day, she'd spotted it and instantly fallen in love. It had reminded her of the Frances Hodgson Burnett novels she'd loved as a young girl.

Now, lying on her back, staring up at a crack in the ceiling shaped like a question mark, Kitty thought of *A Little Princess*—in which young Sara's hope, in the face of all evidence to the contrary, triumphed when she found her father alive. With the flat of her hand, she traced the raised pattern of the wedding ring quilt pressing into her legs and back, plump and sweet as kittens' paws. She thought of the last time she and Sean had made love on this bed, how slowly and carefully he'd undressed her, how he'd examined and stroked each patch of skin as it was laid bare, then bent—like a thirsty traveler to a pool of water—to kiss her there.

The memory brought hot tears that creased her temples and ran into her hair. It was several minutes before she felt strong enough to pull herself upright and reach for the phone on the painted nightstand.

But when she reached her sister's house, it was Lori who answered. Her mother wasn't home, she said. In an odd, whispery voice, she informed Kitty, "She's up at *the house.*"

"*Grandma's* house?" Kitty sat there with the phone

to her ear, stunned speechless. What on earth could Alex be thinking of, rambling around up there before they'd even gotten the place cleaned up? The police had completed their investigation, but even so, it was . . . well, it was _morbid._

There was a pause, then her niece volunteered, "It's not the first time, Aunt Kitty. She's been going there a lot lately."

"Oh, dear." Kitty struggled to keep the dismay from her voice. "Did she say _why?_"

"She _says_ it's to water the plants." Even Lori sounded dubious.

Kitty didn't like what she was hearing, not one bit, but she didn't want to upset her niece any further. Maintaining an even tone, she said, "You know how your mom is—she probably thinks it's her duty to single-handedly keep the old place from falling apart. Why don't I take a run up there and see if she needs a hand with anything?"

Another brief pause, then in an oddly formal voice tinged with relief, her niece agreed, "I think that would be a good idea, Aunt Kitty." She added in a whisper, "Dad is worried about her, you know. But Mom would kill me if she knew I'd told _him_ about some of the stuff that's been going on."

Knowing her sister, Kitty didn't doubt it.

Grabbing her purse, she dashed back downstairs to give Daphne an update, hoping that she and Roger weren't still arguing. But when she stepped into the front room, Daphne was alone. She sat slumped at a table strewn with Kyle's Legos, chin in hand, staring out the window. When she looked up, Kitty saw that she'd been crying.

"Want some company?" Kitty asked gently. "Or would you rather be left alone?"

Daphne managed a wan smile. "What I'd like," she said, "is to be shipwrecked on a desert island for the next twenty years. Maybe by then I'd have it all figured out."

"What exactly?" Kitty cocked her head in bemusement and wondered if most writers were like her sister, with a tendency toward the melodramatic.

"Just my whole life," Daphne moaned.

"Your whole life . . . or just you and Roger?"

Daphne winced and a blush spread across her cheeks nearly as deep as the strawberries that had stained her children's mouths. "Is it that obvious?"

"Only to someone who loves you as much as I do." Kitty took her hand. "Come on, there is something you can do that'll take your mind off all this. It's Alex. She's in more trouble than we thought."

"Moneywise?"

"Not that kind of trouble. *Real* trouble." Though they were alone—at the table where Father Sebastian had sat there was only a crumpled bill amid a handful of change—she dropped her voice. "The kind that can get you put away in the psych ward on a seventy-two-hour hold."

Daphne straightened, her eyes widening in alarm. "Why didn't you say something?"

"I didn't know myself until a few minutes ago," Kitty said. "I just got off the phone with Lori. She told me that Alex was up at the house." She didn't have to spell out that it was *Mother's* house.

The color drained from Daphne's face, and she leaped to her feet. "Come on, what are we waiting for? Roger can watch the kids. And as for me," she managed a tremulous smile, "I can sit around feeling sorry for myself some other time."

Minutes later, they were chugging up the hill to Agua Fria Point in Kitty's elderly Honda. It was almost dark, but the fog that lay in a long gray smudge against the purpling horizon, like on a badly erased homework assignment, had yet to roll in. *Good,* she thought, because lately driving at night made her nervous. Kitty had developed an unreasonable fear of falling prey to some gruesome accident. She would picture herself flung into some muddy ditch, like the broken, rusted appliances littering the dirt road to Barranco—refrigerators, stoves, washing machines that had outlived their usefulness.

Who would mourn her? Her sisters, Daphne most of

all. Her nieces and nephew. Her friends . . . and to a lesser degree, her loyal patrons. But no one whose heart had once lain alongside her bones, whose blood and memories were inextricably intertwined with her own. No son to smile at the memory of her struggling to help build a tree house. No daughter to remember her mother lifting her up to reach the highest branches of the Christmas tree . . . or pinching off pieces of dough for small hands to roll out.

She thought of her own childhood and was pierced with sorrow.

"Do you remember the days when Mother used to meet our school bus?" she reminisced aloud. "The other mothers were always dressed in cardigans and pressed slacks—like those dopey housewives on TV selling dish soap. Not *ours*. She'd be standing there in her artist's smock with a streak of paint on one cheek."

Kitty glanced over and saw Daphne smile. "What I remember best is that she knew the names of every flower, even the ones that grew wild along the side of the road. I never appreciated that until I had children of my own. Now, when Kyle or Jennie point at one and ask, 'Mommy, what flower is that?' I don't have to look it up in a book."

"I just wish . . ." Kitty bit her lip.

"What?"

"That she'd shared more of herself with us," she went on. "Those things—they were like the frosting on the cake. She never talked much about what *really* mattered. Like how she *felt*. You and Johnny, for instance. I don't know if Mother disapproved, or if it was just Daddy."

Daphne fell silent, lost in thought as Kitty wound her way up the hill, past the shadows cast by hulking houses and the sweep of lawns that seemed to rise on either side of them like ocean swells. She roused from her reverie at last and said, "I spoke to her about it. Just once. She said I should listen to Daddy, that he knew best." She paused. "I'm not so sure she'd give me the same advice today."

"Why?" Kitty asked. "Because she finally figured out that Daddy didn't have all the answers?"

"That's not it, exactly," Daphne said, staring out the window. "I think it's more that Mother is finally coming to terms with her own feelings. They've been forced out in the open, and now she can't squash them back down again." She turned to Kitty. "Is that what I've been doing all these years, Kitty, squashing everything down to make it fit?"

Kitty shook her head, a lump forming in her throat. "I don't know, Daph. I think *all* of us have been kidding ourselves, one way or another. The question now isn't so much what we should have known, but what we can learn from this."

Daphne gave a short bitter laugh. "I don't know what I've learned, except that love hurts."

Kitty blinked, and the taillights of the car several blocks ahead of her dissolved in a watery red blur. *Sean,* she thought. The ache in her chest deepened, and her insides dipped and rocked like the fractured moon reflected in the waves rolling onto the point. Would he miss her for long? Probably not. He'd move on, find someone new to love . . . with all the fury of a young man's passion.

The sentiment made her feel noble somehow—with a dash of bittersweet like the pectin in jam that made it gel—but did nothing to stop the dull throb in her veins. By the time she pulled into the driveway of her childhood home, Kitty had no room left over for the heartache waiting for her inside. She had enough of her own to fill a wishing well.

Letting herself in the front door, with Daphne bringing up the rear, Kitty called out in trepidation, "Alex?"

No reply. But she heard a noise, a rhythmic *shush-shush-shush* that made her think of a plank being sanded. Puzzled, she crossed the vestibule, her heart climbing into her throat. In the parlor, she found Alex on her knees with a bucket of soapy water and a brush, scrubbing furiously at the bloodstained carpet.

"Alex! What in God's name—"

Behind her, Kitty heard Daphne gasp at the face that turned up to them. Alex was wearing the glazed, empty look of someone lost in a nightmare. Her normally perfect hair was clumped about her shoulders, the once-fluffy bangs pasted to a forehead polished with greasy sweat. Her red-rimmed eyes blinked up at her two sisters uncomprehendingly for a moment, then she abruptly sat back on her haunches, seemingly unaware of the scrub brush dripping soapy water over her taupe slacks.

"It won't come out. No matter how hard I scrub." Alex's weary voice held a note of childlike petulance. Then she cocked her head brightly as if something had just occurred to her. "Remember how she was always after us. 'Girls,'" her sister scolded in eerie imitation of their mother, "'how many times do I have to remind you to *soak* your panties before putting them in the wash.' As if our periods were something to be ashamed of. As if a tiny little bloodstain were the end of the world." She began to giggle helplessly, a fat tear rolling down one cheek.

Kitty stared down at the carpet, glistening dark with water and scummy pinkish suds. Suddenly, she felt as if she were going to throw up. "Oh, Alex," she breathed.

It was Daphne who took charge, stepping around her to squat down next to Alex. "It's too much for one person, Alex. You'd better let us help you."

"How? *How* can you help?" Alex demanded, her voice rising. "He's dead. Nothing's going to bring him back."

"No," Kitty agreed sorrowfully.

Feeling dizzy, she cast about to get her bearings, taking in the overstuffed chairs, the bric-a-brac crowding every surface, the heavy floor lamp that appeared to be rooted to the carpet. The room held almost no trace of her mother, whose lighter touch was evident only in the delicate watercolors wedged, almost as an afterthought, between the dark formal paintings favored by her father. It struck her then that perhaps she hadn't known her mother at all. Maybe none of them had.

The only thing she knew for certain was that the time for weeping and wailing was over. Her gaze returned to Alex, the sister with whom she had the least in common . . . but whom lately she'd begun to see in a new light.

The compassion that had come so naturally that day in the garden, when Alex broke down and confessed that she was in trouble, welled up in Kitty once more. But this time she had to resist it, stow it away on a high shelf until it would be truly useful. What Alex needed even more right now, she knew, was to snap out of this.

Kitty marched over and grabbed her sister's arm, dragging Alex to her feet. "Get up. *Get up this instant.*" Hearing herself, she recognized the exact tone her mother had used when they were children and one of them was having a tantrum.

It had the desired effect. Alex jerked away, rubbing her arm as she scowled at Kitty. "Where the hell do *you* get off?"

"I could ask the same of you." Kitty faced her squarely, hands on hips.

"In case you haven't noticed, I'm making myself useful. Which is more than I can say for either of you." Alex glanced from her to Daphne, her mouth pursing in annoyance.

"Maybe some of us are too busy worrying about Mother," Daphne reminded her. She rose beside them and walked over to the window to yank the cord on the venetian blinds. They descended with a skeletal rattling that caused Kitty to jump, reminding her of what Daphne clearly hadn't forgotten: there could very well be a reporter lurking outside.

Yet if the same thought had occurred to Alex, she showed no sign of it. "There was dust everywhere," she went on snippily, as if Daphne hadn't spoken. "I found stuff in the refrigerator you could have made penicillin out of. And the plants—most of them were dead."

Alex drifted over to the Boston fern in the window. Brown tendrils with a few yellowing leaves still clinging to them trailed down to brush the sofa back. She began pulling them off, one by one, like the daisy petals they'd plucked as children. *He loves me . . . he loves me not . . .*

"This is crazy." Kitty marched over and planted a hand on Alex's shoulder, forcing her around. "The twins are worried sick, and frankly, so am I." More gently, she urged, "Go home, Alex. Go home to your children. *Leave* all this."

"I will. As soon as I'm done." As if in a trance, Alex shrugged her off and walked back over to the bucket. She'd started to sink to her knees, but Daphne was too quick for her. She darted over to seize hold of Alex's wrist, hauling her to her feet.

"We'll do it together," she repeated, slowly this time, as if for the benefit of a dull fifth-grader. "*All* of us." She darted a glance at Kitty. "Do you think we're strong enough to lift the sofa?"

Catching her meaning, Kitty replied, "If one of us pulls on the rug at the same time." She pondered for a moment, wondering aloud, "The question is, will it fit in the back of my car?"

"What—the sofa or the rug?" Daphne was suppressing a laugh, she could see, but from the high color in her cheeks and the way her eyes were glittering, Kitty suspected she wasn't too far from utter hysteria.

Don't, she warned with her eyes. *Or I'll lose it, too.*

She looked over at Alex, who was staring at them in horror. "You can't," she said in a small strangled voice, staring down at the rug. "You can't just . . . just get rid of it."

"Yes, we can," Kitty told her. "We *have* to."

"But Mother would—" Alex started to say.

"Mother doesn't have to know," Daphne told her, careful to add, "Not right away."

Alex started backing away, as if from something that might hurt her, her eyes wide and panicky. Then, bumping up against the old-fashioned curve-backed sofa, she abruptly sank down, the tension draining from her as suddenly as from an overstimulated child who's wound herself down into a stupor. "Oh God, what am I *doing?*" She covered her eyes, and in a muffled whisper confessed, "I can't let go. The nightmares . . . I thought if I could just get the stain out . . . ."

A sudden lurid image of her father in his coffin leaped into Kitty's mind. And when she reached to switch on the Tiffany lamp by the sofa, she saw that her hand was shaking. As the light flared on, a gentle violet glow that spilled like strewn petals over the worn chocolate plush and onto the carpet at their feet, she thought, *We're like this house. No amount of fixing will ever make us whole again.*

"Whatever's eating you, Alex, it's going to take more than soap and water to get rid of it," Kitty admonished gently.

"Oh, what do *you* know?" The look of disgust Alex shot her was all too familiar. It was as if the humbled woman who'd opened up to her that day in the garden had vanished, leaving only the pesky younger sister who'd tagged after her and Daphne when they were children, whining when they wouldn't let her play with them.

Kitty had to force herself to speak softly. "I don't know everything, Alex. But what I *see* is someone cleaning up a mess she didn't make."

"Kitty's right," Daphne said. "What happened here—" she glanced down at the carpet and swallowed hard, looking back up with an expression of grim resolve—"is not your fault."

"You still don't get it, do you? I'm to blame for *all* this." Alex glared up at them, her eyes bright with unshed tears. "I knew what he was doing behind her back. I should have told Mother . . . *warned* her somehow."

"What good would it have done?" Kitty asked.

But Alex just sat there, shaking her head. "I believed him. All his reasons that were really just excuses. He made it seem like he was doing her a *favor* almost, that deep down Mother actually preferred it that way. I never thought anyone could get hurt."

"It hurt *you,*" Daphne pointed out.

"You don't know the half of it." Alex turned away, her mouth pinching shut.

Whatever she was biting back, Kitty knew better than to try and pry it out of her. Alex was like a sea anemone that buttoned up tight with the slightest poke. Instead, she urged softly, "Why don't you tell us then? Maybe it would help."

In the silence that followed, Kitty was acutely aware of every noise: the prowling murmur of cars abruptly slowing as they passed the house, the creaks and groans of an old house settling, the ticking of the pedestal clock on the mantel, full of portent somehow.

At last, Alex cleared her throat and in a voice as haunted as the house, replied, "The woman you're looking for—the nurse he was seeing. I know who she is."

Kitty felt the strength go out of her knees as abruptly as a spring-loaded hinge popping loose. With a groan, she sank down on the sofa next to Alex. "Why do I get the feeling I'm not going to like what I hear."

Alex gave her a long look filled with signs of an eternal struggle. A muscle twitched alongside her hard flat mouth, and her eyes brimmed with angry tears. In a low wrenched voice, she said, "It was Leanne."

Daphne dropped onto the sofa arm nearest Kitty. "Oh, Alex. Are you sure?"

Alex nodded wearily. "Ninety-nine percent."

Kitty thought, *My sister's best friend? Impossible. Even Daddy wouldn't sink that low.* Then she realized, with a dull thump in her stomach that spiraled up in a wave of dizziness, that any man who would cheat on his wife with *her* best friend—however many years ago it had been—would stop at nothing.

"How . . . how did you find out?" she stammered.

"I was thinking about what you said. About the earring. It turns out Leanne is missing one."

"That doesn't necessarily prove anything," Daphne said.

"Not by itself maybe," she agreed. "But there were other signs. Little things I ignored until they all added up."

Kitty didn't have to ask if Alex was sure. The grim certainty in her face told the whole story. "What happened when you confronted her?"

"I haven't. Not yet. As you can see, I've been . . . busy." Alex looked down in sudden disgust at the scrub brush lying discarded on the floor in a puddle of congealing suds. "All that work, and look—it hasn't made one bit of difference."

"Mother was right," Daphne said in an oddly shrill

voice, a giggle of hysteria just below the surface, "once a stain sets, you never get it out."

Alex's mouth twisted in a small pained smile. "You could write a book about all the things Mother warned us not to do. Too bad nobody warned *her*. About Daddy. Years ago, before it was too late."

"Alex, listen to me." Kitty, seated beside her sister on the sofa, swiveled around to take hold of both her hands, gripping them tightly. "There was nothing you could have done to prevent it."

"Whose fault *was* it then?"

"Maybe no one's. Maybe everyone's. It was like a conspiracy in some ways, wasn't it? A pact of silence that wouldn't have held up if we hadn't *all* played along. You, by guarding Daddy's secrets. Me, by pretending not to know for the sake of keeping the family peace. And, Daphne," she paused to smile ruefully at her elder sister, perched on the sofa arm, "by being Daphne." As Kitty spoke, the picture grew sharper, like a photograph in a darkroom emerging from what had been a ghostly blur. "Maybe the moral, if there is one, is that silence isn't always golden."

"What *I* want to know is, where does Leanne fit in?" Daphne said, her expression turning grave.

"That's what we have to find out," Kitty said.

"She works the night shift," Alex told them. "We'll have to wait until tomorrow to talk to her."

"Says who? Come on," Kitty stood up, and headed for the door. "Leave all that. We'll come back later and get rid of the damn thing. I never liked that rug anyway."

"Me neither," Alex confessed. Kitty turned and caught a hint of the old Alex in her younger sister's eyes as she rose to follow her.

"I think there's an old braided rug of Nana's up in the attic," Daphne called after them. She caught up with them in the foyer, her cheeks flushed. "It's not as big, but at least the floor won't look so bare."

"I'm glad we can all agree on one thing, at least." Kitty took a deep breath and stepped out onto the porch, where the paint had been rubbed off the railing

in spots by the police tape and a single moth was me-
thodically beating itself to death against the light by
the door.

She felt a peculiar sense of anticipation mixed with
dread. What if they ended up not just solving a mystery,
but opening up a Pandora's box that would bring more
harm than good?

K itty slowed as the sign rose into view, bathed in foot-
lights like a nativity scene. MIRAMONTE GENERAL.
Growing up, she and her sisters *had* seen it as somehow
holy. The temple to which their father had gone every
day, not to worship, but *be* worshiped. As chief of pathology, his doctoring skills had been confined to the
dead, but that had only enhanced Kitty's image of him
as someone godlike, unafraid to walk where few others
dared. When she was much younger—young enough to
believe everything she saw in movies—she'd gone so far
as to imagine he could bring a dead person back to life.

Her fantasies had flourished in part because her father
seldom talked about his work. It wasn't a suitable topic
of conversation, he'd admonish in a tight, clipped tone
whenever someone had the temerity to ask. Yet however
diligently he scrubbed at the end of his day, he'd never
failed to bring it home with him: the faint antiseptic
smell of the hospital morgue, a smell inextricably associated in Kitty's mind with death.

Now, as she pulled into a space near the emergency
room entrance, she found herself growing as chilled as
she had felt standing before her father's open grave.

She waited with Daphne in the Honda until Alex, following in her own car, joined them. The three of them
were heading for the covered walkway that led up to
a pair of swinging double doors when Daphne spoke
up nervously.

"What will Leanne think when she sees us all descending on her at once?"

"I hope she'll know the game is up," Alex shot back,
her bitterness toward her friend as readily apparent as

the bloodstained slacks visible through her loosely belted raincoat.

Alex was back in her old fighting form, Kitty noted with relief.

Inside, the waiting area was teeming and no one paid the slightest bit of attention to the three neatly dressed women hurrying past. A burly bearded man with a bloody towel pressed to his forehead was the only one who looked up. They were nearly at the elevators when they heard someone cry out, "Kitty!"

Sean. As she turned in the direction of his voice, Kitty felt as if she were slowly pivoting on the spike that had been driven through her heart. Dear God, what was *he* doing here? For a wild, unfocused moment it occurred to her that he might have been following her, then she remembered that Sean had far too much pride for that.

She spotted him not ten feet away, leaning up against a vending machine—a dark-haired young man in ratty Levis, with the guarded eyes of someone far older. Beneath his purposefully relaxed pose he was like one, large contracted muscle ready to spring into action.

Kitty hesitated a moment, torn between the desire to run to him . . . and wanting to dive into the elevator she heard thump open behind her. Slowly, she walked over to him. In a low voice, she asked, "Sean, what are you doing here?" Her gaze skated over him, looking for blood or bruises, an arm that didn't hang right.

Her concern wasn't lost on him. A corner of his mouth lifted in a small knowing smile. "Don't worry, I'm fine. It's Heather—she fainted. It's probably nothing, but I thought she should have it checked out." He jerked his head in the direction of his sister, seated several dozen yards away by the admissions desk.

Heather, flipping through a tattered magazine, didn't see her and appeared to be suffering from nothing more than a case of terminal boredom.

All at once, Kitty became acutely aware of the curious looks she was getting from her sisters. Turning to them, she said, "Five minutes, okay? I'll meet you upstairs."

Neither commented, for which she would be eternally

grateful. Alex merely nodded and said, "Fifth floor. We'll wait for you in the visitors' lounge."

Watching the elevator doors close on them, Sean asked, "Your sister?" He was referring to Alex, of course; Daphne, he'd already met.

Kitty nodded. "Sorry, I should have introduced you."

He shrugged, straightening as he pulled away from the vending machine. "Another time."

Kitty glanced again at Heather, noting that the bulge under her sweatshirt was bigger than the last time she'd seen her. Her heart twisted with a sharpness that brought a bitter, metallic taste to the back of her tongue. Forcing herself to meet Sean's unremitting gaze, she asked softly, "How's it going? I mean, in general."

"Okay. You?" His eyes slid away from hers, and he became suddenly absorbed in prying at a slip of paper taped to the machine's panel, on which someone had scrawled with a ballpoint pen: OUT OF ORDER.

"To tell the truth, not so good."

"Sorry to hear that." The look he gave her wasn't very sympathetic, but the glimmer of hurt in his eyes told another story.

She took a deep breath and let it out slowly, as if too sudden an exhalation might be painful with her heart thumping savagely in her chest. "Look, Sean. What happened with us . . . well, let's just say I didn't want it to end this way."

"Why does it have to end at all?"

"It just does."

Sean cocked his head, his spiky dark hair seeming to bristle like that of a wild animal sensing a threat. "Yeah? My whole life, I been hearing that line. *Don't ask so many questions, son. Just accept things the way they are.* Bullshit." He socked the vending machine with a clenched fist, evoking a hollow, tinny rattle from inside. "It's a fucking cop-out, and you know it. You don't want to see me anymore? Okay. I don't have to like it, but at least I know where it's coming from. I can *fight* it."

"Some things you can't fight."

He took a breath and in a low, battened-down voice

said, "Whatever you might think, I had nothing to do with Heather choosing that couple over you."

"I'm not accusing you of anything."

"Then why do I feel like I'm being punished?"

"This isn't about *you,* Sean," she cried in exasperation.

"What *is* it then?"

Kitty sighed. "I don't know. I can't explain it any more than I can explain what happened in *my* family." She glanced down, unable to meet his eyes—hot and black, like two holes scorched into wood too green for a fire. "The only thing I *do* know is that there's no way I can go on seeing you and at the same time put all this behind me."

He regarded her steadily for a moment, then said, "Where I come from, we have another word for it—chickenshit. You don't like it when something smacks you in the head? Too bad. You deal with it anyway."

"It's not that simple."

"Simple? Who the fuck said it had to be simple? All I ever asked was that you give enough of a shit to at least *try.* But if you don't want to, well, what can I say? It's been fun. Have a nice life." Sean spun on his heel. If not for the tightness in his shoulders and the fierce angle of his neck, she might have been able to convince herself he didn't care as much as he claimed to. But she knew better. She knew even before Sean tossed over his shoulder, "You know, maybe Heather made the right choice after all. One thing about raising kids—you're in it for the long haul. It's not something you can back out of when the going gets tough."

Sean's words hit home like a blow. "Sean, I—"

But he was already out of earshot. She watched through a film of tears as he joined his sister, now conferring with one of the nurses. As Heather bobbed clumsily to her feet, he gently took her arm, guiding her in the direction the nurse had pointed.

He'll make a good father someday. The thought rang clear and sweet as a carillon amid the crowd of emotions that bumped and elbowed her as Kitty stepped into the elevator.

Punching the button for the fifth floor, she angrily brushed the tears from her eyes and ordered herself, *Not now. Later you can think about Sean. Tonight, when you're lying in bed counting all your sensible reasons instead of sheep.*

Upstairs, in the visitors' lounge catty-corner to the nurses' station, Alex jumped up from her chair to demand, "Who was *that?*"

"A friend." Kitty cast a grateful glance at Daphne, making a mental note to thank her later on for not spilling the beans. She couldn't cope with any long-winded explanations about Sean, not now. Dropping her voice, she asked, "Did you have Leanne paged?"

Alex shook her head. "She'd wonder what we're doing here and maybe get suspicious. It's better if we just surprise her." Her eyes narrowed, any thoughts of Kitty's love life clearly eclipsed by the prospect of what lay ahead. Then she abruptly turned, leading the way down the corridor to the neonatal intensive care unit, where Leanne was on duty.

Reaching a pair of stainless steel double doors marked ALYCE BUNT THAYER WING, Alex pushed her way inside. Kitty and Daphne followed her into a large windowless space like something from another planet. Behind the cluster of desks that made up the nurses' station stood rows of isolettes, their tiny occupants scarcely recognizable as human, each one monitored by a thicket of tubes and electronic devices.

Kitty's gaze fell on the smallest of the preemies, the fluttering of its tiny chest making her think of a fish gasping in the bottom of a boat. The card on the isolette read, "Baby Boy Roper." Below it was taped a photo of a smiling dark-haired woman, facing inward, where her infant might have seen it had his eyes not been covered with patches—a mother making a desperate bid for her child's life the only way she knew how.

Choking back a cry, Kitty thought, *If he were mine, I would love him just as much . . . maybe more.* There'd be no need for a photo of his mother because she would never leave his side.

At the desk closest to them, a stout gray-haired nurse

barely glanced up from a chart she was scribbling in. "Visiting hours are between two and eight," she informed them mechanically, "unless you're a family member; in which case, you're welcome anytime as long as you scrub." She gestured vaguely in the direction of the sink.

Alex cleared her throat. "We're here to see Leanne Chapman."

This time, the woman didn't even bother to look up. "Leanne? She's in the critical-care room, I think. I'll go see . . . if you'll just give me a minute to finish this."

"I know the way. I've been here before," Alex informed her in the businesslike voice of a top-notch realtor who didn't take no for an answer.

"We're relatives," Daphne was quick to interject. Not a lie exactly. They *were* related . . . to each other. But Kitty was surprised nonetheless. She wouldn't have thought her straight-arrow sister capable of fibbing. Daphne really *had* changed, she thought, not without admiration.

The gray-haired nurse paused to eye them more closely. Was she wondering why they'd asked for Leanne? If so, she must have concluded that, as relatives of a sick baby, it wouldn't have been unusual for them to have developed close ties with one of the nurses. In any event, she pointed toward a doorway in back, merely repeating, "Don't forget to scrub."

At the stainless-steel sink to the right of the double doors, the three sisters removed their bracelets and rings and took turns squirting Exedine over their hands, scrubbing until they were raw. They were their father's daughters; they knew the drill.

A few minutes later, as they were making their way through the forest of isolettes and monitors, Daphne murmured under her breath, "I don't know how she does it with that little boy of hers to go home to every day. You'd think it would be more than any one person could handle."

"She must have imagined Daddy was going to rescue her," Alex whispered back in a voice heavy with scorn.

Kitty said nothing. In her own mind, she was suddenly

seeing it from Leanne's point of view—how a single mom with a severely handicapped child, struggling to make ends meet, might be attracted to a man as old as their father, a revered doctor, no less, who must have represented the stability so glaringly absent from her own life.

The thought sickened her nonetheless. Following Alex down a short corridor that led to a glass door with a sign that said, CRITICAL CARE, PLEASE KNOCK BEFORE ENTERING, Kitty had to make a conscious effort to rearrange her features into a pleasant mask.

Alex didn't bother knocking. She just sailed on in. The room was smaller than the one in front and contained only four isolettes—occupied by the very sickest babies. Leanne appeared to be the only nurse on duty. She stood before an open isolette, expertly changing a preemie scarcely bigger than her hand despite the wires taped to its chest and the tubes sprouting from its nose and mouth. Seeing them, she blinked in astonishment and seemed to falter for a moment.

Then she pulled herself together and smiled, quipping, "If this is a fund-raising drive, I gave at the office." She slid the tiniest of diapers under a bottom that would have fit into a tablespoon. "Seriously, what gives? This is sort of off the beaten track for you guys. You visiting someone on one of the other floors?"

Noting Alex's thunderous expression, Kitty was quick to step up to the plate. "We came to see *you*." She spoke lightly, casually almost.

In the glare of overhead fluorescents Leanne wore a strange, almost luminous pallor—like someone swimming toward them underwater. A tiny frown creased her pale forehead. "I appreciate the thought, ladies, but as you can see, I sort of have my hands full right now."

Alex found her voice at last. "This won't take long."

"Why do I get the feeling this isn't an invitation to a Tupperware party?" Leanne laughed nervously, glancing from Alex to Kitty, then at Daphne, who hung back with her arms crossed over her chest.

"I'm curious about something, Leanne," Alex said

softly. "The earring you said was missing. Any idea where you might have lost it?"

Something flashed in Leanne's eyes. Something that made Kitty think of a small fleet-footed animal leaping from a clearing into the underbrush. Then it was gone.

"You came all the way here to ask about an *earring?*" Leanne secured the diaper in place and gently replaced the infant in its isolette. She carried the wet diaper to a scale on the Formica counter behind her, weighed it for urine output, then scribbled a note on the baby's chart. "If this is your idea of a fun evening, you must be pretty desperate," she laughed. "Anyway, I thought you said you found it."

"I was lying." Alex's voice cut like a sharp instrument through the soft beeping of monitors. "An earring *was* found—in a room at the Surfside Motel out in Barranco. I'm assuming it's yours."

Leanne's head shot up, and before she could stop herself the tip of her tongue darted out to lick her lips. "Why . . . why would you think that?"

Daphne stepped up alongside Kitty. "You were there," she said. "With our father."

Leanne's mouth twitched in a sick smile that didn't reach her flat, staring eyes. "That's crazy! I don't know what you're talking about."

"Give it up, Leanne," Alex growled.

Leanne stared at them a long moment longer, then with a low moan she sank into the padded rocking chair by the door—compassionately provided for visiting parents. Kitty, expecting remorse, tears of shame even, was taken aback when Leanne lifted her chin, showing patches of mottled redness that stood out in her cheeks like defiant banners. Her eyes glittered, and her mouth was set in a hard line.

In a low unrepentant voice she said, "You think you have it all figured out, don't you? Well, you're wrong. It wasn't some cheap affair. We were in love. We were going to get married. As soon as—" her voice broke, and her eyes filled with tears. "Stop looking at me like I'm some kind of monster! It didn't start out that way. He was good to me . . . not just when we were kids.

After I came to work here, we'd meet for a bite to eat in the cafeteria sometimes. Alex, you remember what it was like with Chip at the end? I was a wreck. I don't know what I would have done if it hadn't been for your dad. When Chip left, right after I'd found out I was pregnant, he was the only one who kept me going. After I had Tyler, too, when it became obvious he wasn't going to grow up to be . . . well, normal, and everyone was saying, 'Just take it a day at a time,' and I wanted to scream that I didn't know how I was going to survive the next five *minutes,* I couldn't have gotten through it without Vern. I would have *died.*"

She glared accusingly at Alex. "*You* couldn't even stand to touch him. Do you know what it was like for me, having my best friend shrink from the sight of my own son? To know that you thought of me as some kind of charity case? Your father was the only one who treated him like a real person!"

Alex stared back at her with a mixture of horror and disgust. "You didn't care that he was . . . he was my father? And that he'd slept with your own *mother?*"

Leanne shrugged with a lack of concern that seemed exaggerated, as if she'd gone over it hundreds of times in her own mind, carefully constructing a rationale that fit. "I'm sorry I had to lie to you, Alex," she said with what seemed like genuine contriteness. "But as far as what happened between him and my mother, that was *decades* ago, before I was even born. And it was never all that serious."

"Your dad must have thought so," Alex replied coldly. "That *is* the reason your parents got divorced, isn't it?"

Leanne's mouth trembled, and her chin lifted, as if to keep her tears from spilling over. "You're just trying to hurt me, and . . . and . . . I guess I don't blame you. I know I should have told you. I was going to, but then . . ." she stopped to let loose a gasping sob, clutching at her chest as if in pain. "After he . . . afterward, there didn't seem any point."

"You *bitch,*" Alex swore. "All this time pretending to be my best friend. You're the one who should rot in prison!'' She started toward Leanne, one tightly clenched fist raised as if to strike her.

Daphne stepped forward to slip a restraining arm about Alex's shoulders. In the harsh light, she, too, appeared ghostly. But the hot gaze she fixed on Leanne was very much of this earth.

A heavy silence fell, interrupted only by the frantic beeping of an alarm in the next room: a baby that had stopped breathing. A fairly regular occurrence, Kitty knew, one requiring little more than a light tap against its chest. But at this particular moment, in this sterile room under the eternal high noon of fluorescents whose cold light would burn long after many of these littlest of lives had been extinguished, it felt as if *she* were the one who was unable to breathe. Her senses seemed to loop out of focus, the air around her growing fuzzy and dense, sounds coming at her as if through a narrow iron pipe.

As if from a great distance, she heard Leanne give a hollow laugh. "Prison?" she scoffed. "I wish I were *dead*. Anything would be better than having to hide how I feel, pretend he was nothing more than a family friend.''

Kitty reached for—and grasped hold of—a grain of understanding amid the anger and disgust welling in her. What Leanne had done was unforgivable, yes, but she hadn't acted out of malice. "Whatever you did, it's not too late to help our mother," she urged softly. "Leanne, we need to know what happened. Did she find out about you and Daddy? Is that why she killed him?''

Leanne's face crumpled, and suddenly she looked thirteen again, Alex's skinny little friend trailing along on every family outing. She shook her head. "It wasn't Vern. *I* told her. But the weird thing was she didn't act shocked or anything. She said very calmly that she knew about the others . . . but that he hadn't loved any of those women.''

"But you told her this was different, right?" Daphne prompted.

Leanne had the decency to look ashamed. "I didn't have to tell her. Your mother *knew*. Still, she . . . she wouldn't listen when I said that Vern wanted to marry

me. She got upset then, and shouted that it was wrong.
Evil. That it had to stop. That—" she bit her lip, shaking
her head.

"What?" Alex almost screamed. Her hair, already disheveled, had become a fright wig, and she'd taken on
the wild-eyed look she'd worn back at the house. *"Tell
us."*

Leanne didn't look at her. Rocking back and forth in
the underwater light, the chair's runners making faint
crackling sounds against the linoleum, she stared with
blank eyes at something only she could see. Finally, with
a high idiot's chuckle that sent a chill up Kitty's spine,
she said, "She claimed he was my father, that we were
committing incest, not adultery. Have you ever heard
anything so insane?"

Chapter 15

Alex thought if she could just make her heart stop its racing, everything would be okay somehow. It was long after midnight, and she lay in bed with the lights out, the twins fast asleep in their rooms downstairs. The only sounds were the faint whirring of her digital clock and the ceaseless barking of her neighbor's golden retriever in the yard below. Her lost hours up at the house, the trip to the hospital with her sisters, then driving home in a fog that seemed to have emanated from the dark shoals of her own mind—all of it might have been nothing more than a ghastly dream . . . except that, for the past five hours, she hadn't slept so much as a wink. Rigid, she stared up at the ceiling in which bright specks glittered like stars in a remote galaxy, every circuit in her brain humming.

How could Leanne have done this to me? Her closest friend since kindergarten. Alex remembered when they were thirteen, Leanne's crush on their art teacher, and how Leanne had sobbed in her arms, brokenhearted when Mr. Simms moved back east to teach at another school. She'd been there for Leanne, too, the time she nearly died from meningitis . . . and in school she'd once covered for her when Leanne was accused of cheating on a test. And then there were the hours upon hours of listening to her rant and rave about Chip.

Each memory was another twist of the knife in Alex's heart. It had been several days since the seeds of suspicion had taken root, but she hadn't known for *sure,* until now, tonight. Now the vastness of her friend's betrayal smashed over her like a huge wave, leaving her too flattened even to sit up.

She would never, ever forgive Leanne.

Then a voice whispered: *What about Daddy?*

Hadn't *he* betrayed her as well, sleeping with her best friend behind her back? He had to have known how it would hurt her. But he'd done it anyway. Without regard to her feelings or the deep bond she'd imagined they had.

She didn't believe for a minute that Daddy had planned on leaving Mother for Leanne. Any more than she gave credence to the delusion that Daddy had fathered Leanne—which only proved that Mother really *had* lost her mind.

What came to her now, clear as the snap of bone breaking, was the unavoidable truth at the center of it all: *He couldn't have loved me.* How could he have, and still done this to her? She'd guarded his secrets as jealously as her own and rushed to meet his every need, often at the expense of her husband and daughters—oh yes, Jim had hit a nerve there—and for *what?*

She pictured him with Leanne, the two of them making fun of her blind loyalty . . . as if she were some sort of family pet, too stupid to know better . . . mocking her, the way they probably had Mother, for her silly pride in thinking *she* was the only one he truly cared about.

Alex closed her eyes, holding them screwed shut until the effort became too much and they sprang open. Her head throbbed painfully. And her heart—was she having some sort of attack? Anxiety so severe she'd wind up in the psychiatric ward, in a bed next to the one that was being saved for Mother?

She thought of a recurring dream she'd had growing up, one that still plagued her on occasion, in which she was standing in the middle of a deserted road in her nightgown, a huge truck bearing down on her. The road was narrow, with steep gravel embankments falling away on either side, and when she'd jump out of the way of the truck, she'd find herself tumbling over and over down an endless slope, a silent scream wedged in her throat.

Deep down, was that how she'd felt about Daddy all

along? she wondered now. Trapped in some way, with nowhere to turn? Kitty had wanted to know what kind of parent would burden a young girl with such confidences. Now, after all these years, Alex knew.

I was his sin eater.

Was she like the untouchables of the Appalachian Mountains, for whom offerings of food were traditionally left out on coffins at funerals? They were outcasts, in the eyes of their backwoods neighbors, who also performed a vital function—just as *she* had.

Jim had seen it all along. He'd accused her of worshiping Daddy to the exclusion of her own family. And now she was beginning to understand. Not just the role she'd played . . . but how perfectly it had suited her father. In assuming his guilt, she'd allowed herself to become, not only his confidante, but his *conscience*. So he could ultimately arrive sin free in heaven, while she . . .

Went through hell here on earth.

All this time, she'd believed herself so utterly in control—more so than either of her sisters—yet how could she have failed to notice she was driving away her husband, and alienating her children? Even now, with her daughters, she was keeping them at arm's length in many ways; not trusting them to love her in spite of her flaws.

Why? Maybe because deep down she felt dirty, as if she didn't deserve them. For hadn't that been her father's *real* legacy to her? The sins she'd eaten that were now consuming *her*?

A low, dark chord hummed in Alex's chest. Stretched out in bed, staring up into the darkness, she willed herself to cry. Anything to relieve this dry aching pressure behind her eyes. But it was no good. Her tears were too deep, stones buried in the bitter soil of her awareness. There was only one person who could have comforted her: the man who, in some ways, had hurt her most of all.

Before she knew what she was doing, Alex was rolling onto her side and reaching for the phone on the night table. It wasn't until she'd punched in her ex-husband's number—which for some reason, she'd memorized—that she remembered how late it was. On the heels of that thought came an even more sobering one: Jim might not be alone.

She nearly hung up, but something kept her from doing so . . . even with her hand trembling and her tongue sticking to the roof of a mouth that was suddenly as dry as Styrofoam.

Jim picked up on the third ring with a groggy, "Hunh?"

"Jim, it's me." She hesitated, then asked, "Are you alone?"

There was a pause, and she pictured him adjusting the pillows, punching them into place as he settled back against the headboard. Then a low growl of laughter rumbled down the line. "Nothing like getting straight to the point," he said. "Aren't you supposed to apologize first for waking me from a sound sleep?"

"Sorry." Alex heard the edge in her voice and was quick to add, "I didn't realize how late it was." Like a steady beat in the back of her head, though, was the knowledge that he hadn't answered her question. She remained alert, waiting.

Then Jim muttered thickly, "I was having the most incredible dream—me on the beach at St. John, basking in the sun and trade winds, not another soul in sight."

"I thought your idea of paradise was a pitcher of margaritas and a beautiful woman in a string bikini," she replied acidly.

"Then you don't know me as well as you thought." She heard the rustle of bedclothes. He yawned, then observed drily, "Being as you're not hyperventilating, I take it this isn't an emergency. Did you phone me at one-thirty in the morning just to tell me what an asshole I am?"

Alex took a shallow breath and rolled back onto her pillow. "No," she said. "I'm sorry if it sounded that way."

He gave a low whistle. "Two apologies in a row. Wow, this must be my lucky day."

She squeezed her eyes shut. "You're not an asshole, Jim. It's *me*," she confessed softly. "In case you hadn't heard, I've been kind of a mess lately."

"Now that you mention it, I *do* remember seeing something on the evening news," he joked. Either he wasn't taking her seriously, she thought, or he didn't want to get all wrapped up in her troubles. Whichever, it was a mistake to have confided in him. Alex was grasping for a face-saving exit line when he said with perfect seriousness, "Christ, Alex. After what happened to your parents, who *wouldn't* be a mess?"

"Someone who'd paid more attention to what *really* counted before it was too late." Alex fell silent, waiting with her heart in her throat for Jim to make the next move.

"Nobody's perfect," he said cautiously.

"Aiming for perfect is what got me in trouble." She sighed. "In case you still have one foot on that beach—which, by the way, I remember perfectly well from our honeymoon, and it was St. *Thomas*—this is my way of saying maybe it wasn't all your fault, our divorce."

"I'm listening."

She told him then. About Leanne and her father. About her sisters, and what they'd talked about up at the house. "You were right all along," she acknowledged bitterly. "I was valuable to my father . . . but not the way *I* thought. He needed me to make it all seem more palatable somehow. To launder it like . . . like dirty money."

There was silence while he mulled this over, then Jim asked, "Do you think your mother was telling the truth—about Leanne being his kid?"

Alex fought the urge to snap, *Don't be an idiot.* But she couldn't curb her disgust. "Of course not! For one thing, Leanne was five when her parents got divorced. That would have meant Beryl and my father had been sneaking around all those years. Among other things, don't you think Beryl's husband would have caught on before then?"

"Look how long it took your mother," Jim pointed out.

Despite everything she now knew, Alex felt a burning desire to defend her father. "No," she said. "Daddy might have been selfish . . . but he wasn't a monster. If

Leanne had been his, he never would have . . ." she stopped, too sickened by the thought to finish.

"What if he didn't know?"

"That's impossible. Beryl would have told him. A woman doesn't keep a secret like that."

"Why not? *You* certainly kept your share."

Alex massaged an aching temple with her thumb. "Look, I know I'm the one who brought it up, but would you mind if we didn't talk about this anymore? I'm on overload as it is."

She listened to the sound of his breathing, as comforting in its own way as the ocean she'd fallen asleep to every night growing up. When he asked softly, "Want some company?" the question seemed as natural as a wave breaking against the shore.

Her heart stopped its shallow racing and began to pound.

It was what she wanted, desperately, but she hesitated nonetheless. If she said yes, what would it imply? That she was willing to start over? And suppose Jim was only asking out of pity. The last thing she needed was a mercy fuck.

When she found her voice at last, it was almost as if another person, someone inside her bumping around in the dark, were speaking. Softly, she said, "I'll leave the back door unlocked."

Alex felt the tension inside her abruptly ease, and as soon as she hung up, she was overcome with tiredness. Suddenly, eyes that had refused to close wouldn't stay open. She'd rest them for just a minute, no more—she had things to do before Jim showed up. Change out of her flannel nightie into something sexier, brush her teeth, unlock the door . . .

Alex was still asleep, dreaming of a different shore, colder and less agreeable than St. Thomas—the one she and her father had strolled along nearly every evening after supper—when a part of her dimly registered someone slipping in beside her. A familiar presence whose scent she recognized and instinctively inched toward.

"Alex." She felt the flutter of warm breath against her cheek.

Still half asleep, she groaned softly and flung an arm out. Beside her, Jim lay naked, the warm shock of his bare flesh like a dream from which she didn't dare waken. Somewhere, fathoms below the stony shores of conscious thought, Alex felt the stirrings of a desire long ago put on ice.

She allowed it to float upward, not resisting, savoring it as if it were some new delicious taste as Jim lightly ran the tip of his tongue over her mouth before teasing her lips apart. When he kissed her, it was as if the two years they'd been apart had never been, as if that whole painful period had been a dream, and this the only thing that was real. With her eyes still shut, she snuggled up against him, savoring the length of him along her legs and torso, all taut muscle and long planed shanks—savoring, too, the familiar coves into which her curves fit so perfectly. She felt him stir against her leg and heard him moan softly in the darkness as she reached down under the covers to stroke him.

Alex willed herself not to think of the women he'd been with since their divorce, but the images crept in regardless, prodding her further into wakefulness and, in a perverse way, exciting her even more. The warmth seeping through her gathered into a hot, white knot of urgency.

She tugged her nightgown over her head and lay back to allow him the same liberty with what was between her own thighs. Feeling herself unfold a little further with each expert brush of his fingers, she thought, *How could I have let go of this?* Suddenly, the lonely nights she'd lain awake, convincing herself she was better off without him, seemed as far away as when Lori and Nina were little . . . and as naive as when her daughters had believed a night-light could banish any threat of the boogeyman.

"You haven't forgotten," she whispered.

"The beach maybe, never the woman." She caught the flash of teeth in the darkness before he scooted down, pushing the covers aside, his tongue taking up where his hand had left off.

She spread her legs and arched her back, each sensation more exquisite than the next. *There . . . oh yes . . . he knows me so well.* She began to quiver uncontrollably all over . . . then was carried over the brink with a soaring effortlessness that took her breath away. Wave after wave of pleasure washed through her, drenching her in luxurious release, leaving her scoured and pink and delirious . . .

. . . and free to do whatever came naturally.

There was no rush, she told herself. They could take all night if they wanted. She rolled out from under him, wanting to pleasure Jim the same way he had her . . . but he was impatient and pulled her on top instead.

Moments later, as she looked down at his face—fierce with concentration, a wild faraway glint in his eyes—the desire that had been satisfied rose up once more, higher and brighter with each rolling thrust until she once again exploded . . . and Jim caught the wave, too, meeting it with hard short thrusts.

Warm liquid trickled down the inside of one thigh as she fell back onto the mattress, out of breath, weightless, as if springing free from something that had been tightly wound.

In the darkness, she listened as her ex-husband struggled to catch his breath. After a minute or so, he rolled onto his side, facing her, and cupped a hand lightly against her cheek. "I have a confession to make," he whispered. "Well, two actually. The first is that I've been wanting to do this for the past year and a half."

She smiled at him. "What's the second one?"

"This." He reached up and palmed something on the nightstand. It glinted in the half-light as he held it up. "The key to your door. Lori gave it to me—just in case."

"In case of what?"

"Oh, I don't know. Fire. Flood. Or . . ." she felt his stubbled jaw lightly graze her shoulder, ". . . the outside chance that you'd ask me over one night in a moment of weakness."

She vaguely remembered promising to unlock the door, just before she'd drifted off to sleep. "I suppose I ought to be angry," she said with a breathless little laugh. "But it's a good thing—what would you have done without it?"

"Kicked the door in most likely." He grinned. "You know us cavemen—we let nothing stand in our way."

She arched a brow. "So I've noticed."

"Any complaints?"

"One."

"Oh?" He moved down and began nuzzling her throat.

"Once definitely wasn't enough."

"My sentiments exactly."

"You don't have a plane to catch?" she teased.

"There's nowhere I'd rather be than right here."

The kiss he gave her then made any further comment not only impossible, but unnecessary.

Hours later, as they sat sipping tea in her kitchen, she thought, *How perfectly at home he seems.* As if he'd lived here at one time. She had the oddest feeling that if she were to get up and check, she'd find his clothes hanging in the closet, his toothbrush parked in the medicine cabinet next to hers. How could she have been in this house nearly a year and not have noticed that the easy chair she could see through the doorway into the living room was exactly like his favorite one in the home they'd shared?

"Remember just after the girls were born?" Jim recalled. "This time of day—or should I say night—was the only chance we had to be by ourselves." He'd thrown on his clothes in case one of the girls was to wander in for a late-night snack, but it hadn't escaped her notice that his shirt was untucked in back and his belt buckle undone. Under the table, he slid his bare feet closer to hers until their toes were overlapping.

She smiled, blowing on her tea. "We were afraid that if we spoke above a whisper they'd wake up and start screaming."

"Look at us—still whispering. Some things never change." He chuckled softly.

Thoughtfully, she fingered her tea bag, vaguely alarmed at the thought of the girls seeing them like this. She didn't want them to get their hopes up. Keeping her voice light, Alex ventured, "The question is, where do we go from here?"

Jim pondered this for a moment, then said slowly, "I'm not sure . . . but it might be fun finding out."

She nodded, swallowing against a sudden tightness in her throat. "It might be," she agreed. "That is, if you're not seeing anyone at the moment."

When Jim didn't answer right away, she began to tremble a little, fearful of hearing the answer she dreaded. Then he shook his head in amused exasperation and reached across the table to lightly cuff her cheek, scolding, "You could start by trusting me a little."

Alex felt her tension ease and she smiled. "I will. As soon as I learn to trust myself." Haltingly, she added, "Jim, there . . . there are some things I haven't told you. Things you'd need to know before . . . well, before we go any further."

Thinking of her money troubles, she felt herself begin to grow tense once more. But that wasn't all. There was damage to repair in the bulwark of her family as well. Was Jim ready for the rough task that lay ahead? Was *she?*

He leaned onto his elbows, the hard angles of his face softened by the wisps of rising steam. With an offhandedness belied by the intensity of his gaze, he asked, "What are you doing tomorrow? I have the afternoon off. We could hike up to Lighthouse Point. Can't think of a better place to air things out."

Alex hesitated. She was showing a house tomorrow— a split-level that had been listed with her agency for close to a year—but the seller wasn't interested in coming down in price, and she knew almost nothing about the prospective buyers, an older couple who probably weren't all that serious.

"What would I tell the girls?" she hedged.

"That you have a date with someone tall, dark, and handsome." He flashed her a grin that faded quickly, replaced by a searching look. "But then again, a lot of guys fit that description." Pause. "Are *you* seeing someone?"

Alex nearly laughed out loud at the idea—not that

she hadn't had her share of opportunities, but her life had been so crazy lately that the bumps and false starts of getting to know someone from scratch would have been just one more thing to cope with.

"It would serve you right if I were," she teased, pressing her lips together to keep from smiling. She grew pensive then, her mind playing back over the day's events like a weaver working a loom—pulling, threading, tying off loose strands. "Could we make it the day *after* tomorrow? There's someone I need to see."

"Anyone I should know about? Not that it's any of my business." That little frown line, like a hash mark carved just above the bridge of his nose—it always gave him away, even when he was doing his best to conceal his emotions.

Jim was jealous.

Now Alex *did* smile. And told him the truth, which in some ways was even more worrisome—to her, at any rate—than any loose ends she might have had to tie up with a lover.

"My mother," she said.

Chapter 16

Johnny paced his boss's office, somewhat larger than his own, and certainly neater, but with the same soporific view: an expanse of sloping lawn dotted with redwood-bark coves in which dwarf conifers and clumps of pyracantha huddled as forlornly as shipwrecked sailors. It was the second week in June, and already the mock cherries lining the walkway had spent their blossoms, some of which still littered the grass like confetti from a parade long since passed by.

"Flight risk?" he echoed. "You're shitting me, right? She's practically *handing* us a conviction on a silver fucking platter." Johnny had to fight to keep from shouting. "I'm talking about three, four weeks max here. Enough to put her affairs in order, spend some time with the family. She's not going anywhere, believe me." He stopped pacing and spun around. "Kendall will give it to her if we back down. I say we do it. Makes *you* look good to the bleeding hearts out there. And the old lady has a few weeks of freedom before she's locked away for good."

Bruce Cho, squeezed in behind his desk, eyed him with the stony impassivity that was his trademark. "You think because she's old she won't jump bail? Most people would have laughed at the idea of a sixty-six-year-old woman murdering her husband." His basso rumble of a voice—the kind that children and dogs instantly obeyed—gave no quarter. "But for the sake of argument, let's assume she stays put. There's another problem. Since you brought it up, my guess is that in the court of public opinion, a move like that could just as easily backfire. What kind of message would it send?

That the DA is willing to bend over backward if you're a certain age, or race, or religion?"

Cho, a six-foot-five meat locker of a man, the product of Samoan and Filipino heritage, had met with every prejudice a small town could dish out in his rocky ascent to district attorney—and had a chip on his shoulder to match. Convincing him to give in, Johnny knew, would have to be handled with extreme care.

"A few weeks—you'd give that much to a sick dog," Johnny argued.

"Not if it was rabid." Cho's eyes narrowed—glittering chips of anthracite deeply embedded in their surrounding folds. "One thing's for sure, the lady sure has people wondering," he said. "I say she stays where we can keep an eye on her. She must have money put away. Enough to live like a queen in Rio de Janeiro."

Johnny gave a short mirthless laugh. "Maybe, but from the looks of it, I doubt she could cross the street on her own."

"The same was said about that wise guy, Vinnie Gigante. By eight shrinks."

"All paid for by the mob, no doubt," Johnny noted drily.

Cho regarded him thoughtfully, nodding as if in response to some inner dialogue, his large square hands steepled under his chin. This was the same man, Johnny thought, who could hammer a conviction through by sheer force alone—like that tomato farmer he'd sent upriver on three counts of manslaughter for holding migrant workers in a locked shed under a broiling summer sun. Two had perished. He hadn't meant to hurt them, Joe Cunningham had protested, just teach them a lesson. But in the end, it was Cunningham who'd gotten the lesson: forty years in Lompoc.

"If I didn't know better, John, I'd say you had a personal stake in all this." The DA's voice was like a pin dropping in the silence.

Johnny felt the room grow warm all of a sudden. His gaze drifted to the file cabinet, on which sat a framed eight-by-ten of Cho in his glory days as a star fullback for Notre Dame. He'd been singled out for the pros, but a bad knee had sidelined him into law school. What hadn't changed, though, was the thrill of the game so evident in that photo. For Cho, winning was everything.

Johnny took a different, though not necessarily opposing, view. He saw the gray area between what was legal and what was simply the moral thing to do, and wondered just where, exactly, *his* motives fit. Did the fact that he was acting out of love make him better than someone motivated primarily by ambition? Were either of them being strictly honest here? Cho wanted nothing to get in the way of his being reelected. For Johnny, the goal was much simpler, and at the same time, a whole lot more complicated: Daphne. He wanted Daphne. And in seeking his help, she'd unwittingly provided him with the opportunity he'd been looking for.

But first, he needed to level with Cho.

Johnny dragged a chair over and sat down, leaning close to establish eye contact the way Cho had taught him to do with jurors. "We go way back, Bruce. The night before the election, that night we got wasted at Manny's? You told me if you didn't win, you were going to throw in the towel . . . coach football for underprivileged kids."

Cho's stone face creased in faint amusement. "Too many margaritas on an empty stomach." His smile dropped away, and he growled softly, "Just for the record, I meant it."

"You were probably too drunk to remember it, but I told you about a woman," Johnny went on. "Someone I was in love with a long time ago and haven't been able to get out of my mind since." He felt a slow heat building inside him, compressing his heart into a tight, hard ball. "What I didn't tell you—because it wasn't important then—was her name." He paused, then said, "Bruce, it's Daphne Seagrave."

Cho jerked a little in surprise, but true to form, didn't bat an eye. "Are you telling me there's a conflict of interest here?"

Johnny drew in a breath. "I'm not gonna bullshit you," he said straight out. "I love my job, and I think you know you can count on my integrity. I just wanted you to hear it from me first . . . that I have a personal interest in all this. As far as this case goes, you have my word that nothing she and I have talked about has been out of bounds."

Cho frowned, clearly unhappy with this new spin Johnny had put on an already sticky situation. "Never mind what *I* might think. People in small towns talk. It's risking a lot for an old flame."

Johnny flashed back on the one and only time he'd been burglarized, a few years after he and Sara were married. He remembered staring at the empty spaces where the TV and stereo had stood, blocked off by squares of gray dust, and thinking how depressing it all was. Not just the fact that it was gone, but that some sorry son of a bitch had risked getting caught and, quite possibly, killed—what if Johnny had been home and lying in wait with a shotgun? And all for a few crummy appliances that had cost enough new but wouldn't net more than a hundred used.

This was different. The risks were high, sure, but what he stood to gain was beyond measure. Should he lie to Cho?

Johnny settled on the simplest of truths instead. "I'm not sleeping with her, if that's what you mean."

He specifically avoided the use of past tense. What his boss didn't know about that night on the beach wouldn't hurt him. And until this trial was over, there would *be* no repeat of that night. Daphne had her own reasons— reasons that didn't entirely make sense to him—but he realized now that, if only for her mother's sake, she was right to keep her distance. For the time being, anyway.

After this was over? Her husband, Cho, the entire Notre Dame line of defense couldn't keep him away.

"Let me put it another way." For the first time, Cho sounded a little ticked off. "On this bail issue, you wouldn't happen to have some kind of ulterior motive, would you?"

Johnny felt a little bump inside, where the smooth pavement of rationalizations ended, and the rutted road of instinct began. As a young man, he'd slayed dragons for Daphne with his fists. Now he had to rely on his wits alone. But it all boiled down to the same thing, didn't it? Man's nature, despite thousands of years of civilization, was to fight, even kill, for what he wanted. In that sense, he was no different from Cho.

"I've told you everything you need to know," Johnny said. It was as close to the truth as he dared get, though he knew how it must sound—as if he were hiding something.

A shadow moved across Cho's expressionless face like storm clouds passing over an uninhabitable plain. "It's not just a matter of what's legal . . . or even ethical, John. If the press *were* to get hold of this, it could be damn embarrassing."

A muscle twitched in Johnny's cheek. "They won't."

"How the hell can you promise a thing like that?"

"You have my word, that's how. And if somebody wants to dig up dirt on what a couple of eighteen-year-olds were up to back in seventy-seven, it might make a cute story, but it'd be pretty thin soup."

He remembered kissing her on the pier, right out in the open. That had been dumb, though he didn't regret it, not for a minute.

Cho didn't say anything, and Johnny waited in tense silence. His boss was only testing him, he knew. Seeing if there was any more he could sweat out of his assistant DA. It was Cho's best line of defense in cross-examining a witness: that .22-gauge stare of his. And though unmarried—his office was his wife and mistress, courthouse regulars liked to joke—his boss was savvy enough to know that a guy with a soft spot for an old flame was far less a threat than one whose heart might take him places his conscience dared not go.

After what seemed an eternity, Cho leaned back and coughed into his fist—a single explosive bark, like a gun firing. When he looked back up at Johnny, his eyes glittered coldly. "You said you were in love with her once. You didn't say how you feel about her now."

Johnny visualized a lever, the heavy-duty kind used to manually override industrial machinery, and pictured himself pressing down on it with all his might. He chose his words carefully. "You don't have to worry. She's married."

Cho didn't need to know how he felt about Daphne or that her husband, absent lo these many weeks, had sensed a shift in the wind and come running. Johnny was privy to that fact because yesterday he'd spotted the guy barreling out the front entrance of Jasper with Daphne in tow—a big man who wore the look of someone inordinately pleased with himself and who perfectly fit the picture he'd formed in his mind.

Now seated in his boss's office, part of Johnny would have welcomed the chance to tick off, one by one, all the reasons Daphne ought to divorce the jerk, but Cho luckily didn't press that particular point. Glancing at his watch, he swore, "Shit, I have to be in court in less than ten minutes. Munson again—would you believe that asswipe had his lawyer submit a motion for retrial?" As he rose heavily to his feet, the overloaded springs of his chair released with an audible pop. He seemed to have forgotten all about Cathcart's motion. Johnny was preparing to launch his final salvo when Cho abruptly leaned forward, far enough to partially eclipse the sun streaming in through the window at his back. His hands planted firmly in the center of his desk, he said with soft emphasis, "One word of advice, John. I don't care *who* you're fucking. But if we give in on this, and anything— I mean *anything*—happens while she's out on bail to prevent Lydia Seagrave from standing trial, getting fired will be the least of your worries. You got that?"

Johnny pressed down harder on the lever in his head and felt it start to buck—a hard grinding resistance that caused the muscles in his arms and chest to clench. But he didn't flinch, or even look away. Meeting his boss's gaze squarely, he answered, "Loud and clear."

The following morning at eleven-thirty, Daphne, seated in Judge Harold Kendall's courtroom, watched in fearful silence as her mother was brought before the bench. The courtroom that had been so packed the day of her arraignment was nearly deserted on this sunny

Wednesday morning in June, more than two months later, but she hardly noticed. Even the proceedings, mercifully brief, passed in a blur. Except for Johnny stating tersely that the prosecution was withdrawing its objection to the motion seeking bail, she'd hadn't heard a word. But now her gaze was fixed on the judge, with his face like an overgrown English bulldog.

"If prosecution has no objection, I'm inclined to grant the motion. Bail is set at five hundred thousand," Kendall declared, bringing his gavel down with a decisive bang.

Daphne reeled as if from a blow. Until that moment, she hadn't realized how tense she was. It was a moment or two before she was able to unlock her clenched fingers and reach over to squeeze Kitty's hand. The ordeal was far from over, she knew, but it was a small triumph nonetheless.

On her left, Roger shifted, clearing his throat loudly. Was he thinking of the money they'd have to come up with to post bond? Knowing him, probably. A flash of annoyance momentarily distracted Daphne from the sense of joy welling in her. Her father had invested in mutual funds, she knew, but if for some reason they couldn't get their hands on those assets, she would damn well pay for it out of her own pocket.

When Roger looked over at her, though, she was instantly chastised by the look of naked relief on his face. She kept her eyes fastened on him so she wouldn't have to look at Johnny, making his way down the aisle.

She didn't know how he'd pulled it off, but Johnny had made this happen. There could be no other explanation for the abruptness with which the prosecution had backed down. And it wasn't just that. In her heart, hadn't she known all along that he wouldn't let her down?

As she followed Roger and Kitty out of the courtroom into the glass-walled corridor that overlooked the grounds below, she caught sight of Johnny, in huddled conference with his boss. Her pulse quickened. Throughout the hearing, she'd been far more aware of him than of her own husband, seated beside her. Even now, as

Roger excused himself to go off with Cathcart to discuss arrangements for posting bail, Daphne couldn't shake the feeling that it was Johnny, not her husband, setting her mother free.

The hardest part was that she couldn't let him know how much it meant to her: the strings he must have pulled at his own expense, judging from the expression on Cho's stone tablet of a face. She had to keep her distance, never mind that it was killing her, because whatever happened in the end, one thing was certain: she had to give Roger this chance, even if meant sacrificing her own with Johnny.

Daphne started toward her sister, who stood a short distance down the corridor chatting with Cathcart's pixieish blond paralegal. She hadn't taken more than a few steps when she was intercepted by a firm hand on her elbow.

"Got a moment?" Johnny's breath against her ear was warm.

She turned slowly to face him, her pulse quickening. The first thing that struck her was the red nick on his jaw where he'd cut himself shaving. She hadn't noticed it in the courtroom—he'd been too far away. Now, though they stood a discreet distance apart, he seemed far too close, and his eyes seemed to burn into her.

"Johnny, I don't think this is the—" she started to protest.

"It won't take long." He guided the way down the corridor and around a bend, to a shorter corridor that opened onto a small atrium in which chairs and benches were scattered amid large potted ficus and planters dripping with maidenhair ferns.

Daphne, realizing how her reluctance might have been interpreted, hastened to apologize. "I'm sorry if it sounded like I was brushing you off. You went out on a limb to make this happen, didn't you? You don't have to say anything. I know you, Johnny. And . . . and I'm grateful. Truly, I am."

"You're under no obligation," he said.

"Oh, Johnny . . ." She ducked her head so he wouldn't

see the tears in her eyes. "I wish you could know how much this means to me."

Abruptly changing the subject, he asked, "Was that guy I saw you with your husband?"

She nodded. "Roger flew in unexpectedly the day before yesterday. He . . . he wanted to surprise me." Her mouth flattened in a smile that was more of a grimace.

Johnny regarded her in bleak silence for a moment. "When I said you were under no obligation, I meant to *me*. That doesn't mean you don't owe anything to yourself." His expression softened. "Think about it, will you? That's all I ask."

"Things are complicated right now."

"I know. I can wait."

"Johnny, I have *children*."

"I love kids. I have one of my own, remember?"

"You're divorced. I'm not."

"So I've noticed." He glanced past her, as if half expecting to see Roger stride through the doorway . . . and maybe even *hoping* for a confrontation that would force things to a head. She thought she saw something savage flare in his smoky eyes. Then he said mildly, "I'll be honest with you, Daphne. From what I've heard so far, I had your husband pegged as the type who, in the old days, wouldn't have had to do more than open his mouth to give me an excuse to take a swing at him. But seeing him, there is one thing that surprised me, I'll admit."

She waited, her heart beating unsteadily. A few dozen yards away, a mismatched crew that could only have been prospective jurors sat on benches among the potted ficus, not speaking to one another, just waiting, like people in a bus station with nothing in common but a shared destination.

"He loves you," Johnny said.

His words caught her by surprise. "How can you know that?"

"It's my job to size up the competition, and I'm good at it." He grinned, but his eyes remained flat and unsmiling. "I saw the way he looks at you. He tries to hide it, a little *too* hard."

Daphne felt shaken and confused. She didn't need Johnny to tell her. Didn't she know already? It was why she'd stayed with Roger.

Why she was giving him this second chance. He might not show it, but, yes, he loved her. And in the end, that might be the very thing that doomed her.

"Johnny, why are you doing this?" she asked in a low stricken voice.

He brought his hand up, and for a panicked moment she thought he was going to touch her. But he let it fall back to his side. "Loving someone ain't a ticket to ride, it's just the price of admission," he told her. "Whatever you decide, Daphne, don't do it for your husband, or your kids. Or me. We'll survive. Do it for *you.*"

Daphne blinked back her tears, allowing a tiny smile to surface. "For someone who flunked English, you sure have a way with words."

He smiled back, that easy crooked grin she'd fallen in love with all those years ago, in the smoker's pit behind the science building. "It doesn't take a genius. You get knocked in the head enough times, you eventually figure it out."

Daphne looked past him, and there was Roger—not striding with his usual take-no-prisoners gusto, but walking with slow, deliberate steps . . . like someone who knows where he's headed, but isn't quite sure what he'll find when he gets there. She felt her throat tighten, and realized that for the first time in their eighteen years of marriage, *she* had the upper hand. But she derived no satisfaction from it, as she once might have. Instead, she almost pitied her husband. Things would be better once this trial was over and they were back in New York, but they still had a long way to go, and Johnny wasn't making it any easier.

From a distance, as he walked toward them, she saw Roger's eyes flick questioningly from her to Johnny, and was relieved when Johnny reached out to grip her hand and give it a brief, businesslike shake. She willed herself not to blush at the flood of memories released by the firm warm pressure of his fingers.

"Good-bye, Johnny. And thanks . . . for everything."

"Don't mention it." A split-second before Roger's presence would have forced an introduction, Johnny gave her hand one last squeeze, and was gone.

As she stood there, struggling to fix into place an expression neutral enough to pass her husband's scrutiny, it felt like the hardest thing Daphne had ever had to do. Harder than visiting her mother in jail, and learning the ugly truth about her father. Harder even than the last time she'd let go of Johnny.

Chapter 17

In the end, nothing went as planned. On the drive back, Lydia, wearing the flowered silk dress Kitty had grabbed from her closet—which, in addition to being all wrong for the occasion, was now miles too big—turned away from the backseat window she'd been staring out of to remark pleasantly that she was looking forward to seeing if the begonias on her porch had come back after that cold snap last winter.

Roger was making the turn onto San Pedro Avenue in his rented Chrysler LeBaron and he cut the steering wheel so sharply that the tires let out a squeal, leaving a skid mark in the shape of a fat comma on the pavement in front of Friendly Planet Natural Foods, with its mural of cavorting dolphins. He abruptly slowed, and they glided past the neighboring Hiz n' Herz hair salon. In the exaggeratedly patient voice that put Kitty's teeth on edge, Roger told his mother-in-law that it had been *discussed*, and they had decided she'd be better off at Kitty's for the time being.

Kitty, buckled in beside her mother, held her tongue. *Once Mother sees the sense in it,* she thought, *she'll change her mind.* The house would be too full of reminders. And she couldn't exactly stay with Alex.

She thought of yesterday's somewhat strained phone conversation with her younger sister. Alex had asked after their mother, seeming unusually concerned, if a bit self-conscious of the fact. But when Kitty urged her to attend the hearing, Alex had backed off at once.

"I'd rather wait until we can be alone," she'd said, sounding nervous, but sincere. "There's something I need to tell her. And I can't say it with a lot of other people around."

Kitty didn't doubt her little sister had plenty to get off her chest. She just hoped their mother was strong enough to hear it.

She darted a concerned glance at Lydia. who smiled back at her, as if to say, *What's all this fuss about?* "I appreciate the offer, dear, but I really *must* be getting home," she politely insisted. "It's been so long. you see. and there's so much to take care of before . . ." her voice wavered for just a moment ". . . before the trial."

"It's out of the question." Daphne twisted around to frown at her over the front seat. "You can't stay in that big house all by yourself. It's . . ." she looked about to swallow the word, but spoke it anyway. "It's *ghoulish.*"

"To you, maybe." Lydia leaned forward to pat her shoulder comfortingly. "To me, it's home."

Thank God they'd gotten rid of the carpet. Kitty thought. She and Daphne had gone over there last night. and between the two of them, they'd managed to roll it up and carry it out to Kitty's Honda. in which they'd immediately carted it off to the city dump. Kitty nonetheless felt as skittish as an accomplice to murder. disposing of the body under cover of darkness.

"But wouldn't you be happier at my place?" she cajoled. "For one thing, you wouldn't be alone. And you'd get to see Kyle and Jennie."

Her mother seemed to brighten. and when she asked anxiously, "Who's watching them now?" Kitty was heartened to note that she was still the same person who'd once fussed over her and her sisters.

"Willa offered to sit with them," Kitty told her. "She's really good with children. She has two of her own." She spoke with a lightness that might have fooled her mother but did nothing to still the sudden reminder of her own loss that unfurled inside her like a blood-red rose out of season.

From the wistful expression that crossed her mother's face, it looked as if she might relent. Then with a sigh. she folded her hands resolutely in her lap. "I'll see them soon enough. I want you all to come for supper, in a day or two . . . after I've had a chance to settle in."

Daphne, who could be equally stubborn, tried a different tack. "Why don't I stay with *you* then? That way you'd have some company."

Lydia shook her head in regret. "I'd like that, dear. Some other time." Behind her smile, Kitty caught a glimpse of the strain she'd been under. "Right now, I need to be by myself."

Daphne argued that *she* would rest easier up at the house, presumably where she could keep an eye on Mother. She didn't need to add that she was worried about her health—not even Lydia could have denied how frail she'd become.

But their mother remained steadfast. In the end, there was simply no talking her out of it. As if, Kitty thought, this were a lifeboat, with Mother manning the rudder, guiding them through the stormy seas that had claimed the ship carrying their family's precious cargo of memories and illusions.

Holding fast to her course, she navigated the way up the hill to Agua Fria Point, where Kitty and Daphne, flanking her at each elbow, and with Roger leading the way, escorted their mother up the steps to the house she'd first come to forty years ago as a young bride . . . and last walked out of in handcuffs.

Kitty hadn't realized how shaky she herself was until a toe of the high heels she was unaccustomed to wearing caught on a warped board in the porch, and she nearly tripped. Catching herself, she rocked back, her heart galloping all out of proportion, as if she'd narrowly missed plunging off the cliff opposite the house, on the far side of the road where Agua Fria Point dropped off into the shimmering expanse of ocean below.

At the same time, she was gratified to note that the begonias, in their hanging baskets under the eaves, showed signs of life. Fleshy leaves the purple-green of day-old bruises had begun to sprout from blackened stems. She watched her mother reach up in passing to lightly finger a leaf, and felt her own spirits lift slightly.

Maybe there's still hope, she thought. *For Mother . . . and all of us.*

Lydia, too, must have felt it. Stopping just inside the front door, she turned to face them: a thin white-haired woman wearing a baggy flowered dress and looking easily ten years older than her age, someone who seemed smaller, too—as if the weight of her sorrow had left her diminished in some fundamental way. But bathed in the celestial glow of the stained-glass fanlight so admired by visitors, her eyes sparkled with a renewed vigor.

"My dears, don't think me ungrateful," she said. "I'm deeply touched by everything you've done."

"But . . ." Daphne started to say. In a navy linen suit that did nothing to flatter her coloring, she looked pale and drawn. Her sea-green eyes were huge and luminous as they searched her mother's face.

Bracing herself with one hand held tightly to the doorknob, Lydia brought the other to rest on Daphne's arm. "Please, you mustn't worry. I'll be fine, I promise."

She gave them each a dry little peck on the cheek, then quietly, but firmly, pulled the door shut.

In the three days that had passed since then, Kitty had kept busy with the tea room, refusing to dwell on what might go wrong up at the house. Yes, she agreed with Daphne, their mother could fall down the stairs and break a bone. Or become ill, and be too weak to get to the phone. But what would all their worrying accomplish? And what, Kitty had pointed out, could be worse than the terrible thing that already *had* happened?

Yet by Saturday afternoon, as she stood in her kitchen grating lemons for pound cake, Kitty found herself seriously pondering another possibility: that her mother really was as crazy as everyone seemed to think. They'd spoken over the phone, yes—half a dozen times, at least—but it was always Daphne or Kitty who initiated the call. And though unfailingly polite, it was clear that Lydia's mind was on other things.

When asked how she was managing on her own, she'd reply, "Just fine." There was still so much to do, she'd say with a breathless little sigh. Friends and relatives with whom she needed to get in touch, *stacks* of mail she'd only begun to sift through. She would have them all over, just like she'd promised, the very minute she was caught up. But Kitty was beginning to wonder.

Never once had her mother mentioned her father, or the trial just three weeks away. No reference was made, either, of the handful of reporters who'd gotten wind of her release and were camped out front—Kitty had had to hear it from Mrs. McCrae, next door, who'd phoned to say she was "keeping an eye on the situation." And if her mother fretted that her homecoming might be short-lived, she showed no outward sign of it. It was, Kitty thought, merely as though she were returning home from a long and exhausting trip.

Whatever Lydia might have felt in the anguished days leading up to the night when she'd picked up a gun and fired the shots that had shattered the lives of everyone in the family, she appeared to have arrived at some sort of peace. Kitty wished she could do the same. Leanne's tale had left her badly shaken. It was all so sordid. And so sad—that one man could have caused such harm, over the course of so many years. Ironic, too—because he was a man who in some ways had been worthy of admiration, and yes, even love.

Did she believe that Leanne was her father's child? Anything was possible, she supposed. But in the end, what really mattered was that her mother believed it. That, more than anything, Kitty felt convinced, was what had cost him his life.

And now he would be butchered all over again, in court. Wasn't that the source of her mother's deafening silence? And Leanne's reluctance to testify? They were protecting him. Just as Alex always had.

Sadness welled in her, filling her to the brim. That was the real tragedy, she thought, fully comprehending now what she'd only begun to realize the other night up at the house, with Daphne and Alex: the conspiracy of silence that had cost them *all* so dearly. In her bright kitchen, with the early summer sunshine spread in banners of gold over the old tile floor, she felt as if they'd gotten stuck somehow—she and her sisters—and were spinning in aimless circles, like the honeybees she could see from her window, stitching their endless loops above the grass.

Her thoughts turned to Sean, and she wondered if he knew how deeply his words had cut. What he'd said the other night about taking the bad with the good, suggesting that maybe she wasn't fit for the challenges of motherhood. Suppose he was right? Had she been looking for the storybook ending in a situation that was bound to be messy and tangled? All that time she'd been rolling her eyes at Daphne's tendency to look at life through rose-colored glasses, hadn't she been doing the same? Drawing up blueprints that had left no room for the unexpected, the strange, and yes, even the wondrous.

All her life, she'd been what was deemed the highest praise in her house: a good girl. Though not perfect, she'd been brought up to believe a kind heart counted more than material success and that honesty was the foundation on which lasting friendships were built. Yet she'd fallen short of the mark somehow and allowed her desire for a child—a desire that had become an obsession—to eclipse all that *was* within her reach.

She saw the same thing happening with her sisters. Daphne, confusing duty with love. And Alex . . . she had lived in their father's shadow so long Kitty doubted she'd known where his needs ended and hers began.

She sighed as she scooped the grated lemon rind into a small bowl and reached up to retrieve a measuring cup from the shelf above her. *What if I were to call Sean right now, this very minute?* she wondered.

She'd missed him more than she ever would have imagined possible. Even the memory of him seemed to heighten each of her senses, intensifying the ordinary elements of her day in a way that illuminated their beauty somehow—the scent of lemons that filled the kitchen with the most fragrant of perfumes, the contented purring of the cats curled up by the stove, the sunlight lending the heart-shaped leaves of the nasturtium creeping up over the porch railing a lacy-green translucence. Love? She didn't trust herself to know the true meaning of it. Not just because she'd never felt this way before, but because her mother had loved the same man for forty years . . . and look what had come of it.

But, Lord, if this feeling—as if she'd been scraped as thoroughly as the naked lemons now piled on the counter—were anything to go by, it had to be the next closest thing.

"Mami says if you want a man, put something of his under your pillow at night."

Kitty turned to find Willa standing inside the doorway, balancing a tray laden with dirty plates and cups while she scratched at one ankle with the polished pink toe-nails of the opposite foot. She was smiling mischievously, as if she'd somehow read Kitty's mind. "I don't know if it works or not," she added, "but you'll have sweet dreams at least." She carried the tray over to the sink, and began loading the plates into the dishwasher.

Today's traffic-stopping outfit was a red tank top and sarong skirt printed with splashy pink hibiscus, rounded off by a pair of open-toed espadrilles. She was sporting a new tattoo as well—on one plump brown shoulder was a thumbnail-size apple with a bite taken out of it.

Kitty smiled in spite of herself. "I don't know about sweet dreams," she said. "But I sure could use a good night's sleep."

"I know something that'd help," Willa ventured slyly. "It don't come in a pill, though."

Kitty felt herself grow warm. "If you're referring to Sean, I'm not seeing him anymore," she informed Willa somewhat primly, then relented with a sigh, "It's proba-bly just as well. We really don't have that much in common."

"Says who? People are always saying you're too young or too old or too fat. Look at me—if I'd listened to all the advice I've been getting all my life, no way would I have my two boys." Willa's expression turned pensive, and in that moment Kitty saw a glimmer of wisdom amid the mismatched clothes and blithely chaotic lifestyle.

Yet she replied nonetheless, "With some things you don't always have a choice." Kitty sighed and resumed her task. Measuring flour and sugar, separating eggs—
these were the things she had control over.

Kitty felt a warm, slightly sticky hand come to rest on her arm. "Hey, I didn't mean to rub it in . . . about kids. You know me, stuff comes out of my mouth before I even know I'm thinking it." She turned to find Willa's sweet round face filled with concern.

Kitty gave a small good-natured shrug. "It's not your fault everything's such a mess."

Willa stepped back to peer at her. "Hey, you okay? You look kinda pale. Maybe you should lie down."

"No thanks. The way I feel, I'd never get up." Kitty hoisted the canister of sugar off the shelf and plunked it down in front of Willa. "Measure this while I see if my sister needs help with anything, okay? Two cups. And cream the butter while you're at it." She spoke kindly, but briskly.

Since Daphne's arrival, she and her sister had fallen into a routine: Daphne helped out in the tea room mornings and afternoons, for an hour or two, disappearing upstairs in between to type furiously on her laptop. She was now on a first-name basis with all the regulars—who'd evolved into a sort of free-floating baby-sitting service—and could manage just fine on her own, Kitty was sure. It was *she* who needed a break from Willa's well-meaning, but ultimately maddening conviction, that for everything wrong in life there was a simple solution: a man.

She found Daphne setting out tea and blackberry scones for Mac MacArthur. The editor-in-chief of the *Miramonte Mirror,* with his fleecy graying sideburns and face as scored as her old butcher block, was carrying on to her sister about his pet peeve.

"Two-headed babies! Alien abductions! That's all people want to read about these days. Know why they sell those rags in supermarkets? Because it's the same as junk food—a load of crap dressed up to look like Hostess cupcakes." He cocked a gimlet eye at her. "They tried, you know—the younger ones. About twisted my arm out of my socket to get me to run stories on your folks like the ones in the tabloids. I told 'em the day I sink as low as that, they can dig me a plot in Twin Oaks Cemetery alongside Vernon Seagrave's!"

Daphne, to her credit, didn't flinch. Exchanging a glance with Kitty, she replied evenly, "I hope it doesn't come to that, Mac. We need more journalists like you."

He patted her hand clumsily. "Speaking of what's in print—I see your book everywhere I go. Ashamed to say I haven't read it yet. I'll have to pick up a copy at The Bookworm." He winked at Kitty. "You must be pretty proud of your big sister."

"I am," Kitty said. *But not just because she's a gifted author.*

Kitty watched her sister's hand bobble in the midst of pouring his tea. "They say to be careful what you wish for. If I'd known . . ." Daphne stopped and shook her head. "Let's just say success isn't always what it's cracked up to be."

Mac nodded in commiseration, brightening only when Kitty asked if he'd mind sharing his table. She'd just caught sight of Gladys Honeick poised in the doorway, scanning the room anxiously for an empty seat. These past months Mac had been doing everything he could to catch her eye, while the henna-haired proprietress of Glad Tide-ins pretended not to notice. And now, when Kitty went over and proposed that she sit with him, Gladys regarded her with a long measuring look over the tops of her parrot-green sunglasses.

"I could come back later," she said.

"He's says it's no bother, really," Kitty assured her, quick to add, "I'm sure he means it."

"Well . . ." Gladys's gaze flicked over Mac, then, as if satisfied that no trickery was afoot, marched over to his table and slid into the chair opposite him.

He disarmed her at once by sliding his untouched mug across the table to her. "Go ahead," he growled. "It won't bite."

Fluttering her eyelashes, she purred, "I take mine with lemon. How do you take yours?"

"Black as sin and strong enough to cut with a knife." The aging but still spry editor-in-chief gave her a roguish wink as he poured what was left of the tea in his pot into the fresh mug Kitty hastened to put in front of him.

When Kitty glanced over next, they were deep in conversation, their heads bent over a plate sprinkled with crumbs. She smiled. Maybe there *was* hope, after all . . . for a lucky handful.

She glanced about, reassured by the safe warm sameness of it all: Josie Hendricks, sipping tea and gazing fondly at little Jennie, playing with her dolls on the floor at her feet; Tim from the tannery, enjoying a break with several of his buddies while they devoured a platter of sticky buns; and Father Sebastian, at his usual table, engaged in a lively game of solitaire. The other day, when her nephew arrived home from school in tears because he didn't understand how to subtract, it was the unorthodox young priest who'd sat him down and demonstrated a method he claimed was infallible: using poker chips.

Through the bay window, she could see her nephew now, out in the front yard, tossing a rubber ball for Romulus—again and again, neither boy nor dog seeming to tire of the game. Ever since Daphne's children had come to live with them, Rommie had apparently decided that Kyle was the Lone Ranger to his Tonto. The dog followed him everywhere, standing guard at his chair during meals and curling up by his bed at night. Watching them now, Kitty was struck by the odd pair they made— her towheaded nephew, who hadn't yet lost all his baby fat . . . and the fierce-looking half-breed, with his pale eyes and bristling mane.

Serena Featherstone, at the table by the window, was watching them, too. The self-styled psychic, looking less gothic than usual in a flowing cotton batik dress the soft blue of a summer sky, was seated alongside her lover, a woman. Oh yes, Kitty knew, there were some who would lift an eyebrow—even in a town as laid-back as this one—but she nevertheless found herself smiling at the obvious affection between the two. There was little enough happiness in the world as it was, she thought, for it to be parceled out only to those deemed worthy by popular vote.

She recalled Serena's eerie prediction of two months ago—that there would be a death in her family. The psychic had also divined that she would fall in love. Both had come true, she recalled with a faint ripple of alarm.

What would Serena predict were she to sidle over there now? Suppressing a shudder, Kitty decided she didn't want to know. The future, like the past, had no business intruding on the present.

She brought her gaze back to Josie Hendricks instead. Something was different about the old woman, she thought. It wasn't just that Josie's normally disheveled bun was neatly screwed on for a change: Kitty couldn't recall the last time she'd pointed out a leak or crack or faulty wire. Maybe it had something to do with her new role as little Jennie's self-appointed godmother. Kitty's niece had climbed onto Josie's lap and was happily scribbling on a napkin with her crayons while the old woman looked on—no doubt offering encouraging and cogent remarks on Jennie's lopsided house and stick figures. And if the weight of the three-year-old pained Josie's arthritic hip in any way, she didn't show it. Or maybe she just didn't notice.

Kitty squinted against the sunlight pouring in the windows that suddenly seemed too bright. When she felt her sister's arm slip about her waist, she leaned into Daphne's shoulder, remembering when she had been Jennie's age, how secure she'd felt in her big sister's presence.

"You okay?" Daphne asked.

"I'm fine. Just a little tired." She pulled away and stepped around behind the counter, where she noted that several of the baskets were running low. Rearranging muffins and fat slices of tea bread to cover the bare spots, she asked, "What about you?"

"About the same."

"It's Johnny, isn't it?" Kitty dropped her voice to a near whisper. "It's no use pretending, Daph. Not with me."

Daphne lowered her gaze, but not before Kitty caught the troubled look in her eyes. "We're all out of sticky buns," she said. "Do you want me to get some more from the kitchen?"

"There aren't any left. And you still haven't answered my question."

"For heaven's sake, Kitty, not *now*." Daphne glanced

nervously over her shoulder, and Kitty knew she was thinking about Roger, on the phone upstairs. Abruptly changing the subject, she asked, "Any word from Alex?"

Kitty smoothed a lace doily that had gotten crumpled. "She phoned again this morning to ask about Mother. For someone who's been keeping her distance, she seems awfully concerned all of a sudden."

"Maybe Alex has finally decided to forgive her."

"Or forgive herself."

Daphne followed Kitty back into the kitchen. Drifting over to the sink, she grabbed a pitcher from the counter, and began filling it with water. "Speaking of Mother," she said over the rush of the faucet, "don't you think this has gone on long enough? I keep feeling we should *do* something."

"Like what?" Kitty asked. Thankfully, they were alone—Willa had gone back to clear the rest of the tables—but even so, she kept her voice low.

"We could simply show up," Daphne suggested. "Confront her with what we know and see what she has to say."

Kitty thought for a moment, then said, "That could just as easily backfire. I say we sit tight until she's ready."

"When will *that* be exactly?" Daphne shut off the water and turned to face her, the stainless pitcher cradled against her chest like some sort of armor. As if in eerie echo of Kitty's earlier thoughts, she ventured nervously, "Kitty, what if she really is incapable of making any kind of rational decision? Cathcart might be right, you know. The best thing might be to have her declared legally incompetent."

"Judging by her actions so far, I can't think of a good argument against it," Kitty said, a familiar grain of doubt chafing in the pit of her stomach like a pebble in the toe of a shoe. "But something about it still doesn't sit right. I can't put my finger on it, but I have a feeling we'll know soon enough."

"Whether or not Mother really *is* crazy, you mean?"

"I was thinking more that we'll know which course to take."

"I wonder," Daphne said, her pretty, earnest face filled with an odd sorrowing acceptance, "if we'll *ever* know what really happened that night. We may have to settle for what we can get—a lot of little pieces that don't necessarily add up."

Kitty was on the verge of saying that Mother, in her own obtuse way, might know exactly what she was doing—that it was only *they* who'd been struggling to fit a square peg into a round hole—when the phone rang.

Kitty snatched it up, expecting it to be a deliveryman, or the handyman calling about a part for the oven she'd ordered, or a customer wanting to know how late they stayed open . . . but it was her mother's voice that came on the line, as soft and lilting as Kitty remembered from childhood. "Am I interrupting anything?" she asked.

Caught by surprise, Kitty stammered, "No, not really. Daphne and I were just cleaning up. Is . . . is everything all right?"

"Everything's fine," she replied, as always. "I called to ask you girls to supper tomorrow. Roger and the children, too, of course."

She spoke as if it were no different from countless Sunday suppers over the years. Yet something in her mother's voice made Kitty wonder if the lifeboat she had been navigating—their family's own private ship of fools—was at last being guided to shore.

Suppose supper wasn't the only thing being dished out? Tomorrow they might finally have the answers they'd been seeking. A tiny chill of anticipation prickled along her spine.

"Are you there?" Lydia fluted anxiously.

Kitty took a breath, thinking about all the times she'd tried to wriggle out of it—those awful Sunday suppers up at the house, with her mother attempting to shoehorn them into roles formed when they were children, before they'd moved out and established lives of their own. She thought of her father at the head of the table, wielding his carving knife as skillfully as a scalpel, while her mother ferried back and forth from the kitchen with bowls and platters, calling, "The roast isn't too done in the middle, is it, dear?" as if it weren't too late to do anything about it. And her father booming gallantly, "Tender as the lady who cooked it."

Somewhere between the wine and the decaf, Alex would invariably start in on one of her daughters. And if Kitty happened to take Nina's or Lori's side, Alex was sure to remind her that *she* had no children of her own, so she couldn't talk. By the time they finished helping their mother wash up, Kitty would be so exhausted it'd be an effort just to put on her coat.

But if the habits of a lifetime hadn't changed, the familiar terrain to which they'd all clung had crumbled away, leaving them grasping at thin air. This opportunity for all of them to get together might be the turning point, the fulcrum on which the future hung in balance. Not just for Mother. For *all* of them.

Holding her hand pressed to her chest, where her heart thumped with a mixture of hope and dread, Kitty said softly into the phone, "Sunday supper sounds wonderful. I'll bring dessert."

Chapter 18

Later that same day, as Alex was pulling up in front of Leanne's house, a family of mud hens forced her to a stop a few yards short of the driveway. Four small brown ducks with black heads and necks, a mother and three half-grown babies, ambled leisurely in the direction of the salt marsh a few hundred yards to the west of where Sandpiper Lane ended in a mucky field of bayberry and sea grape. For an endangered species that had succeeded in mobilizing local activists and politicians, arresting real estate development, and royally pissing off neighboring homeowners, the drab little creatures, she observed, were singularly unremarkable.

A thin smile broke the layer of ice that seemed to envelope her, like frost on a windowpane, as she thought, *Proof that the race doesn't always go to the swift or the strong.* Sometimes the swift and the strong were felled by those who appeared weaker and less able to cope, like friends who smiled and put their hands out while secretly stabbing you in the back.

Alex parked her Tercel and got out. Fog had settled over the potholed lane like a thin blanket through which the setting sun glimmered faintly. Her shadow stretched across Leanne's scruffy little yard as she walked up the front path, her throat tight and a burning sensation just below her windpipe. This time Leanne wasn't going to wriggle out from under her, she thought. *I'll make her pay for what she's done.* Leanne *owed* it to her, and to Mother, to get up on that witness stand. And, dammit, she would—even if Alex had to personally haul her up there by the scruff of her neck.

It wouldn't be easy, she knew. Once Leanne dug her

heels in, she was impossible to budge. She could get downright belligerent, even. Alex remembered when her friend was being harassed by a collection agency over a bill Chip had stuck her with when he walked out. After a series of calls and increasingly nasty letters, a heavyset man had shown up at her door one day and threatened her with prosecution. Refusing to be intimidated, Leanne had chased him down the driveway with the garden hose turned on full blast, cursing like a sailor all the way.

Now it was Alex's turn to chase what she'd been running from: a situation not entirely of her mother's making . . . and, in all fairness, not Leanne's, either. What had killed her father, she understood at last, wasn't a single person or event, but a whole series of wrongdoings and misguided actions: each on its own relatively harmless, but like neutrons when clustered together, they'd created a devastating explosion.

When she arrived at her mother's doorstep tomorrow, she wouldn't be asking for forgiveness, nor would she be offering it. What she hoped to give was something more concrete: the guarantee of Leanne's testimony.

She was halfway up the path when she spotted Leanne's mother's Lincoln parked in the gravel alley alongside the garage. Alex froze. What was *she* doing here? Beryl hardly ever visited. Had she finally decided to play grandma to the little boy she'd all but ignored since his birth? If so, Alex couldn't imagine what might be in it for her. Tyler wasn't exactly a grandson a woman like Beryl took pride in showing off.

Alex stepped up onto the narrow concrete porch, where a dusty-green welcome mat with some of its letters scuffed off beckoned w COM. *Why come indeed?* she thought with cold amusement. What did she expect to accomplish here? Once Leanne got wind of her mission, she'd chase her away like that bill collector. With Beryl bringing up the rear.

Poised at the door with her heart knocking in her chest, Alex was on the verge of walking away, but something forced her to knock. Something gritty and abrasive at her core, like carborundum, formed by years of pushing herself to the limit and beyond, that had honed her to a fine gleaming point. This was about more than just Mother. For her own sake, she wanted answers: answers only Leanne could provide.

How long had she and Daddy been seeing one another before he died? And when had Beryl found out about the affair? Was that why Beryl let the cat out of the bag to Mother about her *own* long-ago involvement with him? It made sense, as far as timing was concerned: a few weeks before the party . . . long enough for the shock and denial to have worn off, and for the pressure that had to have been mounting in her mother to have finally exploded.

Maybe it was a good thing after all, she thought, that Beryl happened to be here. In a way, weren't they *both* in this together? As much as it sickened Alex to see her father in that light—as someone unscrupulous enough to have slept with the daughter of a woman with whom he'd once had an affair, who also happened to have been *her* best friend, she had to face facts. Together, Beryl and Leanne would paint a picture lurid enough to sway even the most hard-hearted juror. *That is, if she could get them to agree to testify. And it was a big if.*

But if someone had once said she could sell ice cubes to Eskimos now was her chance to prove it. Kitty had phoned a short while ago to let her know about tomorrow's supper up at the house. It was the chance Alex had been waiting for, a chance to explain to her mother that she hadn't meant to harm her, and she didn't intend to show up empty-handed.

Waiting for her knock to be answered, she stood motionless on the doorstep, a pulse in one temple thudding in time to each leaden beat of her heart. She wished Jim were here. He had a way of sanding down her sharp corners and soothing her fears. Earlier this week, if he hadn't come when she'd called, she honestly didn't know *what* she'd have done.

They'd sat up most of the night, sipping tea and talking until it had begun to grow light outside. She'd confessed to him about the hole she'd dug for herself financially. And Jim, rather than blaming or belittling her, had mapped out a plan for consolidating her debts.

It was more than he personally could scrape together, he'd said, but he knew someone—an executive at one of the companies he did business with. The guy owed him a favor and might advance her the money at an affordable interest rate.

Alex, for her part, had listened with newfound humility to advice that only a short while ago she'd have thrown back in his face. Huddled at the kitchen table, idly tracing the moist circle left by her mug—the way she'd once, as a teenager, traced their initials in steamed-up car windows—she had been filled, not with resentment, but with gratitude—for this man she'd never stopped loving and for the fact that he wasn't here to save her . . . just to show her how to save herself.

And isn't that why she'd *really* come here? To save herself along with, she hoped, her mother. She only prayed it wasn't too late . . .

Alex heard a chain rattle on the other side, then the door cracked open. But the face peering out at her wasn't Leanne's. For a ghastly split-second, it was as if Alex were glimpsing a hideously aged Dorian Gray version of her friend. How was it she'd never before noticed the strong resemblance Leanne bore to her mother?

Maybe you weren't looking.

With a sickening jolt, Alex realized she hadn't paid much attention until now because there had been no reason to question which of her parents Leanne might take after. But she quickly brushed the thought aside, forcing herself to concentrate on the task that lay ahead.

"Leanne's not here," Beryl rasped, her heavily made-up eyes narrowed at Alex over the door chain. Stale air smelling of cigarettes wafted out at her.

"When do you expect her back?" Alex inquired with all the politeness she could muster.

"Any minute. But it won't do any good to wait. She doesn't want to see you."

Beryl's flat reptilian gaze sent a chill down her spine. Alex tightened her grip on the strap of her shoulder bag, squeezing until it felt as if her knuckles would pop right through her skin. "I'll leave a message then. May I come in? I don't have anything to write on."

She had no intention of leaving until Leanne *did* show up, but Beryl didn't have to know that. Even so, the woman seemed suspicious. Alex waited for what seemed an eternity after Beryl's gaunt horror show of a face had disappeared from view. Then the chain rattled again, and this time the door swung all the way open.

Stepping inside, Alex was at once enveloped in a haze of cigarette smoke. Ever since she could remember, Leanne's mother had been trying to cut down, which Beryl defined as merely going from four packs a day to two or three. It wasn't just smoking, either. As kids, Alex and Leanne used to riffle through her mother's medicine chest and count all the prescription vials. They'd numbered in the dozens.

Now, as she led the way into the darkened living room, Beryl, in tight-fitting black slacks and a turtleneck that showed every rib, made her think of a frayed rope about to snap.

Beryl carefully lowered herself onto the sofa and retrieved a pack of Winston Lights from the coffee table, absently extending it to Alex before remembering she didn't smoke. With a shrug, she lit one for herself, her long manicured nails flickering jewellike in the shuttered dimness, lit only by the yellowish glow emanating from the kitchen.

"I'll need a pad and pencil," Alex reminded her.

Beryl gave a hoarse, rattling laugh that ended in a cough. It was a moment before she caught her breath, and almost in the same instant she took a deep drag from her cigarette. "You can drop the pretense. I know why you're here. It's payback time, isn't it?" She blew a plume of smoke upward, her cold gaze fixing on Alex. "Yes, I know—someone has to be at fault. And it couldn't possibly be your dear sainted father. And your mother . . . well, we all know she was driven to it. So I guess that leaves Leanne."

Alex, taken aback, sank down across from her in a plush easy chair, which gave way with a seat-sprung sigh. Through the closed door to Tyler's room, she heard a single mewing cry. Something twisted in her gut, and for a moment she didn't think she could go on. Then she thought: *I have to.* "You found out a few weeks before the party, didn't you? Right after Leanne had gone to my mother." The whole ugly picture was coagulating in Alex's mind as she spoke. "That's what forced you to tell Mother about *you* and Daddy, isn't it? You couldn't stop what was happening—Leanne wouldn't listen to you—so you wanted Mother to do it for you."

Behind a film of smoke, Beryl's eyes gleamed. "I wish I'd told your mother *years* ago, back when Phil and I were getting divorced. If I had, maybe I would have been able to face what I've spent the past thirty-five years trying to bury." She crossed her legs and sat back, her cigarette smoldering unnoticed in the forked fingers of the hand she held propped on one knee. As she stared off into the distance, Alex had the eerie feeling Beryl wasn't so much remembering as struggling to forget.

"You didn't have to go on pretending to be her friend," she accused. "Even a snake shows itself for what it is."

"Hard as it may be for you to believe, she *was* my friend." Beryl's mouth twisted up in a mirthless smile. "You've probably wondered what we have in common, your mother and I," she said without irony. "We don't share the same interests, true. But we're birds of a feather. If something doesn't fit our rosy picture of how it's supposed to be, why, we just trim the edges until it *does*."

"My mother wasn't the one sleeping with her best friend's husband!"

"True." In the half-light, Beryl's cigarette seemed to float up to the crimson slash of her mouth. "Do you know something? I used to wish she would go off and have an affair of her own. Poor Lydia. You know what the real crime was? She loved him, far more than he deserved."

"What about Leanne? Apparently she was under the impression that he was going to *marry* her." Alex remained perfectly still, sensing that even the slightest move might break the spell.

Beryl shook her head in grim bemusement. "He made

the same promise to me. Thirty-four years ago . . . just before I found out I was pregnant with Leanne."

Alex shuddered as if a window had been thrown wide open, letting in a blast of chilly air. Coming here had been a terrible mistake, she realized. What she needed to do right now was simply get up and walk out. Before she had to listen to any more of this . . . this . . .

Horse twaddle.

The old-fashioned epithet reverberated inside her head, but it was her *mother's* voice delivering it—the cursory tone with which Mother would dismiss an opinion or version of events that differed from her own. Alex remembered how angry it always made her, and now, instead of bolting for the door, she held herself very straight, her hands clasped tightly in her lap. She *had* to listen. To know. Ironically, for Mother's sake.

"Why are you telling me this?" she asked hoarsely.

Beryl hesitated. When she spoke, there was an odd catch in her voice. "Isn't that what you came for? The truth?"

"Why should I believe anything you say? You hated my father."

"True. But it wasn't always that way. Once, I loved him." Her hard expression grew soft around the edges, like something worn down with caressing.

"Why?" Alex choked, anguish rising thick and hot in her throat. "Why couldn't she have just divorced him? Why did she have to kill him? Was it just because he was making a fool of her with someone his daughter's age?"

"Not his daughter's age. His *daughter*."

The dreadful words hissing out of Beryl brought back the recurring image of a snake. But now Alex could feel its fangs in her flesh, its poison spreading through her in a hot, numbing wave.

It's true, a voice hammered in her head. *You know it's true . . . you've known ever since Leanne told you what Mother said. You just didn't want to face it.*

"In the beginning, I wasn't sure," Beryl went on in that hollow whispery voice like something scraping the bottom of a boat. "Vern and I had been seeing one another for *years,* and we'd always been careful. Well, as careful as one could be, back in those days. When I found out I was pregnant, I wanted to believe it was my husband's, from the one time I'd been with Phil the month before. The timing was all wrong, of course, but desperation can convince you of almost anything." She tapped her cigarette against an ashtray piled with lipstick-stained butts. "When Leanne was growing up, there were so many times I'd think, *she's just like Vern.* Then I'd catch myself, and the process of convincing myself would start all over again. It wasn't until Tyler was born that I knew for sure."

Alex felt her stomach drop out from under her, as if she were ascending rapidly in an elevator. "You mean . . . oh, God."

Beryl's ravaged face lit briefly with a volcanic hatred, long capped and simmering . . . and directed mostly at herself, Alex now realized. "It was history repeating itself. Whatever she might have told you, Leanne had been seeing Vernon for *months* before that no-good husband walked out on her."

Alex's fingers crawled up over her face, digging into her eyes to make the horrid images stop. Oh God . . . poor Mother . . .

Beryl went on, relentless. "When Tyler was diagnosed, it didn't take a genius to put two and two together. I'd known about Vern and Leanne. She had to confide in someone, I suppose, and who would understand better than I?" She started to laugh, and broke out coughing again. It was a moment before her hacking subsided and she could wheeze, "She was hell-bent on telling your mother, too, even though I'd begged her not to. That's when I went to Vern." She paused. "He just laughed. He accused me of being a crazy old woman who'd been medicating herself for too long. He didn't believe Leanne was his daughter . . . any more than he had all those years ago when I told him what I suspected."

"Was it true?" Alex dragged her gaze up to meet Beryl's. "*Was* he planning to leave Mother?"

"I don't know." Beryl sounded dubious enough to be telling the truth. "I don't suppose we'll ever know."

Something else occurred to Alex and suddenly the

mists cleared. "It was *you*," she said. "You got to Mother before Leanne did. You couldn't take a chance she'd think of it as just another one of Daddy's cheap affairs, and do nothing to stop it. You had to make sure she knew. *Everything.*"

Beryl stared back at her, stone faced except for her crimson lips, pressed so tightly together they twitched. "Yes, I told her. The whole nine yards, as they say."

Alex felt sick. "Oh God. How did she react?"

"She said absolutely nothing. Just turned white as a sheet and showed me the door." Beryl dropped her head into her hands with a harsh sob. "Poor, poor Lydia."

When Alex could bring herself to speak, she choked, "If you knew all this, why in God's name have you kept quiet? She could go to prison for the rest of her life!"

Beryl's eyes, when she raised them again, were ringed with mascara, giving her the look of a ghoulish Halloween mask. "I had to choose, don't you see? Your mother isn't the only one on trial. When Leanne's case goes to court, how will it look for her? If people find out Tyler is the child of incest, they'll also know there's a very good chance he was *born* this way. It would kill any chance Leanne might have for a normal life. Without some sort of settlement—enough to get that boy the full-time care he needs—she might as well be in prison herself."

"So the rest of us can just go to hell, is that it?" When Alex stood up, she felt as though she were towering over Beryl, like in that ridiculous movie—*Attack of the Fifty Foot Woman*—she and Leanne had howled over as kids.

Beryl looked up at her with a hollow laugh. "You think your mother wants it any different? She could have said something. Have you ever asked yourself why she's kept her mouth shut all this time?"

"What gives you the right to decide what's best for my mother?" Alex demanded. Her skin felt stretched and hot, as if too small for her frame.

"Isn't that what *you* did? By keeping his dirty little secrets?" Beryl eyed her with disdain. "Oh, don't look so surprised. I know all about it. I used to watch you two together—thick as thieves. He told you everything,

didn't he? And you just lapped it up. But I'll bet he
didn't tell you about Leanne."

Standing there, shaking all over, Alex understood. Everything. Like a flash of lightning illuminating a sulfurous sky, she saw how it had happened—how each of
them had deluded themselves both separately and as a
whole. And how her father had played on that, using
them, extracting only what he needed and discarding the
rest, as he had the cadavers he'd autopsied—bones and
flesh where a breathing, thinking person had once stood.

In the darkened living room, Alex took a step back,
her legs trembling. "I have to go," she announced in a
toneless voice. Her reason for being here in the first
place was no longer valid; it had been punched out, like
a ticket made worthless. The only trial at which Leanne
was going to testify was her own.

It wasn't until she'd reached the door that Alex
thought of something else. She stopped and turned
slowly around. "Why do you think my mother still loved
him? After all *that?*"

Beryl stubbed out her cigarette and leaned back. Her
eyes gleamed in the mask of her ravaged face. In a soft
voice, almost as if marveling to herself, she replied,
"There was no one else like him. That's the hell of it
all, don't you see? Once he'd had you, there was no
forgetting."

A lex was picking her way down the front path in near
darkness when a pair of headlights swung into view,
cutting across the yard and momentarily blinding her.
Throwing a hand up against the glare, she saw Leanne's
car pull into the driveway. A moment later, Leanne
climbed out, heaving something with her. Slowly, she
walked to meet Alex, a bag of groceries clutched against
her like a shield.

"Hi, Alex."

"Hi," Alex managed to choke.

"You should've called first."

"Why? Would you have asked me over?"

Leanne's harsh laugh was an eerie echo of her mother's. "Probably not." In the anemic glow of the porch light, she looked sallow and tired. Saturday was her one full day off—the only time she had to run errands and catch up on chores. An odd pity stole over Alex. She hated what Leanne had done, yes, but seeing her face to face was another matter. The eyes fixed on Alex over the serrated edge of the Albertson's grocery bag were those of a haunted woman, not a Jezebel.

"Anyway, I was just leaving," Alex said.

"You talked to my mother?" Leanne looked worried.

"Yes. We had a long talk." Alex hooked a thumb around her purse, and felt its strap dig into her shoulder. "In all the years I've known her, I think it's the longest talk we've ever had."

"You know Mom—she hardly said two words to me the whole time I was growing up. And I'm her daughter." Leanne's attempt at laughter fell flat, and Alex caught a tremulous note in her voice. She was hoping to cash in on the long years of familiar bantering, Alex knew. But this time it wasn't going to work.

"She hasn't forgotten that fact, believe me." Alex fixed her with an unforgiving stare. "You should thank her, you know. She's looking out for your best interests. And I don't just mean baby-sitting Tyler."

"I know." Leanne had the decency to flush. "Alex, what about you? You're not going to have me subpoenaed, are you? Because I'll deny everything. I swear I will." Her voice took on a desperate, ranting quality. "Everything I've worked for in this community would be destroyed. I wouldn't be able to hold my head up at the hospital. And Tyler . . ." she stopped, her eyes filling with tears. "You just don't *know* . . . what it's like to feel like you're pushing a boulder up a hill with every move you make, what it's like to love someone who can never love you back."

"As a matter of fact, I *do* know," Alex said. For hadn't it been that way with Daddy? However much he'd pretended to, he hadn't loved her. Not in the way that counted.

Leanne shifted the bag to her other arm. Standing there, her groceries balanced against one hip, she struck an unintentionally insolent pose. "I'm sorry," she said in an oddly choked voice. "If that's what you wanted to hear, okay. I was a shitty friend. I lied to you. But, Alex, I didn't mean to hurt you. I never meant to hurt you."

"Why do people always say that?" Alex gave a dry laugh. "Nobody ever *means* any harm. And yet somebody always get hurt. Or in some cases, killed."

Leanne grew very still and seemed to waver unsteadily on her feet. Then, as if an invisible string attached to her spine had been pulled taut, Leanne straightened. "I think you'd better leave," she said.

"Believe me, I can't get out of here fast enough." Alex, her heart pounding in sick uneven thuds, moved forward briskly. She was brushing past Leanne when her purse bumped up against the bag of groceries, knocking it from Leanne's grasp.

The bag split open as it hit the concrete, spilling groceries onto the scruffy grass and frost-heaved brick path: a carton of milk, boxes of cookies and cereal, an open bag of grapefruit that rolled like croquet balls to bump up against the muddy hose snaking across the grass. Alex looked down at a carton of eggs at her feet, oozing glistening whites and broken yolks.

Instinctively, she bent to help retrieve the scattered items. But Leanne, already kneeling in the grass, a four-pack of toilet paper absurdly tucked under one arm, shouted tearfully, "Go! Just *go!* I don't need your help. I don't need anything from you."

Alex shook her head and began backing away. It was crazy. *She* should be the one screaming at Leanne. And yet a horrible sympathy was welling up in her. She didn't blame her friend any less, but she understood somehow. They'd been caught in the same trap, a trap woven of lies and an overarching love for one man.

Like their mothers before them.

Minutes later, in her car snaking along Quartz Cliff Drive, she thought about telling her sisters what she'd learned. But what would be the point? Beryl and Leanne weren't going to testify, and if forced, they would only lie. And Daphne and Kitty—hadn't they absorbed enough already? Would it be fair to rob them of any last bit of affection they might have for their father? *One last secret,* she thought, *only this time, it's not for Daddy's sake that I'm keeping it.*

Wisps of fog swirled in her headlights, and the ocean murmured somewhere below the guardrail gleaming white in the purple twilight. Her thoughts turned to her mother. *For weeks, she knew and kept it to herself—while I was out hunting down napkins, candlesticks, and tablecloths for the party. She knew, and didn't let on . . .*

Alex shuddered. That night, had her mother finally gotten up the nerve to confront her father? Or had he come to her on his own and told her he wanted a divorce?

Either way, one thing was clear: whatever was said, there had been no turning back. No exit. No place to go from there.

There had been only one thing left for her mother to do. And she had done it. Whatever became of her now, she had made her choice. Nothing any of them could do would change that.

Tears filled Alex's eyes, momentarily blurring the road ahead, which appeared to be rushing at her. *All I can do,* she thought, *is tell her what I should have years ago. That I love her. That I'll always love her, no matter what.*

Chapter 19

The first thing that hit Daphne when she walked in was the mouth-watering smell of roasting chicken, a smell she associated, not just with Sunday supper, but with everything that was safe and warm and happy. Memories of years past, before she'd gone away to college and gotten married, rose up as one; and it seemed to Daphne, as she stood there in the hallway, inhaling the scents of roast chicken and lemon Pledge, that she'd never moved away, that every Sunday of her life she'd sat down to supper at her parents' heavy clawfoot table, surrounded by her mother and father and two sisters.

In spite of the apprehension she felt, Daphne smiled. From the kitchen, she heard her mother call brightly, "Be right with you, girls! Just let me get this bird out of the oven."

"Need any help?" Daphne called back, though at the moment, with Kyle and Jennie clinging to her legs like a pair of limpets, she was having enough trouble simply negotiating the short stretch of hallway between the front door and the coat closet.

"I'll go." Kitty pried Kyle away from her and helped him wriggle out of his jacket before breezing on ahead into the kitchen.

Roger, standing inside the doorway shaking off the rain that had begun to fall on their way in, strode over to scoop Jennie up into his arms before she became lost in the folds of the raincoat Daphne was struggling to take off.

Both children had fussed nonstop the whole way over. Though Daphne and Roger had been deliberately vague about their grandmother's absence while in jail—saying only that Grandma had to go away for a while and would be back as soon as she could—they'd sensed something amiss about her sudden return. In the car, as Daphne was strapping her into her car seat, Jennie began to cry and kick. Kyle had been teasing her about not being big enough for a real seat belt, and it was several minutes before Daphne could calm her. Then Kyle started in about only getting to watch the first half of *Free Willy* before it was time to go—never mind that his favorite video was practically worn out from being played so often. He'd whined and bucked in his seat. Why did they have to go to Grandma's? Why couldn't they have supper at Aunt Kitty's?

Daphne hadn't the heart to scold them too hard. It was their only way of communicating the feelings for which they had no words: that there was something different about this visit with their grandmother. They didn't know what—but whatever it was, it scared them.

Perhaps the children were picking it up from her. Since yesterday, when Kitty told her about the invitation to supper, Daphne's stomach had been in knots. Now, glancing about, at the freshly polished furniture and vases of cut flowers from the garden—asters, daisies, Spanish bluebells—she couldn't help thinking how normal everything looked. *Too* normal. As if the past two months had been nothing more than an unexpected absence. The mail that had piled up on the hall table was gone. In the parlor, the furniture had been pushed back into place, and the braided rug she and Kitty had hauled down from the attic covered the area left bare by the old carpet.

What should she say, Daphne wondered, if her mother asked what had happened to that carpet? She shuddered at the memory of rolling it up and securing it with twine. But if that was bad, this was even worse, to be here and have to act as if nothing out of the ordinary had tainted every memory she held dear.

While Roger herded the children into the kitchen to say hello to their grandmother, Daphne found herself lingering behind. She drifted into the parlor, as polished and vacuumed as when Daddy was alive, and sank down on the sofa. *This is crazy,* she thought. *We should be all over Mother, pacing the floor and tearing our hair out.* Instead, her first impulse was to head for the dining room, where it had been her job, since she'd been old enough to be trusted with the good china, to make sure the table was properly set.

She resisted the urge, peering instead out the rain-streaked window for any sign of Alex, who ought to be arriving any minute. The prospect worried her more than a little. Alex hadn't spoken to their mother since her arrest, so things were bound to be tense. And Alex had never been her mother's favorite. On the other hand, she thought, it might be good if her sister were to shake things up a bit—like a good hard slap to jolt their mother out of her make-believe world.

Is that what this is—Mother hiding her head in the sand? Or is it you who's not seeing clearly?

Yes, she admitted to herself, there just might be a method to her mother's madness. For however calm things appeared on the surface, Daphne sensed an underlying current tugging inexorably in a direction none of them had anticipated. She didn't yet know what it was, but one thing she felt sure of: her mother had a plan. She hadn't asked them to supper just for the joy of seeing them all seated around the table as one big happy family. Whatever she'd been up to these past few days, all alone in this house full of memories and ghosts, Daphne had a feeling they were about to find out.

Her uneasiness, though, wasn't limited to thoughts of her mother. There was the unsettled nature of her own future as well, throbbing in the back of her head like an infected tooth. The earth had cracked open and swallowed her—body and soul. And yes, heart, too, because without Johnny, she was little more than an empty shell, simply going through the motions, hoping against hope that by treading the familiar grooves, long enough and hard enough, she'd begin to feel again and grow a new heart—one with room in it for Roger.

Despite her resolve, hardly an hour passed when she wasn't reminded of Johnny in some way. Picking Kyle up from school, she'd remember the long-ago nights she and Johnny had met there after dusk, after everyone had gone home. She'd see them in her mind, as clearly as their initials—worn but still visible on the trunk of the huge old live oak shading the playground—two naive kids who'd thought they'd known it all, perched side by side on the jungle gym, holding hands and smoking cigarettes in the soft buggy twilight. Or running errands downtown, she'd spot someone at a distance who brought her heart to a standstill, but when she drove slowly past, the man would look nothing at all like Johnny, and she'd start to catalog this innocent stranger's flaws as if it were *his* fault somehow.

Had Roger noticed? If so, he was keeping it to himself. She'd caught him eyeing her strangely a few times, nothing more. He'd been pretty distracted himself lately—on the phone to his office half a dozen times a day, handling crises with staff and patients while attempting to broker some sort of a deal with his partners. She supposed she ought to give him credit just simply for being here . . . but she was unable to summon the necessary gratitude. She felt only resentment. Daphne resented the fact that she had to *try,* for the children's sake and for Roger's. She resented the fact that he was being nice when she wanted him to be a shit—that he was *here,* dammit, keeping her from Johnny.

The only good thing was that her husband hadn't pushed too hard to make love. Oh yes, he'd made a few half-hearted attempts that were more, she suspected, a show of willingness than anything else. Roger's pride wouldn't permit him to go too far out on a limb. If she wanted him, she'd have to make the first move.

Daphne had no idea when that might be. Right now, everything in her—every need, fear, desire—was raised in a single cry, both piercingly sweet and exquisitely agonizing: *Johnny.*

She was pulled from her thoughts by the sizzle of tires slowing at the curb out front. Through sheets of rain that billowed and twisted, she recognized the green Tercel for which her sister had traded in her BMW. Moments later, Alex and her girls were at the front door, shaking out umbrellas and slickers, stomping on the mat.

It was at that exact moment that their mother emerged from the kitchen, Kitty at her heels. Seeing Alex, she stopped short. Cheeks flushed from the kitchen's heat deepened to a hectic glow, and as she stood there with her hands behind her back like a guilty schoolgirl, frozen in the act of untying her apron strings, she looked impossibly youthful . . . more like the carefree young woman in the framed snapshot taken of her and Vernon on their honeymoon, hanging on the wall beside her.

Then, with a tiny cry, she brought her arms up, spreading them wide as if in exultation . . . or maybe to welcome back into the fold a daughter lost, but not forgotten.

Alex, framed in the open doorway with strands of wet hair pasted to her cheeks and her eyes dark with some pent-up emotion, didn't move. The twins hung back as well, exchanging nervous looks. A gust of wind blew in, scattering a handful of wet leaves over the hall runner and sending a shiver through Daphne. She drew in a sharp breath. Was Alex going to say something about their father? Or merely pretend, like the rest of them, that this was just another Sunday supper like all the hundreds of Sunday suppers before it.

The awkward moment seemed to stretch out, becoming almost unbearable. Then at last, Alex stepped forward with a queer stilted dignity to accept the embrace that was being offered, bowing her head against their mother's shoulder with a barely audible sob.

When she drew back, her eyes were glistening. "Sorry we're late," she apologized with a heartiness that seemed artificial. "It's really pouring out there. I couldn't see two feet in front of me."

Kitty, who wasn't exactly dry-eyed either, Daphne noted, crept around to shut the door, taking the opportunity to give each of the twins an encouraging little pat.

"Never mind. You're just in time." Lydia turned her attention to Nina and Lori, their downturned faces half hidden by the collars of their matching denim jackets. "Goodness, let's have a look at you two. Don't be shy. Whatever you might have heard, I still have most of my marbles . . . and haven't forgotten what it's like to hug my granddaughters."

When she'd finished fussing over them and hanging up everyone's coats, Lydia slipped her arm through Alex's and announced, "Supper is on the table, everyone. Come, let's sit down before it gets cold."

All things considered, the meal went smoothly enough. There was an uncomfortable moment when Roger began to carve the chicken—a ritual Daphne identified so strongly with her father that the sight of her husband at the head of the table carefully sawing the meat into paper-thin slices seemed almost a sacrilege. She wasn't the only one who felt it. A heavy silence fell over the table, followed by a flurry of bowls and platters being passed around. Then suddenly everyone was talking at once.

For once, Daphne was grateful for Roger's tendency to hold forth. She laughed with her sisters at stories she'd heard a thousand times, taking a sip from her wineglass whenever the forced jollity began to seem like so much rearranging of the deck chairs. Faintly but decidedly tipsy, she calmly wiped Kyle's chin and cut Jennie's chicken into tiny bites, while inside a voice was screaming, *Why doesn't someone say something?*

A passerby who happened to glance in the window would have seen nothing out of the ordinary, she thought. There was Mother, in her usual place at the head of the table closest to the kitchen, her haggard look of the past two months replaced by one that was almost beatific. She wore a yellow-checked shirtwaist that softened her edges and made her seem more slender than gaunt. And her silver hair, tucked neatly behind her ears, glowed like the sterling at her plate.

On her right, Alex sipped her wine and nibbled at her food, maintaining a cheeriness that only partly masked a tension that was like catgut strung too tight. Avoiding any subject that might summon the ghost of their father, she talked about the houses she was showing, the ribbons the girls had won in gymnastics, the family that had moved in next door . . . until Daphne began to feel like one of her clients, subjected to a stream of bright chatter designed to obscure any flaws they might encounter while touring a house that had been on the market a while. No one appeared to notice the way Alex nervously toyed with her pearls throughout the meal . . . or the return of her childhood habit of endlessly sculpting the mashed potatoes on her plate.

Except for Alex's daughters, who seemed absolutely fixated by what was on their plates—while managing not to eat very much of it—the one who was most subdued was Kitty. When she did join in, her conversation was stilted, like lines rehearsed for a play.

Daphne felt a pang of sympathy. *At least I have my children,* she thought.

It wasn't until Daphne and her sisters began to clear the table that Lydia seemed to stir from her rose-hued bubble. Rising from her chair, she said, "Leave all that. Nina and Lori can wash up." Turning to her granddaughters, she asked sweetly, "You don't mind, do you, girls? I need a moment alone with your mother and aunts. We'll be back in time to help with the drying."

Kyle and Jennie shot her anxious looks, as if fearful of being away from their mother, if only for a short while, and Daphne was grateful when Roger, without missing a beat, asked in a jolly voice, "How would you two like to watch TV with me in the den? Come on, let's go see if there's something good on."

As she and her sisters followed their mother upstairs, to the bedroom in which Lydia had slept alongside her husband for nearly forty years—the husband whose children she'd borne, whose clothes she'd washed and meals she'd cooked, and whose secrets she'd kept, even from herself—Daphne felt queasy, as if she'd eaten too much. She wondered if the hour had come, if this was the reckoning they'd been hoping for, and at the same time dreading. Was their mother going to reveal at last what had happened the night she'd climbed these very same stairs in search of the gun in the locked box on the top shelf of the closet?

Kitty slid her an uneasy glance. Whatever was in the

air, her sister felt it, too. Even Alex, trudging up the stairs ahead of them, seemed to drag her feet, as if of two minds.

We've all had something taken from us, Daphne thought. *Not just Daddy . . . but some essential part of ourselves.*

In her parents' bedroom, she sank onto the loveseat between the pair of windows that looked out over the Point, which at the moment appeared only as a sketchy outline, half obscured by a sheeting gray mist. Rain was predicted for tomorrow as well, which meant the children would be cranky from having to be indoors all day. Daphne remembered, too, her mother expressing a wish to go swimming in the cove. Had she abandoned the idea? Or was she merely waiting for the weather to clear? She found herself thinking, *I should have insisted on staying. She shouldn't be here all by herself.*

Daphne glanced about the room, marveling at how little had changed since she was a child. Even the mirror over the dressing table was tilted at the same exact angle, reflecting the silver-backed brushes engraved with Lydia's initials and the cluster of framed family photos at one end. Her mother's touch was more evident here than anywhere else in the house, in the simple oak bed and dresser and delicate watercolors scattered over pale yellow-striped walls. There were only a few antiques— treasured heirlooms from her mother's side of the family, like the bird's-eye rocker in which Kitty sat, which had been handed down from their great-grandmother, Agnes Lowell.

What could have been going through her mother's head that night as she climbed the wooden stool in the closet and reached up to feel along the top shelf? As she groped among the extra blankets and ski sweaters, her fingertips dancing over the metal box, did it enter her mind that she was about to cross the boundary of all that was safe and predictable, with no hope of ever turning back? That she'd be entering a savage wilderness where the habits and relationships of a lifetime would be snatched from underfoot?

Daphne, her mind racing with these questions and

more, watched in silent dread as her mother retrieved a
hatbox from atop the dresser . . . and for a feverish
moment saw a metal box instead: shiny gray steel, with
a lock in which a small key would fit—not unlike the one
bagged in plastic in the police morgue in the basement of
the justice administration.

Feeling dizzy, she closed her eyes a moment . . . and
an image of Johnny swam into view, his crooked smile
and cool measuring eyes that gave no quarter and asked
no favors. Growing up, the ugly things she was familiar
with only through newspapers—people getting robbed
and beaten up, fires set by careless smokers—had been
frequent occurrences in Johnny's neck of the woods.
And suddenly she yearned, not for a pair of capable
arms—her own would do just fine—but for the hard acceptance that had been burned into him and the practiced agility with which he negotiated his way through a
world rigged with hidden trapdoors and trip wires.

Lord, give me strength . . .

The room grew still with a silence as leaden as the
sky, which swelled like a ghostly gray ocean against the
eaves and old uneven windowpanes as they waited for
Mother to make her move.

Settling into the narrow bench at the foot of the bed,
the hatbox perched on her lap, Lydia said at last, "There
are some mementos I'd like you girls to have. Something
special for each of you." She smiled, and Daphne took
note of the deep lines in her cheeks, where once there
had been dimples. "I know it's not what you were expecting. But *that*, I'm afraid, I can't give you. There's no
way I can explain what happened with your father. It's
more complicated than you realize, though by now I'm
sure you know some of it, maybe even most of it."

She glanced at Daphne and Kitty before allowing her
gaze to settle on Alex with an expression that was both
loving and wistful. When she spread her hands, as if in
regret, Daphne saw that the gold band that had been
absent during her stay in jail was back in its rightful
place, on the third finger of her left hand.

Alex, perched on a corner of the bed, started to say
something but was silenced when her mother continued,

"It doesn't take away, of course, from everything you've done to help." Lydia's soft voice was oddly mesmerizing, like the slippery rustling of taffeta Daphne remembered from when she was a child—her mother bending down to kiss her in the darkness, smelling of perfume and the one martini she allowed herself before a party. "You've shown tremendous courage under the most difficult of circumstances. Yes, even you, Alex. I know it's been harder on you in some ways than on your sisters, and you did the best you could. It's enough for me that you came tonight."

"Can't you at least try to explain?" Kitty cried in frustration.

Mother shook her head sadly. "It doesn't matter, not really, because whatever happens in the end, I'll never be free. And as incredible as it might seem to you, I'm at peace with that. The only thing I want—with all my heart—is for you, each one of you, to be at peace, too." She pried the lid off the hatbox—an old one covered in a rosebud-printed fabric faded from long exposure to the sun. It contained all the odds and ends too good to throw away, but for which there was no readily apparent use: scraps of lace and stray buttons, balls of yarn left-over from knitting, an old tortoiseshell comb with half its teeth missing.

Now, from its lavender-scented depths, their mother withdrew a velvet jewelry box, which she held out to Alex. "It's the diamond brooch your father gave me for our twenty-fifth anniversary," she said. "You can keep it, or sell it if you like. It makes no difference to me. Your father only gave it to me because—" she stopped, her eyes filling with tears. "Let's just say it's a bit too ostentatious for my taste."

Alex, looking stunned and a bit sheepish, stared at the box for a moment before opening it. When Daphne got up, walking over to peer over her shoulder, she couldn't help but gasp. Ostentatious wasn't the word for it. This was—well, there was no getting around it—*magnificent:* a delicate basket woven of platinum, from which rose a flower-shaped spray of diamonds.

Yet to her knowledge, Lydia had never worn it; none

of them had even known of its existence. Daphne stared down at it, speechless. Even Alex, who could be unsentimental and hard nosed, appeared overwhelmed.

Her eyes gleamed with unshed tears, and she seemed to be struggling to find the words to thank her mother. When at last she spoke, it was as if all her hard outer layers had been stripped away, leaving her as soft and vulnerable as the newborn Daphne had once, as a four-year-old, gingerly cradled in her arms.

"I . . . I don't know what to say," Alex stammered. "I certainly wasn't expecting this. It's . . . it's very generous of you, Mother."

"No need to thank me." Mother smiled. "It's a gift, free and clear. My only wish is that you put it to good use, whatever you decide to do with it. Now, for you, Daphne . . ." There was a rustling of tissue paper, and she reached once more into the box, pulling out a diary bound in faded red leather. Placing it in Daphne's outstretched hands, as reverently as if it were an ancient scroll containing secrets of a lost civilization, she said, "This, more than any explanation I could give you, may help you to understand some of what you need to know. I kept it from the time I was sixteen, until I had you. After that, there weren't enough minutes in the day for everything that needed doing." She smiled in fond recollection. "When you write about what happened, and I know you will—you *must*—I hope this will provide some insight."

"*Write* about it?" Daphne echoed in horrified confusion. "How could you think I'd do that? Put our family on display like . . . like some kind of freak show. Make *money* off what happened?"

Lydia shook her head, and a tear slipped down her cheek. "No, Daphne, you're looking at it the wrong way. You'd be setting the record straight, don't you see? People will want someone tortured, a monster or a victim . . . they always do. It might surprise them to know that my hopes and dreams, the things I worried about, however overwhelming they might have seemed at the time—they were really quite ordinary. When you write about this, it'll be to let people know I wasn't so different from them."

Daphne clutched the diary to her chest, fighting back tears of her own. A ray of sunshine found its way through the clouds and onto the hand resting atop the hatbox, and for an instant the light seemed to be radiating from the gold wedding band it wore.

Swallowing hard, she said, "I . . . I'll try."

"Last but not least . . ." Mother turned her gaze on Kitty, who until this minute had sat motionless, taking it all in. Now her sister straightened and leaned forward in the rocking chair as their mother began to speak, in a way that Daphne had never before heard her address Kitty—with a kind of puzzled tenderness. "You were my biggest challenge," she said. "But the other day, as we were leaving the courtroom, I *knew*. The perfect thing." She reached once more into the hatbox.

As the light winked on the small silver cup in her hand, Kitty let out a choked cry. It was the baby cup that had been passed down from one generation of their mother's family to the next, starting with her great-great-grandmother, more than a hundred years ago. On it were engraved the initials KML: Katherine Marie Lowell.

Daphne was stunned by the insensitivity of such a gift. Why was Mother doing this? How could she not *know* how painful it would be to Kitty? She wanted to snatch the cup from her and hide it, quickly . . . before it could do any more harm. But it was too late. The look of hurt and loss on her sister's face as her fingers closed woodenly about the cup was as deeply etched as its engraved initials.

"I've been saving it for the baby you would have someday," Lydia explained gently.

Clearly embarrassed, Kitty struggled for words. "I don't know what you heard, or who told you . . . but it's not true. The . . . the baby I'd hoped to adopt . . . its mother changed her mind."

Mother looked at her in confusion and for the first time tonight seemed hesitant. "Oh, well, I wouldn't know anything about . . . I mean, no one told me . . ."

She stopped and pulled herself up, adding more firmly, "I meant *your* baby. The one you're going to have."

The color drained from Kitty's face, leaving it a sick, pasty gray. She stared long and hard at their mother, as if trying to decide whether this was some sort of cruel joke . . . or whether her mother really *had* gone mad. Then she turned, and with what little was left of her composure, gently set the cup down on the dressing table. In the mirror above it, Daphne could see her anguished eyes reflected. "I'll never have a child of my own," she said. "I don't know if I'll be able to adopt one, either. You'd better save this for someone who'll need it."

In the stillness that followed, the startled laugh Lydia gave seemed to reverberate through the room like a shock wave following an earthquake. "You mean you don't . . . oh, dear . . ." She got up and walked over to put her arms around Kitty. "I thought you *knew*."

"What?" Kitty demanded in confusion.

"You're pregnant. I can always tell—call it a sixth sense. I knew it the moment I was expecting each of you girls . . . and with Alex, too, before she told me she was pregnant with the twins. When was your last period?"

"I . . . I've never been regular," Kitty replied somewhat testily, as if she didn't dare believe what her mother was saying. "It's been a few months, I think . . ." Suddenly, she clapped a hand over her mouth, and her eyes widened. "Oh, God, what if *that's* why I've felt so tired lately? And sick all the time." She straightened as suddenly as if she'd stepped on something sharp, and then burst into tears.

Lydia patted her awkwardly on the back. "Go ahead, cry all you want. God knows enough tears have been shed over what's dead and gone. It's time we cried over something good to come."

Hours later, Kitty lay on her bed, staring up at the angel on the ceiling. Not a real angel, if such things even existed, only an ancient water stain in the shape of one, left from a long-ago burst pipe. She thought of the angel Gabriel appearing before the Virgin Mary to herald her immaculate conception and nearly laughed out loud. She knew exactly where *this* baby had come from.

Sean.

She was having his baby. The realization hit home with an impact so great the room seemed to sway—as if she were inside a bell, a huge church bell, pealing out the glad tidings, over and over, until every part of her sang with it, and her heart soared.

On the ride back tonight, still reeling from her mother's unexpected gift, Kitty had asked Roger to stop at Long's Drugs, where she'd bought a pregnancy test. Arriving home, she'd wished everyone good night and gone straight up to her room, locking the door behind her. What if it was all a cruel mistake? Better to let Daphne know in the morning, after she'd had a chance to swallow her disappointment in private.

Yet as Kitty had sat shivering on the toilet, clutching the white plastic indicator, she'd begun to think her mother wasn't so crazy after all. A blue line appeared in the test window, then two. Positive.

She'd nearly fainted from the shock of it, right then and there, on the blue-and-white tiled bathroom floor. But somehow, her knees buckling with every step, she'd managed to stagger into the next room and climb into bed, pulling the covers over herself as gently as she might have a damp towel over rising dough.

It was now half past midnight. She knew only because the little brass carriage clock ticking on her night table told her so. It could have been minutes or hours since she'd been lying here, still in the violet dress she'd worn to supper. She hadn't bothered to undress because she saw no point in even trying to sleep. How could she sleep with her mind racing, feeling as if it were about to burst open like a ripe plum? If this was anywhere near how Mary had felt when she'd received Gabriel's news, Kitty could appreciate now the rapturous glow that surrounded her in religious paintings. Her own miracle was in many ways just as astounding: why now, after all these years? Why *this* man?

You weren't in love with the others, a voice whispered.

But, oh, what did it matter who had fathered it? It was *her* baby. Her own flesh-and-blood child no one could take away. There were angels after all, and they'd heard her prayers.

Kitty brought her hands to rest on her still-flat belly, from which a warm glow seemed to emanate. She became aware of a pulse, most likely her own, that seemed to flutter like a tiny heart. Closing her eyes, she tried to imagine what it would be like to hold her child in her arms . . . and for a moment, could actually *feel* it—the weight of a small bottom cupped in her palm, a baby's head with hair soft as kitten's fur brushing the underside of her chin. A tingly warmth started in her toes, like a tap slowly filling her until she could hold no more, until she was floating, carried off by the fathomless wonder of it all.

She'd convert the guest room, in which Daphne was installed for the time being, into a nursery. But instead of ducks and bunnies, she'd decorate it with her mother's watercolors. The crib would face the window, so that when her baby woke from its nap, it would see swallows swooping and darting in and out of the eaves and the ocean glimmering in the distance. And on a high shelf, she'd place birds' nests and seashells and bits of driftwood, so that he or she could gaze at them and know the world as a friendly place to go into, full of magic and mystery and wonderful surprises.

Her mind afloat on a sea of happy plans, she drifted to sleep in spite of herself. When she woke up, it was still dark, but she felt more refreshed than she had in weeks. She knew what she had to do. Climbing out of bed, she peeled off her wrinkled dress and threw on jeans and a T-shirt. She then tiptoed downstairs, careful to step over the middle stair that creaked loud enough to wake the whole house.

Without traffic, the drive to Sean's house seemed shorter this time. And the rain had stopped, leaving the road glistening in her headlights like a black river on which she was being borne effortlessly. She found her way easily, without even fretting about whether or not

she should have phoned first. It was as if her third eye—
her *truest* eye, according to Hindu belief—were guiding
her.

How would he react when she told him the news?
Would it scare him as much as it ought to? Would he
change his mind about wanting to be with her?

She'd let him know at once that she wasn't going to
burden him with this baby. She could handle it on her
own, thank you very much, and had, in fact, been preparing for this for some time. In an odd sense, Kitty
couldn't help feeling this wasn't Sean's baby, or *anyone's,* for that matter; it had been willed into existence
by the mere intensity of her yearning.

She found the door to Sean's little studio in back unlocked. Kitty didn't bother to knock. Nor did it occur to
her that he might be away . . . or, worse, with another
woman. Nothing could disturb the warm current on
which she seemed to float. She was blessed. She was . . .

Pregnant.

Sean was fast asleep on the mattress on the floor, and
when she crouched down to gently shake him, he didn't
stir. Without pausing to consider what her next move
should be, Kitty crawled in under the covers next to him.

Sean muttered something thickly and drew closer,
throwing an arm about her as if, even in sleep, he'd
sensed the need to protect her. Then his eyes opened.
For a long moment he simply lay there, staring in
disbelief.

"Kitty," he murmured. Just that, her name. As if he'd
been half expecting her.

"I'm sorry I woke you," she whispered.

"Everything okay?"

"Never better."

"Glad to hear it." He was fully awake now, his head
propped on one elbow. "But you didn't come all this
way just to let me know you're okay. What's up?"
Under the warm covers redolent of his outdoorsy scent,
she could feel him tensing.

"I needed to see you."

"Yeah?" His eyes searched her face in the darkness.
"You weren't so desperate to see me the other day."

He was hurt, and not quite ready to forgive her. Or maybe it was just that he didn't quite trust her motives. In a perverse way, she found the thought somewhat reassuring. If sex had been the only thing on Sean's mind, they wouldn't be having this conversation.

She looked down, smoothing a wrinkle in the madras spread. "I'm sorry if it seemed like I didn't care. I *do* care. Very much."

"You have a funny way of showing it."

"Do you want me to leave?" she asked softly.

She waited, listening to the rustle of wet leaves in the wind that had kicked up and the distant splashing of tires along the freeway. When he reached up to trace the line of her jaw with his fingertip, the shiver it sent through her seemed to come from a place deeper than mere flesh and bone.

"No," he said.

She caught his hand and brought it to her mouth, feeling the pulse in his wrist beating sure and steady. "I'm glad. Because there's something I need to tell you . . ."

A guarded hopefulness flickered in his eyes. In the ghostly light filtering from the skylight, they remained fixed on her, black as the ocean under a moonless nighttime sky. In his dark cropped hair, she saw a few flecks of sawdust he'd missed, like tiny reflected stars.

Kitty hesitated, feeling torn. The knowledge of her pregnancy was so new her impulse was to horde it, to selfishly revel in her joy. But it would be unfair to keep it from him. Whatever his reaction, he deserved to know. It wasn't an angel who'd given her this baby. It was Sean. He'd opened her heart somehow, let in enough light for it to grow.

"I'm pregnant," she said.

Sean stared back at her, utterly expressionless, as if he hadn't heard . . . or maybe didn't *want* to hear.

Something that had been gently unfurling inside Kitty retracted into a tight hard ball.

It doesn't matter, she told herself. She didn't need anything from him. She wasn't some penniless teenager. She was a thirty-six-year-old woman with a thriving business who could raise this baby on her own just fine.

She was about to tell him so when Sean asked softly, "When did you find out?"

"Tonight. A few hours ago."

"So that isn't why you wanted to stop seeing me?"

She looked at him, too startled at first to think of a response. Then cried, "God, no. Oh, Sean, how could you even *think* such a thing?"

A look of relief came over him, but his expression remained hard. Slowly, he said, "So you *do* want me to be a part of this baby's life?"

Kitty struggled to put into words what she wanted from him, but nothing concrete emerged. "Well, yes. I hadn't thought that far ahead. But, of course, if you want." She hesitated, then said, "To be honest, I wasn't a hundred percent positive you would."

She could see a clenched muscle working in his jaw. "I'm glad to hear it," he said in an odd constricted voice. "Because you have no fucking idea what I've been going through. When I saw you the other night . . . oh, *Christ*." With a hoarse cry he caught her to him, burying his head against her breasts, which felt tender and swollen, and clutching at her shirt as if it were the only thing keeping him from sliding down a steep precipice. After a moment, she recognized the strangled noises coming from him: he was crying.

"Sssh. It's okay." Struggling against her own tears, she stroked the back of his head, the soft bristles of his hair springing up against her palm. When he lifted his face to her, it was furrowed, angry almost. In a voice tight with emotion, he said, "You think I'm too young to know what love is, but you're wrong. I'll tell you something else you might not want to hear—I'm glad you're having my kid. Over the fucking moon." He started to laugh, loosely and a little insanely. Then he whooped: "Jesus! We're having a kid! I don't believe it."

"I don't believe it, either." She grinned. "I've been lying awake for the past few hours trying to convince myself it's true."

Sean drew himself up. He seemed more in control now. "Let's get one thing straight, okay? However you want to handle it, this kid is going to have a father."

"I don't think anyone could argue that," she laughed.

Sean scowled at her. "You know what I'm talking about. We'll have to work out some kind of a plan."

"What did you have in mind?" she asked.

"Would it do any good to ask you to marry me?"

Kitty thought for a moment, then shook her head. "Don't take this the wrong way, Sean. In some ways, I'd love nothing more. But I don't think that would be a very good idea. Not right now, anyway, with everything so up in the air. Maybe down the line . . . we'll see."

Sean, though clearly disappointed, didn't appear to have taken offense. With a shrug, he said simply, "I'm warning you, though, it won't stop me from coming over every chance I get."

"Who's stopping you?"

"I thought you wanted to cool it for a while."

"I'm the one who woke you up, remember?" She smiled and slid her hand down his leg. He had on a T-shirt but wasn't wearing any briefs.

Sean's reaction was immediate. He reached for her, hungrily, holding her so tightly that for a moment she couldn't breathe. Then as if suddenly aware of her supposedly delicate state, he abruptly released her. "We'd better not," he murmured. "Won't it hurt the baby?"

"Not at this stage," she assured him. Having read every book on the subject, Kitty felt like a seasoned pro.

Without further ado, he peeled her shirt off, then helped her wriggle out of her jeans. She'd removed her panties before taking the pregnancy test, and underneath she was naked. When Sean saw her, he didn't wait for a second invitation.

"You're so beautiful," he said. It was the closest she would ever get to poetry from Sean, but right now the words didn't matter. There was only his palm smoothing up her thigh, his fingers igniting her with their touch—the sure touch of a man, never mind his youth, who knew instinctively what it took to please a lover.

She moaned, arching up into the hand cupped between her thighs. His gaze locked with hers, and after a long sweet time in which she became lost in the delicious sensations crowding in on her, he brought it to his face,

the hand with which he'd been pleasuring her, inhaling
her scent as if it were the sweetest perfume.

Something released in her—a balloon that spiraled up
into her head before dropping down to settle just south
of her belly button. Kitty laughed with delight and shook
her head, her long crinkly hair falling down her bare
shoulders and back like a silken shawl.

She burrowed in next to Sean and caught the faint
smell of resin on his skin, mingled with soap and the
plain forward scent that was his alone. She felt a slow
liquid heat roll through her. She wanted him to take her.
Now. This instant. But when he started to push her legs
apart, she drew back. "No," she ordered gently, sliding
down to take him in her mouth instead.

After only a minute or so, he pulled away. "I'll come,"
he said, his voice husky. "I want it to be inside you."

Then he *was* inside her, on top of her, with Kitty guiding him into her, nearly sick with desire. She'd never felt
this way before, even with Sean—buffeted by emotions
stronger than any she'd known, each sensation so exquisite it trembled on the verge of agony. *The baby.* It
wasn't just that she was hungry for Sean, it was the baby,
too, knowing it was inside her, growing even as she lay
there beneath him.

Droplets of sweat dripped from his face onto hers like
warm sweet rain. He was holding back, and suddenly
she didn't want him to. She wanted only to feel him, *it,*
spilling into her as it had the night that she'd conceived—a life force with the power, not only to create,
but to revive hopes and dreams she'd believed dead.

Kitty thrust up into him, gasping and crying out with
the unbearable sweetness of it. She clutched his hips as
she would have a glass of water to her mouth, not wanting a single drop of it to spill out. In the same instant,
he came, too, rearing up as he pushed into her. Hard,
but at the same time as if, somewhere deep in the blind
rush of his release, he was being careful not to hurt her,
or the baby. She could feel him holding back a little,
and when he was finished, he didn't collapse on top of
her as he normally would have. He eased from her, and
rolled onto his side, facing her.

Gently, he pressed a hand to her belly. She smiled and covered his hand with her own, saying, "I wonder if she felt that."

"How do you know it's a girl?"

"Just a feeling. I'd be just as happy with a boy."

"You sure about that?"

"Positive." Her smile widened into a grin. "In case you haven't noticed, I happen to like boys."

He grinned back. "I've noticed." Sobering, he added, "I was serious, you know, about what I said before. Whenever I think of my sister's kid, not knowing its own flesh and blood . . . well, I don't want that to happen to *my* kid. Even if we aren't married, or even living together, I want us to be a family."

Kitty thought of her own family and how different it was from the one she'd imagined growing up. As a child, she'd taken it all for granted—the days strung out as if in endless supply, the little rituals that bound them to one another like the nearly invisible stitches in the quilts her mother made out of scraps of outgrown dresses. But now the crazy quilt that was her family had come apart, and they each had to fashion their own out of what fabric was left.

Their mother's gifts made perfect sense, she realized, not just for reasons that were obvious, but as reminders that their history hadn't *all* been a lie, that some parts were worth remembering and even treasuring. In the days to come, they would act as compasses—things to guide them as they negotiated the shoals that lay ahead still.

Kitty looked into Sean's deeply tanned face, which wore the outdoors like a badge, noting the pale creases at the corners of his eyes from squinting into the sun. *He'll make a good father,* she thought, just as she had that night she'd seen him at the hospital with his sister. About the rest, well, they'd have to see.

She touched his chest, as solid as the trees he climbed for a living. She could just as easily picture him snuggling a baby or pushing a stroller. Kitty smiled. "I'm not sure I even know the real definition of a family anymore," she said. "Maybe it's one of those recipes you make up as you go along—a little of this and a pinch of that. We could certainly try, couldn't we? Who knows, we might even end up with something worth keeping."

"**M**om?"

Alex, hearing Nina call out softly from the darkness of her room, paused at the foot of the stairs. Unable to sleep, she'd stayed up late watching TV, only to drift off to sleep on the sofa in the middle of Jay Leno's monologue—some stupid joke about men who cheat on their wives—she remembered *that* much. Now her head felt stuffed full of those maddening Styrofoam peanuts you have to dig through to get to what's at the bottom of the package. It was a moment before she remembered to stop and reverse her steps, crossing the short length of hallway to Nina's room.

Her daughter was sitting up cross-legged in bed when she walked in. Alex smiled at the picture she made in the soft pool of light from the lamp on the night table, eyes blinking sleepily, her thick dark hair ruffled up in back like when she was little, when Alex used to tuck the twins in every night. Nina was wearing a cast-off T-shirt of her father's, faded and splotched from the time Jim had absentmindedly tossed bleach into the washing machine before it had finished filling with water. Alex had really given it to him that time. Did she have to work all week *and* be a hundred percent responsible for household duties? she'd railed. The memory made her cringe. God, she could be such a bitch. It was a wonder Jim hadn't divorced her years ago.

And the girls . . . oh, she loved them dearly, no question. But over the years, in the blizzard of days that had piled up like sand dunes, when it was all she could do simply to trudge from one dune to the next, her mothering had become diffused somehow. Lately, when she thought of her daughters it was in terms of schedules and lists and appointments. She'd lost touch with the time when the mere sight of her toddlers, in their matching OshKosh overalls, pulling themselves up to view the world from the wobbly perch of their newfound legs, could move her to tears.

Alex sank down on the bed and patted the knee that stuck up under the quilted spread. Nina, despite her alarmingly mature appearance, was still a little girl in many ways. When they had moved here, she'd insisted on having her room done up in Laura Ashley—flowery fabrics edged in ruffles, matching white wicker bureau and headboard, an antique trunk lined with calico and filled with all the dolls and stuffed animals she hadn't the heart to give away. Only the vintage poster tacked to the closet door—Marlon Brando in torn T-shirt, of all things—was representative of a young woman as quirky as she was headstrong, a young woman Alex wanted very much to get to know.

"I heard you in the living room." Nina yawned, screwing her fists into her eyes exactly the way she had when she was little. "What are you doing up so late? Is everything okay?"

"I was on my way to bed." Alex started to say that everything was okay, just fine and dandy, when she realized that wasn't strictly true. Though in a way she *was* fine—or to put it more accurately, past the point of feeling unable to cope, when the better part of each day was spent wondering which section of the sky was going to come crashing down on her first—but she was far from dandy. With a sigh, she confessed, "The truth is, I still have trouble sleeping alone. Even Jay Leno is better than no one."

Nina smirked, and rolled her eyes. "That's pretty pathetic, all right. But you know what's worse?" She dropped her voice, confiding in a stagey whisper, "I still check under the bed every single night before I put the light out, just to make *sure*."

Alex didn't have to ask of what. Since she'd been a toddler, Nina's bedtime ritual had included a thorough investigation of every corner and hidden spot in which a boogeyman might be lurking. Lori, more trusting and perhaps less imaginative, would settle for a goodnight kiss.

Keeping a straight face, Alex replied with mock gravity, "I think it's fair to say that if a boogeyman were lurking around, we'd have scared *him* off by now."

"Things haven't exactly been what you'd call *normal*," Nina agreed.

"I have a feeling that's about to change. We're about due for some sunny skies, wouldn't you say?"

Nina pursed her mouth in thoughtful speculation. "By any chance, would these sunny skies have something to do with Dad?"

Alex felt the old tension automatically kick in. Did everything have to revolve around Jim? Didn't she get *some* credit for holding the fort down?

She thought of the diamond brooch her mother had given her. Upon closer examination she'd found a receipt inside the box, folded in a square tucked into the lid, for the staggering sum of slightly over ten thousand dollars—more than she could ever have imagined her father paying for a piece of jewelry. Had it been a token of his love . . . or merely a guilt offering?

At the thought of her mother keeping it hidden in a drawer all this time—apparently her only avenue of expressing the silent hurt and rage she dared not let out of *its* box—she grew cold. She should be grateful to Mother, not just for somehow sensing her need . . . but for forcing her, albeit by an act too terrible to contemplate, to confront her own boogeyman. Daddy . . . Leanne . . . Beryl . . . she'd shone the bright light of day on them and discovered that there *were* no such things as monsters, after all. There were no superheroes, either, just human beings who were weak and flawed, some more deeply than others; a few, like her father, fatally so.

Jim? He was one of the good ones. She just hadn't recognized it until now.

"Your father and I—" Alex stopped, growing suspicious all of a sudden. "I know that look, Nina Marie Cardoza. You've been spying on me, haven't you?"

"Not spying, exactly," her daughter hedged. "I just happened to pick up the phone when you were talking last night. Cross my heart, hope to die, I didn't mean to listen in." She pulled her pillow up over her chin to muffle her giggles.

Alex struggled not to smile. "Very funny, Sherlock. How much did you just *happen* to hear?"

Nina pried the pillow away from her mouth. "Only the part where you were talking about whether or not it was going to clear up tomorrow, so you could have your picnic up at Lighthouse Point." Slyly, she added, "We're *all* going, right?"

"What if I told you it was just your dad and me?"

Nina thought for a moment before replying, "I'd say it was a good idea . . . as long as you promise to tell me absolutely everything when you get home." She blushed. "Well, maybe not *everything*. Just the parts that are PG rated."

"And if I don't?"

Nina gave an elaborate shrug, her T-shirt slipping off one shoulder. "Oh, I don't know, I guess I'd have to make up a lot of the stuff I told Lori. Sort of fill in the blanks."

"Sounds like blackmail to me," Alex growled.

Firmly, but not without a touch of mischief, she replied, "Okay, I admit it. I'm not above whatever it takes to get you two back together." After a moment, she added wistfully, "I wish he could have been with us tonight. It was weird being at Grandma's—half the time I didn't know what to say. I kept wanting to tell her I was sorry about what happened, that I'd missed her, but . . . I don't know, there never seemed to be a good time. Do you think she minded?"

Tears came unexpectedly to Alex's eyes. "No, honey. I'm sure she didn't." She thought of all the times she, too, could have reached out to her mother . . . but had chosen to take refuge in her father's memory instead.

Nina yawned again, her eyelids beginning to droop. She wriggled down under the covers, squashing her pillow behind her head, then socking it into place for good measure. "I guess you're right," she muttered thickly. "She didn't seem that upset when we were leaving. In fact, she was kind of cheerful. She told me that in the morning, if it cleared up, she was going swimming."

"Swimming?" Alex echoed in surprise.

"In the cove. Like she used to back when . . ." Nina's eyes were closed now, her voice barely audible. She muttered something Alex couldn't quite hear—something that made her wince nonetheless, like the time she'd stuck her hand into a sinkful of soapy water . . . and accidentally cut her thumb on a broken glass. It had sounded like, *Back when we were a family.*

Chapter 20

The following morning, the first thing Daphne saw when she opened her eyes was the sun coming up in a cloudless pink and blue sky. Sometime in the night it had stopped raining. Groggily, she reached for her husband, but the bed beside her was empty. She could hear him in the bathroom, the gurgling sound of his brushing his teeth that made her think of someone . . .

Drowning.

She sat up, scrubbing arms gone tight with gooseflesh. Her head felt thick and grainy from a dream that stubbornly refused to let go—a *bad* dream in which her mother had been drowning. Daphne had tried to save her, but as she ran toward the water, her feet had become stuck in the sand. Far out beyond the waves she could see the bobbing shape that was her mother . . . but as she struggled to pull herself free, she only sank deeper in the wet, sucking sand. A foghorn was moaning off in the distance, and she remembered thinking, *How strange.* Because it wasn't the least bit foggy. The sun was shining, in fact, twinkling on the waves like a net beaded with thousands of tiny diamonds . . .

In the iron bed in Kitty's guest room, Daphne squinted into the sun slanting in bright spears over the gabled roof of the house next door. The curlicued hands of the antique clock beside the bed stood at a quarter to seven. Around the time Mother usually got up. She imagined her mother peering out the bedroom window and seeing what a perfect day it was shaping up to be. Saying to herself, as Daphne had so often heard her remark . . .

"A lovely day for a swim," she whispered aloud.

A distinct unease spread through Daphne. She wondered if her mother's desire to go swimming had been so innocent after all. Thinking of last night's gifts that had been more than gifts, really—treasures to remember her by?—Daphne shuddered.

When her husband emerged from the bathroom, still in his pajamas with his hair all fluffed up and a smudge of toothpaste in one corner of his mouth, Daphne warned herself, *Stay calm. Roger will think you're being hysterical, and you know how he hates that.*

"Roger?" she called softly. "I'm worried about Mother."

"What else is new?" He laughed as he was peeling off his pajama bottoms—a laugh intended as light-hearted that came out sounding faintly sarcastic.

She forced herself to take a deep breath. *Nice and easy.*

"I'm not talking about the trial," she said. "I was thinking of last night—did it seem to you she was acting a little strange?"

Roger, hopping on one foot as he pulled the other one free, stopped to stare at her, with one leg of his pajama bottoms snaking across the old pine floor. "Strange?" he echoed incredulously. "Strange isn't the word for it. I'd say any woman who seems perfectly content to rot in jail for the rest of her life was *certifiable.*"

Daphne bristled. "Well, if you're going to take that tone . . ."

Instantly Roger was contrite. He walked over to the bed and sank down next to her, the old bed frame creaking in protest. "I'm sorry, hon. This has been tough on me, too. I wasn't going to say anything until after breakfast . . . but I have to catch a plane home today. That idiot mediator has us all dancing like circus bears. He's scheduled another meeting for early tomorrow morning, and I have to be there."

Daphne felt herself grow very still. "You must have known all weekend. Why did you wait until now to tell me?"

"I didn't want to worry you." His gaze cut away, and the old injured tone crept back into his voice. "Hell, you think I *want* this?"

Quite suddenly Daphne couldn't bear the sight of him: his carefully averted eyes and the patented droop of his shoulders. The thick shock of hair that sprang from a peak in the middle of his forehead made her think of a handful of weeds needing to be yanked out by their roots.

"Honestly? I have no idea." He opened his mouth to say something, but she held out a hand to stop him. "Let's not get into it, okay? You go on ahead and take your shower. I'll get the kids up." Then she added with forced casualness, "Look, Roger, there's no point in you sticking around for the trial. Why don't you just stay in New York until it's all over?"

She held her breath, not at all sure what his response would be. She imagined him saying something like, *And risk losing you for good? I know I haven't been the most sensitive of husbands, but I'm not stupid . . . or blind, either. I can see how much is at stake here . . .*

But Roger didn't argue. She caught him giving her a look—or was it just her imagination?—as if he sensed he might be walking into a trap. Then, as if seeing nothing in her demeanor to arouse his suspicions, he said simply, "We'll see. Depends on how tomorrow's meeting goes." He started to get up, then as if remembering something, sank back down, focusing on her with a sudden, disquieting intensity. "Look, Daph, I know we have a few wrinkles of our own to iron out. And as soon as you get back, we'll work on it, okay? Go to a counselor, if that's what you want. I'm serious. Anything it takes."

"Sure," she said, but her heart wasn't in it. For Roger, marriage was always going to be an appointment penciled in on his calendar for some time next week, or next month . . . or next year, when what *she* wanted was today, this morning, this minute.

She watched him get up and walk toward the bathroom, not the solid bulwark she'd once hoped would shelter her . . . just an ordinary man a tad past his prime, with a rear end beginning to droop and more than an inch to pinch around his middle, who had a plane to catch and better things to do than calm his wife's fears.

"Roger?" she called after him.

He stopped, and turned around. "Mmm." But she could see that she'd already lost him. His mind was on what awaited him in New York.

"I was just wondering," she said. "If you've ever . . . you know, been with another woman. Since we've been together." Stunned by her own boldness, she wasn't surprised to see Roger's eyes widen.

"What would make you ask a thing like *that?*" he demanded.

"I don't know. My father, maybe." She didn't remind him of the woman in the bookstore, merely waited a beat before adding, "Well, *have* you?"

He stared at her for a moment before saying sternly, "I'm not even going to dignify that with an answer." Then his eyes narrowed, and he asked, "Is it Kitty? Has she been filling your head with this nonsense? I know she's never liked me."

"No," Daphne replied honestly. "I don't think I've ever heard Kitty say a mean word against anyone, much less you."

It's me, she wanted to shout. *I don't trust you.* Not just to be faithful, for suddenly it didn't really matter whether or not Roger had slept with that woman, or *any* woman. She didn't trust him with her hopes and dreams. And certainly not with her future.

"Well, I should hope not." Roger eyed her reproachfully. In a voice rich with sarcasm, he asked, "May I take my shower now? Or is there something else you'd like to know about my dark and shadowy past?"

"I'm sorry I brought it up," she said. "Go on, take your shower."

Daphne felt sad, and a tiny bit relieved as well. For the most part, she was struck by the quietness of it all. She'd have expected a marriage of eighteen years to go with a bang, not a whimper. Hearing the shower crank on, she wondered if he would even remember to leave her a dry towel.

Well, she certainly wasn't going to wait around to find out. Throwing on an old beach cover-up she'd found in the closet, Daphne dashed upstairs to wake the children, only to find them both on the floor in Kyle's room, ab-

sorbed in a game of pickup sticks thoughtfully provided
by their Aunt Kitty. Reluctantly, she herded them down
to the kitchen, where her sister was up to her elbows in
a mound of dough.

Daphne couldn't help noticing how pretty she looked
this morning—her eyes sparkling and her cheeks rosy,
as if from the sun. Was it true, then, what their mother
had seemed so certain of? She eyed Kitty questioningly,
and over the pair of blond heads bobbing and weaving
between them, her sister caught her glance and nodded
shyly.

Daphne gave a whoop of joy and ran to hug her. "Oh,
Kitty, I'm so happy for you," she murmured. "Think
how much fun it'll be. Our kids growing up together . . .
oh, God, I can hardly stand it."

She didn't add that it looked as if there were a better
than even chance she'd be out here longer than expected.

Kitty smelled faintly of cinnamon and rain-washed
hair. "I want you to be godmother. And another thing:
you can stay as long as you like." She spoke in a voice
choked with emotion. "If it sounds like I'm twisting your
arm, you're not wrong. Forever would suit me just fine."

An image of Johnny resurfaced in Daphne's mind:
Johnny, standing at the end of the pier with his fists
shoved deep in his pockets and the wind snatching at
his hair. For a long deliciously agonizing moment she
allowed herself to wallow in it, to take long draughts
of the moony longing held at bay for the sake of her
floundering marriage.

Then she remembered what she'd come downstairs
for.

"I'm going over to Mother's," she announced. "Mind
watching the kids for an hour or so?"

It was probably silly of her to worry, she knew, but
some sixth sense kept urging her to go see for herself.
No doubt, she'd find her mother lingering over a cup of
coffee or perhaps even headed for the beach. Mother
would be surprised to see her so soon after last night
but only too happy to have her daughter join her for a
swim. And why not? Daphne thought. The water would

be cold still, but bracing. And just the thing to clear her head.

"Sure thing." Peering at her closely, Kitty asked, "What's up? You're not still worried about Mother are you? She seemed fine last night."

"Maybe a little *too* fine." The words were out before Daphne realized she'd spoken them. Quickly, she added, "I'll tell you about it when I get back." No sense getting her sister all worked up over what would probably turn out to be nothing.

But Kitty wasn't letting her off so easy. "If something's wrong, I want to know about it."

"It's nothing, Kitty. Really. Just my stupid paranoia."

Daphne turned away and began searching for her thongs among the pile of sandy shoes and sandals by the back door. She would explain later. Right now she needed to hurry. Just in case . . .

Nevertheless, on her way out the door, she found herself blurting, only half facetiously, "Give me forty-five minutes. If you don't hear from me by then, send in the marines."

It was half past seven by the time she pulled up in front of her mother's house. The sun had climbed up over the tops of the Monterey cypresses that grew in tortured splendor along the cliff, their wind-flattened branches resembling the outstretched arms of sirens luring sailors to their death. A mild wind had kicked up, and the freshly scrubbed sky gleamed overhead. She could smell the tall grass along the point, still wet from last night's rain. Just off shore, a pelican skimmed over a surface bright as polished chrome.

All in all, a perfect day for swimming.

Daphne decided to head straight for the cove. If her mother was nowhere in sight . . . well, all the better. She'd pop into the house for a cup of coffee. And it *was* such a lovely morning . . . lovely enough to almost make her forget the reason she was here.

Almost, but not quite.

She descended the flight of steep wooden stairs that zigzagged its way down the cliff to the beach below. Growing up, how many times had she climbed these

stairs? Those endless breezy summers when she and her
sisters had practically lived in their bathing suits, they
must have scampered up and down a thousand times. In
her mind, she could see her mother poised at the top,
wearing her favorite blue terry cover-up, her pale gold
hair blowing up to catch sparks of sun. Daphne could
hear her calling out through cupped hands, *Be careful,
girls . . .*

For just as they'd been warned not to accept rides
from strangers or cross a street without looking both
ways, they'd been taught the dangers of riptides that
could sweep you out to sea. They knew to swim in pairs
and to stay out of the water just after they'd eaten.

Now, as she made her way down the ice plant-festooned
cliff, Daphne wondered what, if anything, could have
prepared them for the danger of a family coming apart
at the seams? Was there an early warning system for
such things? A lighthouse flashing on a distant shore
they could have heeded?

The beach, no more than a deep pocket of sand really,
appeared deserted at first glance. Then Daphne spotted
it, farther down by the rocks that jutted out to form one
of the cove's sheltering arms: a towel folded neatly atop
a straw tote bag.

Mother's? Yes, of course. Who else would be out for
a swim this time of day?

Scanning the horizon, she was nearly blinded by the
sunlight glancing off the waves in sharp, jagged points.
No sign of life . . . only the seagulls circling overhead.
Their cries, reedy and plaintive somehow, sent an icy
prickle up the back of her neck.

That's when she saw it, a hundred yards or so out—a
pale spherical shape that might have been a bathing cap,
dipping in and out among the swells. Not appearing to
flounder. Just . . . drifting. Daphne recalled her dream
and her heart lurched in dread.

Without thinking, she stripped off her shift and dashed
toward the water, the cool air slipping like silk along her
naked skin.

Diving under a wave, she gasped. God, who would
have thought it would be so *cold?* No one could be out

there, she thought. Certainly not for the fun of it. She nearly turned back, but some instinct kept her from doing so.

She began to swim.

Stroking hard, she struggled to block out the panic threatening to overwhelm her. Swells that had appeared small from shore loomed over her now like tidal waves. It had been a long time since she'd ventured out this far. With the children, she spent most of her time watching them paddle in the shallow surf. She'd joked about being out of condition, but it was no longer funny.

Still Daphne pushed on, her arms slicing the swells in practiced, deliberate strokes. Icy waves rose up to slap her in the face. Choking, she once again fought the urge to turn back.

High overhead a gull screamed. Minutes later, she felt like screaming, too. The freezing water had numbed her, causing her limbs to grow heavy. She felt herself being dragged down by their weight and rolled onto her back. The sky tipped into view, staring down at her like a vast unblinking eye. She drew in a breath tasting of brine and shouted at the top of her lungs, *"Mother!"*

No answer. Daphne floated in shivering silence, rocked by swells that seemed to be carrying her farther from the pale sphere she could see out of the corner of her eye, bobbing not more than a dozen yards away.

Go back, a voice in her head urged. She thought of Kyle and Jennie, and her chest grew tight with panic. If she drowned, her children would be motherless.

But if she turned back now, so would *she*.

Daphne plowed on. The shape seemed to grow nearer. She narrowed her burning eyes to slits and kicked harder. A memory came to her—her sophomore year in high school, taking home first prize in the statewide Emily Houghton short-story contest for aspiring young writers. Her father had had the certificate framed and hung on the wall in her bedroom, saying, "Every time you look at it, you'll be reminded, that you can do anything. Anything at all you put your mind to."

But that knowledge had become lost in the thicket of

marriage and raising children—her sense of herself as a person capable of remarkable feats.

Daphne reached deep inside herself and in a frenzied burst managed to close the short distance separating her from her mother. It wasn't until she saw what she'd swum all this way for—the thing she'd been so sure was a bathing cap—that she felt her heart sink. A float . . . a dirty Styrofoam float off some fishing net . . .

A fierce sense of loss tore through her. She felt somehow . . . *cheated*. Dog-paddling in place, she frantically searched the horizon. But it stared back at her, bright and vast and blank.

Not until she had reversed direction and was swimming back to shore did Daphne realize how far she'd come. The wind was against her now. It had picked up, sweeping the waves in long swells that were beginning to pile up on one another. And the current, dear God, she could feel it tugging at her . . . drawing her inexorably out to sea.

In her panic, she began to flag. Her strokes grew weaker, and her legs scissored without seeming to propel her forward. It felt as though she were merely swimming in place. Or perhaps . . . sinking. Then it struck her: mother must not have wanted to be saved. And now she herself—who had everything to live for—was going to die.

The irony of it caused a harsh little laugh to bubble up in her throat. She wasn't a heroine. She couldn't even manage to save her marriage. *I'm just another casualty of this crazy, mixed-up family.*

She felt exhausted and out of breath. All she wanted to do was drift. Allow the current to carry her wherever it wanted. Would it be so hard to simply let go? She'd let go of so much lately: her father and mother, Johnny . . . and now Roger.

Only the thought of her children spurred her on. Not to know their sweet faces blinking sleepily up at her from their pillows at night, or feel their firm slippery flesh, rosy from the bath as she towelled them off—no, it was unthinkable.

Through a stinging red haze, she thought she saw

something: a dark figure silhouetted against a shore that seemed impossibly far away, separated from her by acres and acres of heaving ocean. Then she blinked, and it was gone.

The waves rushed at her, one after another . . . until she felt as if she were under assault. Barely able to keep her head above the surface, she spat out the salty water that flooded her mouth. The sea and sky seemed to darken and blend together, dissolving in a mass of dancing gray particles. She no longer had any sensation in her legs. *God, help me . . .*

"Daphne!"

She was going under when she heard someone shout her name.

Johnny. It sounded like Johnny.

But, no, that couldn't be. How would he have known to look for her here? The warm rush of joy she'd felt was replaced by cold confusion.

Even so, she somehow found the last thimbleful of strength needed to go on. *Backstroke . . . use your backstroke.* Daphne rolled over, gulping in air until she felt her light-headedness begin to recede. Color seeped back into a sky gone flat and gray as old flannel. She began to stroke . . .

She hadn't gone more than a few feet when a wave crashed over her. Daphne was yanked under, her mouth and nose flooding, her feet tangled in churning water that felt like yards and yards of writhing rope.

Fighting to reach the surface, her lungs on fire, she reached out blindly . . .

. . . and was seized by a pair of strong arms. Even as she blindly fought them in her panic, they tugged at her, dragging her to the surface. The sky broke open overhead, and a burst of sweet air flooded her lungs.

"It's okay . . . you're okay now, Daphne."

Johnny. Gasping and sobbing at the same time, she clung to him. *How . . . ?*

"Just relax," he panted. "We're almost there."

Water streamed down her face and into her eyes. His face blinked in and out of focus. But his presence, solid as timber, had an instantaneous effect, causing her to go limp as he circled her chest with one arm and began dragging her to safety with strong sure strokes. *Johnny, oh Johnny . . . you found me.*

"It's not far," he panted.

Trusting him, she stopped trying to scissor kick in tandem—which only seemed to be slowing them down—and maybe she even lost consciousness for a little while because the next thing she was aware of was something solid scraping underfoot.

Daphne landed in a heap on the wet sand. She lay there for a moment, gasping for breath, covered in sand and bits of kelp like some poor half-dead creature washed ashore by last night's storm. Then the bright sun was eclipsed by a pair of broad shoulders. Strong hands dragged her upright.

"Daphne? Are you all right?" Johnny was squatting down beside her, peering anxiously into her face. His eyes were the gray of the ocean at his back.

She coughed again, bringing up a mouthful of water, and sagged against him. Shoving back the sopping strands of hair plastered to her eyes and cheeks, she looked up at Johnny and began to laugh weakly—laughter that quickly melted into tears.

He didn't try to stop them. He just held her as she sobbed. Beneath his warming skin she could hear his heartbeat, steady and reassuring, and feel his hands moving over her, touching every part of her as if to make sure she really *was* okay.

"Daphne, thank God . . . thank God . . ." he murmured over and over.

When she could drag herself up to take him in, she saw that he was naked, like her. Water trickled down his arms and chest, and his hair was plastered to his skull. But it was his eyes that made her know she was really, truly alive—that she wasn't dreaming this while floating somewhere below. In that instant, they weren't gray like the ocean, not gray at all . . . but blue, as blue as the brilliant sky soaring overhead. The eyes of a man who would do anything for love.

"How . . . how did you—"

"Sssh," he soothed, cradling her against his chest.

"Thank God for your sister. When Kitty couldn't reach you at your mother's, she was worried enough to call me." He smiled. "Did you think I was going to wait around until I heard back that something had happened to you?"

"My mother. She . . ." Daphne choked on the words, and once again began to cry.

"Later," he soothed. "We'll deal with it later. Right now we have to get you dried off and into your clothes. Can you walk?"

"I . . . I think I can manage." Daphne tried to stand, but her knees buckled under her like wet cardboard. Then Johnny was scooping her up in his arms . . . just like in her girlhood fantasies, where the heroine lives happily ever after, and no one ever gets hurt or dies.

It can't last, she thought. Sooner or later, life, *real* life, would come crashing back in. But in her half-drowned state, Daphne knew one thing to be true: never again would she face it alone. Good, bad, or ugly, whatever happened, Johnny would be there with her. If not to rescue her—she'd had quite enough of that for the time being—to walk alongside her, sleep in her bed, march to the beat of the same drummer.

"I forgot to thank you," she murmured into his chest as they were bumping up the steep wooden stairs.

"Take your time," he answered with a gruffness that told her of the mighty struggle he was having with his own emotions. "We have the rest of our lives."

Epilogue

It was one of those warm spells older residents of Mira-monte would reminisce about in the months, even years, to come—an unbroken string of cloudless days with the digital display over the Wells Fargo building showing a steady temperature of just under eighty and colorful beach umbrellas blooming along stretches of shoreline where the fog that rolled in each morning was only a faint memory by noon. An early gift, courtesy of June, before the summer crowds commenced flocking in by the busload and the state beach parking lots, crammed with Winnebagos, began to resemble a herd of behemoths peacefully grazing.

It was exactly one year from the date inscribed on the granite headstone marking the grave beside the one in which Vernon Seagrave lay buried, under a spreading locust in Twin Oaks Cemetery. It read simply: *Lydia Beatrice Seagrave, devoted wife and mother.*

Her daughters didn't doubt that some would find it ironic. And during the storm of press that erupted in the aftermath of her death—referred to by the tabloids as her "mysterious disappearance," as if she were having the last laugh from a lavish hacienda somewhere south of the border—there were times when even Daphne, Kitty, and Alex had to wonder. After all, no body ever washed ashore. And their mother's affairs, while neatly placed in order, could have been evidence of nothing more than a practical woman on the eve of standing trial for murder, for whom time was quite simply of the essence.

But each had arrived separately at her own conclu-sion, which they then collectively agreed on. In the dark

still marrow of those nights following their mother's disappearance, when sleep eluded them and an eternity of
unanswered questions spread out before them, a picture
slowly began to develop—the portrait of a wife who'd
loved her husband beyond all reason and perhaps even
sanity . . . enough to kill him in order to save him from
an act for which there could be no coming back, no
possibility of redemption. An ordinary woman in most
respects, not without talent and a sense of humor, whom
love had pushed to extraordinary lengths.

For Kitty, it had been a season of renewal as much
as loss. Following a gloriously uneventful pregnancy—
through which she sailed without experiencing any of
the dire mishaps every late-in-life mom she met up with
felt compelled to warn her about—she gave birth to a
healthy eight-pound girl, at home, in the Victorian sleigh
bed in which her child had been conceived. Sean, who
hadn't missed a single Lamaze class, was at her side
throughout the sixteen hours of labor. And when it came
time to cut the cord, and the midwife handed him the scis-
sors, he executed his duty with all the swelled pride of a
master of ceremonies launching an ocean liner. When his
newborn daughter was placed in his arms, he took one
look at her shock of red hair and with a laugh that didn't
disguise the catch in his throat, remarked drily, "She's
got my eyes, at least."

Like everything else in Kitty's life, her new family was
unorthodox, to say the least. They'd planned to wait
until Sean had finished college before making any decisions about the future. But that hadn't stopped him from
coming over almost every night, when it was a toss-up
between Kitty and the baby as to who got the lion's
share of his attention. In the end, it had been Sean
who'd come up with the name they settled on: Made-
leine, which the doting patrons of Tea & Sympathy immediately shortened to "Maddie."

There was no doubt as to who was in charge, though.
Daphne's youngest quickly assumed the role of little
mother, hovering over the cradle Sean had had made by
a local cabinetmaker in exchange for two days' work
trimming trees. She engaged Maddie in endless whis-

pered conversations, as if the baby could understand every word, and was magnanimous about sharing her dolls and toys. Strangers who leaned in too close would find an indignant four-year-old glaring fiercely up at them. "*My* baby," Jennie would announce loudly.

As for Daphne, her stay in Miramonte became permanent. A few months after her mother's disappearance she announced to Roger that she wanted a divorce, and rented a modest bungalow a few blocks from Kitty. It had been rocky in the beginning, but Roger, after an initial scene or two and several wild threats, had proven surprisingly fair minded about the whole thing. In the end, they'd hammered out an agreement they both felt they could live with. He would keep the penthouse in New York and have the children six weeks every summer, plus every other Christmas and Easter. She would retain custody of Kyle and Jennie, along with the sizable advance for her memoir about her family, to be published in the fall.

Alex, a veteran of *that* war, assured her it would all work out for the best. She was certainly in a position to know—in December, she and her ex-husband had quietly remarried. They'd sold their respective homes, thus freeing Alex to pay off all her debts, and surprised everyone by moving into the house on Agua Fria Point. It had been left to all three of them, but Kitty and Daphne agreed to accept their share in monthly installments.

On this fine day, the afternoon of the anniversary of their mother's death, they were gathered on the porch where as girls they'd spent endless hours, their feet tucked under them on the glider, devouring the latest *Nancy Drew* along with an illicit box of See's, or brushing their wet hair dry on the front steps. In the yard below, Jennie was trundling Maddie along the front path in her pink doll buggy, while the baby bounced and crowed in delight, her gingery curls flashing red in the sun. The twins had taken Kyle down to the cove with them, swearing on six Bibles they wouldn't let him out of their sight.

Daphne wasn't worried about her son, whose cousins doted on him. As she sat in the green wicker chair by the steps, flanked by her sisters, a suitcase packed and ready just inside the door, something quite different weighed on her mind.

"Should I make lemonade?" Kitty asked, sounding a little anxious herself. "It might be nice to take along a thermos. It's a long drive."

"Never mind. We'll stop along the way," Daphne told her.

"They'll be drinking *champagne*, you idiot." Alex laughed wickedly, tossing the melted ice from her glass into the hydrangea bushes below the porch. With Jim in Taiwan on business, she and the girls had been living off iced tea and cookies all week, and Alex complained that she'd gained enough weight to sink a boat—though neither of her sisters could detect a single ounce of it.

Kitty sighed. "I just wish . . . oh, I don't know. A *real* ceremony would have been nice. With flowers and a cake. And rice. What's a wedding without Uncle Ben's?"

"You're one to talk," Alex scoffed affectionately. "Look at you and Sean. By the time you two even get around to moving in together, you'll be applying for Social Security."

Kitty tossed her head in mock indignation. "At least I'll have someone to push me around in my wheelchair."

"He'll have to apply for his driver's license first," Daphne teased. Sobering, she added, "Look, I know you think I'm crazy, and maybe I am. But after all that's happened . . . well, it just seemed like a good idea. Remember, twenty years ago we almost *did* elope."

"It's been so long. I forget what happened exactly." Alex leaned forward, suddenly curious.

"It was Johnny who pulled the plug," Daphne reminded her.

"After what Daddy did to him, I'm not surprised," Kitty recalled, her expression darkening.

Daphne shook her head. "It wasn't just that. He was afraid for me, too. Of everything I'd be missing out on. We were so young. And in a way, it did work out for the best. For one thing, I wouldn't have had Kyle and Jennie."

"Lucky you—for an entire week you won't even know

they exist." Alex had volunteered to baby-sit the children while Daphne was on her honeymoon and wasn't
going to let her forget.

Quietly, Kitty put in, "The main thing is that you're
happy." Her gaze softened as it fell on Maddie, and
when she looked back at Daphne, her eyes shone
brighter than any gem. "Who needs Uncle Ben when
you've got a man who gave up the throne for the woman
he loves?"

Daphne laughed uncomfortably. "It wasn't quite that
dramatic. He's still a lawyer . . . only not in the DA's
office."

"I'm sure private practice has its pluses." Alex
winked broadly.

"At least you won't starve," Kitty said.

"Like anyone *could,* living down the street from you!"
Alex frowned in despair at the Tupperware container of
cookies Kitty had brought over.

That's when Daphne heard it—the distant growl of an
engine. She remembered twilights long past when she'd
sat on this very porch, waiting. This time it was a midnight-blue Thunderbird that rounded the corner onto
Cypress Lane. Yet the face of the man behind the wheel
wore the same dangerous squint, a cigarette tucked reck-
lessly in one corner of his mouth. He caught sight of her
and honked. She waved back, feeling sixteen again, the
red carpet of her life rolled out in front of her, both
wondrous and terrifying.

Slowly, she stood up, her legs weak as melted butter
and her knees buckling. Taking care not to trip over feet
that were suddenly the only thing holding her up,
Daphne went to retrieve her suitcase and hugged each
of her sisters good-bye. Then, pausing to take a deep
breath laced with the scent of brine and juniper, she
reached into the pocket of her blazer to finger a pair of
old tickets worn to the softness of fabric before stepping
off the porch, on which it seemed she'd been waiting all
her life for this moment. With her heart and chin high,
she walked to meet the man striding toward her up
the path.

Dear Reader,

In the twelve years since the publication of my first novel, *Garden of Lies*, which was subsequently translated into twenty-five languages, I've gotten letters from all over the world. A retired British army colonel wrote that he couldn't remember when he'd last enjoyed such a "cracking good tale." A Japanese student was moved by parallels in her own life. An elderly shut-in from Florida confided that she didn't get out much these days, and treasured most those books which brought temporary respite from her aches and pains—she'd read mine several times!

My greatest pleasure is hearing what you think. Writing for the most part is a solitary pursuit . . . and mail from readers makes it all worthwhile. On that note, I invite you to drop in at my website . . . and throw in your two cents while you're at it. Or write me at home with any questions you might have, or to let me know if you enjoyed this, or any of my other books. If you'd like to be on the mailing list for my free newsletter, which will give you an update on current appearances and future books, please let me know. From my point of view, it's the next best thing to getting together for a cup of coffee and a piece of cake. Speaking of which, did I mention my hobby is baking? So you can expect a few of my favorite recipes now and then. (I'd love to hear how they came out!) Until then, happy reading . . .

Warmly,

Eileen Goudge

Website: www.eileengoudge.com
E-mail: info@eileengoudge.com
Address: P.O. Box 1396—Murray Hill Sta.
New York, N.Y. 10016

Enter the world of *The Second Silence,* where a mother's worst nightmare brought to life unites a family and even awakens the possibility of new love. Eileen Goudge's engrossing new drama, her most suspenseful yet, will appear in stores summer 2000 in hardcover.

Noelle sat motionless on a bench in the town square. Somehow the entire afternoon had slipped by unnoticed. She had a vague memory of leaving the courthouse and of feeling the need to rest a bit before driving home, knowing that if she didn't, she might not make it in one piece. Now she saw that the children scampering over the jungle gym had all gone home. Shadows were beginning to creep out from under ladders and slides to slither over the churned-up sand below. Even the surrounding benches were mostly empty.

Noting the clerks and secretaries making their way down the steps of the courthouse, she glanced at her watch and saw that it was a few minutes past five.

Do they know? she wondered with a dull ache. *All the forms they staple and punch and stamp, all the duplicates and triplicates stuffed into files and envelopes—do any of them have the slightest notion of the impact it can have on someone's life?*

Probably not. The men and women hurrying past were concerned with little else besides beating the quickest path possible to home. No one cared about a little girl named Emma. While they thought about what they were going to have for supper or if their favorite TV show was going to be a new episode or a rerun, Noelle sat dying a slow death at the prospect of each visit with her daughter ending like this last one—with Emma having to be pried from her arms. Mrs. Scheffert, the old biddy who'd seemed so nice at first, had shot her a reproving look over Emma's head . . . as if it were all Noelle's fault somehow.

It felt as though something vital had been torn from her. What she wanted was so natural the very simplicity of it was a cruel irony—like a trick mirror fooling you into thinking there's a doorway where there isn't. She wanted her daughter. Nothing more, nothing less. She wanted to be among the mothers who'd stood calling to their children through cupped hands that it was time to go. She wanted to walk along the sidewalk with her daughter's small hand in hers. She—

"Mind if I join you?"

Startled, Noelle glanced up. A man stood before her, the sun at his back throwing his face into shadow. It was an instant before she recognized him. In chinos and a short-sleeve shirt, minus his doctor's coat, Hank Reynolds might have been just another passerby . . . someone of medium height, with light brown hair, whose muscled arms and shoulders suggested regular workouts at the gym. Except for his eyes, which caught the sun as he lowered himself onto the bench—eyes the dark amber of tea laced with brandy.

"I'm afraid I'm not very good company right now," she warned.

Hank smiled warmly. "I'll take my chances."

He had a newspaper tucked under one arm and a grocery sack balanced in the crook of his elbow. He lowered the sack onto the grass at his feet. "I usually take the short way home, but it's such a beautiful day I decided to walk through the park instead." He nodded in the direction of her foot. "Looks a lot better than the last time I saw it. How does it feel?"

Noelle shrugged. "All I can say is, it's the least of my worries."

Hank was silent for a moment, looking out over the lawn where a couple of teenage boys were tossing a Frisbee. "If you feel like talking, fine," he said at last. "If not, we can just sit. I'm in no rush."

"As you can see, neither am I." Her voice cracked, and she suddenly found herself on the verge of tears.

He glanced at her in concern. "That bad, huh?"

"You don't want to know."

Hank touched her arm. "Try me."

He's just being nice, she told herself. *Nice Dr. Hank, beloved of children and old ladies alike.* "I'm afraid it's a bit out of your bailiwick," she said with an attempt at an airy laugh that fell far short of its mark.

"You'd be surprised. In my line of work I'm exposed to pretty much everything—even the stuff that isn't catching." A rueful smile tugged at one corner of his mouth.

In the old days, she would have said, *Thank you, I appreciate the offer . . . but I'll be fine in a minute or two.* But that was before. The dutiful daughter who from age ten through eighteen had smiled her way through the rounds of parties, openings, and premieres that were essential to her mother's line of work . . . while secretly longing for the solitude of her old room back at Nana's. The company wife who'd found respite, amid the bright clamor of cocktail parties and boring business dinners, in stolen sips from the bottle hidden in her pantry. But the woman emerging from the too-tight skin of her former self didn't seem to have those reservations. Without further ado, Noelle burst into tears.

"I'm sorry," she gulped when she could at last trust herself to speak. "I'm making a fool of myself. You should go home. Your ice cream will melt." She gestured toward the pint of rocky road poking from his grocery sack.

"I can always buy more."

To her profound gratitude, Hank didn't pat her on the back or murmur false reassurances. He merely handed her his handkerchief, a neatly pressed square that smelled freshly ironed.

They sat together in silence while Noelle mopped her face and struggled to regain her composure. Finally, she said, "It's a long story."

"I'm a good listener."

She studied him out of the corner of her eye. He might not be the kind that inspired strange women to slip him their business cards—home number scribbled on the back—as regularly happened with Robert. Hank's appeal wasn't so obvious. But it was undeniable nonetheless. Even the slight overbite that reminded her of Pete Caswell, an altar boy at St. Vincent's that she'd had the biggest crush on back in the fifth grade. Despite her mood, she felt her heart quicken.

"Maybe another time," she told him.

"In that case, I'll treat you to a cold drink instead." He reached into the sack and pulled out a Seven-Up, thoughtfully popping the tab before handing it to her.

"Thanks." She tilted her head back and drank deeply. She thought she'd never tasted anything so delicious.

Long brush strokes of orange and purple tinted the horizon, which twinkled in the golden rays of the setting sun. From where she and Hank sat, as companionable as an old married couple, the distant slamming of car doors had dwindled to an occasional *thunk*. A breeze had kicked up, stirring the stagnant air and rustling the leaves overhead. Noelle became aware of Hank's hand, curled loosely on his knee. Against the tan fabric of his slacks, it looked large and capable. Unexpectedly, she felt a stab of longing—for what exactly, she couldn't have said.

She pointed toward the fountain at the center of the square, featured on postcards sold at Gleason's Pharmacy—a graceful Art Noveau nymph ringed with spouts in the shape of lily pads. "If that girl could talk, think of the stories *she'd* tell."

Hank smiled, the creases at the corners of his tea-brown eyes flaring. "Maybe that's why she spends her days weeping instead."

She shot him a sharp glance. "A good shoulder to cry on isn't always the answer."

"No, but it helps."

She looked into Hank's kind face and saw something she hadn't seen before: a quiet strength that seemed to rise from a place deep within. He reminded her of her father, that look Dad sometimes got—of an immovable object meeting an irresistible force.

"I saw my daughter this afternoon," she began, the words coming easily now, rising like the water bubbling to the surface of the fountain. "I have supervised visitation twice a week, for three hours. We sat in a room with the door open so a social worker could keep an eye on me, to make sure—" She broke off, staring down at the grass and imagining the look of pity she was certain Hank wore—pity mixed with wariness perhaps. And suddenly she didn't want his sympathy. What she wanted—*needed*—was simply for this nightmare to end. "It's all so unbelievable, the very idea that I would ever hurt my little girl. . . ." She cleared her throat. "When she was a baby, I made all her baby food from scratch. I wouldn't have dreamed of feeding her from a jar. It might sound paranoid, but I even kept the cleaning supplies on a high shelf. I didn't trust those safety latches."

"I see plently of kids who'd have been spared a trip to the hospital if their mothers had been as paranoid," Hank observed mildly.

"The worst of it is that I can't protect her *now*. She's suffering and I can't do a thing to prevent it." Noelle paused to blow her nose into Hank's wonderfully voluminous white handkerchief. When she lifted her head, she felt rinsed clean, the soggy gray weight of her sorrow drained away and in its place a gleaming sharp anger. "I'm sure you hear a lot of women say their husbands are evil, but mine really is. I used to believe he loved his daughter, but now I'm not so sure. He's using her to crush me . . . and the awful thing is, it's working."

"From where I sit, that's not how it looks." Meeting his gaze, she saw that Hank didn't pity her. His expression was coolly assessing, even admiring.

"What . . . what are you saying?" she stammered.

"That the woman I see is perfectly capable of kicking down any door that stands in her way."

Noelle smiled reluctantly at the image of herself as Xena, Warrior Princess. "Emma's five," she said softly. "That age when every other sentence is a question. I just wish I had all the answers."

"Then you'd be like that guy over there. They'd erect a statue of you in some park." He gestured toward the one of Luther Burbank, a gray squirrel perched like a miniature aide de camp on one bronze shoulder.

Noelle laughed, watching the squirrel scamper back down to retrieve an acorn from the grass below. With the toe of one sneaker she nudged a wet spot on Hank's grocery sack. "Looks like you're too late to save that rocky road."

"Story of my life." He shrugged and stood up, hoisting the groceries under one arm before offering her the other. "Will you allow a fellow wayfarer to walk you to your car?"

This time, when Noelle rose to her feet, her legs didn't threaten to collapse. She found she could walk quite steadily, one arm resting lightly in the crook of Hank's elbow. Her fingertips brushed the fine hairs along his muscled forearm and she was acutely aware of the heat of his skin against hers. Nana and her mother would be wondering what was keeping her, she thought. They'd be worried. But at that moment, for the first time in days, Noelle felt safe and strong.

SIGNET (0451)

NATIONAL BESTSELLER
Family drama and intrigue from
New York Times bestselling author

EILEEN GOUDGE

"Double-dipped passion...in a glamorous, cut-throat world...satisfying...irresistible." —*San Francisco Chronicle*

"Love and deceit in a tainted world of glamour and money...will find a devoted audience!"—*Chicago Sun-Times*

❏ THORNS OF TRUTH   (185277—$7.50)
❏ BLESSING IN DISGUISE   (184041—$7.50)
❏ SUCH DEVOTED SISTERS   (173376—$7.50)
❏ GARDEN OF LIES   (162919—$7.50)
❏ TRAIL OF SECRETS   (187741—$7.50)

Prices slightly higher in Canada

Payable in U.S. funds only. No cash/COD accepted. Postage & handling: U.S./CAN. $2.75 for one book, $1.00 for each additional, not to exceed $6.75; Int'l $5.00 for one book, $1.00 each additional. We accept Visa, Amex, MC ($10.00 min.), checks ($15.00 fee for returned checks) and money orders. Call 800-788-6262 or 201-933-9292, fax 201-896-8569; refer to ad # N121 (12/99)

Penguin Putnam Inc.	Bill my: ❏ Visa ❏ MasterCard ❏ Amex _____ (expires)
P.O. Box 12289, Dept. B	Card# _____
Newark, NJ 07101-5289	Signature _____
Please allow 4-6 weeks for delivery.	
Foreign and Canadian delivery 6-8 weeks.	

Bill to:
Name _____
Address _____ City _____
State/ZIP _____ Daytime Phone # _____

Ship to:
Name _____ Book Total $ _____
Address _____ Applicable Sales Tax $ _____
City _____ Postage & Handling $ _____
State/ZIP _____ Total Amount Due $ _____

This offer subject to change without notice.

PENGUIN PUTNAM INC.
Online

Your Internet gateway to a virtual environment with
hundreds of entertaining and enlightening books
from Penguin Putnam Inc.

*While you're there, get the latest buzz on
the best authors and books around—*

Tom Clancy, Patricia Cornwell, W.E.B. Griffin,
Nora Roberts, William Gibson, Robin Cook,
Brian Jacques, Catherine Coulter, Stephen King,
Jacquelyn Mitchard, and many more!

**Penguin Putnam Online is located at
http://www.penguinputnam.com**

PENGUIN PUTNAM NEWS

Every month you'll get an inside look at our upcom-
ing books and new features on our site. This is an
ongoing effort to provide you with the most
up-to-date information about
our books and authors.

**Subscribe to Penguin Putnam News at
http://www.penguinputnam.com/ClubPPI**